❧ THE ❧
CASEBOOK OF
NEWBURY & HOBBES

Newbury AND Hobbes
Investigation

Also by George Mann and available from Titan Books

Newbury & Hobbes: The Executioner's Heart
Encounters of Sherlock Holmes

COMING SOON

Sherlock Holmes: The Will of the Dead (November 2013)
Further Encounters of Sherlock Holmes (February 2014)
Newbury & Hobbes: The Revenant Express (July 2014)

THE
CASEBOOK OF
NEWBURY & HOBBES

A Newbury AND Hobbes Investigation

GEORGE MANN

TITAN BOOKS

THE CASEBOOK OF NEWBURY & HOBBES
Print edition ISBN: 9781781167427
E-book edition ISBN: 9781781167434

Published by Titan Books
A division of Titan Publishing Group Ltd
144 Southwark Street, London SE1 0UP

First edition: September 2013
10 9 8 7 6 5 4 3 2 1

Cover design by Amazing15.com

What did you think of this book? We love to hear from our readers.
Please email us at: readerfeedback@titanemail.com,
or write to us at the above address.

To receive advance information, news, competitions, and exclusive
offers online, please sign up for the Titan newsletter on our website:

WWW.TITANBOOKS.COM

FOR PAUL MAGRS AND STUART DOUGLAS
No one could ask for better friends

TABLE OF CONTENTS

INTRODUCTION

I can barely believe it's been five years since *The Affinity Bridge* was first published. It seems as if only a few months have passed. I've been astounded by people's response to the series, by how many people have found something to enjoy in these madcap tales of derring-do and adventure in the dark streets of a Victorian London that never was.

When I set out to write *The Affinity Bridge* it was purely an exercise in self-gratification. I wanted to write the type of story I love to read, something that would be sheer, unadulterated *fun.* I wanted to write a book for the sheer pleasure of it. The irony, of course, is that the book and the series it spawned has proved to be by far the most successful I've ever written. Which only goes to prove that old adage about writing for yourself, rather than writing what you think people are going to want to read...

Four novels and a handful of stories later and the characters have taken on something of a life of their own. Now it seems like they've always been there, a part of my psyche. Perhaps they have.

I originally conceived of Sir Maurice Newbury long before I wrote *The Affinity Bridge.* I think he was born out of my desire to write a sequence of stories in the mould of those classic Victorian and Edwardian tales about supernatural sleuths – Aylmer Vance, Eugene Valmont, Flaxman Low and, of course, Carnacki the Ghost Finder. I've always had a passion for those stories, along with Sherlock Holmes and *Doctor Who* – tales of high adventure, of foggy streets and bizarre encounters. Of bold heroes and larger-than-life villains.

Newbury was always going to explore bizarre and supernatural crimes in a weird, fantastical version of Victorian London. And his desire to understand the occult and his drug addiction would mean he always walked a fine line between being an expert in the dark arts and becoming a practitioner. That, you see, is Newbury's flaw – he is drawn to the darkness. And it may yet prove to be his undoing.

It wasn't, however, until Veronica Hobbes came into being that everything gelled and *The Affinity Bridge* began to take shape. Veronica was only ever intended to be Newbury's sidekick, but almost as soon as I started writing I realised that this had to be a true partnership, a meeting of equals in a time of inequality. Veronica, a strong woman battling against the prejudice of her age, her clairvoyant sister locked in a lunatic asylum – she had a story of her own to tell. And secrets, too. Dark secrets that she couldn't share with Newbury, no matter how much she longed to do so.

Then, of course, there was Charles Bainbridge, Newbury's friend and confidant, a fellow agent to the Queen and an inspector at Scotland Yard. Bainbridge was never going to be a bumbling Lestrade, the ineffectual policeman who was there only to allow our hero to shine. Rather, he is a man of steady nerves – solid, dependable – quite the opposite of Newbury, and in his own way as essential a member of the team. Bainbridge solves crimes through hard work, process and resolve, whereas Newbury relies on flashes of insight and inspiration. Method as opposed to action; Bainbridge is yin to

Newbury's yang. They need each other to function effectively.

It soon became clear to me that these books are as much Veronica's and Bainbridge's story as they are Newbury's, and the more of them I write, the more evident I think that becomes. Newbury – the man who started it all – is made greater by the presence of his friends and loved ones, just the same as us all.

So, as I sit here at my desk working on the fifth novel in the series, it seems strange to reflect back to the beginning of the saga. Things have changed so much for these characters – loyalties and battles have been fought and won; friends have been made and lost. But the core of these stories – the trio of Newbury, Veronica and Bainbridge – remain as constant as ever. Hopefully their adventures will continue for a long time to come.

Here, then, in this collection, are a selection of those adventures, tales that detail some of the exploits of these characters during the times between novels, and for anyone encountering them for the first time, offer a flavour of the series as a whole.

Alongside all the regulars we also meet in these pages some of the other characters that later turn up in the novels, or enjoy associated adventures of their own: Professor Archibald Angelchrist, Lady Arkwell, Peter Rutherford, to name a few. Plus, of course, the occasional dalliance with famous peers, such as Sherlock Holmes and Dr Watson.

Also included here is a timeline of stories set in the alternate world which Newbury, Veronica and Bainbridge – and in fact nearly all of my characters, across all of my different novels, stories and series – inhabit. Since *The Affinity Bridge* the world of Newbury and Hobbes has grown and evolved, spreading out in all manner of unexpected directions, encompassing other characters and stories and weaving them into the same fictional strata. Some of the stories included in this book draw some of those other characters in, helping to forge a more cohesive and diverse alternate history of the world.

I hope the timeline, and the stories in this volume, may prove to be something of a guide to navigating this fictional history. Most of all, however, I hope they prove to be *fun*.

George Mann
Grantham, April 2013

THE DARK PATH

I

"I make a point of only smoking Guinea Gold cigarettes and drinking French brandy, Benson. I fear nothing else will do." Templeton Black exhaled slowly, smoke pluming from his nostrils. His cigarette drooped languidly from his bottom lip.

"Then you, sir," replied Benson, striking the billiard ball with the tip of his cue, "are nothing but a frightful bore." He stood back, admiring his handiwork as two balls clacked together and a red one tumbled into a pocket at the far end of the table. He took a swig from a near-empty whisky bottle he'd left resting on the raised lip of the billiard table.

Black raised a disapproving eyebrow. "You understand, Benson, that it's terribly uncouth to drink from the bottle like that?"

Benson laughed, nearly spluttering on his drink, and Black chuckled heartily, reaching out his hand. "Oh go on, give it here, foul stuff that it is." He took the proffered bottle and downed the last of the caramel-coloured spirit, shuddering as it hit his palate.

"A drink's a drink, Templeton," said Benson, placing his cue on the table. "And a win's a win. That's a guinea you owe me. Unless you want to up the stakes for a rematch?"

Black shook his head, taking another long draw on his

cigarette. "No," he said, hopping down from where he'd been sitting on a window ledge and blowing smoke from the corner of his mouth. "I must find Newbury. Apparently there's something he wants to discuss."

"Hmm," murmured Benson, unhappy to be losing his playmate. "I'm not sure why you bother attending these house parties, you know. You're never here for more than five minutes before you go and get yourself caught up in another ridiculous investigation. You should tell Newbury to keep his mysteries to himself."

Black laughed, slapping Benson heartily on the back. "Now you're being drunk and petulant," he said, warmly. "Go on, go and find someone else to beat at billiards." He looked up at the sound of footsteps to see a pretty young woman in a black, floor-length gown enter the room. "Jocasta will play, won't you?" he said, laughing.

"In this dress?" she replied, with a winning smile.

"Oh, come on, old girl!" said Black. "Otherwise Benson will lapse into another of his foul moods and spend the rest of the party scowling at everyone. You know how he is."

Jocasta laughed as she closed the gap between them. She put a hand on his arm. "Do you like it?" she asked, demurely. "The dress, I mean."

Black grinned. "Oh, come on, old girl. You know you're not my type."

Jocasta rolled her eyes. "Yes, well, more's the pity. I suppose I shall *have* to make do with Benson and his billiards."

"I *can* hear you, you know," said Benson, with mock hurt. "And *I* think your dress is terribly pretty," he added.

"There you are, then," said Black. "Benson has someone to beat at billiards, and you have someone to appreciate your dress. The world is a happy place."

"Go on," replied Jocasta, sighing, "go and find Newbury before I change my mind."

Black started toward the door. "Play nicely," he called over his shoulder.

"You still owe me a guinea!" bellowed Benson, behind him.

II

Sir Maurice Newbury was lounging on a sofa when Black found him in the drawing room a few minutes later.

He was a handsome man in his late thirties, with a pale complexion and a square-set jaw. He wore his raven-black hair in a neat side parting, falling in a comma across his forehead, and tended toward black suits with starched white collars and colourful silk cravats.

Now, he was nursing a half-empty glass of claret, and appeared to be deep in conversation with an older man who sported an impressive set of white whiskers.

Newbury looked up when Black entered the room, and beckoned him over with a wave of his hand.

Dutifully, Black made a beeline toward them, ignoring the two other conversations that were taking place in the large drawing room: a cluster of four women had gathered on a seat beneath a tall, mullioned window, while two other men spoke in hushed tones across the far side of the room, standing before the fire. Black had been introduced to them all, of course, but he was damned if he could remember their names. He realised this was something of a weakness in a Crown investigator, but he seemed to get by.

"Ah, Templeton, have you been properly introduced to our host, Sir Geoffrey Potterstone?" said Newbury, as Black joined them.

Black turned to regard the older man, extending his hand. "I believe not, although I do fear I've rather been taking advantage of your hospitality, Sir Geoffrey."

Potterstone laughed warmly. He was a ruddy-faced man,

in his late fifties, with narrow blue eyes and the scarlet nose of a heavy drinker. He took Black's hand in his own, giving it a firm squeeze. Black resisted the urge to grimace in pain. "You're most welcome, Mr Black. Most welcome indeed. Any friend of Sir Maurice is a friend of mine." He finally released Black's hand, adding, "And besides, he speaks most highly of you."

"Does he, indeed?" replied Black, with a quick glance at Newbury, whose expression was giving nothing away. "Well, it's both a pleasure and an honour to be considered a guest at your impressive house, Sir Geoffrey." Black glanced at the empty chair beside Newbury. "May I join you?"

Sir Geoffrey waved a hand dismissively. "Oh, don't mind me, Mr Black. I've been ignoring my other guests for too long as it is." He planted his hands firmly on the arms of his chair and pulled himself up. He was not a large man, but portly, and was clearly having some difficulty with his right foot. *Probably gout*, considered Black, *given the overall appearance of the fellow and the evidence of his most comfortable lifestyle.*

Sir Geoffrey turned to Newbury. "Regarding that other matter, Sir Maurice…?"

"In hand, Sir Geoffrey," replied Newbury. "Say no more."

"Excellent," replied the other man. "Then I'll ask the two of you to excuse me while I mingle for a while." He turned and tottered off in the direction of the four women by the window.

Black turned to Newbury. "What was all that about?" he enquired, searching out his silver cigarette case and withdrawing another Guinea Gold. He lit it, leaning back and taking a long, pleasurable draw.

Newbury watched him for a moment, smiling. "A little problem he's asked me to look into," he said, after a moment. "That's what I wanted to talk to you about. I rather fear I've volunteered our services."

Black laughed. "I imagined you might."

Newbury grinned. "I could use your help. And besides, I thought you might find it interesting."

"Don't I always," replied Black, with a chuckle. "So, go ahead, enlighten me."

"It's the valet," said Newbury. "He's missing."

"Missing?" enquired Black.

"For three days," replied Newbury. "No one has seen hide or hair of him. He requested the morning off on Wednesday, claiming he had a personal errand to run. Said he was heading into the village. He never returned."

"And no one here has any idea where he might have gone?" asked Black.

"Apparently not. Sir Geoffrey says he's a very private man. Keeps himself to himself, spends most of his free time alone in his room, reading novels. His name is Henry Blakemore." Newbury shrugged.

"Family? Might he have received word of an emergency and taken off without notice?"

"Hardly the actions of a dutiful valet. Even if he'd been called away by an emergency, it's been three days. He'd have sent word by now." Newbury took a swig from his brandy. "And besides, he has no family left. No parents, no siblings. No one to run to."

Black smiled. "A real mystery." He exhaled another cloud of cigarette smoke. "So, where do we start?"

"Apparently the servants are saying all sorts of fascinating things about the haunted woods on the edge of the estate," Newbury became more animated as he spoke, and his face seemed to light up at the very prospect, "but I imagine our first port of call should be to search his room in the morning."

Black laughed. "Don't think for a minute that you can pretend you didn't know about these so-called 'haunted woods' before we set out for this party. I can see now that's the *only* reason we're here."

Newbury looked scandalised. "I'm shocked that you'd think that, Templeton." He leaned forward, lowering his voice to a conspiratorial whisper. "I had heard that Sir Geoffrey has a rather impressive and plentiful wine cellar, too."

Black shook his head in mock dismay. "You're incorrigible. I'm turning in. I suppose I'll see you at breakfast?" He stood, crushing the stub of his cigarette into a nearby ashtray.

"Indeed," confirmed Newbury. "And then our investigation can begin."

"I can hardly wait," said Black, with as deadpan a tone as he could muster.

III

Breakfast consisted of a small portion of bacon and eggs, followed by copious amounts of black coffee and cigarettes. Black had risen early, unable to sleep, and having eaten, he decided to take a stroll around the extensive grounds of the manor.

It had rained during the night and the air smelled damp and earthy. Water droplets glistened on the immaculate lawns as the sun attempted to break through the canopy of grey clouds, spearing shafts of brilliant light onto the ground.

Black paused for a moment on the stone terrace at the front of the house, surveying the horizon. There, on the far edge of the estate, were the "haunted woods" Newbury had mentioned the previous evening. Black didn't put much stock in talk of ghosts and ghouls but, he had to admit, the dark, spiky stretch of woodland did not appear particularly inviting. The leafless trees seemed somehow threatening as they clawed at the sky with their jagged fingers. He could see why they'd attracted such a sinister reputation.

He turned at the sound of footsteps on the terrace behind him.

"Ah, there you are," said Newbury, coming to stand beside

him. "Your friend Benson said you'd be out here."

"Benson?" asked Black, surprised. "I'm astonished he's managed to rouse himself so early."

"It seems he couldn't keep away from the bacon and eggs," replied Newbury, deadpan. "And I gather he's smarting from losing at billiards."

Black almost snorted as he attempted to fight back a guffaw.

Newbury smiled. "I must say, Templeton – you do seem to have a fondness for rather raffish company."

Black grinned. "We *are* here for a party, Sir Maurice."

"Well, some of us, perhaps," replied Newbury. "Are you ready to assist me in examining Mr Blakemore's room?"

"Mmm," mumbled Black, taking a final draw on his cigarette and stubbing out the still-smouldering butt on the stone balustrade. "Yes. Coming."

He turned to find Newbury was already holding the French doors open for him, but he couldn't resist one final glance over his shoulder at the brooding, ominous woods in the middle distance.

IV

Henry Blakemore's room was immaculately kept, ordered to an almost military precision. The furnishings were sparse and functional: a bed, a wooden nightstand, a small gentleman's wardrobe. The man's belongings appeared just as minimal, with very few personal effects, save for a hairbrush and toiletries, a handful of neatly shelved novels and a drawer full of papers and old photographs. A few carefully pressed suits hung in the wardrobe. A small window looked out upon the gardens. To Black it seemed more like a prison than a home.

"It seems he lives a rather spartan existence," he said, picking out one of the novels and turning it over in his hands. He read the title on the spine: *The Moonstone* by Wilkie Collins.

It looked well thumbed, with some of the page corners turned over. He returned it to its place on the shelf.

"A military man, I'd suggest," said Newbury, glancing around. "We can confirm that with Sir Geoffrey, of course."

"You think it's pertinent?" asked Black.

Newbury shrugged. "Anything could be pertinent at this stage. It would certainly explain why he doesn't appear to place much value in material acquisitions. Perhaps also why he leads such a private existence, and why he might have chosen not to share his problems with the rest of the staff."

Black nodded. "Makes sense." He crossed to the dresser. "There's little here that might help us to discover what's happened to him, though. The whole place seems devoid of personality."

"Hmm," murmured Newbury, distractedly. Black turned to see him folding back the bed sheets and lifting the pillow. "Ah-ha!" exclaimed Newbury a moment later, fumbling beneath the pillow for something small and blue.

"What have you got there?" asked Black, joining him by the bedside.

"A small bottle," replied Newbury, holding it up to the light. It was corked and no more than six inches tall. A dark liquid sloshed around inside as Newbury turned it over in his hand, searching for a label. A little square of brown paper had been pasted on the side, with a handwritten legend scrawled upon it. It read: *WARNER'S LUNG TONIC.*

"Quack medicine," said Newbury, with distaste. He handed the bottle to Black, who took it, bemused. He shrugged and pulled the stopper free, bringing the vessel up to his nose, before recoiling in abject disgust.

"Who the blazes could even consider ingesting such a foul concoction?" he asked, quickly forcing the stopper back into the neck of the bottle. He fought a brief wave of nausea, hoping that the oily, acrid scent of the tonic would soon clear from his throat and nostrils.

"Someone who was very desperate," said Newbury, thoughtfully. "Someone who had nothing to lose."

Black placed the bottle on the bedside table and glared at it balefully as if it were a living thing. "Someone with an iron stomach and no taste buds," he said.

"Nevertheless," said Newbury, "it gives us something to go on."

"You think he might have disappeared because of an illness or affliction?" prompted Black, when it seemed clear that Newbury was not going to elaborate. "What if he simply collapsed somewhere by the side of the road? He could be lying in a hospital, or even dead."

"Quite," replied Newbury. "But let's not alarm everyone just yet. We don't know anything for certain."

Black nodded. "Of course, if he *is* seriously unwell, then someone must have noticed. No matter how private a man he might be. You can't hide things in a house like this. Not from everyone. We should speak to the servants, see if anyone has observed any change in his behaviour."

"Yes, you're right," said Newbury. "Sir Geoffrey told me he'd spoken with them all, and that no one knew where Blakemore might have gone. But this is a different question entirely, isn't it?" He smiled brightly. "I'll start with the footmen if you begin in the kitchens."

"Excellent," replied Black. "That way I might be able to charm the cook into rustling me up some elevenses."

"It's not even ten!" said Newbury, with a disbelieving shake of his head.

"Details," said Black. "Mere details."

V

It was the cook – the portly and generous Mrs Braddock – who turned out to be just the mine of information that

Newbury and Black had been searching for.

Black had spent the two hours following their brief search of Blakemore's room enjoying varied and enlightening discourse with the four women who inhabited the kitchens, sitting on a stool by the fire while they buzzed around him, readying a cold buffet for lunch and making early preparations for dinner. The pungent scent of herbs and spices filled his nostrils, causing his stomach to rumble.

Mrs Braddock had a colourful turn of phrase – one that might have caused a less worldly man to blush – but Black could tell she had a kind heart and, rather than embarrassment, he derived a great deal of enjoyment from her outrageous asides.

"I'd always considered him a bit of an arse," she said of Blakemore, when finally she found time to take a short break, joining Black by the fire for a cup of tea. She was red-faced and hassled, but still smiling. "Bit aloof, if you know what I mean. As if he didn't want anything much to do with the rest of us. Up 'imself, like." She fixed him with a stern gaze, gesturing upward with bunched fingers as if mimicking something unspeakable. "But I was wrong. Very wrong."

"You were?" prompted Black.

She faltered slightly. "Well, I don't think that I should say any more…"

"What's the matter, Mrs Braddock?" asked Black in his most reassuring tone.

"It's just… well, I'd be betraying a confidence, is all. That's the problem with bloody secrets, ain't it? You're supposed to keep 'em to yourself." She looked rueful.

"Ah. I see your dilemma. But then, there are secrets, and there are *secrets*, if you follow me?" said Black, conspiratorially.

"Not really, love. No," replied Mrs Braddock, with a frown.

Black sighed. "Mr Blakemore is missing, and quite possibly in need of urgent assistance. Surely, if it results in his safe return, he won't hold it against you if you've told me in confidence whatever it is you're keeping secret for him."

Mrs Braddock slurped noisily at her tea. "Oh well, when you put it like that," she said, hurriedly, "then I don't suppose I have a choice!"

"I'd say not," encouraged Black, stifling a laugh.

"It was last week, it happened. It was late in the evening and I'd popped down for a tot of rum." She cupped her hand around her mouth and leaned closer to Black, as if worried that someone might overhear. "I'm in the habit of takin' a small measure before bed, you see. Just a snifter." She sat back, straightening up on the stool and acting as if her little aside had never occurred. "Well, he was bent double by the back door, hacking his guts up. Bloody disgusting, it was. Literally. It was all over the floor."

"What did you do?" asked Black.

"What do you think?" replied Mrs Braddock, incredulous that he should even ask such a thing. "I went to offer my help. He was flushed and disoriented, so I loosened his collar and opened the back door to let in some fresh air. The place stank." She took another swig of her tea, which, Black decided, must have been tepid by this point. "The cold air seemed to bring him round a bit and his coughing subsided. I got him up and walked him through here, to the kitchen, where I cleaned him up. At first he was all apologetic, a bit sheepish, like, but he thanked me for my efforts, once he realised there was no need to be embarrassed. So I fixed him a hot toddy and dragged out a bucket and mop to sort out his mess."

"I take it he hadn't simply over-indulged at the village pub?" asked Black.

Mrs Braddock shook her head. "Not the way he was carrying on. You should've heard him. Sounded like he was about to expire. His lungs were giving him gyp. And all that blood..." She trailed off. "Well, it was clear as the day is long that he was in a bad way."

"Did he talk to you about it?"

Mrs Braddock nodded. "Aye, and in truth they might have been the first real words we'd shared since he joined us over a year ago. Possibly the last, too."

"And?"

"He told me it'd been going on for weeks. That he'd been to see the doctor, who explained there was nothing they could do. He has a lung condition, you see, and it's only a matter of time…" She looked stricken at the memory, and Black remained tight-lipped while she composed herself.

"He said he'd tried everything. Tonics and potions, the lot. But nothing was working. So I… I told him about Martha." She shook her head and issued a long, heartfelt sigh. "Look at me, ruddy fool that I am. Getting all maudlin."

"Tell me about Martha," said Black. "Tell me what you told Mr Blakemore."

Mrs Braddock frowned. "I should never have said anything. I shouldn't have given him hope. It's just that…"

"Go on."

"Martha's my sister-in-law, annoying bat that she is. She told me a story, about a woman who can heal people, using the old ways. Claims she knows a man who was brought back from the brink of death."

"The old ways?" asked Black.

"Magic," replied Mrs Braddock, in a sepulchral whisper. "Funny stuff. Rituals with herbs and plants. That sort of thing."

"Herbs like the ones you're using in your kitchen? They smell delightful," said Black.

Mrs Braddock frowned. "No." She paused. "Well, perhaps. But it's all about how you *use* them," she said, a little defensively.

"I see," said Black, trying to keep the scepticism from his voice. "And you think Mr Blakemore might have gone in search of this woman?"

"Wouldn't you? If you'd run out of options, if you'd tried

everything else. Wouldn't you at least want to try?"

"Yes. I rather think I would," conceded Black. "Do you know where I might find her?"

Mrs Braddock shook her head. "I told Mr Blakemore to ask in the village."

"Then Sir Maurice and I shall do the same," said Black. "My thanks to you, Mrs Braddock. You've been most helpful."

"Do you think you'll find him?" she asked suddenly, her guard slipping.

Black shrugged. "We'll try."

She nodded, getting down from her stool and smoothing the front of her apron. "Was there anything else?"

"A crumpet, perhaps? Or a piece of that rather spiffing-looking pie?" chanced Black, with a grin.

"You cheeky bugger!" was her only response.

VI

The village, it transpired, was little more than a hamlet: a cluster of small stone cottages around a central square, with a single inn – The Saracen's Head – and an old, decommissioned well. It was picturesque and welcoming, but Black couldn't help thinking that, if forced to remain in such environs for more than a few days, he'd be at serious risk of dying from boredom. Quite literally, in fact, given there was nothing to do but ensconce oneself at the inn and drink. And he did like a drink.

Save for the gentle wisps of curling smoke that rose from a handful of chimney stacks, the village appeared utterly devoid of activity. No figures could be seen on the quiet lanes; no sounds of chatter or toil from the surrounding fields.

Given this apparent paucity of life, Newbury and Black settled on The Saracen's Head as the most obvious destination at which to glean the information they sought.

Inside, the inn was an austere, functional sort of place, with roughly hewn wooden tables and stools, and a spitting open fire. Two rust-coloured spaniels lounged luxuriously before the hearth, warming their bellies, and a gaunt-looking man with a balding pate was propped against the bar, apparently engaged in deep thought.

Black hovered by the door and lit a cigarette while Newbury approached the man, coughing politely to gain his attention.

The man – evidently startled by the unexpected arrival of customers – turned to Newbury with a surprised smile. "Oh, ah, hello gentlemen," he stammered. He moved smoothly around to the other side of the bar, looking at Newbury expectantly. "What'll it be?"

"Oh, well..." began Newbury, as if to explain to the man that they were only there to ask a few questions, but Black cut in when he saw the crestfallen expression on the barman's face.

"A gin and tonic, please," he said, taking two strides forward to join Newbury by the bar, "and whatever my colleague is having."

Newbury glanced at him with a raised eyebrow. "Well, I don't suppose a small brandy would do any harm," he conceded.

The barman nodded, shooting a grateful look at Black, and reached for two glasses.

"Gin and tonic? At this hour?" whispered Newbury when the man's back was turned.

"Trust me," replied Black, with a cheery smile. "Buying a drink will help loosen his tongue." He took a pull on his cigarette, expelling the smoke from the corner of his mouth. "And besides, I'm thirsty."

Newbury sighed and reached for his wallet.

"There we go, gents," said the barman as he placed their drinks on the wooden counter. He glanced at Black. "Sloe gin. Made from local berries."

Black took his glass and peered at it for a moment, then took a swig. "That's very good," he said, enthused. "Do you cultivate the berries yourself?"

"No," replied the barman. "They grow wild in these parts. Wild things seem to flourish here." He glanced at Newbury, who passed him a few coins. "Will you be requiring accommodation?"

Newbury shook his head, reaching for his glass. "No, thank you. We're not planning to stay."

The barman gave him a quizzical look. "If you don't mind me saying, gentlemen, you make an unlikely pair of visitors to these parts. Are you guests up at the big house?"

Newbury grinned. "Guilty as charged."

The barman laughed. "It's not often we receive patronage from the manor, but you're the second in as many weeks. There must be something in the air."

Newbury glanced at Black. "Well, that's actually why we're here. We're looking for someone."

The barman narrowed his eyes. "Now don't go expecting me to get involved in anything nefarious. I prefer to keep my nose clean."

Newbury put his drink down and spread his hands in a placatory fashion. "Oh no, nothing nefarious. It's Sir Geoffrey's valet from the manor. He's gone missing. No one has seen him for three days, and we're trying to help. We were led to believe he might have come this way to enquire about the location of an old woman, a healer?"

The barman's shoulders sagged. "Not been seen for three days, you say?" He dashed his hand against the counter in obvious frustration. "He didn't listen to me, then. The damn fool."

"So you *did* speak with him?" prompted Black.

"Oh, yes. I spoke with him. Warned him off. Told him to give it up. But the dogged idiot didn't listen, and now he's missing." The barman's voice raised in pitch as he spoke, as if the anxiety was physically strangling him.

"Warned him off?" asked Newbury. "From what?"

The barman grabbed a bottle of brandy from beneath the counter and poured himself a generous measure. He swallowed it in one, quick slug, gasping as he dropped the glass on the bar. "He's not coming back, you know."

"Tell us," said Black, levelly.

The barman raised his head, meeting Black's gaze. "The old woman," he said. "No one's seen or heard anything of her for months. She used to be a familiar face around these parts. She lives in a cottage in the woods, and people would go to see her with their ailments, pay her a few coins for her help. She'd recommend herbal remedies or find ways to heal people. Some of the methods she employed were... old fashioned. Ancient ways, handed down through the generations. Always worked, though. Whatever she did, she always found a way to help." He paused to pour himself another brandy. "Some people – superstitious types – called her a witch and wanted nothing to do with her, but most of us know her as Old Mab, and she's a kindly sort. A little eccentric, perhaps, but harmless."

"And this is the woman Mr Blakemore, the valet, came looking for?" asked Newbury.

The barman nodded. "Yes. He said he needed her help."

"Then why did you warn him off?" said Black. "It sounds as if this 'Mab' character might have been able to help him." He glanced around for an ashtray, and finding none, extinguished his cigarette in his now-empty glass. Newbury shook his head in dismay.

"As I said, no one's seen anything of her for months," replied the barman, draining his second glass.

"What's become of her?" asked Newbury, his brow furrowed. "Has anyone been to search for the woman?"

"That's exactly the problem," said the barman, quietly. "They have."

"And she's missing?" asked Black.

"No. *They* are." He looked from Newbury to Black, as if judging their reactions. "No one who's gone into those woods in the last four months has come out again. God knows what's become of them. Whatever fate has befallen Old Mab has befallen them, too. There's something in there. Something unnatural."

"The 'haunted woods' that Sir Geoffrey spoke of," said Newbury. "That's why you warned Mr Blakemore against searching for Mab."

"Precisely," said the barman. "No matter how desperate he was, he should never have gone near that wood."

"How many people are unaccounted for?" asked Black.

"Half a dozen, including Mab," said the barman. "And the local bobby, too. He went in looking for some of the missing village folk. Never returned."

Newbury pulled his pocket watch from his jacket and popped open the cover. He consulted the dial. "We still have a couple of hours of light," he said to Black.

"You can't be serious!" exclaimed the barman, clearly taken aback. "After everything I've just said, you're considering going in there?"

Newbury shrugged. "Someone has to get to the bottom of what's going on," he said. "And I do enjoy some old-fashioned haunted woods."

"You're mad!" said the barman, shaking his head.

"Quite possibly," said Newbury. "Are you with me, Templeton?"

"I wouldn't miss it for the world," replied Black, clapping Newbury on the shoulder.

"Then God help you both," muttered the barman, dramatically. "God help you both."

VII

The woods were as sinister up close as they had appeared from the terrace at the manor that morning. Towering trees, divested of their foliage for the season, stood like stoop-backed sentries, guardians protecting some impregnable realm. Their branches were spiky and gnarled, and to Black seemed like the jagged limbs of an ancient, tentacled beast, poised and waiting to strike. A dark path, shrouded in shadow, led deeper into the heart of the wood.

"It does seem rather... unwelcoming," said Newbury. "I can understand why the villagers have come to believe there's something supernatural going on. There's a definite atmosphere about the place."

"You can say that again," said Black. "Are you sure you want to go in there?" He paused, and then decided to say what was on his mind. "We could come back tomorrow, when there's more light. We could be better prepared."

"For what?" said Newbury. "How can we prepare for something that may not even exist? We don't know what we're going up against, if, indeed, we're going up against anything at all. There may be a perfectly reasonable explanation for the missing people."

"Like a wild animal with a big appetite," muttered Black, knowing all too well that Newbury was not to be dissuaded from his current plan.

"You have your revolver?" asked Newbury, as if that would be an end to the matter.

Black looked surprised. "What revolver? I never carry a revolver."

"You don't?" said Newbury, frowning. "Then what about last week, when I went charging into the midst of all those oriental gangsters? You were covering me with a revolver then, weren't you?"

"I was not," replied Black.

Newbury swallowed. "But... I told you to cover me. What if I hadn't been able to fend them off?"

"You bellowed 'cover me' as you went barging in," said Black. "You didn't give me chance to ask what with!"

Newbury raised both eyebrows, and then shook his head. "Remind me to buy you a revolver," he said. He clapped his hands abruptly. "Right, come on. No time like the present." He trudged off in the direction of the tree line.

Sighing, Black hurried to keep up.

VIII

The path through the woods was flanked on either side by an avenue of ancient oaks, and had obviously been cleared many years earlier to form a bridle path. Now, the fingers of the old trees were beginning to encroach, feeling their way out tentatively into the human world, reclaiming the habitat that was once theirs. Black found himself twisting and weaving to avoid them where the path became narrow.

Underfoot, the dirt track had given way to a spongy carpet of moss that was slowly consuming everything, including the fallen branches of long-dead trees, and the trunks of those still living. He wondered how many people had come this way in recent years – he suspected very few. With a shudder, he considered whether the missing villagers might be under that mossy carpet somewhere, their corpses slowly succumbing to its cloying embrace. There was certainly no sign of them or their recent passing, and the place had an air of desolation about it; wild and untamed.

The light was beginning to fade and the setting sun cast long, eerie shadows all about them. Black couldn't help feeling hemmed in by the looming trees. He had the ridiculous notion that their progress was being observed. He pressed on regardless, however, trying to keep up with Newbury, who seemed intent on pushing ever deeper into the woods in search of answers. He'd noticed this tendency in Newbury before – an unrelenting need to get to the truth, no matter the consequences or personal risk. It was an admirable trait, but also a deeply infuriating one. Black considered suggesting they turn back for the day, try again the following morning, but there would be no stopping Newbury, not now his mind was made up. Black trudged on, his feet sinking in the bracken.

Presently, the trees on either side of the path began to thin and open out, and the path itself became wider, eventually giving way to a large copse. From here the path wound away deeper into the heart of the wood, but it was the presence of an old, tumbledown cottage that drew Black's immediate attention.

The building was small and constructed from local stone, and was in a terrible state of disrepair. It had about it the sense of somewhere that had been abandoned for years; trees had forced their way inside the structure, their branches poking through the shattered windows and splintered stonework, or growing up and out through large holes in the thatched roof. Moss and lichen clung to the lintels; vines and creepers dripped from the guttering. No lights burned in the windows, and Black suspected they had not for some time. If this was the house belonging to Old Mab, then she had clearly quit the place a good while ago – far longer than the handful of months implied by the barman at The Saracen's Head. Everything about the cottage suggested it was returning to nature, left to spoil and degenerate, given over to the trees and the moss.

"I think this must be the place Mr Blackstone was searching for," said Newbury, approaching the building and peering in through one of the windows. What remained of the glass was smeared with mossy spores, and a thick bundle of ropey branches erupted from the hole, obscuring the interior from view. The door, however, was hanging open on one damaged hinge, hinting at a shadowy room beyond.

"Well, there's clearly no one living here," said Black, glad for the brief respite from their forced march through the trees. He reached into his jacket and withdrew his silver cigarette tin, popping it open and extracting a Guinea Gold. He rested it between his lips while he sought out his box of Lucifers. "Perhaps Old Mab has moved on, and when the valet discovered the house, he abandoned his search."

The light was thin and pale now, peeking through the treetops in narrow shafts and pooling on the mulch by their feet.

"Then why didn't he return to the manor?" asked Newbury as he circled the decrepit building, searching for any signs of life. The wind whistled loudly through the overhead branches. Pools of dead leaves stirred near Black's boots. "Surely even the most stubborn of men would want to be surrounded by familiar faces as he faced death?"

Black shrugged, blowing smoke from his nostrils. "Perhaps," he said, noncommittally. "Or perhaps he wasn't ready to give up yet. Either way, it doesn't appear that he found what he was looking for here."

"Hmm," said Newbury, unsure. "I'm going to take a quick look inside. You wait here."

Black watched as Newbury picked his way around a twisted knot of tree roots that had erupted from the soil by the threshold, and pushed at the door. The rusted hinge creaked in protest and the door broke free, clattering noisily to the ground. The sudden sound was like a thunderclap in the clearing, and startled birds burst out of the surrounding trees, cawing as they took flight. Startled, Newbury stepped back, glancing over his shoulder at Black. Then, with a shrug, he turned and disappeared inside.

Black took another long draw on his cigarette, kicking idly at the dry leaves. Newbury would return in a few moments to report the house was empty, and then hopefully he'd relent, allowing them to make the long trek back to the manor before night set in. They'd have to resume their search for the missing valet in the morning.

"That was qui—" Black sensed movement and glanced up at the cottage expecting to see Newbury in the doorway, but everything was still and the words died on his lips. He paused, listening intently, tuning out the background sounds of the wood. There it was again: a noise like the rustling of dry leaves. This time it was followed by something that sounded very much like a strangled gasp.

"Sir Maurice?" Without hesitation Black rushed to the door of the cottage, ducking his head beneath the lintel and scrabbling in to look for Newbury. It was gloomy inside, and the first thing that struck him was the thick, mouldy stench of the place. The second was that Newbury appeared to be grappling with a writhing tree root that had snaked around his neck and was attempting to lift him off his feet.

"Get... it... off... me!" gurgled Newbury, when he caught sight of Black in the doorway, cigarette still drooping from his lips. Newbury's arms flailed dramatically, beating ineffectually at his wooden attacker.

In the dim light of the building it was difficult to ascertain exactly what was happening, how best to help. The single room that comprised the ground floor of the building was festooned with hanging roots and branches, curling down from the ceiling, sprouting up through the broken floor, or worming in through cracks in the dry stone walls. They curled and writhed like the tentacles of some dreadful sea monster, alive and full of malicious intent.

Dead leaves covered the floor like a shifting carpet, and the detritus of a former, inhabited home created bizarre juxtapositions: a framed tapestry of two herons nestled amongst sinewy vines; a mahogany tea trolley clutched in the embrace of two claw-like branches; the contents of a bookcase blooming open like paper flowers, speared on the ends of new shoots.

Most disturbingly, at the heart of all this, a figure sat in the ruins of an armchair, nestled amongst the rustling branches. She had once been human – most likely the old witch whom Newbury, Black and the valet before them had sought – but now she was something else entirely, a twisted amalgam of a human being and a tree. Five or six supple branches erupted through the front of her chest, curling about her like probing tentacles; vines snaked around her throat; a thick, translucent root burst from the back of her skull. Her eyes had taken on a dead, milky aspect, and her flesh was dry and smooth, as if it were slowly transforming into the pliable bark of the parasite that had infested her body.

All around her, discarded amongst the dry, brown leaves, lay the desiccated husks of the dead, their hollow bodies ensnared in the web-like roots. One of them was attired in the remnants of a police constable's uniform. Others were less discernible, left for too long to degrade amongst the mulch. These, then, were the missing villagers, the people who had come to Old Mab in search of her help. Black felt bile rising in his gullet.

At her feet lay the recently dead corpse of a man – the valet, Black presumed. More of the translucent roots pierced his chest, slowly draining the fluid from inside of him. Black could see it being drawn into the root system as if it were being sucked through a straw.

"Temple... ton!" bellowed Newbury, and Black fell back just in time to avoid the lash of one of Old Mab's branches as it whipped out toward his head. He stumbled and caught hold of the doorframe, and the witch-thing cackled loudly, dead leaves tumbling from her open mouth as she turned to glower at him with her dead eyes.

Black fought rising panic. They had to get out of there

before they ended up like the valet, like the dead villagers.

Black rushed to Newbury's side, leaping over a trailing branch and grasping hold of the limb that held him. Black wrenched sharply but the branch simply flexed in his grip, and Newbury spluttered and hacked as it constricted around his throat.

Black cast around for something he could use as a weapon, but the branches were all around him now, curling around to ensnare him. He felt something close around his calf and glanced down to see roots snaking up from the ground, weaving around his boots and left leg. All the while, the witch-thing continued her hollow laugh.

Newbury's breathing was constricted, his face swelling, his cheeks flushed. Black had moments to act.

He reached for the cigarette that still dangled from his bottom lip. Steadying himself, he took one last, long draw, and then twisted in the grip of the roots that were now clawing at his waist and flicked the butt towards the old woman. It landed amongst the dry leaves on her lap, disappearing from view.

Newbury kicked out as the branch lifted him wholly off the ground, and his thrashing uncovered the remnants of a shattered mirror amongst the fallen leaves. Jagged teeth of glass were scattered around a gilded oval frame.

Straining against his bonds, Black stooped low and snatched up a fragment of broken glass, curling his fingers around it as the roots that clutched his legs constricted more tightly, twisting him about. He thrashed, lashing out, jabbing the sharp edge into the sinewy branch that held Newbury, slicing deep into the thick, pulpy flesh. The witch-thing screamed, and Black struck again and again, worrying away at the limb that held his friend. Its grip loosened fractionally, and Newbury frantically dragged air into his starving lungs.

By this time the leaves in the woman's lap had begun to

smoulder. Black could smell them burning, and he twisted, watching as the smoke thickened and intensified until sprightly flames began to lick at the edges of the chair. He felt the grip on his ankles loosen and began to pull free, but was forced to watch in horror as Newbury was flung bodily across the room. He crashed into an old sideboard and dropped heavily to the ground. Empty tumblers and shards of broken glass rained down upon his back as he lay still and silent, face down in the dirt.

Old Mab threw her head back and screamed – a shrill, guttural shriek that caused the hair on the nape of Black's neck to stand on end – and one of her branches flicked out, striking him painfully in the chest and sending him sprawling to the floor.

He bashed the side of his head against an overturned lamp stand and rolled, fighting a wave of nausea. He scrambled to his knees, dodging a flailing appendage as she took another swipe at him, this time narrowly missing his face.

His right palm was bleeding where he'd caught it on something in the fall, but he had no time to worry about it. He had to get to Newbury.

He could feel the heat of the fire on the side of his face as he dragged himself to his feet, and a quick glance at the witch-thing told him the Guinea Gold had done its job. The flames had spread to Old Mab herself, hungrily consuming her ancient, tattered clothes and her strange wooden flesh. As she squirmed, her flaming limbs served to spread the fire, dripping incendiary puddles around the room and igniting more of the brittle leaves and dry twigs.

Black staggered across to where Newbury was lying, dropping to his knees and rolling the other man over. Newbury's head lolled, his complexion pale. His eyes were closed, and blood streamed from a deep laceration in his left cheek.

Black felt his heart race, panicked that he was too late, that the witch had already squeezed the life out of Newbury, or that the sudden blow that had tossed him across the room had caused his heart to give out. He put a hand on Newbury's chest, and felt a flood of relief when he realised the man was still drawing shallow, but regular, breath.

"Sir Maurice?" he said, his voice an urgent croak. "Newbury?"

Newbury stirred, his face creasing in a deep frown as his head turned slowly towards Black. He didn't open his eyes. "Templeton?" he said, quietly.

The crackling of the flames had now become a desperate roar as the fire crept up the walls, licking at the ceiling. Oily smoke stung Black's eyes, causing him to hack and splutter. All the while, the screaming, violent death throes of the witch-thing continued behind him.

"Get up!" bellowed Black, grabbing Newbury beneath the shoulders and hauling him up to a sitting position. "Now!"

Newbury opened his eyes and looked woozily at Black, struggling to focus.

"My apologies, Sir Maurice," said Black, drawing back his hand, "but please don't consider this my resignation." He brought his palm back round with a sharp swing, striking Newbury hard across the right cheek.

Newbury howled in shock, lurching back, pushing at Black. For a moment he glowered at Black accusingly, but then his eyes appeared to regain their focus and he shook his head as if clearing the fog. He glanced from side to side, getting his bearings.

"I... I..." he stammered, searching for words.

"Can you walk?" asked Black, getting to his feet. He kept his back stooped to avoid the thick pall of smoke that was settling over the room.

"I think so," replied Newbury. Black grabbed him by the forearms and pulled him up, taking care to steady him as he tottered.

It was difficult now to discern the opening of the door from the walls of angry flame that surrounded it; difficult even to be clear about which direction they were facing. Black decided he would have to trust his instinct. Any longer at the heart of the inferno and the two of them would be asphyxiated or roasted alive.

"This way," he said, grabbing Newbury's upper arm and leading him carefully – but swiftly – towards where he thought the door to be. The interior of the cottage now resembled a Hellish inferno, and the two men were forced to run a gauntlet around blazing stumps, flaming coffee tables and collapsing timbers from above.

"There!" bellowed Newbury from beside him, pulling free and staggering towards the door. Black stumbled after him, gasping for breath. The heat of the fire was searing his lungs, the smoke making it almost impossible to see. He watched, his eyes streaming, as Newbury almost fell out into the clearing beyond, and then paused on the threshold to glance over his shoulder at the burning form of Old Mab, still poised in her armchair at the heart of the conflagration as the flames utterly engulfed her.

Then, with every inch of his body screaming at him to get as far away from the burning cottage as possible, he turned and ran.

IX

It was hours later when the two men – tired, dishevelled and aching – tramped their way along the gravel driveway to Sir Geoffrey's manor. They'd barely spoken during the long walk back, despite numerous attempts by Black to engage Newbury in conversation. Newbury was brooding, Black realised, distracted as he mulled over the day's events, and so they had trudged side by side along the gloomy dirt tracks, each of them pleased to be putting some distance between themselves and that diabolical cottage in the woods.

They paused for a moment on the terrace, standing in the shadow of the great house. It was dark now and the moon cast a watery, silver light upon the grounds, shimmering upon the surface of the lake. Music and chattering voices spilled out from an open window somewhere in the house, the gaiety incongruous, sitting ill with Black's mood.

He turned, glancing back at the woods on the horizon. Even from here he could see that the cottage still burned fiercely, a funeral pyre flickering brightly in the darkness.

"What are we going to tell Sir Geoffrey?" he asked, as Newbury came over to stand beside him. "Surely we can't tell him what *really* happened?"

Newbury sighed. "I'll deal with that. You should get some rest. You've earned it."

Black nodded, although he wasn't sure if the gesture was wasted on the other man, who now seemed fixated on the view.

"Sir Maurice…?" ventured Black. He paused, but when no response appeared forthcoming, decided to press on regardless. "What…" He trailed off, then decided to rephrase his question. "How did she end up like that? Old Mab, I mean."

Newbury kept his eyes fixed on the burning cottage in the distance. "Only she knows for certain," he said, "but I'd wager I have a notion."

"Well?"

"She fell foul of the darkness, Templeton," said Newbury. "I have no doubt she set out with the best of intentions – a little arcane knowledge, a little ritual here or there to heal people's ills, remedies passed down through the ages. I believe she was drawing strength from the plant life around her, imparting it to the ailing people who came to her for help. But she took a step too far. She consorted with things she could not control, bonding with the trees to absorb more of their energy, doing it to help more people, with ever greater ailments." He paused for a moment, as if weighing his words. "I believe I understand that impulse, Templeton. That desire to help people, to sacrifice oneself to achieve one's goals. The draw of it, however, becomes too strong. At some point Old Mab lost sight of who she was, blurring the distinction between herself and the trees. In doing so she became something terrible. She began to draw the life from anything and everything indiscriminately, including the people who came to her for assistance. That hunger was all that was left. It consumed her, just like the trees."

"And she ended up like *that.* A monster, feeding on people," added Black, quietly. "Quite a cautionary tale."

"Indeed," replied Newbury.

They lapsed into silence for a few moments, standing side by side on the terrace, Newbury's words weighing heavily on their minds.

"Well, I suppose I should seek out Sir Geoffrey and apprise him of the situation," said Newbury, after a while. He clapped a hand on Black's shoulder. "I rather fear I've ruined your weekend, Templeton."

Black waved a hand dismissively. "I wouldn't have it any other way."

"I'm glad to hear it," said Newbury, with a grin. He crossed to the door. "Are you coming?"

Black shook his head. "No. Not yet. I think I'll stay out here and… well, have another cigarette."

Newbury laughed. "Yes, you do that." He hesitated. "And Templeton?"

"Yes?"

"Thank you." Newbury opened the door and slipped quietly inside.

Alone on the terrace, smiling, Black reached for his silver cigarette case and extracted another Guinea Gold. He struck a Lucifer on the stone balustrade and brought it up to the tip of his cigarette, enjoying the sound of the crackling paper as the tobacco took to the flame. He filled his lungs with the pungent smoke.

Then, with a sigh, he turned his back on the view and decided he would follow Newbury indoors, regardless. It was time he challenged Benson to a rematch. The poor man was probably going stir-crazy with only Jocasta to keep him company, and besides – Black wanted to see if he couldn't win that guinea back, after all.

THE HAMBLETON AFFAIR

LONDON, NOVEMBER 1901

"You never did tell me about the Hambleton Affair, Newbury."

Sir Charles Bainbridge leaned back in his chair, sipped at his brandy and regarded his friend through a wreath of pungent cigar smoke. Around him, the gas lamps flickered momentarily in their fittings, as if a sudden breeze had passed through Newbury's Chelsea living room. Unperturbed, the chief inspector crossed his legs and stifled a yawn.

Across the room, Newbury was leaning on the mantelpiece, staring silently into the fire. He turned towards the older man, the flames casting his face in stark relief. He nodded. "Indeed not. Although I will warn you, Charles, it's not a tale with a heart-warming end."

Bainbridge sighed. "Are they ever?"

Newbury smiled as he started across the living room to join his friend. "No, I suppose not." He paused beside the drinks cabinet, his expression suddenly serious. He placed a hand on his left side, just above the hip.

Bainbridge furrowed his brow. "The injuries are still troubling you?"

Newbury shrugged. "A little. It's this damnable cold weather." He sucked in his breath. His tone was playful. "I heartily commend to you, Charles, to avoid getting yourself injured in the winter. The experience is rather detrimental to one's constitution."

Bainbridge chuckled and took another draw on his cigar.

"Still, I suppose it would do no harm to relate my little tale," said Newbury, before taking the last few strides across the room and lowering himself gingerly into the chair opposite the other man. His black suit crumpled as he shifted to make himself comfortable. He eyed his friend.

Tonight, Newbury considered, the chief inspector was wearing his age. His white hair was swept back from his forehead and his eyes were rheumy and rimmed with the dark stains of too many sleepless nights. It was clear that he was in need of a rest. Newbury smiled warmly. "You look tired, Charles. Are you sure you wouldn't rather turn in for the night?"

Bainbridge shook his head. "No. Not yet." He raised his glass, a forlorn look in his eyes. "Tonight is the anniversary of Isobel's death. I'd rather keep from dwelling on the matter, if it's all the same." He took a swig of his brandy, shuddering as the alcohol assaulted his palate. "I still think of her, you know. In the quiet times." He shook his head. "Besides, I can't bring myself to abandon a decent brandy." He smiled, his bushy moustache twitching. "Come on, you've put this one off too many times before. Give it up!"

Newbury nodded and placed his own glass on the coffee table between them. He took up his pipe from the arm of the Chesterfield and tapped out the dottles in the palm of his hand. Discarding these, he began to fill the pipe from a small leather tobacco pouch that he searched out from amongst the scattered debris on the tabletop. A moment later he leaned back, puffing gently on the mouthpiece to kindle the flame. He had a haunted expression on his face.

"It was the spring of 'ninety-eight. April, to be precise.

Just a few months before Templeton Black and the disaster at Fairview House, if you recall."

Bainbridge looked sullen. "All too well."

"Indeed. Well, I had just drawn a close to a particularly disturbing case involving a series of brutal murders at an archaeological site, when I received a letter from a man named Crawford, the physician of the Hambleton family of Richmond, North Yorkshire. I had schooled with Sir Clive Hambleton at Oxford, briefly, and while I couldn't claim him as a friend, I knew him as a man of integrity and science. Anyway, the letter went on to describe the most bizarre of affairs." Newbury paused whilst he drew on his pipe, and Bainbridge leaned forward in his chair, urging him to go on.

Newbury smiled. "It appeared that Hambleton had a new wife – a young wife of only eighteen years, named Frances – who had taken up residence with him at Hambleton Manor. Life had proved harmonious for the newlyweds for nearly twelve months, until, only a handful of days before the letter was dated, she had simply vanished from her room without a trace."

Bainbridge took another long slug of his brandy. He eyed Newbury warily. "Well, it sounds pretty clear to me. She'd finally realised that she had inadvertently committed herself to a life of drudgery in rural Yorkshire, with an older man as her only companion. It doesn't sound like the sort of matter I would usually associate with your field of expertise. Had she taken flight?"

Newbury shook his head. "No. Not as simple as all that. But I'll admit that was the first thing that crossed my mind upon reading the missive. Until I read on, that is." Newbury cleared his throat. "It seemed that, after dinner, Mrs Hambleton had retired to her room, as was typical of her daily routine. Only on this occasion, she failed to reappear in the drawing room an hour later. Believing that she had likely fallen into a light doze, her husband made his way up to her room to look in on her, only to find that the bed was undisturbed and that his wife was nowhere to be found."

Bainbridge frowned. "You've lost me, Newbury. I still can't see how it could be anything other than the woman's desire to take flight from her circumstances."

"Quite. And Hambleton initially believed the same. Until he discovered that her belongings were all still *in situ* and had not been disturbed since that morning. Clothes were still in the dresser. Jewellery was still on the dressing table. Precious childhood mementoes were still in a box beneath the bed. Not to mention the fact that the lady had no money of her own.

"Distraught, Hambleton interviewed the servants, none of whom had seen the lady leave the premises. He had them tear the place apart looking for her, but she was nowhere to be found in the house or the grounds. It seemed that, somehow, Hambleton's new wife had simply vanished without a trace."

"Kidnap, then?"

"It remained a distinct possibility, and the local constabulary was indeed called in to investigate. But they could find no evidence of any wrongdoing, and the days that followed brought none of the expected demands from the imagined kidnapper in question. The entire affair remained a mystery, and Crawford, concerned for his charge, had been forced to watch as Hambleton had fallen into a deep funk from which he could not be roused. It was as if the life had gone out of him, leaving behind nothing but a shadow of the former man."

Bainbridge eased himself back in his chair and clamped his cigar between his teeth. "Quite a singular case. I can see now why the man was drawn to write to you. What else did he say?"

"The letter stated that Crawford was aware of my reputation as a man who had experience of the occult and, since there appeared to be no other explanation for what had become of Mrs Hambleton, asked if I would pay a visit to Hambleton Manor to investigate. At the very least, he hoped that I would be able to rule out any occult interference. Hambleton himself, of course, knew nothing of the letter." Newbury shrugged. "Of course, I'm a rational man and knew there had to be a rational explanation for the lady's disappearance, but one finds it difficult to resist a challenge. I set out that very morning, taking the twelve o'clock train from Euston to York." Newbury puffed thoughtfully on his pipe. After a moment he took it from his mouth and waved it at his companion. "Feel free to pour yourself another, Charles. You'll forgive me for not getting up?"

Bainbridge nodded. "Of course. You stay put, Newbury. I'll fetch the decanter over." The chief inspector placed his glass on the table beside Newbury's and pulled himself to his feet. He crossed the room, retrieved the bulbous, flat-bottomed vessel and returned to his seat. He removed the glass stopper with a light *clink* and began sloshing the brown liquid into his glass. He looked up. "Well, keep going man!"

Newbury laughed. "All this police work is starting to show on you, Charles. Patience certainly isn't one of your strong points."

"*Starting* to show! By God, Newbury, after thirty years at the Yard I'd expect even the most fresh-faced shoeshine to be able to discern *that* much."

Newbury grinned. He retrieved his glass from the table. "I hadn't had time to send a telegram ahead to alert Crawford of my impending arrival, so there was no escort awaiting me at the station when the train finally pulled in at York that evening. Collecting my bag from the steward, I took a cab immediately out to Hambleton Manor, which proved to be a pleasant – if brisk – drive through the countryside. The light was starting to wane by this time, and my first sight of the house itself was almost enough to cause me to reconsider my initial thoughts about the case. The place was a rambling wreck, more a farmhouse than a country estate, and appeared so dilapidated that I had to allow for the possibility that my earlier reasoning may in fact have been correct. At that point I admit I would not have been surprised to discover that the young Mrs Hambleton had indeed fled the estate in sheer desperation at her circumstances."

Bainbridge coughed noisily and placed the stub of his cigar in the ashtray. "I take it from your tone that this was not to be the case?"

"Quite so. In fact, as the hansom drew up outside of the house it became clear that the structure was not in such an alarming state of disrepair as it had at first seemed. Certainly, it was in need of urgent cosmetic attention, but the building itself appeared to be sound and the welcome I received from the manservant, Chester, was enough to immediately put me at my ease. I clambered down from the cab and followed the wispy-haired old chap into the house.

"Once inside I was taken directly to the drawing room to meet Crawford, whom – judging by his expression – was more than a little relieved to see another friendly face. He pumped my hand rather vigorously and bade me to take a seat.

"I could tell almost immediately that Crawford was an honourable man. He was clearly concerned for his old friend, and the strain of the situation had begun to show in his face. He was in his mid-forties, with a shock of red hair and a full moustache and beard. His skin was pale and he was obviously tired. He sent Chester away to fetch tea. I asked him where Hambleton was and he offered me a rather sheepish look. He said that he'd sedated him an hour earlier and left him in his room to get some rest. Apparently it was the only way that Crawford had so far managed to force his friend to sleep."

"Sounds like a rum job for a medical man. Was there no

housekeeper who could have helped with all that?"

Newbury shook his head and regarded the bowl of his pipe thoughtfully. "I think they were all a little in awe of the man. Later I would witness the manner in which Hambleton bustled around the house barking directions at his staff, giving orders like he was running some sort of military operation. Which I suppose he was, in many respects, marshalling his troops to search the local area for evidence of his missing wife." He paused. "Still, I'm getting ahead of myself." He smiled, and Bainbridge nodded for him to continue.

"With Hambleton asleep in his room, Crawford took the opportunity to fill me in on the circumstances of the case. He explained that Hambleton had barely spoken a word for days, and spent all of his time waiting on news of his missing wife, or sitting in her room staring at her belongings, as if they could somehow reveal to him what had become of her. It was soon clear from Crawford's testimony that Hambleton was on the verge of a complete breakdown.

"After Crawford had finished recapping the details he had already disclosed in his letter, I explained that I had not had any real contact with the family since my time at Oxford, and asked Crawford to fill in any gaps. He went on to explain that Hambleton had inherited the family fortune – such as it was – after his father had died a few years earlier and had invested heavily in farming and agriculture. He was currently engaged in a project to develop a method of better preserving fruit and vegetables after harvesting, and until recently had spent long hours locked away in his workshop; time, Crawford was not afraid to add, that he felt Hambleton should have been spending with his wife. Nevertheless, Crawford was quick to establish that Hambleton did in fact dote on his young wife, and that if truth be told the doctor was worried about how Hambleton would be able to carry on without her.

"Soon after, Chester returned with the tea, and our

conversation moved on to more practical considerations. I promised I would do all that I could to help resolve the sorry situation, and that, first thing in the morning, I would examine Mrs Hambleton's room for any signs of evidence that may have been missed. Crawford promised that I would be reacquainted with Hambleton later that evening over dinner, and while the doctor was yet to enlighten his friend about my visit, he was sure that Hambleton would be pleased to see an old friend from Oxford." Newbury smiled. He eyed Bainbridge over the rim of his glass as he took a sip. "Can you begin to imagine how Hambleton *really* felt about my unannounced visit?"

Bainbridge shrugged. "Well, I'd imagine he'd be less inclined to reminisce about his schooldays than Crawford seemed to be suggesting, but glad of the extra help in searching for his missing wife, no doubt."

Newbury shook his head. "I fear that could not be further from the truth. I parted from Crawford after tea and Chester kindly showed me to my room. It was small but pleasant enough, furnished with oak panelling and an ostentatious four-poster bed, but with a wonderful view of the grounds. I unpacked my case and took a while to refresh myself, before heading down to the dining room to meet the others for dinner.

"No sooner had I approached the door to the dining hall, however, than I became aware of a heated debate being played out on the other side. Unsure what else I could do, I hesitated on the threshold, awaiting an opportunity to politely make an entrance.

"It seemed that Crawford had finally informed Hambleton about his invitation and my subsequent arrival at the house, and the news had not been received well. I heard Hambleton cursing the doctor. 'She's left me, Crawford, can't you see that? I need to be left alone to my misery.' Crawford then uttered some sort of bumbling reply, and I decided that was the point at which to make my entrance. I strolled through the door as if oblivious to the tension between the two men, and made a point of greeting Hambleton like an old school friend would."

"Did he alter his temperament upon seeing you?"

"Not at all. He greeted me gruffly and without emotion. He refused to look me in the eye, and showed no real sign that he recognised me from our time at Oxford together. It was as if he saw me as an interloper, come to interfere and ogle at him as he wallowed in his misery. He hardly spoke a word throughout dinner, and then made his excuses and repaired to his room, claiming he needed an early night to be fresh for the morning." Newbury shrugged, pausing to gather his thoughts. "Crawford had certainly been right about one thing. Hambleton was indeed in a funk, and a dire one at that. The man looked as if he hadn't slept for a week. His hair was in disarray, he had neglected to shave, his shirtsleeves were filthy and he bore the haunted look of a man who was carrying the weight of the world on his shoulders. It was clear that he truly cared for this girl, and that he blamed himself for whatever had become of her, to the exclusion of all else."

"So how did you handle the man? It can't have been easy trying to help someone in that state of mind, no matter how understandable their disposition."

"I decided to carry on regardless. At that point in proceedings I was still unsure whether I'd actually be able to shed any light on the case, but with no other means to help the poor fellow I decided to follow Crawford's example, and together we retreated to the drawing room to plot our next move. Over a brandy we discussed how we could get to the bottom of the situation. We both felt that our influence on Hambleton could only prove beneficial, and that, whatever had happened to his wife, it was clear he was in need of answers. If we were able to shed even the tiniest sliver of light on the subject, we should do our damnedest to try. I reiterated my intention to search the lady's room at first light. Then, downing the rest of my brandy and offering Crawford all the reassurance I could muster, I retreated to my bed to take some rest.

"It was at this point, however, that things began to take a turn in an entirely different direction."

Newbury stared at the flickering gas lamp on the wall, lost momentarily in his reminiscences. Bainbridge edged forward in his seat. He was caught up in Newbury's story now, anxious to know what happened next.

"How so?"

Newbury smiled. He ran a hand over his face before continuing. "Wearily I made my way to my room, tired from my long journey and more than a little distracted by the shocking appearance of my old school friend. I spent my usual hour reading before settling in for the night – a rather lurid novel entitled *The Beetle* – and a short while later fell into a light doze. Sometime after that I found myself rudely awakened by a terrible banging sound from elsewhere in the house. I sat bolt upright in bed, unsure what to make of the despicable racket. It was as if someone was beating panels of metal sheeting, and the sound of it quite startled me from my bed.

"Pulling my robe around my shoulders, I took up a candle and crept from my room, anxious to understand the nature of the bizarre noise. The hallway outside of my room was dark and deserted. The entire episode had the quality of an intangible dream and I wondered, briefly, if I weren't acting out the fantasies of a nightmare, inspired by the gothic novel I had indulged myself with just a few hours earlier. Yet the banging was so loud and persistent that I knew it had to be real. I crossed the hall, feeling the chill draught as it swelled up the stairwell. The sound was coming from deep within the bowels of the house, far below where I was standing. I wondered why there was no sign of Crawford or any of the staff. Surely they must have been awoken by the thunderous sounds?"

"Remarkable. Did you find out what it was?"

Newbury laughed. "Yes. Indeed. And I fear it was nothing as sensational as you might have imagined, Charles. At the time, however, I admit I was perplexed. I made my way down the stairs in the darkness, my candle guttering and threatening to leave me stranded alone in the shadowy hallway at the foot of the stairs. Then, startled, I heard the shuffling sound of approaching footsteps and all of a sudden Chester was upon me."

Bainbridge frowned. "The manservant? Had he set upon you in the darkness?"

"No, no. But he certainly gave me a fright. His face loomed out of the gloom like some sort of ancient, other-worldly spirit. He was dressed in a robe and his candle had been extinguished, burned down in its holder. He appeared to be heading towards the stairway, returning from a brief sojourn elsewhere in the house. He asked if he could help me with anything, evidently unclear as to the reason for my appearance in the hallway at such a late hour. Puzzled, I enquired about the banging sounds, which were still ringing loudly beneath us – underneath, I realised, the ground floor of the house itself. I surmised that there was obviously a large cellar somewhere far below.

"Chester, who seemed entirely nonplussed by the intolerable sound, shook his head and smiled. 'Nothing to be alarmed about, sir. The master often works late into the night. Best to leave him to his labours.' He put his hand on my arm as if to shepherd me back to bed. Unsure how else to respond, and realising there was little I could do about the noise, I resigned myself to a sleepless night and retraced my steps, following Chester up the creaking stairs and along the galleried landing to my room. After I had heard Chester retreat to the servants' quarters I lay awake for some time, disturbed by the noise, but also suspicious of the manservant and the reasons for his midnight stroll around the house."

Bainbridge stroked his moustache thoughtfully and searched around in his jacket pockets until he located his walnut cigar case. Withdrawing a cigar, he snipped the end with his silver cutter and flicked the brown cap skilfully into the ashtray. Then, taking up one of Newbury's matches, he lit the fat tube with a brief flourish and sat back in his chair, regarding the younger man. "For how long did Hambleton continue with his bizarre nocturnal pursuit?"

"Hours. There was little peace that night, and if truth be told, I rather abused Crawford's patience by taking the opportunity to rise late the next day. I was still groggy from lack of sleep and I admit I found myself a little out of sorts.

"The others were finishing their breakfast when I finally made my way down to the dining room, and even though I was suffering from a terrible bout of lethargy, I was keen to discover more about the nature of the work that had kept Hambleton busy so late into the night."

"I suspect he looked done in, after spending most of the night beating metal?"

Newbury shook his head. "That was one of the strangest things about the entire episode. Hambleton looked fresh-faced and clean-shaven, as if he'd had a good night's rest and had risen early for breakfast. He was sitting at the table finishing a plate of eggs and bacon when I entered the room. I remember it distinctly, the manner in which he eyed me warily as I took a seat beside him. Of course, the first thing I did was enquire about the banging and the nature of his work in the cellar."

"And was he forthcoming?"

"Only in as much as he acknowledged that he *had* been working through the night and apologised for keeping me awake. I pressed him further on the matter, politely at first, but he was loath to give away any real details. I held firm in my questioning, and eventually he relented. His explanation tallied with what Crawford had told me the previous day. He said he was working on a machine that would aid in the preservation of fruit and vegetables after picking, a means by which to maintain the freshness of the produce before it found its way to market."

"Did he show it to you?"

"No. He was dismissive of the whole enterprise. Told me it was 'far from finished' and that there was 'very little of consequence to see'."

"How odd. Did this not raise your suspicions about the man in any way?"

"I certainly had a sense that there was more going on at Hambleton Manor than I had initially suspected. Nevertheless, I was also acutely aware that Hambleton was suffering a great deal of distress following the disappearance of his wife, so perhaps I was a little more forgiving than I may have been in different circumstances.

"Feeling that I should not press the matter any further, I finished my breakfast – indulging in copious amounts of coffee to stave off the fatigue – and agreed with Crawford that he would show me to the missing woman's bedchamber directly. Hambleton, for his part, did nothing but stare at his empty plate as we left the room.

"As we crossed the hall I felt the tension dissipating, and Crawford gave an audible sigh of relief. 'He's not his usual self. Poor man. Please forgive him his brevity of conversation. At any other time I'm sure he would be delighted to reacquaint himself with an old school friend, but with Frances gone…' The doctor clearly felt he needed to apologise for his friend and patient. I allowed him to do so, offering platitudes where necessary. I am much too long in the tooth to let such minor offences concern me.

"I still had little notion of what had occurred at the house, and hoped that the coming day's investigations would yield quick, obvious results. That way I could be on my way back to London as quickly as possible. One sleepless night was already enough for my constitution." Newbury shuffled uncomfortably in his seat, putting a hand to his side. He grimaced with obvious discomfort.

Bainbridge smiled warmly. "I'm sure it won't be too long before you're fully recovered, Newbury. I take it you're now a little more accustomed to sleepless nights?"

Newbury laughed. "Quite right. Quite right." He sucked at his pipe.

"So did the lady's room reveal everything that Crawford hoped it would? Evidence of foul play?"

Newbury shook his head. "Not a bit of it. I went through the place in minute detail. There was nothing of any consequence. No markings, no untoward smells, no evidence of occult activity. Hambleton had been right; the room was completely undisturbed, as if Lady Hambleton had simply disappeared into thin air. There was evidence that her husband had searched the place, of course, but nothing to suggest that she had taken flight. That is, nothing to suggest that she had *planned* to take flight. There was still the slight possibility that she had fled the house on a whim, bearing none of her effects, but that seemed increasingly unlikely. Having been driven along the approach to the house in a hansom the previous day, I found it difficult to believe that anyone could have been able to flee the grounds without being seen, or else without requiring vehicular assistance of some kind. If the lady *had* run away, it was clear to me that she must have had an accomplice.

"Nevertheless, I spent a good hour searching the room, attempting to build an impression of Lady Hambleton and the manner in which she went about her business. You can learn a lot from a victim's personal effects, Charles, something your chaps at Scotland Yard could spend a little more time considering."

Bainbridge shook his head in exasperation.

"Of course, Crawford was getting desperate by this point, and was very insistent in announcing his theories. 'You see, Sir Maurice. The disappearance simply has to have a supernatural explanation. There's no other way to satisfactorily account for it', or words to that effect. I admit his zeal was growing somewhat tiresome. I typically find in situations such as these that the simplest explanation is usually the correct one, and I counselled Crawford that he would do well to keep that fact in mind. While the circumstances were clearly unusual, I was confident that the missing woman had not been abducted through supernatural or occult endeavour, and I resolved to put my finger on the solution before the day was out."

Bainbridge leaned forward to dribble cigar ash into the glass tray on the table. "Ah, so we are nearing some answers."

Newbury smiled and shook his head. "Alas, my hopes of resolving the mystery so quickly were soon dashed. I had a notion that someone in the house knew more than they were letting on, so I next took it upon myself to interview each and every member of the staff. Crawford and I arranged ourselves in the drawing room and, in turn, each of Hambleton's servants were called upon to give account of the events leading up to Lady Hambleton's disappearance. It was a day-long endeavour, and to my frustration we came away from the exercise with nothing of any real import or relevance to the case. Most of the staff proved anxious to stress that they were unaware of any furtive behaviour and that nothing out of the ordinary had occurred in the household on the day that Lady Hambleton went missing. The cook had prepared meals to her normal routine; the maids had stripped and made the beds in typical order. Even Chester, whom I had reason to suspect after finding him wandering the halls the previous night, provided a satisfactory explanation of his activities when pressed."

"Which was?"

"Simply that he'd been woken by the banging from the cellar and had risen to ensure that his master was not in need of his services. Having received no response to his query and finding the door to the cellar locked, he had come away to return to bed. He added that this was not an unusual occurrence and that while Hambleton himself often kept unsociable hours, he in no way expected his staff to accommodate him in such pursuits. His explanation seemed eminently reasonable and seemed to fit with the facts of the matter. In giving his account of the day that Lady Hambleton had disappeared, he accounted well for his whereabouts, the details of which were corroborated by at least two other members of the household staff.

"I admit at this juncture in proceedings I was very nearly dumbfounded by the lack of evidence, but I knew I still had one further line of enquiry to pursue. I needed to see what Hambleton was building in his cellar.

"By this time the day was drawing to a close. Hambleton himself had been out on the grounds of his estate for much of the afternoon. I suggested to Crawford that when Hambleton returned from his excursion we should question him like the other members of the household, allowing him to give his account of the hours leading up to Lady Hambleton's disappearance, and also to enlighten us further as to the nature of the device he was constructing underneath the house. Crawford, of course, was utterly appalled by this notion and rejected the idea immediately. He felt that it was not only a grave imposition on our host, but an unwise course of action, to submit a man in such a terrible state of anguish to probing questions about the loss of his wife. He went on to argue that, as a doctor, he was concerned about the health of his charge and that forcing the man to recall the events of that day would likely be enough to break him."

"Pah! I think this man Crawford was a little wet behind the ears." Bainbridge shook his head with a sigh.

Newbury laughed. "Perhaps so. But at the time I went along with his argument. I'd already resigned myself to spending another night at the manor, and I hoped that the evening might present an opportunity to discuss the matter with Hambleton to the same end. Tired, and unable to do anything more until Hambleton returned, I took myself off to my room to gain what rest I could before dinner.

"I slept for two or three hours, before being woken by a loud rap on my door. Chester had come to inform me that dinner would be served within the hour, and that the master had returned to the house and was taking a brandy in the drawing room. A little dazed from the rude awakening, I thanked the manservant and then stumbled out of bed. Fifteen minutes later I was washed, dressed and on my way to the drawing room, having decided that joining Hambleton for a brandy would be a most excellent idea.

"As it transpired, however, Hambleton had finished his drink and was now on his way to his room to change for dinner. I passed him on the stairs and he stopped momentarily as I bid him good evening. We eyed each other warily. 'I hear from Crawford that your search for supernatural activity on the premises has yet to bear fruit?' I couldn't help but catch the sneer that accompanied this gruff comment. I explained that I now felt beyond any doubt that there were no supernatural or occult elements involved in the disappearance of his wife, and that I was doing all I could to aid in her recovery. At this he seemed genuinely surprised, as if he'd expected me to react defensively to his offhand remark, and I could sense an immediate mellowing in his attitude towards me, as if, for the first time, he had realised that I was genuinely there to

GEORGE MANN

help. He smiled sadly, and said that he'd see me shortly for
dinner, but that I could find Crawford in the drawing room
in the meantime.

"I thanked him as he set off in the direction of his room
once again, but I couldn't help thinking how far removed this
person was from the distraught wreck of a man I'd seen that
morning over breakfast. Evidently his turn around the estate
had done him some good.

"I joined Crawford in the drawing room. He was sitting
in a large armchair knocking back the brandy at a rate I had
rarely seen in a gentleman. He was no longer sober, and
I could tell from the manner in which he looked up and
greeted me that he had been there for some time. The man
was evidently at his wits' end, even more so than Hambleton
had seemed that evening. It occurred to me that I hadn't yet
taken the opportunity to question the doctor. I took a seat
opposite him and poured myself a small measure. Then,
when the opportunity presented itself, I steered the topic of
conversation around to his relationship with the family and
his arrival at the house. I asked him how long he'd been here
at the manor and whether he'd also been the physician of
Lady Hambleton following her marriage to Sir Clive."

Bainbridge coughed and glowered accusingly at the end of
his cigar. His moustache twitched as he considered the facts.
"Very interesting indeed. So you'd come around to wondering
whether Crawford himself was involved in the disappearance.
Did he give a satisfactory account of himself?"

"He did, although it manifested as a rather garbled slurry
of words, as the man was by then too inebriated to sensibly
string his sentences together with any meaning. Nevertheless,
I managed to decipher the gist of it. He claimed he'd arrived
at the house the day after the disappearance, following an
urgent telegram from Hambleton requesting his help. And
while he had indeed been acting as physician to the missing

lady, he claimed he'd had little cause to treat her as yet, as she was young and in perfect health. I had no reason to doubt his claims – the facts were easy to corroborate. I believe his state at that time was derived simply from his frustration at being unable to help his old friend.

"A short while later Hambleton appeared again, dressed for dinner. It was clear by that time, however, that Crawford was in no fit state to eat, so together we carted him off to his room to sleep off the brandy. As a result, dinner itself was a relatively low-key affair, and although Hambleton was beginning to open up to me, he would talk only about our old days at Oxford together, or tell inconsequential stories of his family. When pressed to answer questions regarding his missing wife or his work in the basement, he retreated once again into an impenetrable shell and would not be drawn out.

"With Crawford incapacitated and Hambleton unwilling to talk, I found myself once again at a stalemate. I repaired to my room for an early night. I knew that I had to see what Hambleton was building in his cellar, and I was now near-convinced that it had something to do with the strange disappearance of his wife. There were no other obvious lines of enquiry, and no evidence to suggest that Lady Hambleton had fled the house in a fit of pique.

"That night, I managed to find at least a few hours' sleep before the banging recommenced to startle me from my dreams. I lay awake for some time, listening to the rhythmic hammering that, in the darkness, sounded like some dreadful heartbeat, like the house had somehow come alive while I slept. I stirred from my bed but hesitated at the door. I'd planned to make my way down to the cellar to surprise Hambleton and make sense of what he was doing under the house, but it occurred to me that Chester was probably prowling the house in the darkness, and with Crawford likely still unconscious from the alcohol he had consumed, I thought it better to wait until morning. I planned to get away from the others at the first opportunity and slip down into the cellar to examine the machine. If all was well I would at least have the comfort of knowing that Hambleton was truthfully not involved in his wife's untimely disappearance." Newbury leaned forward in his chair and rubbed a hand over his face. He sighed.

"The next day brought startling revelations, Charles. Perhaps some of the strangest and most disturbing things I have ever seen. But it started typically enough.

"I'd fallen asleep again in the early hours of the morning and woken in good time for breakfast. Expecting to find Hambleton and Crawford in the dining room, I shaved, dressed and hurried down to greet them. I hoped to find an opportunity to steal away while the others were occupied, so that I may find the door to the cellar and investigate what lay beyond. To my surprise, however, Hambleton was nowhere to be seen, and Crawford, looking a little green around the gills, was taking breakfast alone. Or rather he was staring at his plate as if indecisive about whether he should attempt to consume his food or not. He looked up as I came into the room. 'Ah, Sir Maurice. Sir Clive has had to go out on urgent business and extends his apologies. He said he would return by midday and that he hoped everything would soon become clear.'

"Of course, two things immediately crossed my mind. First, that Hambleton's absence from the manor would provide me with the opportunity I had been waiting for, and second, that his message could be deciphered in two different ways: that either he hoped Crawford and I would shortly find an answer to the mystery, or, as I was more inclined to believe, that it was Hambleton himself who had the answer, and that he hoped to be in a position to reveal it to us shortly. I had the sense that things were about to fall into place.

"I took a light breakfast with Crawford, who stoically

attempted to hide the after-effects of his over-zealous consumption of the previous evening. He ate sparingly, with little conversation, and then declared he was in need of fresh air and planned to take a walk to the local village if I wished to join him. Of course, I refused on the grounds that I needed to press on with my investigations and stressed that he should feel at liberty to go on without me. He bid me good morning and took his leave, assuring me that he would return within a couple of hours to help with the matter at hand.

"Being careful not to alert Chester to my plans, I finished my tea in a leisurely fashion, and then, when I was sure that I was alone, I made haste to the cellar door. It wasn't hard to locate, being situated under the staircase in the main hall. I tried the handle, only to find that the door had been locked. Unperturbed, I fished around in my pocket for the tool I had secured there earlier. Glancing from side to side to ensure none of the servants were about, I set to work. I spent nearly five minutes tinkering with the mechanism, attempting to get the latch to spring free. Alas, the lock proved beyond me, as I was far from an expert in such matters in those days. Frustrated, I returned to the drawing room to consider my options."

Bainbridge was confused. "Didn't you put your shoulder to it?"

Newbury shook his head. "You must remember, Charles, that I had no actual evidence of wrong doing. While I had cause to suspect that whatever Hambleton was up to down in that cellar may have somehow been connected to the disappearance of his wife, I had no empirical basis for that belief. None of the staff suspected their master of anything more than a little streak of eccentricity and an inability to keep normal hours. If I went ahead and smashed the door off its hinges, I would have been declaring my suspicion then and there that Hambleton was somehow involved in the disappearance of his wife. If I'd been proved wrong…

well, the recriminations would have been difficult to counter. I had no formal jurisdiction in that house. And more, if I was right about Hambleton's involvement, but unable to find any clear evidence in the cellar to support my claim, then the game would have been up and the villain would have been provided with the perfect opportunity to cover his tracks. It was certainly a quandary, and in the end I decided to sit it out and bide my time.

"As it transpired, however, the case was soon to resolve itself.

"Crawford was true to his word and came bustling into the drawing room around eleven, his cheeks flushed from the exercise. He looked as if the walk had done him good, and he had regained his usual composure. When he saw me sitting by the window with a book on my lap, he offered me a quizzical expression and came to join me, casting off his walking jacket and taking a seat nearby. 'Any developments, Sir Maurice?'

"I assured him I had not been resting on my laurels, and that, while I didn't yet have any evidence to show, I felt that I was drawing closer to a solution. Well, I don't mind telling you, Charles, that while I had indeed managed to spot the culprit in the matter, I had in no way been able to foresee the manner in which the crime had been perpetrated." Newbury paused to smile. "Or indeed the reasons why.

"Anyhow, I asked Crawford to give an account of his morning stroll. He was animated, full of energy. He said he had walked to the local village as planned, enjoying the brisk stroll and the fresh morning air, but had been surprised upon his arrival to find all manner of commotion in the village square. It soon unfolded that a young man had been found dead on the moors – a village lad, the son of the postmaster – and that everyone had gathered to gossip about what had become of the boy. He was seventeen years old and much liked by the community. It seemed a senseless killing. Nevertheless, someone had clearly taken a dislike to the boy, and just a few hours earlier his corpse had been recovered from amongst the heather; battered, bruised and broken.

"Crawford was obviously appalled by such goings-on, but clearly saw no connection to the case in hand. I, on the other hand, believed I now had all the information I needed. This was the motive I had been looking for, and all that remained was to await Hambleton's return. Then, I was convinced, I would have all of the evidence I needed to build my case."

"So what, Hambleton killed this boy on the moors? But why? Did he have something to do with Lady Hambleton's disappearance?"

"In a manner of speaking. But it was much more complicated than all that, as you'll soon hear.

"It was only a short while before Hambleton himself returned to the manor. Crawford and I, sitting silently in the drawing room, were alerted to his arrival by the sound of his horse whinnying noisily in the driveway. We both clambered to our feet. Of course, Chester was the first one out of the door, crossing the hall before either of us had even made it out of the drawing room. And indeed, it was Chester who was to inadvertently give his master away. Coming out into the hall, both Crawford and I heard the manservant exclaim upon seeing his master. 'Sir? Are you hurt?' Hambleton's reply was sharp. 'Don't be ridiculous, man. It's not my blood. Here, take the reins.'

"Glancing cautiously at each other, Crawford and I made our way out into the bright afternoon to get a measure of the situation. Chester was leading the horse away across the gravelled courtyard. Hambleton, still wearing his hat and cape, was spattered with blood. It was all over him; up his arms, over his chest. Even flecked over his collar and chin. His gloves were dripping in the stuff. He gave us a cursory glance, before pushing past us and into the hall, his boots leaving muddy footprints behind him.

"Crawford was appalled. 'Look here, Sir Clive. What's the meaning of all this blood? What the devil have you been up to? This morning you said that you hoped everything would become clear, but as yet, things continue to be as murky as ever!'

"Hambleton stared at his friend for a long while. His shoulders fell. It was as if a light had gone out behind his eyes. 'Very well, Crawford. I had hoped to at least find myself some clean attire, but I suppose it is time. You too, Newbury. You've probably worked it out by now, anyway.'

"He led us across the hall, stopping at the door to his cellar. There, he fished a key out from under his coat, smearing oily blood all over his clothes. He turned the key hastily in the lock and then, pulling the door open, revealed a staircase, which he quickly descended into the darkness. Crawford hesitated on the top step, but I was quick to push past him and followed Hambleton down into the stygian depths of the workshop. A moment later I heard Crawford's footfalls on the stairs behind me." Newbury sighed and took a long draw on his brandy. Bainbridge was on the edge of his seat. He'd allowed his cigar to burn down in the ashtray as Newbury talked, and he was watching his friend intently, anxious to know how the mystery would resolve itself.

"The workshop was a sight to behold. It was a large room that must have filled a space equal to half the footprint of the manor itself. It was lit by only the weak glow of a handful of gas lamps and the crackling blue light of Hambleton's bizarre machine, which filled a good third of the space and was wired to a small generator that whined with an insistent hum. Valves hissed noisily and the machine throbbed with a strange, pulsating energy; a huge brass edifice like an altar, with two immense arms that jutted out on either side of it, terminating in large discs between which electrical light crackled like caged lightning. And in the centre of all this, prone on the top of the dais, was Lady Hambleton. Her face was lit by the flickering blue light, and it was clear that she was no longer breathing.

"Hambleton stepped up to take a place beside her.

"Crawford, appearing behind me from the stairway, gave a terrible shout and rushed forward, as if to make a grab for Hambleton. He stopped short, however, when Hambleton raised his hand to produce a gun from beneath the folds of his coat. He waved it at Crawford. 'Don't come any closer, Crawford. I don't want you to inadvertently come to any harm. This is only for your own good.'

"Crawford was incensed, but stayed back, putting himself between me and the gun. He caught my eye, trying to get a measure of how I planned to respond to the situation. He turned back to Hambleton, his voice firm. 'What's going on, man? What's happened to Frances?'

"Hambleton sighed and lowered his gun. He met Crawford's eye, and spoke to his friend as if I were not there in the room with them at all. I listened to his terrible tale as he recounted it.

"'I knew the danger of marrying a young wife was that she may quickly grow tired of an older man, or at least weary of my company as I grew only older and more stuck in my ways. I loved Frances more than it is possible to say. I love her still.' He glanced at his wife, serene on the contraption behind him. 'I had miscalculated just how soon she would begin to look for companionship elsewhere, however, and had not expected after only twelve months to find her making merry with the postmaster's son in the stables. I was enraged, and stormed out of there with fire in my belly. The boy had scarpered and I had refused to see Frances for the rest of the day. That night, however, we had a blazing row over dinner, and Frances had declared her love for the boy, claiming that I was a terrible husband who had trapped her in a drafty old house and paid her no attention. This cut me dreadfully, and I found myself seething as she fled the room.' Hambleton offered Crawford a pleading look, as if willing him to try to understand. 'That is when the insanity took hold of me. I knew I was losing her, and I couldn't stand it, couldn't stand the thought of another man laying his hands on her. In a fit of madness I waited until the servants were all engaged elsewhere in the house and stormed up to her room, dragged her to the cellar and activated the machine.'

"Crawford's voice was barely a whisper. 'What is the machine?'

"'An experimental preserving device, designed to maintain the integrity of food after harvesting. It holds things in a form of stasis field, a bubble of energy that preserves them indefinitely, preventing them from decaying or altering in any way.' He paused, as if choking on his own words.

"'I threw Frances into the stasis field in a fit of rage, believing that I was saving her from herself, that it was the only way to stop her from leaving me forever. Too late, when the madness and rage had passed, I realised I had not yet perfected the means to bring her out of it again. All of my experiments with fruit and vegetables had ended in disaster. The integrity of the flesh had not been able to withstand the process of being withdrawn from the preserving field. Anything organic I put in there would simply fall apart when the field was terminated. Frances was trapped. Frozen in time, unable to be woken, unable to live her life. I couldn't bring myself to end it, and for days I've been searching for an answer, a means to free her from this God-forsaken prison I've created.'

"Crawford edged forward, and Hambleton raised his firearm once again. Tears were rolling down his cheeks. 'Oh no, Crawford. You don't get to save me this time. This time I deserve my fate. Besides, it's too late now, anyway. I killed the boy this morning; practically tore the poor bastard apart.

There's no going back now. The only choice I have is to submit myself to the stasis field, to join the woman I love in the prison I have created. Goodbye, Crawford. Do not think ill of me.'

"Hambleton turned and threw himself onto the dais beside his wife, his gun clattering to the floor. Crawford cried out. The machine fizzed and crackled, static energy causing my hackles to rise. A moment later Hambleton was overcome, and he collapsed into a peaceful sleep beside his wife."

Bainbridge looked aghast. "So what did you do? How did you get them out?"

"That's just it, Charles. We didn't. There was no way to free them from their fate. Neither Crawford nor I had any notion of how to engage the controls of the machine, and although we spent hours reading through Hambleton's notes, we could find no evidence of a method by which to safely deactivate the preserving field. Hambleton had been telling the truth. They were frozen there, in that bizarre machine, and there was nothing at all we could do about it.

"At a loss for how else to handle the situation, Crawford and I sealed up the basement and went directly to the local constabulary. We told them that we'd all been out walking on the moors and that Hambleton, overcome with distress about his missing wife, had thrown himself in the river. We'd tried to save him, of course, but he'd been swept away and lost. The police set about dredging the river for his body, but of course there was nothing to find. The servants could not dispute the facts, either, as only Chester had seen his master return from the village that morning, and he was loyal until the end."

Bainbridge shook his head. "My God. What a terrible tale. What became of them?"

"A while later Hambleton was declared dead and the house passed on to his nephew. Chester retired from service and Crawford had the door to the cellar panelled over before the new incumbent could move in. The missing lady was never found, presumed dead on the moor, having fled the house of her own volition."

"So, they're still there? Trapped in that cellar, I mean?"

Newbury nodded. "For all I know, yes, they're still there. Perhaps there will come a time when technological achievement is such that the machine can be deactivated and the two disenchanted lovers can be reunited. For now, though, their story ends there, in a basement beneath a manor house." Newbury paused. He eyed his friend. "As I've said before, Charles, revenge can make people do terrible things."

Bainbridge eyed Newbury over the rim of his brandy glass. "Hmm. Well there's a lesson there for all of us, I feel. And for you in particular, Newbury."

Newbury frowned. "How so?"

"I don't think revenge has got anything to do with it. Women, Newbury. Women can make people do terrible things." His eyes sparkled. "Better keep an eye on that assistant of yours, eh?" He winked mischievously.

Newbury flushed red. "Right, you old fool. That's quite enough of that. Time you were getting some rest. I'm in need of my own bed, and you're keeping me from it."

Bainbridge laughed. "Right you are, old man. Right you are." He placed his brandy glass on the table and rose, a little unsteadily, to his feet. He crossed the room, took up his coat and hat and, his cane tapping gently against the floor as he walked, bid his friend goodnight and made his way out into the fog-laden night. Newbury watched from the window as the chief inspector clambered into a waiting cab. Then, hesitating only long enough to bank the fire, he extinguished the gas lamps and made his way slowly to bed.

THE SHATTERED TEACUP

♕

LONDON, DECEMBER 1901

"Newbury! Thank God you're here."

Sir Maurice Newbury swept into the hallway, his overcoat billowing open behind him as he marched across the marble floor towards his friend. His expression was serious. "Don't thank God, Charles. Thank the cabbie who agreed to take my fare this close to Christmas." His face was ruddy from the biting cold and his breath was shallow with exertion. He began removing his black leather gloves, one finger at a time, eyeing the older man for any clue as to why he'd been called from his bed at such an early hour of the morning.

Sir Charles Bainbridge, his grey moustache twitching with irritation, glanced over Newbury's shoulder as if he were expecting someone else. "Miss Hobbes?" He looked flustered.

Newbury shot his friend a stern look. "Charles. It's Christmas Eve!"

Bainbridge nodded in acknowledgement, as if the date had only just dawned on the chief inspector. He glanced at his pocket watch. "Quite so, old man. Quite so." He shook his head. "Well, Christmas or not, I'm afraid the situation here is rather grave."

Newbury nodded. He was a young-looking man approaching

his fortieth year, with jet-black hair and a hawkish nose. His eyes were a startling emerald green. He glanced into the open doorway behind Bainbridge. "Lord Carruthers?"

"In there. Dead."

Newbury raised an eyebrow. "Indeed?" He shrugged out of his overcoat and scarf and handed them both to Bainbridge, who accepted them with a begrudging sigh. Newbury paused for a moment to examine the burst lock and splintered frame where the door had been forced, and then stepped over the threshold into the dimly lit room beyond. He took a moment to survey the scene. "The drawing room, then."

"Yes. Not the most auspicious place to die."

Newbury frowned, glancing round at the dusty stacks of books and trophies. "Oh, I don't know…" Then he caught sight of Carruthers's corpse, sprawled out on the floor before the desk and contorted into a shape that it was never meant to achieve in life. He turned to Bainbridge. "Ah. Well, perhaps not."

He paced further into the room, taking in his surroundings. The room was panelled in dark oak, giving it a gloomy cast, despite the large sash window in the south wall that looked out over an expanse of lawned garden. There was a large wooden writing desk, a bookcase full of austere biographies and Dickens novels, and a chair in one corner, a newspaper draped haphazardly over one arm. There was a small occasional table beside the chair, a well-loved pipe and an empty white saucer resting on its surface. The room had a musty smell about it, of old books and stale air. It reminded Newbury of his study back in Chelsea, only lacking the specimen jars and other, more arcane trinkets.

Something trilled in the corner of the room behind the chair. Newbury glanced at Bainbridge.

"One of Carruthers's little toys. We haven't been able to work out how to shut the thing up."

Intrigued, Newbury approached the chair. The noise sounded again, a kind of *tee... tee,* accompanied by a quiet mechanical whirr. Leaning over the back of the chair, Newbury peered into the shadowy corner. A strange brass object was moving about on the floorboards, its metal feet clacking against the smooth lacquer. It was about the size of a human head, but crafted to resemble a barn owl. Its metallic feathers shimmered in the reflected light of the gas lamps. Newbury watched it for a moment as it paced about, just like a real bird, its head twitching from side to side as it walked. After a few seconds, it turned its head as if to regard him, gears grinding as its glittering, beady eyes adjusted their focus, turning slowly to settle on his face. Then its brass wings clacked and fluttered noisily, and it began to trill again, shuffling off to hide beneath the chair.

Newbury looked across the room at Bainbridge. "What a marvellous little device. Seems almost as if it's alive."

"Hmm."

Newbury grinned at his friend's disdain. The older man looked tired and exasperated, and was clearly in need of a rest. He decided to press on. "So, before I examine the body, what can you tell me of the circumstances?" He indicated Carruthers's corpse with a wave of his hand. "How did you come to find him like this?"

Bainbridge moved over to stand beside Newbury. He kept his eyes on the body while he talked, as if the dead man was somehow likely to move if he so much as dared to look in the other direction. "Well, it seems to me that he's suffered a massive failure of the heart. The door was locked from the inside when the valet found him this morning. He's been here since some time last night. Alone."

Newbury nodded, urging the other man to continue. "Go on."

Bainbridge cleared his throat. He frowned. "I'll admit it

doesn't sit right with me, Newbury. He was a healthy man, in the prime of his life. He was only thirty-six, for Heaven's sake. What should cause him to drop down dead in such a way?" He rubbed his hands over his face, sighing. "And then there's the note."

"The half-scrawled note on the desk, you mean?"

Bainbridge raised an eyebrow. "Yes, I thought you would have spotted it." He sighed, as if in recognition of the fact that his observations were likely to be redundant in the presence of the other man. "Over here." He led Newbury over to Carruthers's desk, stepping around the contorted body, which lay heaped on a Turkish rug, a wooden chair overturned just beside it. He pointed to a sheet of crisp, vellum paper that was resting on the surface of the desk. "He must have been trying to write it as he died."

Newbury stooped over to examine it. Bainbridge was right – it did look as if the note had been prematurely curtailed. The letters B, R and O had been scrawled untidily in black ink, printed hastily in capital letters with a shaky hand. This half-formed word was followed by a smudged black line that trailed off the page and across the desk, terminating at the lip of the desk as if the pen had been dragged violently across the surface. He noted that the leather writing surface had been severely scored where the nib of the pen had bitten into it, opening a large rent.

Newbury crouched, searching out the missing pen. It lay on the floor a few inches from Carruthers's right hand. He reached for it, turning it over in his fingers. It was a fine specimen, crafted in Switzerland about a decade earlier. He touched the tip against the back of his hand. The nib was dry. The note had been written hours ago.

He glanced under the desk. There was a heap of shredded paper, bits of torn envelope, cream-coloured writing paper, and newspaper. It seemed almost as if the strange clockwork owl had been trying to build a nest.

Newbury turned his attention to the body, noting that the dead man's fingers were stained with black ink. It was clear that Carruthers had been trying to scrawl a message on his notepad when whatever killed him had caused him to convulse to the floor, leaving the message unfinished. He was still dressed from dinner, although he'd obviously retired to the drawing room in his shirtsleeves, as his jacket was absent from the scene. His hair was blond and clipped short. His eyes had once been blue, but had now taken on a milky glaze. His skin, too, had developed a waxy sheen, and his face was twisted in a disturbing rictus. He had clearly been dead for some hours.

Bainbridge cleared his throat. "What do you make of it?"

Newbury, still crouching beside the body, looked thoughtful. "The note? Nothing, as yet." He studied the corpse for a moment longer, before glancing up at Bainbridge, distracted. "What is it that you're not telling me, Charles?" he said.

Bainbridge smiled, caught out. "I believe I have a measure of what that note could mean. Carruthers's valet. His name is Brownlow. I've had him detained in the dining room for questioning. I supposed that Carruthers could have been attempting to identify his killer, if indeed it proves to be anything other than a natural death. The letters, see: *BRO*. The beginning of the name *Brownlow*."

Newbury stood. "Very clever, Charles." He placed the pen carefully on the desk beside the note. "And it was certainly murder. Whatever made him convulse like that? His heart may have stopped, but it wasn't natural."

Bainbridge glanced down at the body. "Strangulation? I didn't see any bruising to the throat."

Newbury shook his head. "Poison."

Bainbridge studied his friend for a moment in silence. It was the last thing he needed to hear on Christmas Eve.

The clockwork owl trilled again from the corner of the room – *tee... tee.*

The moment stretched. Finally, Bainbridge sighed, rubbing a hand over his face. He smiled at Newbury, a wordless appreciation for the other man's help. "Brownlow, then?"

Newbury nodded. "Brownlow."

Together the two men left the drawing room – and the corpse – behind them, heading for the dining room, where Carruthers's valet, Brownlow, was waiting patiently to be questioned.

The dining room was long and grandiose, dominated by a marble fireplace and containing exquisitely moulded cornicing, a large, austere portrait of Lord Carruthers on one wall, and a glittering glass chandelier that hung low over the table. By the door, a uniformed bobby was standing on watch, his hands tucked neatly behind his back. He stood to attention as Bainbridge and Newbury entered the room.

At one end of the table sat an aged man in a black suit. He looked haggard and drawn, his skin pale, his eyes rheumy and tired. He was wringing his hands nervously, glancing from side to side as if he expected someone to sneak up on him from behind. Newbury would have placed him in his mid-sixties. Although, judging by his wisp of white hair and his leathery, liver-spotted skin, he could have been much older. He had evidently been worn down by many years of continual service.

"Mr Brownlow?" Bainbridge asked, his tone authoritative, as the two investigators approached the seated man.

The other man looked up. "Yes."

"We've come to ask you some questions. About the death of Lord Carruthers. My name is Sir Charles Bainbridge, of Scotland Yard."

"Yes," said Brownlow quietly, glancing down at his hands.

Bainbridge pulled out a chair and lowered himself to sit opposite the man. Newbury stood off to one side, observing.

"So, Mr Brownlow. You are Lord Carruthers's valet?"

"Indeed. I've been with the family for many, many years." His voice was reedy and high-pitched. He was clearly distraught. "I was with Lord Carruthers's father before he died. I've lived in this house all of my adult life."

Bainbridge nodded. "I can see this has all been a grave shock to you. Who else was in the house last night, besides yourself and Lord Carruthers?"

"Just Mrs Richards, the housekeeper, and Mr MacKinnon, the butler. Many of the other servants have been dismissed for Christmas."

Bainbridge stroked his moustache. "Can you tell us what occurred when you found your master's body?"

Brownlow looked down at his fingers, and then moved his hands underneath the table, as if suddenly conscious of his own nervousness. "It wasn't until this morning that I discovered anything was awry. Lord Carruthers is..." he caught himself "...*was* an early riser by habit. Consequently, I have grown accustomed to retiring early, so to be ready to rise before my master each morning. Last night he dismissed me after dinner, around eight o'clock, and I went immediately to my room. I spent some time reading before taking to my bed around half-past nine." He cleared his throat, glancing at Newbury, who was studying the man intently. "When I woke this morning I completed my usual round of preparations for the day, before looking in on the master at precisely eight o'clock. That was when I discovered his bed had not been slept in."

Bainbridge leaned back in his chair, looking thoughtful. "What was your first reaction?"

"I know my master's habits well. This was highly irregular. I spoke with Mrs Richards and she informed me that the last she had seen of the master was the previous evening, in the drawing room. I went immediately to the door to that room and found it locked from the inside. I knocked three times but did not elicit a response. I tried my key but found the master's key was still in the lock from the other side. Fearing the worst, I shouldered the door from its hinges and found the master dead on the floor before his desk. I sent for the police immediately."

Newbury stepped forward. "Did you touch anything in the room, Mr Brownlow? This is very important. Did you move anything other than Lord Carruthers's body?"

Brownlow shook his head. He looked perplexed. "No. I'm sure of it. I didn't touch a thing."

"Then thank you, Mr Brownlow. I believe you are free to go about your business." Newbury looked to Bainbridge, who frowned, confused, but nodded his approval, trusting Newbury's instincts.

The valet got to his feet and shuffled slowly towards the door. Newbury pulled out a chair beside Bainbridge and lowered himself into it. Then, as if it were an afterthought, he turned around in his seat and called after the valet. "Mr Brownlow? Could you please see if Mrs Richards is available for interview?"

The valet nodded. "Of course. I'll ask her to attend to you immediately." He disappeared into the hall.

Bainbridge turned to Newbury, a question in his eyes. Newbury shook his head. "Bear with me, Charles."

Bainbridge sighed, loudly.

Newbury stared thoughtfully at the fireplace, where the flames were licking hungrily at the yuletide logs.

Mrs Richards was a stout woman in her fifties, with dark brown hair scraped back into a tight bun, and a warm face that showed what Newbury deemed to be genuine shock and sadness at the death of her employer. She sat at the end of the table facing the two investigators, her hands folded neatly on her lap. She was wearing a long, blue flower-print dress beneath a plum-coloured apron.

Newbury leaned forward, looking her straight in the eye. "So tell me, Mrs Richards. Who stands to benefit from the death of Lord Carruthers?"

The woman looked taken aback by the directness of the question. "To be honest with you, sir, I have little to no idea. As you know, the master was not yet married, and his father was buried just a year ago this last spring. There was a younger sibling once, a boy named Harry, but he and his mother died shortly after childbirth and the previous Lord Carruthers never remarried. I expect there is a cousin or an uncle who will benefit from the estate." She shook her head. "I also expect my husband and I will be turned out before too long, once the answer to that question has been successfully ascertained."

Newbury looked thoughtful. "When was the last time you saw Lord Carruthers alive, Mrs Richards?"

"Last night. It was just before ten o'clock. I was on my way to bed when I happened across Mr MacKinnon, the butler, who was taking the master a tray of tea. I offered to deliver it on my way."

Newbury smiled. "And how did you find Lord Carruthers when you knocked on the door to the drawing room?"

Mrs Richards thought for a moment. "Relieved, I should say. I recall thinking he must have been very much looking forward to the refreshment, given the look on his face."

"But aside from that. No sense that he was feeling unwell or troubled in any way?"

"Not unwell, no. But it was unusual for him still to be up and about at that hour. He seemed animated, certainly. Vexed, even. But he was polite enough, and when I asked him if he needed anything else he was kind to me as usual and sent me on my way."

"And what of the tray of tea?"

"I poured him a cup and removed the tray and teapot to the hall. I collected them this morning before I began making preparations for breakfast."

"Excellent!" Newbury stood, then began pacing before the fireplace, lost in thought. The housekeeper watched him with cautious eyes. After a moment, Newbury paused behind Mrs Richards's chair. "You may take your leave now, Mrs Richards. I'd appreciate it very much if you could send Mr MacKinnon along to talk with us."

Mrs Richards got to her feet, clearly relieved. "I'll do so right away, sir."

The two men watched her as she crossed the room and disappeared through the doorway. Bainbridge glanced at Newbury, raising an eyebrow at his friend. "I know... I won't even ask."

Douglas MacKinnon was a smart-looking man in his early thirties. He was wearing an immaculate black suit and tie, and his hair was blonde and worn in a side parting. His eyes were a piercing electric blue. He spoke with a gentle Scottish lilt that Newbury placed as an Edinburgh accent, and his voice itself was soft and even.

Bainbridge was first to start with the questions. "So tell me, Mr MacKinnon. How long have you been with Lord Carruthers's household?"

The man smiled. "Only this last six months, sir. Before then I was engaged as a butler in Edinburgh, to the Collins family."

"And how have you found Lord Carruthers?"

"An excellent man in many regards. He treated his staff well, and I was made very welcome in his household."

"And the rest of the staff. Did they accept you readily?"

MacKinnon shrugged. "They did. It was obviously a difficult time for many of them. They had lost the former Lord Carruthers only six months before my arrival, and they were still recovering from the loss of the previous butler, who had been with the family for many years. But they accepted me readily enough."

Bainbridge cleared his throat. "So when did you last see your former master alive?"

Newbury watched the butler's reaction. He remained steadfastly unemotional. "Last night. Just before ten o'clock. He rang the bell for tea."

Newbury leaned forward. "And did you deliver that tea?"

"No, sir." The butler paused. "After hearing the bell I called on the master in the drawing room to enquire as to his needs. Then I repaired to the kitchen to organise the tea. However, I met Mrs Richards in the passageway outside of the kitchen, and since she was already heading in the direction of the drawing room, she offered to deliver the tray on my behalf."

"So can you explain why Lord Carruthers may have been showing signs of vexation when she knocked on his door just a few minutes later with that very same tray?"

"I cannot."

Newbury drew a deep breath. "You can stop pretending now, Harry. I understand that none of this has been easy."

The butler's eyes opened wide in shock, and he glanced at the door, as if making ready to run. The bobby stiffened and stepped into the opening, blocking his escape route. Bainbridge stood, nearly knocking his chair over as he did. He glared at the butler.

"Harry? Harry Carruthers?"

Newbury nodded. "That's right, isn't it, Mr MacKinnon? That's your real name, although no one would know it. The Scottish accent is an excellent disguise."

The man glowered at Newbury across the table. "It's no disguise. I spent my childhood rotting in an orphanage in the north, abandoned by my father after my mother's death. He couldn't bear to give up his precious Alastair, of course – my dear brother was his pride and joy – but he blamed me for my mother's death and cast me out, telling the world I had died alongside my mother. I was just an infant. I didn't discover this until years later, of course, and by then I'd already been to hell and back. But a few months ago, when my father died, I finally discovered the truth. I was visited by one of the women who had taken me in at the orphanage. She said that she couldn't live with the secret any longer."

"So you decided to get close to the family. The death of the previous butler was the perfect opportunity, I imagine?"

"I was already working as a servant at the Collins house, although my position was that of an underling. But I couldn't let the opportunity pass. I moved to the nearby village and took a cheap room at the inn. I courted one of the maids who worked at the house, and soon enough she put a word in for me with Mr Brownlow. He was quick to take me on when I listed my credentials. By that time they were much in need of another pair of hands."

"And of course, the Scottish accent and the years of harsh living ensured that no one would recognise you. Not least your brother, who had no reason to even suspect a resemblance. For years he'd been labouring under the impression you were dead."

"And I might as well have been, for all the difference it made when I confronted him after dinner last night. He refused to believe me. He claimed that I was dredging up his family's past in the hope of extorting his father's fortune from him. He told me to get out of his house and to never come back."

Newbury nodded. "So you decided to enact your revenge.

You went directly to the kitchen, found the bottle of strychnine you had secured there for just this occasion, and prepared a deadly brew for your sibling. The clever part is how you tricked poor Mrs Richards into delivering the poisoned cup on your behalf, so that you were never anywhere near the room whilst your brother was struggling for his life. Did you plan to come forward later to claim the inheritance?"

"Perhaps. I would have asked for what was rightfully mine."

Bainbridge banged his fist on the table. "You're a despicable wretch." He turned to the bobby, who had been standing patiently by the door, awaiting instructions. "Get him out of here. Throw him in a cell. He can spend Christmas where he belongs."

He slumped back into his chair beside Newbury, and the two of them watched as the young man was led away, his hands cuffed firmly behind his back.

"How the devil did you work it out, Newbury?" said Bainbridge, bemused. He tugged on his moustache, pondering the flames that still danced in the grate.

Newbury laughed. "It was the clockwork owl that gave it away."

Bainbridge turned to look at his friend, his brow furrowed. "How so?"

"It was trying to tell us all along. Those sounds it was making – *tee, tee* – I think it was telling us how the murder was effected. We assumed all along that there were no actual witnesses to the murder. But we were wrong. That automaton saw everything. And that's why it was making that infernal racket. It wasn't just programmed to make those sounds. It was repeating the same word over and over to put us on the right trail – *tea, tea.*"

"My God! Are you sure?"

"I'll wager if we were to go back to the drawing room now and shift that chair we'd find all the pieces of that shattered teacup hidden under there, collected by the owl during the night. That was the first thing I noticed when I walked into the room this morning. There was a saucer on the table, but no matching cup. Carruthers must have dropped it when he'd fallen, and the owl had saved the pieces as evidence, just like the nest it had built from scraps of paper beneath Carruthers's desk. The Scotsman hadn't counted on that. He was nowhere near the room when the cup was smashed, so he had no reason to look for the debris when the valet found Carruthers the next morning. He probably didn't even consider it. But the missing cup was enough to put me on his trail."

Bainbridge shook his head. "Remarkable. But what about the note? It seemed to be pointing to Brownlow."

Newbury grinned. "No, Charles, although you were on the right track. If the note had been intended to implicate Brownlow, why wouldn't he have destroyed it or removed it when he broke the door down and found Carruthers this morning, before calling the police?"

"What was it then?"

"*B, R, O* – he was spelling the word *BROTHER*. He must have realised that MacKinnon had been telling him the truth, and was trying to leave us a note. One more letter and we might have got it sooner."

Bainbridge shrugged. "Well, it wouldn't have helped poor old Carruthers. We were already too late for him." He glanced at his pocket watch. "We should make haste. It'll soon be Christmas. I'll take you home in my carriage."

Newbury eyed his old friend. "Do you have plans for Christmas dinner, Charles? Mrs Bradshaw makes a passable plum pudding, and I've no doubt the goose is big enough for the three of us."

Bainbridge smiled. "Well, now you come to mention it…"

"Come on then, old man. Let's retire to Chelsea for a brandy. We can put this whole affair out of mind and attempt to enjoy what's left of the season's festivities. Douglas MacKinnon – or rather Harry Carruthers – can wait until Boxing Day."

Bainbridge nodded, getting to his feet. "Thank you, Newbury. If you hadn't put your finger on it so quickly I'd be spending my Christmas here, interviewing the staff."

"Think nothing of it, old man. Think nothing of it. But I do ask one thing of you."

"What's that?"

"Keep an eye on what happens to that marvellous bird. If you find it needs a home…"

"It's yours, Newbury." He clapped a hand on Newbury's shoulder, laughing out loud. "Merry Christmas."

"Merry Christmas, Charles."

The two men collected their coats from the stand in the hallway and set out into the fog-laden night, in search of brandy, cigars and Mrs Bradshaw's excellent plum pudding.

WHAT LIES BENEATH

Dear Alice

Soon! Soon we will be together again. It seems like centuries have passed since I was last able to drink in your sweet scent, to caress your pale cheek, to gaze upon your pretty face. I miss watching you dance in the gardens in that delicate floral gown; miss seeing your tousled hair tumble loosely over your shoulder; miss your beaming smile. How much it pains me to be apart from you! Yet we must take care not to arouse suspicion. Our secret must remain safe. We share it, a burden, together. I will come to you soon, and we can be together again, if only for the shortest of times.

How I long for the day when we do not have to consider the thoughts of others. I live for it. My heart thumps in my chest even now as I think of that day, so loud that I wonder Felicity cannot hear it in the next room!

Poor Felicity. How little she knows. Often I sit here, at my desk, and wonder whether it would be kinder to tell her the truth. It amazes me that she does not yet know. Under her own roof! She glides through her days in blissful ignorance, unaware of the love that has blossomed between her husband and another.

She is no sort of wife to me, but I pity her still. I console myself with the knowledge that she will know soon enough. When the time is right, she will know.

Now, my dearest Alice, I must go. An old friend is coming to visit us. Sir Charles Bainbridge, a policeman from Scotland Yard. Think what he would say if he knew! But do not fear, my love. Soon I will hold you again. Soon,

Isambard

Dear Alice

I fear our liaison must be once more delayed. Much to my surprise, Sir Charles has arrived with another visitor in tow – Sir Maurice Newbury – an anthropologist from the British Museum.

The man is neither wanted, nor welcome. I know you shall think harshly of me for such words, Alice, but I admit I find Sir Maurice unpalatable. He has a certain manner about him; overbearing, direct; arrogant, even. Still, it gives me a feeling of secret glee to know that neither he nor Sir Charles are aware of our secret. Nor shall they be, for I shall take great care not to let it slip, even though I feel a burning desire to shout it from the highest rooftops.

Sir Maurice is unwell. I do not know the cause of his illness, but he starts and shivers and has dark rings beneath his eyes. He barely ate at dinner last night, but guzzled brandy readily enough, until he was clearly inebriated. Sir Charles then saw him off to his room. I wonder if he drinks to forget?

Felicity, of course, fawns over him like a pet. It's disgusting to watch. She fetches him brandy and walks around the gardens with him as if he is the most interesting man alive. Little does she pay me, her husband, such attention! (Still, my dear, I have *you. That means more to me than you could possibly imagine. I do not want or need her attention any longer.)*

Sir Charles says that Sir Maurice is in need of a rest, that he has imposed his friend upon me in an effort to get him away from the city for a few days. Clearly there is more to the matter than that, but it remains unspoken. Of course, I have smiled graciously and welcomed them both with open arms, as any worthy gentleman should. In truth, however, I cannot wait for them to leave so that I may pay you a visit. I live in torment, awaiting the time when I can see you next.

Now I must away to dinner.

> *Be patient, my love,*
> *Isambard*

Dear Alice

Questions, questions! Incessant questions! Newbury knows nothing but questions.

Today, my dear, I took the men shooting on the grounds. The pickings were lean, and we returned with only a handful of mangy rabbits. Needless to say, Newbury was near useless. It was all I could do to still my hand from aiming my shotgun at the odious academic. He proved relentless with his conversation, worming his way into our lives, probing for clues; digging, digging, digging. A constant torrent of questions, right up until we broke to change for dinner.

I think he may suspect something. Does he know of our secret? Does he imagine our trysts? I tried to test him with clever questions – eking out a little information and gauging his response – but he is clever, that one, and did not give himself away. I thought I saw a little smile on his lips, however – a secret, knowing smile – and I'll be watching him. Watching his every movement, listening to his every word. I have a measure of the man, dear Alice, and he shall not be allowed to discover our secret. I promise you. He will die before he knows the truth.

I shall leave this note for you tonight, my love, but shall not risk discovery by lingering for too long in the hope of seeing you. Surely they must leave soon! I need so much to hold you in my arms.

Isambard

Dear Alice

Today I almost let it slip! Tonight at dinner, Sir Charles and I we were talking of his late wife, and I said your name when I meant to speak of Felicity. Thankfully no one appeared to notice, save for a sly look from Newbury. More and more I wonder if he has somehow discovered the truth about us, and worse, that he secretly wants you for himself. You would never leave me, would you, my dearest Alice? Not for him. Not for that secretive, conniving academic. No, I know you too well for that. Of course you would not. You made me a promise, and you are mine forever more. Such is my promise to you.

Nevertheless, it gave me something of a thrill to speak of you in public, to let your sweet name form on my lips. I wish I could talk of you to Sir Charles. We were at school together, the two of us, and I long to confide in him. I am sure he would understand. But I dare not. I cannot risk it. What if he brought it up with Newbury? What if he were unable to keep it to himself, to share in the secret, just as you and I do? Then they would be free to spirit you away from me, and I would lose you forever. I could not bear that.

I must get rid of them, and soon. Sir Charles seems insistent *on overstaying his welcome. Two days already! The longer they remain, the longer it will be before we can be together.*

Your love,
Isambard

Dear Alice

Newbury is incorrigible! Today I found him skulking around the entrance hall, examining things, looking for answers, for hidden clues. He'll never work it out, the damn fool. He claimed to be simply admiring the portraits, but I know his words for the lies they are. He is looking for evidence. He plans to expose us.

If he and Sir Charles do not leave after breakfast tomorrow I will have to take action. Newbury is already ill. I will introduce a poison to his meal. I have some hidden in the potting shed. A slow, deadly poison that will offer up all the symptoms of a heart complaint. He will be dead by late afternoon, and no one will suspect a thing. I know you will think me clever and brave for taking such decisive measures.

Tomorrow night, we will be together!

Isambard

Dear Alice

He knows! I can see it in his eyes! That damnable Newbury. He knows our secret!

He is a sly one, I'll give him that. He did not join us for lunch. After all of my efforts! I had taken great care to create an opportunity to be alone with his food. I dosed his soup with the poison, and took my place at the table just in time for Sir

Charles and Felicity to arrive together (after doing Heaven knows what, alone, in the gardens!).

Newbury, however, sent his apologies, claiming he was feeling unwell and would retire to his room for the remainder of the afternoon. Throughout the meal I could do nothing but imagine him creeping around upstairs while I was trapped in the dining room with the others. He was searching for you, Alice, rummaging around where he's not wanted, trying to expose our secret. To take you for himself.

Well, tonight I draw a line. I'm coming for you, dearest. Tonight I shall make my move. I can wait no longer. We shall flee this place, together. I shall make the preparations. Be ready, my love!

Isambard

Dear Alice,

I can barely bring myself to write a word. All is lost. Newbury and Sir Charles are conspiring in the drawing room. I overheard them talking this afternoon. Newbury has seeded insidious thoughts in Sir Charles's mind. He uses words such as 'erratic behaviour' and 'unhinged'. He makes out that I have lost my mind!

I have no doubt, now, my dear. They're coming for me. I have such little time left. We shall not get away.

Hold on, my love. Our secret is exposed. I'm coming now to bid you farewell before they tear you from my arms. Newbury will not have you! I will die before I give you up.

Know this, my sweetest Alice: I have always loved you!

Isambard

Miss Veronica Hobbes placed the sheaf of letters on the low table beside the chaise longue. Her shoulder was still strapped from the bullet wound she had received two weeks earlier, during her encounter with the rogue agent, Dr Aubrey Knox. She winced as she moved, turning to regard the man standing over by the window. She was wearing a serious expression on her pretty face. "These letters are clearly the work of a madman, Sir Charles. What the devil is going on?"

Sir Charles Bainbridge offered her a heartfelt shrug. His bushy grey moustache twitched as he spoke. "The world is going to pieces is what, Miss Hobbes. Dr Isambard Ward was a good man. I spent many of my formative years in his company. It's a damnable affair. I can hardly believe it myself."

Veronica felt lost. "Believe what? What exactly occurred? And what of Sir Maurice?" she added, with trepidation.

Bainbridge crossed to where Veronica was resting on the chaise longue. He glanced at the pile of letters. "It was meant to be a relaxing break. I believed I was taking Newbury to a place of sanctuary, a place where he could cast off his dependence on that wicked poppy." He sighed heavily. "Little did I imagine that an attempt would be made on his life, nor that I was planting him directly in the middle of another mystery."

"So, what? Dr Ward had lost his mind, and fixated on Sir Maurice, believing him to be a villain? But who is Alice? And what did Newbury want with her?"

Bainbridge smiled; a sad, tired smile. "Alice was once a maid in Ward's employ. What's clear now is that he developed an obsession with her, a deep passion that I'd venture she did not reciprocate. I believe it was this unrequited love that drove him to commit the most heinous of crimes. He became unhinged. He poisoned Alice and hid her corpse beneath the floorboards in one of the disused guest rooms. He rubbed salves into her dead flesh in an attempt to preserve her body, and paid her visits on a regular basis, fantasising that they were having an affair." He shuddered, clearly disturbed by the memory of what he had seen. "He wrote her love letters – such as these – and posted them to her through a crack in the floorboards. He couldn't have her in life, so he made sure she couldn't leave him in death. His wife, Felicity, had no notion of what was going on. She was simply told that Alice had left their employ to take up a position as a governess in another nearby household."

Veronica shook her head, clearly dismayed. "I'm so sorry, Sir Charles. It must have been a terrible shock, to discover an old friend had committed such a terrible act. How did it come to light?"

"Newbury. From the time we arrived Newbury knew that something wasn't right with Ward. I knew he was right, but put it down to stress or anxiety. I suppose I was more forgiving of an old friend's eccentricities. But it didn't sit right with Newbury. Not one bit of it. He said that he'd seen the signs before. He thought that Ward was hiding something, and he was right."

"So Ward was right, too. In the letters, I mean. Newbury really was on his trail."

"In a manner of speaking. Newbury suspected that *something* was amiss, but in no way had he fathomed just how depraved and shocking that something would prove to be. And while he was certainly monitoring Ward's behaviour, he really was unwell, and assures me that at no point did he actually spend time snooping around the house as Ward suggests in his letters. Those are just the ravings of a paranoid mind, I fear."

"So what *did* occur?"

"It was Ward himself who gave it away. After writing that last letter, the bundle of which we discovered only after the Yard had been in to clear up the whole damn mess, Ward decided that we were on to him. In a last, desperate attempt to get away, he rushed to the guest room where he'd hidden the girl's body and began ripping up the floorboards. I think he'd intended to steal away with the corpse. Needless to say, all that banging and shouting alerted us downstairs, and we all went rushing up to discover him cradling the dead woman's body like a baby. The stench was near unbearable. Thankfully, Newbury was able to spare Mrs Ward the shock of seeing her husband reduced to such a sorry state. I was able to prise Ward free of that grim embrace, and we sent for the Yard immediately. Ward confessed the whole thing to me later, after we'd taken him back to London and thrown him in a cell."

"I expect he'll hang for his crime?"

"I think it more likely he'll be banished to the asylum. There's no doubting the fact he's now utterly insane."

Veronica reached for a glass of water that was perched on the table beside her. She took a long draught. Bainbridge stood by, watching her, wordless. The silence between them was enough to convey everything they were both thinking.

"It's Mrs Ward that concerns me." Bainbridge turned to gaze out of the window once again, the sunlight dappling the front of his jacket. Veronica watched the dust motes dance lazily in the air. "She doted on Isambard. Hung on his every word. She'll never be the same again, poor woman. How could you go on living after discovering a secret like that about someone you loved?"

Veronica couldn't look at him. "People keep secrets from one another, Sir Charles. Sometimes for the best of reasons."

"Pah. Poppycock. There's never a good reason for keeping something from the people you love. Secrets are never anything but destructive. Believe me. I was married once." He turned to meet her gaze, a warm smile on his lips. "Anyway, I didn't come to regale you with stories of murder and insanity. I came to find out how you were recovering from your injury."

Veronica grinned. "In that case, Sir Charles, I do believe we should have Mrs Grant put the kettle on. Would you mind terribly if I asked you to search her out and have her fetch the tea?"

"Of course not. It would be my pleasure." He turned and quit the room, calling out for Veronica's housekeeper as he made his way along the landing to the top of the stairs.

Veronica lay back on the cushions and sighed. He was right. Of course he was right. Secrets would be the end of them all. Secrets were the foundation upon which she had built her entire life, what lay beneath the thin veneer of her existence. Secrets were her burden, too, and she knew how they had driven Isambard Ward towards insanity.

Veronica placed her empty glass on the table and turned to see Bainbridge open the door and step into the room. Her heart sank. Secrets might be the end of her friendship with this man, and perhaps the end of her relationship with Newbury, too. She only hoped it wasn't too late. She feared it probably was.

Only time would tell. Time, and the truth, and she feared the latter more than she had feared anything else in her entire life.

THE LADY KILLER

👑

I

Ringing, deafening explosions. Bright lights. Chaos. Screaming.
Then silence. Utter, absolute silence.

II

Sir Maurice Newbury came to with a start.

There was a hand on his cheek, soft and cool. Veronica?
He opened his eyes, feeling groggy. The world was spinning.

The hand belonged to a woman. She was pretty, in her
late twenties, with tousled auburn hair, full, pink lips and a
concerned expression on her face. Not Veronica, then.

Newbury opened his mouth to speak but his tongue felt
thick and dry, and all that escaped was a rough croak.

The woman smiled. "Good. You're coming round." She
glanced over her shoulder. Behind her, the world looked as
if it had been turned upside down. Newbury couldn't make
sense of what he was seeing. He tried to focus on the woman's
face instead. She was watching him again. "There's been an
accident," she said. "My name's Clarissa."

Newbury nodded. An accident? He tried to recall what

had happened, where he was. He couldn't think, couldn't seem to focus. Everything felt sluggish, as if he were under water. How long had he been unconscious? He studied the woman's face. "Clarissa?"

She still had her hand on his cheek. "Yes. That's right." Her voice was soft and steady. Calm. "Do you remember what happened?"

Newbury shook his head, and then winced, as the motion seemed to set off another explosion in his head. *Explosion?* A memory bubbled to the surface. *There had been an explosion.* He shifted, pulling himself into a sitting position. His legs were trapped beneath something hard and immovable.

Clarissa withdrew her hand and sat back on her haunches, still watching him intently. For the first time since waking he became aware of other people in the small space, huddled in little groups, their voices audible only as a low, undulating murmur. Someone was crying.

Newbury blinked. *Was it some sort of prison cell? No. That didn't make any sense. The explosion. An accident.*

Newbury swallowed, wishing he had a drink of water. He was hot and uncomfortable. The air inside the small space was stifling. He felt behind him and found there was something solid he could lean against. He blinked, trying to clear the fogginess. Clarissa looked concerned. "What happened?" he managed to ask, eventually. He was still groggy and his voice sounded slurred.

"I'm not sure. The ground train must have hit something. There was an explosion, and then the carriage overturned. I think I must have blacked out for a minute. When I came round, you were unconscious beside me."

The ground train. Yes, that was right. He'd been on a ground train.

He strained to see over her shoulder again. They were still in the carriage. It was lying on its side.

The vehicle had clearly overturned. How long had they

been there? Minutes? Hours? He had no way of knowing. His head was thumping and the world was making no sense. What had he been doing on a ground train?

He rubbed a hand over his face, tried to take in his situation. His legs were trapped beneath the seat in front and his body was twisted at an awkward angle, so that the floor of the carriage was actually supporting his back. He didn't seem to have broken any limbs, but he wasn't quite sure if he was capable of extracting himself without help. He looked up at Clarissa, who was still regarding him with a steady gaze. "Are you a nurse?"

She didn't even attempt to repress her laughter, which was warm and heartfelt and made Newbury smile. "No. I'm afraid you're out of luck. I'm a typist. Just a typist."

Newbury shook his head. "No. I'm sure you're much more than that."

She gave a wry smile, as if he'd touched a nerve. "Are you hurt?"

"What? No. At least, I don't think so."

"It's just you asked if I was a nurse."

Newbury closed his eyes, sucking ragged breath into his lungs. He must have bashed his head in the aftermath of the explosion. Nothing else could explain the fuzziness he was feeling, his inability to think straight. "I was wondering why you were helping me. If you'd come with the rescue crew."

Clarissa shifted from her crouching position onto her knees. She rubbed her arms. "They're not here yet. I don't think they can get to us. The explosion…" She looked over her shoulder, tossed her hair with a nervous gesture that suggested she was more concerned about their situation than she was trying to let on.

"They'll come. I'm sure of it. It's just a matter of time."

Clarissa shrugged. "I hope you're right. It's just I—" She pitched forward suddenly, grabbing for Newbury as the carriage gave a violent shudder. There was a bang like a thunderclap. Newbury felt himself thrown backwards, and then Clarissa was on top of him, clutching at him, trying to prevent herself from sliding away, across the juddering vehicle. He wrapped his arms around her, desperately holding on. Somewhere else in the confined space a woman started screaming: a long, terrified wail, like that of a keening animal.

Newbury gasped for breath. The engine must have gone up. They were lucky they weren't already dead.

The carriage slid across the cobbled road with the grating whine of rending metal, windows shattering as the frames buckled, showering Newbury and Clarissa with glittering diamonds of glass. Newbury's face stung with scores of tiny wounds. He squeezed his eyes shut and clung to the slight figure of the woman until, a few moments later, the world finally stopped spinning and the carriage came to rest.

For a moment, Clarissa didn't move. He could feel her breath fluttering in her chest, the rapid beating of her heart. Her hands were grasping the front of his jacket, hanging on as if he were the only still point in the universe. Her face was close to his. She smelled of lavender. She raised her head, and he saw the terrified expression on her face.

"Are you alright?" No answer. "Clarissa? Are you alright?"

She seemed suddenly to see him; the vacant look passed out of her eyes. "Yes. Yes, I'm alright." Her voice wavered, as if she didn't really believe her own words. She still hadn't moved. She looked down at him, saw the lapels of his jacket bunched in her fists, realised she was crushing him against another seat. "I'm sorry… I…"

Newbury shook his head. "No need."

She released her grip and eased herself free. As she pulled herself up into a sitting position, she glanced momentarily at her hands, a confused expression clouding her face. Then realisation dawned. She turned her palms out towards Newbury, brandishing them before her, eyes wide. "Blood…" Her voice was barely above a whisper. "Oh God, you're bleeding!"

Newbury stared at her bloodied hands, unable to associate what he was seeing with the words she was saying. He didn't know how to react, what to do next; since waking, everything had taken on a dreamlike quality, as if he were watching scenes from someone else's life unfold around him rather than his own. He stared blankly at Clarissa, waiting to see what she would do next.

She didn't hesitate. Pawing at his jacket, she leaned over him, searching for any signs of a wound. There was blood everywhere. "Where does it hurt?" And then: "You said you weren't injured!"

Newbury pinched the bridge of his nose, tried to concentrate. "I didn't think I was. I—"

"Stay still! You don't want to make matters worse!" She'd finished fiddling with the buttons on the front of his jacket and she yanked it open, exposing the clean white cotton of the shirt beneath. They both looked at it for a moment, dumbfounded.

"If it's not your blood, whose is it?" Clarissa glanced down at herself in surprise, her hands automatically going to her midriff. There was blood there, a dark Mandelbrot of it on her pale blouse, but it was only the impression she had picked up from Newbury's jacket while she'd been laying on top of him.

Newbury reached up and grasped the back of a nearby seat, using it for leverage as he extracted his legs from where they were entangled beneath the seat in front. He called out in pain – a broken metal spar had gouged a long scratch in his calf as he dragged it free. He righted himself, still groggy, then turned to face Clarissa. "Someone is obviously injured. We have to help them."

Clarissa looked at him, incredulous. "You're in no fit state… Look, I don't even know your name."

"Newbury. Sir Maurice Newbury."

She smiled. "Well, you might have a knighthood but it doesn't mean you're impervious to injury."

"I'm quite well. A little groggy, perhaps. But I'll be fine. I can't say the same about whoever has lost so much blood." Tentatively, he pulled himself to his feet, wobbling a little as he attempted to orientate himself in the overturned carriage. His head was swimming and he still felt dreadfully woozy, but he had no choice. He had to press on. "We need to find them and see if they're still alive."

Clarissa laughed. "You're a stubborn fool, Sir Maurice Newbury."

Newbury beamed. "Come on. Let's check on the other passengers."

Clarissa offered him a supporting arm, and together they stumbled the length of the overturned carriage, clambering over the ruins of broken seats and baggage that had exploded in a mess of brightly coloured cardigans and coats.

The roof of the carriage had crumpled during the second explosion, shattering any remaining windows and comprehensively trapping them inside. The openings where the windows had been were now nothing but small, ragged-edged holes, too small for even a child to fit through. They were going to have to wait for assistance.

"Ow!" Clarissa winced as she vaulted over a broken table.

"What is it?" asked Newbury. "Are you alright?"

"It's nothing," she replied, dismissively. "It's just… I bashed my leg in the explosion, is all. I'm fine. There are people here who are really hurt. We should focus on them."

Newbury nodded, climbing unsteadily over the obstruction behind her.

Their fellow passengers had formed into little clusters,

huddling around the wounded and trying to calm those who would otherwise have given in to their rising panic. Newbury and Clarissa moved between them, ensuring none of them were seriously hurt. There appeared to be a raft of minor injuries – even a number of broken limbs – but nothing that could have conceivably resulted in so much blood. Not until, that was, they found the passenger at the back of the carriage.

It was Clarissa who spotted her first. "Oh God," she murmured, putting her hand to her mouth. "She's dead." She grabbed Newbury's arm, pointing to the rear of the carriage.

The woman was still slumped in her seat, her lilac hat pulled down over her brow. Her shoulders were hunched forward, and she was unmoving. There was a dark, crimson stain down the front of her white blouse, and as they drew closer, they could see that the bloodstain had spread to her lap, soaking into her grey woollen skirt. Her arms were flopped uselessly by her sides.

The sight of her caused a cascade of memories to bubble up into Newbury's still-sluggish mind. "Oh, no," he said, trailing off as he staggered towards her. He recognised her immediately, from the hat, the clothes. This was the woman he'd been following when he boarded the ground train. He remembered it now. She was the mysterious agent for whom he'd been searching.

The dead woman was Lady Arkwell.

III

The Queen, Newbury reflected, was looking even more decrepit than usual.

Her flesh had taken on a pale, sickly pallor, and the bellows of her breathing apparatus sounded strained, as if even they had begun to protest under the labour of keeping the woman alive. Her now useless legs were bound around the ankles and calves, and as she rolled forward in her life-preserving wheelchair, he saw that even more chemical drips had been added to the metal rack above her head: little, bulging bags of coloured fluid, feeding her body with nutrients, stimulants and preservatives.

She came to rest before him, folding her arms beneath the bundle of fat tubes that coiled out of her chest and away into the darkness. In the near-silence, he mused he could almost hear the ticking of her empty, clockwork heart.

He stood over her, both of them caught in a globe of orange lantern light in the gloomy emptiness of the audience chamber. She looked up at him from her chair, a wicked smile on her lips. "You do enjoy testing our patience, Newbury."

He nodded, but didn't reply. Following the events at the Grayling Institute, during which he'd uncovered the truth about her patronage of Dr Fabian and his diabolical experiments on Veronica's sister, Amelia, he'd taken to ignoring her summons – preferring, instead, to lose himself to the vagaries of London's many opium dens. It was only out of protest and a sense of duty to the Empire – not the monarch – that he was here now.

Victoria laughed at his uncomfortable silence. "Know that we are watching you, Newbury. We tolerate your insolence only because you remain useful to us. Do not forget that."

Newbury swallowed. "You wished to speak with me, Your Majesty?" he prompted, attempting to change the subject. He'd long ago grown tired of the woman's threats, although he understood all too well that they were far from hollow.

"There is a woman, Newbury," said Victoria, her tone suddenly shifting from one of amused scorn to one of stately authority, "who is proving to be something of a thorn in our side." She emitted a wet, spluttering cough, and Newbury saw a trickle of blood ooze from the corner of her mouth. She dabbed it away. Her bellows sighed noisily as they laboured to inflate her diseased lungs.

So, she had a job for him. "A foreign agent?" he prompted, intrigued.

"Perhaps," murmured the Queen. "Perhaps not. She operates under the alias 'Lady Arkwell'. It is imperative that you locate her and bring her to us."

"What has she done?" enquired Newbury.

"Ignored our invitation," replied Victoria, darkly. She grinned. Newbury nodded slowly and waited for her to continue.

"She is a slippery one, this woman. A trickster, a mistress of sleight of hand. A thief. She has many aliases and she always works alone. She has been linked to a number of incidents throughout the Empire, from thefts to sabotage to political assassinations. Her motives are obscure. Some believe she sells her services as a mercenary, working for the highest bidder, others that she is a foreign agent, working for the Russians or Americans. Perhaps she works alone. We, as yet, are undecided."

Newbury shifted slightly, drawing his hand thoughtfully across his stubble-encrusted chin. He'd never come across the name before. "Do we have any notion of her actual nationality?"

Victoria shook her head. "Unclear. Her various guises have at times suggested Russian, Italian and, indeed, English." She gave a wheezing sigh. "It may be, Newbury, that we are dealing with a traitor." She spat the last word as if it stuck in her throat.

Newbury had dealt with "traitors" before – people like William Ashford, the agent Victoria had mechanically rebuilt after his near-death, a man who was declared rogue because he'd come out of cover in Russia to seek revenge on the man who had tried to kill him. Newbury wondered if he was being handed something similar here. It wasn't only *Lady Arkwell's* motives that were obscure.

"Her age?" he asked, trying to ignore the sinking feeling in the pit of his stomach. The Queen wasn't giving him much to go on.

"Indeterminate."

Newbury tried not to sound exasperated. "But we have reason to believe she is active in London? Do we know what she is planning?"

Victoria laughed, detecting his frustration. "We have heard reports that she is operating in the capital, yes. We do not yet know why. You are charged, Newbury, with uncovering her motives and bringing her in. Preferably alive."

Newbury sighed inwardly. Where to even start with such an endeavour? "With respect, Your Majesty, you're describing a needle in a proverbial haystack. Amongst all the teeming multitudes in this city…" He trailed off, his point made.

Victoria watched him for a moment, a curious expression on her face. When she spoke, her voice had a hard edge. "You are resourceful, Newbury. You will find her." Newbury was in no doubt: this was an order. Victoria's will *would* be done.

She reached for the wooden wheel rims that would allow her to roll her chair back into the darkness, drawing Newbury's audience to a close. Then, pausing, she looked up, catching his eye. "Be warned, Newbury. She is utterly ruthless. Do not be fooled. Do not let your guard down for a moment. And what is more," she drew a sharp intake of breath, reaching for her wheels, "do not fail us."

Newbury watched the seated monarch as she was slowly enveloped by the gloom, until, a moment later, she was swallowed utterly, and he was left standing alone in a sea of black. The only sounds in the enormous audience chamber were the creak of the turning wheels against the marble floor and the incessant wheeze of the Queen's breathing apparatus.

IV

"Oh God. This wasn't an accident, was it?"

Clarissa was standing aghast over the corpse of the dead passenger, her hands to her mouth, her eyes wide with shock. Newbury wanted to put his arm around her; she looked so young and vulnerable. Propriety, however, dictated he did not.

"No. Someone has very purposefully slit her throat," he replied, keeping his voice low to avoid any of the other passengers overhearing. He released his hold on the corpse and the head lolled forward again, the body slumping to one side. He straightened the hat on the dead woman's head, arranging it carefully to cover her blood-smeared face in shadow. He straightened his back.

"Oh God," Clarissa repeated. She remained staring at the body for a moment longer, before tearing her eyes away to look at Newbury. "Whoever did this... do you think they caused the accident?"

Newbury blinked, still trying to shake the grogginess. He must have struck his head badly to be so concussed. It was strange there was no pain. "No," he said, "I don't think so. I imagine it was more opportunistic than that. Whoever did this must have remained conscious during the explosion and the ensuing chaos, and acted swiftly while the rest of us were still blacked out."

Clarissa looked wide-eyed at the dark bloodstains on the front of his jacket. "Why is her blood all over you? You were sitting up there at the front of the carriage near me. How do I know it wasn't you who killed her while I was unconscious?" She looked startled and terrified, and she was backing away from him.

"Don't be ridiculous! Of course I didn't do it!" Newbury didn't know what else to say.

"So you can explain the blood?"

"Well not exactly," he said, with a shrug. "There's nothing to say whoever did it didn't move the body afterwards. I don't know. But I didn't do it. You need to believe me." He reached out a hand and leaned heavily on the back of a nearby seat. His legs felt like jelly. "And remember, my legs were trapped beneath that seat. How could I have done it?"

Something about the conviction in his voice must have reassured Clarissa, as she gave a weak smile and stepped forward again. Nevertheless, he could see that she was still wary. Perhaps she could sense that he was holding something back, keeping from her the fact that he knew who this dead woman actually was.

"Alright. Assuming I believe you, that means there's a murderer somewhere on this carriage." Her voice was a whisper. "No one could have got out. We're trapped in here until the firemen arrive to cut us free. So whoever did it is still here." She glanced around as if sizing up the other passengers, looking for a likely suspect.

Newbury could see the sense in her words. The killer still had to be on board the train.

"And why would they do it? This poor, innocent woman? What could have possibly inspired them to cut her throat?" She shuddered as she spoke, as if considering how different things might have been – how it could have been her, slumped there in the seat with her throat opened up.

Newbury knew the answer to that but chose not to elaborate. It wouldn't do to go involving this girl in the affairs of the Crown, and if he did tell her why, it would only give support to her fears that he was somehow involved in the woman's death. Aside from all that, he didn't want her raising the alarm. The other passengers were scared enough as it was, wondering when – and if – they were going to be free from the buckled remains of the carriage, or whether they were only moments away from another explosion. The last thing these people needed to know was that there was also a murderer on board.

Besides, from everything he knew of her, "Lady Arkwell" was far from innocent. Rumour had it that she was involved in everything from political assassinations to high-profile thefts. No doubt she had scores of enemies, with as many different motives for ending her life.

That suggested the killer had to be another agent. But which nation or organisation they were representing was another question entirely. It wouldn't surprise him to discover the Queen had organised a back-up, a second agent on the trail of Lady Arkwell, just in case Newbury failed. Or perhaps the intention had been for Newbury to lead an assassin to their target all along. Whatever the case, this wasn't a motiveless murder. The killer knew what they were doing, and whom they were targeting.

That in itself begged another question: did the killer also know who he was? Was he also at risk? In his current state, with his head still spinning, he knew he wouldn't be able to handle himself in a scuffle. He had to be on guard.

"What are we going to do?" asked Clarissa, tugging insistently on his sleeve. He looked down at her pretty, upturned face, framed by her shock of red hair, and realised that he hadn't answered her questions.

"I don't know," he replied, shaking his head. "You're right. The killer must still be on board. But we have no way of telling who he might be. I suggest we tread very cautiously, and stick together. We should cover up the body and try not to panic anyone. When they finally cut us free, the killer is going to try to slip away. We need to be alert, watching for anything that might give him away. That way we can alert the authorities when the time is right."

"That's it?" she said, with a frown. "That's all we're going to do?"

"I'm not sure we have any other choice," said Newbury, in a placatory fashion. "If we alert the killer that we're on to him, things could turn very bad, very quickly. We're trapped in an overturned train carriage with no exits. A killer loose in a confined space, desperate and wielding a weapon…" He trailed off, his point made.

Clarissa gave a short, conciliatory nod. "Very well." She stooped and collected up a handful of discarded items of clothing – a man's tweed jacket, a woman's shawl, a tartan blanket – and proceeded to set about covering the dead woman.

Newbury leaned against the wall – which had once been the floor – his head drooping. His memories of the events leading up to the accident were hazy at best, but they were slowly returning. It was surely just a matter of time before he could piece together what had occurred. Yet everything felt like such an effort. All he wanted to do was go to sleep. He lifted his hands to rub at his eyes, but realised they were smeared with the dead woman's blood. Grimacing, he put his right hand into his jacket pocket to search out his handkerchief.

His fingers encountered something cold and hard. Frowning, he peered down as he gingerly closed his hand around the object and slid it out of his pocket. His eyes widened in shock, and he quickly stuffed the thing back, glancing around to make sure no one else had seen.

Clarissa was still busying herself covering the corpse.

Newbury took a deep breath, trying to steady himself. What the Hell was going on? His heart was racing, his head pounding, and he couldn't remember what had happened, what he might have done.

He wasn't a killer. He *had* killed, yes, but he'd been a soldier out in India, and latterly an agent of the Crown. He'd killed in self-defence, in the course of duty, but never in cold blood.

So why, then, was the object in his pocket a sticky, bloodied knife?

GEORGE MANN

V

"So, how are you, Charles?" said Newbury, swallowing a slug of brandy and regarding his old friend, Chief Inspector Charles Bainbridge of Scotland Yard, from across the table. The older man looked tired, careworn, out of sorts. As if he had the weight of the world resting on his shoulders, and was beginning to buckle beneath it.

The two men were sitting in a private booth in the drawing room of Newbury's club, the White Friar's. Over the years Newbury had come to consider the place a second home, enjoying the general ambience and the intelligent banter he often overheard in the bar. The clientele was mostly composed of artists, poets and writers, and although he knew Bainbridge didn't approve of this more bohemian of crowds, Newbury often insisted on meeting him there. It was good, he assured himself, for the older man's soul. And besides, Bainbridge's club was generally full of policemen; useful, perhaps, when one needed such things, but hardly a haven away from the busy matters of everyday life.

Bainbridge gave a heavy sigh. "Darn near exhausted, Newbury, if truth be told. That's how I am. This Moyer case is taking everything I've got."

Newbury gave a resigned smile. Bainbridge had been tracking a killer for weeks, a surgeon by the name of Algernon Moyer, who had – for reasons that appeared to be politically motivated – taken to abducting politicians and minor royals, chaining them up in abandoned houses and infecting them with the Revenant plague. He would then move on, disappearing into the great wash of the city, leaving his victims to slowly starve to death as the plague took hold and they degenerated into slavering, half-dead monsters.

Three days following each of the abductions, a letter had turned up at the Yard, addressed to Bainbridge, teasing him with the location of the most recent crime. By the time

Bainbridge got there, of course, it was already too late. The victims would be beyond saving, reduced to nothing but chattering, snarling animals, straining at their chains as they tried desperately to get at the soft, pink flesh of their rescuers. Every one of them had been put down, electrocuted, their corpses burned in the immense plague furnaces at Battersea or dumped far out at sea along with the mounting heaps of bodies from the slums. Bainbridge hadn't even been able to let the victims' families identify the bodies.

There had been four victims to date, and the police expected another to turn up any day. And, as Bainbridge had continued to bemoan, they were no closer to finding Moyer or uncovering the criteria by which he selected his victims. He struck without warning, abducting them in broad daylight, no obvious connections between them. It was a campaign of terror, and politicians and councillors were increasingly growing wary of leaving the relative safety of their homes.

Newbury echoed his friend's sigh. "I wish I could help you, Charles. I really do. But this Arkwell thing – the Queen..." He trailed off. Bainbridge knew all too well what the Queen was like when she had a bit between her teeth.

Bainbridge looked up from the bottom of his glass. A faint smile tugged at the corners of his mouth. "Ah. Well. That's where I might just be able to help *you*, Newbury."

Newbury leaned forward, pushing his empty glass to one side. "Go on."

"One of our informants, a delightful little man named Smythe..." Bainbridge pronounced the man's name as if he were describing a particularly venomous breed of snake "... Paterson Smythe. He's a burglar and a fence, and not a very successful example of either. But he has a secondary trade in information, and that's what makes him valuable to us." He waved his hand in a dismissive gesture. "Times, places, names. You know the sort of thing."

Newbury nodded. "He doesn't sound the type to be involved with a woman of Lady Arkwell's calibre."

Bainbridge laughed. "Well, precisely. It looks like he might have gone and gotten himself in over his head. He turned up at the Yard this morning claiming he had something big for us, but that he needed our protection."

Newbury raised an eyebrow. "And?"

Bainbridge shrugged. "And it sounds as if it could be your Lady Arkwell. Smythe said he'd been doing some work for a woman, 'a right smart 'un', as he described her, sitting in Bloomsbury Square all night and reporting back to her the next morning to describe everything he'd seen."

Newbury frowned. "Interesting. Anything else?"

"He said it had been going on for a week. No specific target or brief. Simply that she'd told him to note all the comings and goings in the area."

"A scoping job?"

"Precisely that. Descriptions of everyone he saw, when they came in and out of their properties, what time the postman or milkman called. But nothing that might give away the actual target. It could be any one of those grand houses she's interested in, for any reason." Bainbridge frowned, tugging unconsciously at his moustache. "She's clearly a clever one, Newbury. She hasn't left us with much to go on, even after her hired help tried his best to sell her up the river."

"It's already more than I've been able to ascertain so far," replied Newbury. "Where do they meet? That would be a start."

Bainbridge shook his head. "As I said, she's a clever one. They always meet in the back of a brougham. She picks him up at Bloomsbury Square and they drive around the city while he hands over all the information he's gleaned. They always take a different route, and she always deposits him in a different street when they're finished, leaving him with the cab fare home."

"Fascinating," said Newbury, impressed. "Does he have a description of the woman?"

"Only that she wears a black veil beneath a wide-brimmed, lilac hat, along with black lace gloves, so as not to be recognised. He says she dresses smartly in the current fashions, and is well spoken, with an educated, English accent. He does most of the talking, and she issues payment and instructions." Bainbridge shrugged. "That's it. That's all we could get out of him."

Newbury sipped at his brandy while he mulled over his friend's story. Was this the mysterious woman he'd been looking for? And if so, what was she up to? It seemed like an extraordinary effort to go to for a simple robbery. But then, perhaps there was more to it than that. Perhaps this was an invitation to dance.

Bainbridge was looking at him expectantly. "Well? What would you have me do?"

Newbury smiled. "Nothing."

"Nothing?" echoed Bainbridge, confounded. His moustache bristled as he tried to form his response. "Nothing!" he said again.

"Precisely," said Newbury. "Tell Smythe to continue just as he is. Tell him to keep reporting back to this woman on all of the comings and goings to the square, and to make a particular effort to ensure he offers accurate descriptions of all the people he sees."

"Is that all?" asked Bainbridge, clearly unimpressed. "I fail to see how that constitutes an effective plan."

"Not at all," said Newbury. "I believe it's time I offered to play Lady Arkwell at her own game."

"Stop being so bloody cryptic, would you, and spit it out."

Newbury laughed. "If she's as clever as I believe her to be, Charles, she won't have chosen a mealy-mouthed snitch like Smythe without reason. She has no intention of effecting a burglary in Bloomsbury Square. She's doing all of this to announce herself to us – to *me*. She knew full well that Smythe would go running to the Yard. It's an invitation."

"An invitation?" asked Bainbridge. He looked utterly perplexed.

"Indeed. An invitation to respond."

Bainbridge shook his head. "If you're right – and I am not yet convinced that you are – what will you do?"

"Show myself in Bloomsbury Square. Smythe will do the rest," replied Newbury, with a grin. "And then we shall see what move she makes next."

"Good Lord," said Bainbridge, draining the last of his brandy. "You're enjoying this, aren't you?"

"Oh yes," said Newbury, laughing. "Absolutely."

VI

Was it possible? Could he have somehow been driven to kill the woman?

Newbury considered the facts. He'd boarded the ground train while trailing the female agent known as Lady Arkwell, the woman who was now dead from a knife wound to the throat. She'd taken a seat at the rear of the carriage, and so, trying to at least make the pretence of conspicuousness, he'd gone to the front on the opposite side, where he'd been able to keep an eye on her reflection in the window glass. The train had started off, rumbling down Oxford Street, and he'd settled back into his seat, content that he had until at least the next stop before he'd have to make a move.

Despite the fuzziness still clouding his thoughts, he was able to recall at least that much.

The next thing he remembered was waking up with a thick head, Clarissa's hand on his cheek, his jacket covered in blood. Now, additionally, he'd discovered he had a bloodied knife in his pocket. He had no notion of what might have occurred in the intervening time.

He supposed there were two possibilities. Firstly, that he'd been forced to end the woman's life during the aftermath of the accident, before he received the blow to his head that had rendered him unconscious and affected his recollection. Secondly, that the killer had taken advantage of his dazed state to plant the weapon on him, thereby making an attempt to implicate him in the murder.

Despite the apparent outlandishness of the notion, he decided the latter was the most likely option. He was, after all, dealing with assassins and spies, people who might have recognised him and decided he'd make a viable scapegoat to cover their tracks.

Newbury searched the faces of the other people in the carriage. There were at least twenty of them, still huddled in little groups on the floor. None of them seemed familiar. A dark-haired young man with a beard was slumped to one side by himself. His black suit was torn and he was bleeding from a wound in his left forearm. He was watching Newbury intently. Could it be him? Or perhaps the middle-aged man at the other end of the carriage, squatting close to where Newbury had been sitting. He was whispering now to two young women, but his eyes were tracing every one of Newbury's movements, his rugged features fixed in a grim expression.

It was useless to speculate. It could have been any one of the other passengers. He'd have to wait to see if they'd give themselves away. There was nothing else for it.

Newbury rubbed his palm over the back of his neck, wishing the fuzziness in his head would clear. He could feel no lump, no tender spot where he had bashed it during the accident. Why, then, did he still feel so sluggish, so groggy? *It was almost as if...*

A thought struck him. Perhaps he hadn't banged his head

at all. If someone really was attempting to frame him for Lady Arkwell's murder, he might have been drugged. A quick prick with a needle while he was down, a dose of sedative to keep him under, to keep him slow. That had to be it. It was the only explanation for why he was feeling like this. Perhaps the killer had been carrying it in his pocket, intending to use it to incapacitate Lady Arkwell when she alighted from the train. The crash had provided him with a different opportunity, and he'd discharged the syringe into Newbury instead, while everyone else on board was still distracted in the midst of the initial panic and confusion.

It all seemed to make a terrible kind of sense to Newbury, but even so, it brought him no closer to identifying the killer, and at present, he had no way of proving any of it. All he knew for sure was that someone on the train was out to get him, or at the very least, was using him to protect their secret.

"Do you think anyone will notice?" whispered Clarissa from beside him.

He glanced round. She'd done an admirable job. The body might have been a heap of clothes, spilt from a burst case. "Not until we draw their attention to it," he replied, "or one of them comes looking for their coat."

Clarissa gave a wry smile. "I'm scared, Sir Maurice. I keep thinking that no one's going to come and find us and we'll remain trapped in here, with someone capable of... *that*." She put her hand on his chest, and, throwing propriety to the wind, he put his arm around her shoulders and drew her in. They stood there for a moment, holding on to one another as if they were the only still point in the universe.

"It'll be alright," he said, with as reassuring a tone as he could muster. But what he really meant to say was: "I'm scared too."

VII

"Sir Maurice Newbury, I presume?"

The voice was cultured and luxurious, like the purr of a well-mannered cat.

Newbury peeled open his eyes, but for a moment saw nothing but darkness. Then, slowly, shapes began to resolve out of the gloom, as if the shadows themselves were somehow coalescing, taking on physical form.

Around him, figures lay supine on low couches, draped across the daybeds as if they had given themselves up to the deepest of sleeps. Their pale faces might have belonged to spirits or wraiths rather than men; ghostly and lost, these waifs, like Newbury, were adrift on the murky oceans of their own minds.

Gas lamps, turned down low, cast everything in a dim, orange glow.

Newbury turned his head marginally in order to take in the appearance of the man who had spoken. It wasn't a face he recognised. The man was Chinese, in the later years of his life – judging by his wizened, careworn appearance – and was standing politely to one side, his hands clasped behind his back. He was dressed in a fine silk robe and wore an elaborate moustache that curled immaculately around his thin lips, draping solemnly from his chin. His eyes were narrowed as he regarded Newbury through the haze of opium smoke.

Newbury blinked and tried to stir himself, but the drug continued to exert its influence. He couldn't even find the motivation to move. "You presume correctly, sir," he replied, his voice a deep slur. "Of whom do I have the pleasure?"

The other man smiled for the briefest of moments, before swiftly regaining his composure. "My name, sir, is Meng Li."

"Meng Li?" echoed Newbury, unable to contain his surprise. He'd heard the name a hundred times before, always spoken in whispered tones, even amongst the upper echelons of Scotland Yard.

Meng Li was perhaps the most significant of the Chinese gang lords to exert his influence on the British Empire. His network stretched from Hong Kong to Vancouver, from Burma to London itself, and was considered to take in everything from the opium trade to people trafficking, and most other illicit trades besides.

That he should be there in the capital was barely conceivable, let alone consorting openly with a British agent in such insalubrious surroundings. This was, after all, a filthy opium den in Soho – about as far from the Ritz as one could imagine. Clearly, Newbury decided, whatever reason Meng Li had for being there, it must have been of grave importance. The Chinaman was putting himself at great risk.

He mustn't have been alone. Newbury craned his neck. He couldn't see any bodyguards, but that didn't mean they weren't there. For all he knew, half of the patrons of the house might be in Meng Li's employ, ready to leap up from their apparent stupors if Newbury tried anything.

Not, he supposed, that there was any risk of that. Meng Li had timed his appearance to perfection, approaching Newbury while he was still incapacitated from the drug, but cognisant enough to hold a meaningful conversation.

The Queen would be furious if she discovered Newbury had been face to face with the crime lord and hadn't killed him on sight, but he was presently far from capable of that, and besides, he was curious to see what the man wanted, why Meng Li would risk his life in such a manner to speak with one of Victoria's agents.

"You do me a great honour," said Newbury, without a hint of irony.

Again, that subtle smile. "I hope that we may – temporarily, at least – speak as friends, Sir Maurice?"

"Friends?" echoed Newbury. Was this to be a proposition? He would have to tread carefully.

Meng Li gave a slight bow of his head, as if conceding some unspoken point. "If not as friends, then perhaps at least as men of a common purpose, who share a common enemy?"

Newbury raised an eyebrow. "Go on," he said, intrigued.

"The operative known as 'Lady Arkwell'. You seek her, do you not, for your English Queen?" The words were wrapped in amusement, not scorn.

Newbury considered his response. Meng Li was obviously well connected, and dangerous, too. Any denial would be seen for the blatant lie that it was, and he didn't wish to anger the man, particularly given his present situation. "Indeed I do," he said, levelly. "I take it, then, that you also have an interest in finding this mysterious woman."

"In a manner of speaking," said Meng Li. "She has taken something that belongs to me, and for that, I owe her a response."

"Ah," said Newbury, "and so you're proposing an alliance in order to find her?"

Meng Li shook his head. The gesture was almost imperceptible in the dim light. "I wish only to impart to you some information," he replied.

Newbury frowned. More games. "I'm listening."

"It is said that Lady Arkwell is an expert at covering her tracks. She passes like a leaf, blown on the wind, and is soon lost amongst the many others that have fallen from the tree. She never repeats herself, and she never returns to the same place twice." He folded his hands together inside the sleeves of his *cheongsam*. "She has, however, one weakness – her fondness for a particular blend of tea. It is a Yunnan leaf, grown in China, and is found in only one establishment in this great city of London. A tearoom on New Bond Street known as the 'Ladies' Own Tea Association'." He withdrew his hands from his sleeves. In one of them he held a small, white card, which he handed to Newbury.

"And you believe she will be found there?" asked Newbury, surprised.

Meng Li inclined his head. "What is more, you may identify her by means of an old injury. Two years ago, a bullet was lodged in her right knee during an incident in Singapore. The bullet was removed, but the knee was damaged. The affliction is barely noticeable, but alters her gait: every third step she takes is uneven."

"Then why tell me?" asked Newbury. "If you know all of this, why not send a handful of your own men after her?"

"Because it amuses me," replied Meng Li, although this time, his smile did not reach his eyes. Newbury had heard others call this man inscrutable, but to his mind, that was simple ignorance. Meng Li was not so hard to read, and although he hid it well, Newbury could see the truth in the man's expression: he was scared. When Meng Li spoke of Lady Arkwell, he had the look about him of a man who knew he was outclassed. He was aiding Newbury because he did not wish to engage the woman in her own games, for fear he might lose. The crime lord, it seemed, was nothing if not a pragmatist.

Newbury nodded. "Tell me – what did she steal from you?"

"An object that has been in my family for many hundreds of years," replied Meng Li. "The Jade Nightingale."

Newbury almost baulked. He'd heard talk of this precious stone before: an enormous, flawless emerald mounted in a gold ring, and dating back to the ancient, early dynasties of the Far East. Many had tried to steal it, but none had ever succeeded. How it had come into Meng Li's possession, Newbury did not know, but now the crime lord had lost it again, to Lady Arkwell.

"And you do not wish to retrieve it?"

"It is merely a bauble. She may keep it." Meng Li shrugged.

"My revenge is simply to assist my good friends of the British Crown to locate her."

Merely a bauble. The Jade Nightingale was priceless. It would sell for thousands of pounds, even on the black market. Newbury could hardly believe how easily Meng Li had dismissed the matter. It had clearly pained him that the gem had been stolen – enough to reveal himself to an agent of the British government and assist them in locating the thief – but to Newbury it seemed that Meng Li was more concerned with revenge, with the embarrassment of the whole matter, than the actual recovery of the stone.

"It is a matter of honour," said Meng Li, as if reading his thoughts. "Do you understand *honour*, Sir Maurice?"

"I believe I do," replied Newbury, meeting Meng Li's unwavering gaze.

"Then I believe we have an understanding," said Meng Li. "You may leave this house unmolested, and you go with my blessings behind you. When we meet again, we will not be friends."

Newbury nodded, slowly.

Meng Li bowed gracefully, and then seemed to melt away into the darkness, leaving Newbury alone on the divan. His head was still swimming with the after-effects of the Chinese poppy, and for a moment he wondered if he might not have dreamed the entire encounter. But then he remembered the card Meng Li had handed him, and turned it over in his palm, casting his bleary gaze over the legend printed there in neat, black ink: *LADIES' OWN TEA ASSOCIATION, 90 NEW BOND STREET.*

Newbury smiled. Tomorrow, he would finally close the net on the elusive Lady Arkwell.

VIII

"Something's wrong. I don't think anyone is coming." Clarissa was perched on an upended seat across the gangway from Newbury, a frown on her pretty face. Her foot was drumming nervously on the floor, and she was clenching and unclenching her hands on her lap. She kept glancing at the other passengers, and then at the heap of clothes she'd piled over the corpse in the corner. Newbury wondered if perhaps she was showing the early signs of claustrophobia, or whether it was simply the proximity of the corpse, and what it represented, that was troubling her. It was certainly troubling him.

He was slouched against the crumpled ceiling of the overturned carriage, fighting a wave of lethargy and nausea. Whatever was in his system – for he was now convinced that he had been drugged – was threatening to send him spiralling back into unconsciousness. He couldn't allow that to happen. Too much was at stake.

When he saw Clarissa was watching him, a pleading look in her eyes, he took a deep breath, forcing himself to stay alert. "You know what London traffic is like these days," he said. "The roads are awash with people, carriages, carts and trains. The fire engines are probably stuck somewhere, trying to get through to us."

Clarissa shook her head. "No. They should be here by now. It's been too long." She dropped down from her perch, crossing the makeshift gangway to stand over him. She offered him her hands, as if to haul him up. "Come on. I think we're going to have to find our own way out of this mess."

Newbury shook his head. "No. I can't. I'm so tired."

Clarissa folded her arms and glared down at him in a matronly fashion. "You need to keep moving. You know I can't let you fall asleep. Not after a blow to the head." She dropped into a crouch, bringing her face close to his. She smelled of roses. "I'm not sure how much longer I can stand being stuck in this tin can, to be honest," she said, in a whisper. Her lips were close to his ear and he could feel her warm breath playing on his cheek. "I've never been comfortable in confined spaces, and the thought that one of those men is a heartless killer is too much to bear. Please, Sir Maurice. Help me to get free."

She pulled back, her eyes searching his face. He could feel himself relenting. "Very well," he said. "What are you planning?"

She grinned, taking his hands in hers. "If we can bash a panel of this crushed roof away from where a window frame has buckled, perhaps we can make enough of a space to crawl free."

Newbury frowned. "It's perfectly mangled. We'd need cutters to even begin making a hole."

"At least help me give it a try," she said, standing and hauling him to his feet, reluctant though he was. His head spun wildly for a moment, and then seemed to settle. "What have we got to lose?"

Our lives, thought Newbury, *if we turn our backs on the wrong person for too long*, but he couldn't muster the will to fight – not least because she had a point.

"Over here," she said, leading him a little further away from the others, towards the body at the rear of the carriage. "This looks like the weakest point." She indicated a spot where the space between the top of the window frame and the side of the car had been reduced to around two inches.

"The frame is completely buckled," said Newbury. He placed both of his palms against the metal panel and pushed with all of his remaining strength. It didn't budge. "We're going to need something heavy to hit it with."

"Like this?" asked Clarissa, and he turned to see her grappling with a wooden seat that had broken free from the floor during the crash. She swung it back like a golf club, gritting her teeth.

"Clarissa..." said Newbury, ducking out the way just in time to watch her slam the seat into the roof panel with all of her might. There was a terrific reverberation throughout the carriage, followed by the clatter of broken wood as the now demolished seat tumbled in a heap to the floor. The window frame hadn't shifted.

A woman started screaming somewhere at the other end of the carriage, and Newbury turned to see three men getting to their feet. "Now you've done it," he said.

"Shhh," hissed Clarissa. She scrabbled for a foothold and pressed her ear to the opening. "Yes! That's it!"

"What is it?"

"Listen!" said Clarissa, with palpable relief. "I can hear ringing bells. They're coming."

Newbury tried to focus, to suppress the dull roar inside his head. Clarissa was right – he could hear the distant jangle of fire carts, brass bells clanging wildly as they raced through the streets towards the site of the accident. He turned to see the rest of the passengers getting to their feet as they, too, heard the signals, awareness of their impending rescue spreading swiftly amongst them.

Newbury put his hand in his jacket pocket, reminding himself of the incriminating knife that was hidden there, of the difficulties still to come. Whatever happened next, he had to be ready. There was still a killer on board the train. While they were all trapped in there, the killer was, too. As soon as they got free, the man would make a break for it, and all chance of apprehending him would be lost.

He turned to Clarissa. "Whatever happens, you and I have to be the first ones out of this carriage," he said. "Remember that, at all costs. Once we're free we need to get the attention of the police, and make sure no one else gets out behind us."

She looked at him quizzically for a moment, before his intention suddenly dawned on her. "Oh," she said, "because that way, the killer will still be on the train."

"Precisely," said Newbury. "Can you do that?"

Clarissa beamed. "I can do anything if I put my mind to it."

Newbury laughed for the first time that day. "When this is over, I'd very much like to take you to dinner," he said.

"Would you, indeed?" she replied, with a crooked smile.

IX

The Ladies' Own Tea Association on New Bond Street was exactly as Newbury had imagined: overstuffed with dainty decorations such as lace doilies, sparkling chandeliers, pastel-coloured upholstery and overbearing floral displays. Young maids darted about between tables, dressed in formal black uniforms with white trim.

As he peered through the window from across the street, Newbury was filled with a dawning sense of astonishment. It all seemed so unnecessarily... *feminine*, as if the proprietors had never considered that the women who took tea in their establishment might have been perfectly comfortable in less exuberant surroundings. Veronica, he knew, would have found the place decidedly over the top. He could imagine the look on her face now, appalled at the very idea of spending time in such a garish environment.

He sighed heavily, leaning against the doorjamb. Perhaps, he reflected, they were simply trying to scare away the men.

Newbury had taken up temporary residence in the doorway of a nearby auction house, sheltering from the persistent, mizzly rain. Mercifully, the auctioneer's was closed for the afternoon and he'd loitered there for two hours unchallenged, attentively watching the comings and goings of the tearoom's clientele.

So far, he'd seen no one matching his – admittedly limited – description of Lady Arkwell, but he decided to wait it out for a short while longer. It wasn't as if he had any other significant leads, after all.

He'd considered enquiring after Lady Arkwell with the staff, posing as a friend, but in the end decided it would be too conspicuous. He didn't wish to show his hand too soon, and if she *had* become a regular patron and the staff alerted her to his questions, he'd have given away his only advantage.

So, with little else in the way of options, he turned his collar up against the spattering rain, hunkered down in the doorway and endeavoured to remain vigilant, despite the gnawing chill.

It was almost half an hour later when the woman in the lilac hat emerged from the tearoom, unfurling her umbrella and stepping out into the street. At first, Newbury dismissed her as simply another of the tearoom's typically middle-class customers, heading home after a late lunch with her friends. She was young and pretty and not at all the sort of woman he was looking for, and he hardly paid attention to her appearance. Except that, as he watched her stroll casually away down the street, she seemed to stumble slightly, as if from a sudden weakness in her right knee.

Frowning, Newbury stepped out from the doorway, ignoring the patter of raindrops on the brim of his hat. He squinted as he studied the dwindling form of the woman. One step, two steps – there it was again, the slightest of stumbles, before she caught herself and corrected her gait.

Newbury's heart thudded in his chest. Was this, then, the woman he was searching for, the woman with whom he was engaged in such an elaborate game? He hesitated, unsure whether to give chase. Given what he knew of Lady Arkwell, it wouldn't have surprised him to discover she had paid someone to affect a limp, simply to throw him off her trail.

He decided he had little to lose. If this woman in the lilac hat proved to be a red herring, then either Lady Arkwell had set up a decoy and was never going to be found at the tearooms, or else it would prove to be a case of mistaken identity, and Newbury could return the following day to continue his observations.

He set out, pulling the brim of his hat down low and hurrying after the young woman, his feet sloshing in the puddles that had formed between the uneven paving stones.

He followed her along New Bond Street, remaining at a reasonable distance so as not to arouse her suspicions. All the while the little stumbles continued, like clockwork, with every third step. Such an injury, he reflected, would be difficult to affect successfully, and the woman had evidentially grown accustomed to it; it did not appear to have a detrimental impact on her speed or confidence.

After a minute or two, the woman turned into Brook Street, which she followed as far as Hanover Square. She halted at an omnibus stop and lowered her umbrella, ducking under the shelter to await the next bus. A small crowd of five or six people were already gathered beneath the shelter, and so Newbury hung back, keeping out of view.

It was no more than five minutes' wait before the rumble of immense wheels announced the arrival of a passenger ground train. The machine was a hulking mass of iron and steam – a traction engine fitted with fat road wheels – and it came surging around the corner into Hanover Square, belching ribbons of black smoke from its broad funnel. It was painted in the green and black livery of the *Thompson & Childs Engineering Company*, and was hauling two long carriages full of people.

The ground train trundled to a rest beside the omnibus stop. Immediately, a number of carriage doors were flung open and a flurry of passengers disembarked. Newbury watched the woman in the lilac hat step up into the second carriage, and quickly dashed forward, hopping up onto the step and into the same carriage, just as the driver's whistle tooted and the engine began to roll forward again, ponderously building up a head of steam.

The woman had already taken a seat at the rear of the carriage, and so Newbury, still wary of drawing her attention, decided to take one of the empty seats on the opposite side, close to the front, from where, if he turned his head, he could just make out her reflection in the window glass.

The carriage was around half full, following the mass disembarkation at Hanover Square, with a mix of people from all walks of life: office workers, shoppers returning home with stuffed bags, a mother with her little girl, socialites returning home from their clubs. Nothing appeared to be out of the ordinary.

Newbury eased himself back into his rather uncomfortable seat, certain that he could relax until at least the next stop, where he would have to make sure he didn't lose the woman if she chose to alight.

He was about to glance out of the window when there was a sudden, jarring jolt, followed by a thunderclap as loud as any he had ever heard.

Everything went black.

X

"We'll have you free in just a minute, miss. Remain calm." The man's gruff voice was accompanied by the sound of bolt cutters snapping into the iron plating of the carriage roof, as the firemen worked to create a makeshift exit.

Clarissa's relief was palpable. She'd followed Newbury's instructions, doing everything possible to ensure they were the first to be freed from the wreckage. She'd rushed to the small opening in the buckled window frame as soon as she heard voices outside, pushing her arm through and waving for attention. Consequently, the firemen had focused their attention on widening the existing gap and forcing their way in.

Despite their imminent rescue, however, Newbury couldn't

shake the feeling of dread that had settled like a weight in the pit of his stomach.

Aside from the injured, the other passengers were all up on their feet, clamouring at whatever openings they could find, calling out to the firemen for help. Soon, someone was going to discover Lady Arkwell's dead body, and Newbury still didn't have sufficient evidence to exonerate himself. He was covered in the dead woman's blood and was carrying a knife that was sticky with his own fingerprints. Discarding it at this point would be a pointless exercise.

Worse still, the real killer had a chance of getting away scot-free in the chaos, or perhaps even implicating Newbury further. After all, they were the only other person on the train who knew that Newbury was carrying the planted murder weapon. All it would take was a quiet word in the ear of the police, and Newbury would likely be restrained and carted away to a cell. Bainbridge and the Queen would, of course, ensure his eventual release, but by then the real murderer would be long gone, and with him, any hope of discovering the truth of what had really happened.

And, just to make matters worse, Newbury was still feeling decidedly woozy.

There was a terrific *clang* of metal striking stone, and he turned to see daylight streaming into the gloomy carriage through a small, ragged hole in the roof. He squinted against the sudden brightness, and rushed forward to Clarissa's side. "Go!" he said urgently, putting his hand on her back and urging her forward.

She did as he said, ducking low and wriggling out through the hole.

Newbury felt a press of people at his back, heard bickering over his shoulder, but paid them no heed. He had to get free and speak to the police before it was too late.

He followed Clarissa out through the hatch, dropping to

his belly and worming his way out on to the wet street. The fresh air hit him like a slap to the face, and he dragged it desperately into his lungs. He felt hands on his shoulders and, a moment later, two firemen had hauled him up to his feet.

"Thank you," he murmured, as he turned on the spot, taking in the scene of utter devastation. The wreckage of the ground train littered the entire street.

The remains of the engine itself were at least a hundred yards further down the road, steam still curling from the hot, spilt coals as they fizzed in the drizzling rain. The engine casing had burst apart, shredding the metal and spewing shrapnel and detritus over the cobbles and surrounding buildings. Nearby windows were shattered, and the front of one building – a hotel – was smeared with streaks of soot.

The first carriage was jackknifed across the road, and appeared to have suffered more damage than the second, bearing the brunt of the explosion. The whole front of it was missing, leaving a jagged, gaping hole where it had once been tethered to the engine. The rest of the carriage was twisted and crushed and, inside, Newbury could see the bodies of passengers, flung around like dolls by the force of the explosion. He'd been lucky – the carriage he'd been travelling in was relatively unscathed in comparison, on its side, its roof crushed flat as it had rolled across the street.

Crowds of onlookers had gathered at either end of the street, and fire carts were parked in a row, their doors still hanging open where their drivers had abandoned them to get to the injured or trapped.

Newbury caught sight of a lone bobby in the midst of it all and staggered over, grabbing the young man by his cuff. The policeman shook him off irritably, looking him up and down.

"You must send for Sir Charles Bainbridge of Scotland Yard immediately," said Newbury. "There's a dead woman in that carriage." He pointed back the way he had come.

The bobby looked at him as if he'd cracked a particularly bad joke. "Yes, sir," he replied, sarcastically. "There's been an accident."

"No, no!" Newbury shook his head in frustration. "You don't understand. She's been murdered."

The bobby raised a skeptical eyebrow. "Indeed, sir?"

"Listen to me!" barked Newbury. "My name is Sir Maurice Newbury, and I'm a good friend of your chief inspector. I'm telling you, a woman has been murdered on that train. The killer is still on board. My friend here can confirm it." He turned to beckon Clarissa over.

She was nowhere to be seen.

"Clarissa?" called Newbury, perplexed. Had she gone back to help free the others from the wreckage? "Clarissa?"

Concerned, he turned his back on the policeman, scanning the scene for any sign of her.

For a moment he stood there, utterly baffled, while the storm of activity raged on around him. She seemed to have disappeared. One moment she'd been standing there beside him, the next she had gone.

He searched the faces in the crowd. It was then that he saw her, about two hundred yards up the street, walking away from the devastation. Where was she going? "Clarissa?" he called again.

She ignored him and continued walking, her back to him. Confused, he watched as she gave a little stumble, as if suffering from a slight weakness in her right knee. Newbury's heart thudded. *No! It couldn't be…*

There it was again, on the third step – another little stumble. His head was swimming. He started after her, but stumbled, still woozy from whatever sedative had been administered to him. He'd never catch her now, not in this state.

He watched for a moment longer as she receded into the distance. Then, at the last moment, she stopped, turned, and blew him a kiss, before disappearing out of sight around the corner.

Newbury stumbled back towards the carriage, ignoring the protests of the bobby behind him. "Get out of my way!" he bellowed, pushing past the firemen and dropping to his knees before the makeshift hatch in the roof.

The other passengers had all been helped from the wreckage now, and as Newbury wriggled back into the gloomy carriage, he realised he was alone. He clambered shakily to his feet and crossed immediately to the heap of clothes at the rear of the carriage, beneath which the dead woman was buried. He began to peel the layers off, flinging coats, cardigans and jackets indiscriminately to the floor.

Moments later he uncovered the head of the bloodied corpse. He wrenched the hat from the head and saw instantly that the woman's hair, pinned up, was in fact a deep, chestnut brown. Blood had been smeared expertly on her face to obscure her features, but it was clear almost immediately that this was a different woman from the one he had followed from the tearooms.

How could he have been so stupid? Clarissa had kept his attentions away from the body, had even taken great pains to cover it up so he wouldn't realise that this dead woman was not, in fact, Lady Arkwell at all. He'd missed all of the signs.

Clarissa – the real Lady Arkwell – must have killed the woman and switched clothes with her while Newbury was out cold from the crash. She'd then drugged him and planted the evidence before bringing him round.

Newbury let the lilac hat fall from his grip and slumped back against the roof of the carriage, sliding to the ground. No wonder Meng Li had been so apprehensive when he'd spoken of the woman. No wonder the Queen had warned him of her ruthlessness. Newbury had been totally outclassed.

"Well played, Clarissa," he mumbled, his face in his hands. "Well played indeed."

XI

"We find it interesting, Newbury, that she deigned to allow you to live. Perhaps she has a weakness for pretty men?"

"With respect, Your Majesty, she is a cold-blooded killer," replied Newbury. "She took that innocent woman's life purely to evade capture. I suspect she allowed me to live only because she considered me useful. I was her intended scapegoat, and she was relying on me to help her to escape from the wreckage."

Victoria gave a disturbing, throaty cackle. "Don't be so naive, Newbury. Do you think for a moment she didn't know what she was doing? That 'innocent woman' you refer to was a German agent, most likely sent to assassinate Lady Arkwell following her alleged involvement in a theft from the Kaiser's court. She probably killed her in self-defence."

Newbury frowned. Perhaps things weren't as black and white as he'd at first imagined. Could she really have killed that woman in self-defence? If so, that put an entirely different complexion on the matter. Perhaps she was more the woman he'd taken her to be, after all. He sighed. "I fear it is a moot point, Your Majesty. She's probably halfway to Paris by now, or some other such destination where she might go to ground to evade capture."

"Perhaps so," the Queen conceded.

"Then that is an end to the matter?"

Victoria laughed. "No. You shall remain focused on the woman, Newbury. You shall track her down and bring her here, to the bosom of the Empire, where we may question her and discover her true motives." Victoria grinned wickedly, baring the blackened stumps of her teeth. "We think she might yet prove useful."

"Of course, Your Majesty," said Newbury. He stifled a smile. He knew that what he'd just been handed was a punishment for allowing the woman – Clarissa – to slip out of his grasp, but in truth, he couldn't help feeling buoyed by the notion that, some day soon, he might see her again.

"Go to it, Newbury. Do not disappoint us again."

"Very good, Your Majesty," he replied, with a short bow, then quit the audience chamber to the sound of the Queen's hacking, tortuous laughter.

XII

"I was played, Charles. There's no other way to look at it."

Newbury crossed the room to where Bainbridge was sitting by the fire and handed him a snifter of brandy. Then, with a heavy sigh, he dropped into his battered old Chesterfield and propped his feet up on a tottering pile of books.

"Don't look so dejected, Newbury," said Bainbridge, unable to hide his amusement. "It's no reflection on you that you were beaten by a pretty young woman."

Newbury offered his best withering glare, but couldn't help but smile at the gentle provocation.

The two of them had met at Newbury's Chelsea home for dinner, and now it was growing late, and the mood more contemplative.

"It's just... I was completely taken in by the woman, Charles," replied Newbury. "As if she'd somehow bewitched me. I can't believe I missed all the signs."

"I refer you to my previous sentiment," said Bainbridge, grinning. "You're not the first man to be distracted by a feisty, intelligent – and beautiful – young woman, and you won't be the last." He took a long slug of brandy. "And let's not forget, your brain was somewhat addled by the sedative. You shouldn't be so hard on yourself."

He knew that Bainbridge was right, but couldn't shake the feeling that, in losing this first round of the little game he had entered into with Lady Arkwell, he was now on the back foot.

He wasn't used to being the one running to catch up.

Newbury shrugged and took a sip of his drink. "What of you, Charles? Are you faring any better? Tell me about Algernon Moyer."

"All over and done with," said Bainbridge, merrily. "It turned out he'd pushed his luck just a little too far. He got careless."

"And you managed to find him?" asked Newbury.

"In a manner of speaking. It looks as if one of his victims might have bitten him after he'd administered the Revenant plague. We found him climbing the walls in a hotel room in Hampstead, utterly degenerated. The hotel called us in because of the noise and the smell."

Newbury wrinkled his nose in disgust. "You had to put him down?"

Bainbridge nodded. "The blighter got what was coming to him. His corpse was incinerated yesterday."

"It brings a whole new complexion to that old adage, 'treat others as you mean to be treated yourself,'" said Newbury.

Bainbridge laughed. "It does that."

There was a polite knock at the drawing room door. Newbury glanced round to see his valet, Scarbright, silhouetted in the doorway. He was still dressed in his immaculate black suit and collar, despite the lateness of the hour.

"I'm sorry to disturb you, gentlemen, but I have a message for Sir Maurice," he said, holding up an envelope.

"Come in, Scarbright," said Newbury, intrigued.

"A message? At this time of night?" exclaimed Bainbridge, with a frown. He sat forward in his chair, glancing at Newbury with a quizzical expression.

Newbury shrugged. He hadn't been expecting anything.

"It arrived just a moment ago," explained Scarbright, "brought to the door by an urchin, who insisted the message it contained was quite urgent." He passed the envelope to

Newbury and waited for a moment while Newbury examined it. "If there's anything else you need…"

"What? Oh, no," said Newbury, distracted. "We're fine, Scarbright. Thank you."

The valet retreated, closing the door behind him.

Newbury turned the envelope over in his hands. There was no addressee. He lifted it to his nose and sniffed the seal. It smelled of roses.

"What the Devil are you doing?" asked Bainbridge. "Just open the ruddy thing, will you?"

Newbury chuckled. "It's advisable when one receives anonymous post, Charles, to first ensure it's not going to kill you."

Bainbridge's eyes widened. "You don't think it's poisoned, do you?"

Newbury shook his head. "Thankfully not." He ran his finger along the seam, tearing it open.

Inside, there was a small, white notecard. He withdrew it. Printed on one side in neat, flowing script were the words: *Still on for dinner?*

Newbury dropped the card on his lap and threw his head back, laughing.

"What is it?" said Bainbridge. "What does it say?"

"It's from her," said Newbury.

"Who? The Queen?"

"No. Lady Arkwell. Clarissa."

Bainbridge looked utterly confused. "And?"

"She's letting me know that the game is still on," replied Newbury. "That there's more still to come." He handed Bainbridge the note.

Bainbridge glanced at it almost cursorily. "The gall of the woman! You should toss this in the fire and forget about it."

"That would hardly be following orders, Charles," said Newbury. He drained the rest of his glass. "You know what Her Majesty had to say on the subject."

"So you'll do as she asks?" said Bainbridge, incredulous. "You'll keep up the search?"

Newbury grinned. He took the card back from Bainbridge and looked wistfully at the note. "Yes, Charles," he said. "I rather think I will."

THE CASE OF THE NIGHT CRAWLER

FROM THE NOTEBOOKS OF JOHN H. WATSON M.D.

During the many years in which I served as both a friend and chronicler of Sherlock Holmes, there was but a rarefied handful of occasions upon which I witnessed that cold logician rendered speechless or flustered by the unexpected outcome of a case. Irene Adler evoked one such response, and the events that I have come to consider as "The Case of the Night Crawler" elicited yet another. It is due in part to the sensitivities of my friend that I have never published my notes regarding this most singular of adventures, but I record them here for the sake of posterity and completeness. I am, if nothing else, a thorough man, and it would not do to allow such a startling series of incidents to go entirely unrecorded.

So, here, in this worn leather journal, where perhaps my words will go forever unread, I shall set it down. I am old now, and I have little better to do with my time but to reflect upon the more adventurous days of my past.

The biggest irony of all, of course, is that Holmes himself had very little to do with the unravelling of the case. Indeed, he resoundingly turned his nose up at the opportunity to involve himself in such "coarse, ridiculous matters," as I remember so well that he put it, plucking violently at his violin strings as if to underline the significance of his words. His dismissive attitude was, in this rare instance, a cause for his later embarrassment, as it would transpire that the matter in question was quite as far from ridiculous as one might ever imagine. Not that Holmes was ever one to learn from such mistakes.

The aforementioned events marked also my first encounter with that remarkable individual Sir Maurice Newbury and his most astonishing associate, Miss Veronica Hobbes. It was not, much to my regret, the beginning of a long-lasting friendship, but Newbury and I nevertheless identified a mutual respect, and there would follow a number of other occasions upon which we would throw our hats in the same ring – most notable among them that dreadful matter of the Kaiser's unhinged spiritualist during the early days of the war.

Holmes, of course, had quite a different opinion of Newbury, but I suppose that was only to be expected; although without equal in his field, Holmes was not above a modicum of professional rivalry if he felt his reputation – or more truthfully, his pride – was at risk. His attitude towards Newbury would change over time, and I believe by the end, following the resolution of that matter in 1915 and the destruction of the spectrograph generator, he might even have granted Newbury the respect he deserved. War does that to a man, I've found. It teaches him to work alongside those he might otherwise have considered, if not enemies, perhaps the unlikeliest of allies.

It was during that bitterly cold autumn of 1902, early in the season, when the leaves were first beginning to turn and the days were growing noticeably shorter, that the seeds of the affair were sown. My friend and fellow medical practitioner, Peter Brownlow, had called on me unexpectedly at my club. It was late in the evening and I'd been enjoying a solitary brandy by the fire when the poor chap practically collapsed into the chair opposite me, his face ashen. He generally suffered from a pale complexion and maintained a rake-thin physique; a condition he claimed was a result of a stomach disorder but which I attributed more to vanity than any inability to digest his food. Nevertheless, he had a good heart and was a fine doctor, but on that blustery September afternoon he had about him the look of a man who'd seen a ghost.

"Whatever is the matter with you, dear chap?" I said, leaning forward in concern and passing him my brandy. "Here, drink this."

Brownlow nodded, grabbed gratefully at the glass and choked it down in one long gulp. I could see his hand was trembling as he placed the glass on the side table beside his chair.

"Now, tell me what has perturbed you so."

Brownlow took a deep breath. "I barely know how to give voice to it, John. I'm sure you'll think me quite insane."

"Oh, I shouldn't worry about that," I said, chuckling. "I've grown quite used to seeing the impossible rendered mundane, and to madmen proved sane. Speak what's on your mind."

Brownlow smiled, but there was no humour in it. "I have seen the most terrible thing, John. A creature... a beast..." He held his hand to his mouth for a moment, unsure how to go on.

I frowned. "A beast?"

"Yes. Yes, that's the only word for it. A beast of the most diabolical appearance, as if it had dragged itself from the very depths of Hades itself." He turned, staring into the grate at the glowing embers of the fire, but I could tell that he was seeing something else.

"Go on," I prompted.

He closed his eyes, as if trying to blink away the after-image of whatever it was he was attempting to describe. "It had a fat, bulbous body, about the size of a hackney cab, and it pulled itself along on eight thick, tentacle-like limbs that wriggled beneath it like those of an octopus. The sound of its passing was like the screeching of a thousand tormented souls. It was devilish, John. The most horrendous thing I have ever seen."

"And where was this, man? Where did you see this beast?" I watched Brownlow shudder at the very thought of this terrible sight to which he claimed to have borne witness. My first thought was that he must have been drunk or otherwise inebriated, but Brownlow had never been much of a drinker, and he was clearly terrified. Whatever the truth of the matter – and I was sure it could not be that he had genuinely encountered such a bizarre specimen – Brownlow believed what he was saying.

"Cheyne Walk," he said. "About an hour ago. The darn thing pulled itself out of the Thames right before me and slithered off down the street."

Well, I admit at this point I was close to rolling my eyes in disbelief, but Brownlow had such a desperate air about him, and I was sure there must have been more to his story.

"I came directly here. It was the closest place to hand. I couldn't think what else to do. And then I saw you sitting here and knew you'd know what to do."

In truth, I had no real notion of what to do with such a remarkable tale. Surely the police would have only sniggered at Brownlow's story and sent him on his way, putting it down to nothing but a hallucination, or the fabrication of an unhinged mind. But, Holmes aside, Brownlow was one of the most rational men I knew, and there was no reason he would lie.

"Well, first of all, I think you need another stiff drink for your nerves. I'll fetch you another brandy." He nodded enthusiastically at this. "Beyond that, I want you to set it out for me again, this time recalling as much of the detail as you can muster." I'd seen Holmes extract information from enough of his potential clients to know that this was the best way to begin unpicking Brownlow's story. Perhaps he might give something away, some little detail he had missed the first time around that might help to shed light on what had truly occurred. I admit, my interest had been piqued, and I felt pity for the chap, who had clearly had the wits scared out of him.

So it was that Brownlow downed another large brandy and set about relating his tale once again, this time in exquisite detail. I must admit the credibility of his words grew somewhat in the retelling, but there was nothing in it that could help me to discern what might truly have occurred. I had seen some things in my time, particularly since returning from Afghanistan and falling in with Holmes, but this tall tale seemed to test the bounds of even my well-trodden credulity.

It was with a heavy heart that I sent Brownlow home to his bachelor's apartment that night, unable to offer him any real comfort, other than a prescription for a mild sedative should he find it necessary in order to sleep. I promised the man I would consider his story, and that I would contact him directly should I happen upon any possible hint of an explanation. There was little else to be done, and so I made haste to my bed, my mind restless with concern.

The next morning I approached breakfast with a mind to refer Brownlow to a nerve specialist I'd worked with on occasion. Having slept on the matter I was now convinced that his ungodly vision could have only been the result of a hallucination, and decided that, if it hadn't been brought about by drink or other mind-altering substances, it was most likely an expression of nervous exhaustion. Brownlow had always had a tendency to throw himself into his work, body and soul. Aside from his private, paying customers, I'd known him to spend hours in aid of the poor, administering free treatment to those wretches who lined the alleyways of the slums, or huddled in their masses beneath the bridges that criss-crossed the banks of the Thames. Perhaps he'd been overdoing it, and he simply needed some rest. Or perhaps he'd succumbed to a mild fever.

My theories were soon dispelled, however, as I set about hungrily tucking into my bacon and eggs. It is my habit to take the morning papers with my breakfast, and upon folding back the covers of *The Times*, I fixed upon a small report on the bottom of the second page. The headline read:

EYEWITNESSES REPORT SIGHTINGS OF STRANGE BEAST

My first thought was that Brownlow had gone to the papers with his story, but I quickly dismissed the notion. The previous night he'd been in no fit state to talk to anyone, and I'd seen him into the back of a cab myself.

I scanned the article quickly, and was surprised to see that there were, in fact, a number of reports that seemed not only to corroborate Brownlow's story, but also to expand somewhat upon it. It appeared the previous evening had been the third in a row during which sightings of this bizarre creature had been reported. Furthermore, one of the reports stated that the woman in question – a Mrs Coulthard of Brixton – had seen the beast give chase to a group of young vagabonds who had been generally up to no good, throwing rocks at nearby boats and jeering at passers-by. Many of the reports claimed, just as Brownlow had, that the creature had dragged itself out of the Thames, and what's more, that it had been seen returning to the water upon completion of its nightly sojourn.

I leaned back in my chair, sipping at my coffee and staring at the remnants of my breakfast in astonishment. So Brownlow had been telling the truth. He *had* seen something down by the river. And if the veracity of his story was no longer in question, then the beast was something truly diabolical. Could it have been some sort of throwback to the prehistoric past, or some previously undocumented variety of gargantuan squid?

I resolved to visit Holmes directly. There was a mystery here, and people were potentially in grave danger. If only I could persuade him to apply his attention to the matter, there was hope that we could uncover precisely what was going on.

The drive to Baker Street passed in a blur. All the while, as the cab bounced and rattled over the cobbled roads, I couldn't help imagining the scene that must have confronted Brownlow and those others, the sight of that hulking beast dragging itself out of the ink-black water. It would surely have been terrifying to behold.

I resolved then and there that I would find a way to look upon this creature with my own eyes. Only then could I be utterly sure of its existence and the nature of any threat it represented.

Upon my arrival at Baker Street I found Holmes in one of his peculiar, erratic moods. He was pacing back and forth before the fireplace, somewhat manically, pulling at his violin strings as if trying to wring some meaning out of the random, screeching sounds the instrument was making. It was icy cold in there, yet the fireplace remained untended to, heaped with ash and charred logs. If Holmes felt the chill he did not show it.

He had his back to me. I coughed politely from the doorway, noting with dismay that my breath actually fogged in the air before my face.

"Yes, yes, Watson. Do come in and stop loitering in the hallway. And since you're here, see about building up this fire, will you? It's perishing in here."

Shaking my head in dismay, but deciding it would do neither of us any good to take umbrage, I set about clearing the grate.

"I expect you're here about those wild reports in the newspapers this morning," he said, strolling over to the window and peering out at the busy street below. He gave a sharp twang on another violin string, and I winced at the sound.

"I won't bother to ask how you managed to discern that, Holmes," I said, sighing as a plume of soot settled on my shirt cuff and then smeared as I attempted to brush it away. "Can't Mrs Hudson do this?" I said, grumpily.

"Mrs Hudson has gone out to the market," he replied, turning back from the window to look at me.

"She was here a moment ago," I said, triumphantly. "She opened the door and let me in."

Holmes held up a single index finger to indicate the need for silence. I watched him for a moment, counting beneath my breath as I begged the gods to grant me patience. Downstairs, I heard the exterior door slam shut with a bang. "There!" he exclaimed with a beaming smile. "Off to the market."

I sighed and continued piling logs on to the fire. "Well, of course you're right."

"About Mrs Hudson?"

"About the reason I'm here. This supposed beast. I had the unhappy task of comforting a friend last night who claimed to have seen it. The poor man was terrified."

"Hmm," said Holmes, resuming his pacing.

I waited for his response until it was evident that I'd already had the entirety of it. "Well?"

"Can't you see I'm in the middle of something, Watson?" he said, a little unkindly.

I glowered at him. "Really, Holmes! I thought you would be glad of the case. I mean, you've been holed up in here for weeks with nothing to occupy your mind. And poor Brownlow—"

"There's nothing in it, Watson. Some idle hoaxer looking to sell his story. Nothing more. I have no interest in such coarse, ridiculous matters." He plucked violently at three strings in succession. "Besides," he continued, his tone softening, "I find myself in the midst of a rather sensitive affair. Mycroft has gone and lost his favourite spy, a government scientist by the name of Mr Xavier Gray. He's quite frantic about the whole matter, and he's prevailing on me to assist him in the search for the missing man."

"Well, what are you doing *here*?" I asked. Sometimes I found it very difficult to fathom the motives of my dear friend.

"Thinking," he replied, as if that explained everything. He reached for the bow that he'd balanced precariously on the arm of a chair and began chopping furiously at the violin, emitting a long, cacophonous screech. I rose from where I'd been crouching by the fire and dusted off my hands. Clearly, I was unlikely to gain anything further from Holmes. As I crossed the room, heading towards the door, the violin stopped abruptly behind me and I turned to see Holmes regarding me, a curious expression on his face. "Send your friend to see a man named Maurice Newbury, of 10 Cleveland Avenue, Chelsea. I understand he's an 'expert' in matters such as these." He spoke the man's name with such disdain that he clearly thought him to be no such thing.

"Very well," I said, curtly. "I hope you find your missing spy." But Holmes had already started up again with his violin.

As I clambered into a hansom outside number 221B, frustrated by Holmes's dismissive attitude, I made the sudden, snap decision to pay a visit to this Newbury character myself. I am not typically given to such rash acts, but I remained intent on discovering the truth about the infernal beast that had so terrified my friend. Brownlow, being so meek, would never call on Newbury of his own account, no matter how I pressed him. I was sure that even now he would be reconciling himself to what had occurred, finding a way to accommodate the bizarre encounter into his own, conservative view of the world. He would rationalise it and carry on, returning to the distractions of his patients and his busy life. My interest, however had been piqued and I was not prepared to allow the matter to rest without explanation.

I must admit that I was also keen to prove Holmes wrong. I realise now how ridiculous that sounds, how petty, but his attitude had galled me and I was anxious to prove to my friend that the matter was not beneath his attention. As things were to transpire, I would be more successful on that count than I could have possibly imagined.

The drive to Chelsea was brisk, and I passed it by staring out of the window, watching the streets flicker by in rapid, stuttering succession. Almost before I knew it we had arrived at Cleveland Avenue. I paid the driver and watched as the cab clattered away down the street, the horse's breaths leaving steaming clouds in the frigid air.

Number 10 was an unassuming terraced house, fronted by a small rose garden that in turn was flanked by a black iron railing. A short path terminated in three large stone steps and a door painted in a bright, pillar-box red. I approached with some hesitation, feeling a little awkward now after my somewhat hasty retreat from Baker Street. What would I say to this Newbury fellow? I was there on behalf of a friend who claimed to have seen a monster? Perhaps Holmes had been right. Perhaps it was ridiculous. But there I was, on the doorstep, and I'd never been a man to shy away from a challenge. I rapped firmly with the door knocker.

A few moments later I heard footsteps rapping on floorboards from within, and then the door swung open and a pale, handsome face peered out at me. The man was dressed in a smart black suit and had an expectant look on his face. "May I help you?" he said, in warm, velvet tones.

"Mr Maurice Newbury?" I replied. "I was told I might find him at this address?"

The man gave a disapproving frown. "*Sir* Maurice is not receiving visitors at present, I'm afraid."

Holmes! He might have saved me that embarrassment if he'd wanted to. "Indeed," I replied, as graciously as I could muster. "I wonder if I might leave a card. My name is John Watson and I'm here on a rather urgent matter. I would speak with him as soon as is convenient. He comes very highly recommended."

The man – whom I now realised was most likely Newbury's valet – raised his eyebrows in what appeared to be genuine surprise. "Dr John Watson? The writer?"

I smiled at this unexpected recognition. "Quite so."

The valet grinned. I had to admit, I was warming to the fellow. "Well, Dr Watson, I think you'd better come in. I'm sure Sir Maurice will be anxious to meet you when he discovers the nature of his caller." He coughed nervously as he closed the door behind me and took my hat and coat. "If you'd like to follow me?"

He led me along the hallway until we reached a panelled door. I could hear voices from inside, two of them, belonging to a man and a woman and talking in the most animated of tones. The valet rapped loudly on the door and stepped inside. I waited in the hallway until I knew I would be welcome.

"You have a visitor, sir."

When it came the man's reply was firm, but not unkind. "I thought I'd explained, Scarbright, that I wished to receive no callers today? I have an urgent matter I must attend to with Miss Hobbes."

"Yes, sir," replied the valet, a little sheepishly. "Only, it's Dr John Watson, sir."

"Dr Watson?" said Newbury, as if attempting to recall the significance of my name. "Ah, yes, the writer chap. You're a follower of his work, aren't you, Scarbright?"

"Indeed sir," said the valet, and I couldn't suppress a little smile as I heard the crack of embarrassment in his voice. "He claims to have a rather urgent matter to discuss with you, sir."

Newbury gave a sigh of resignation. "Very well, Scarbright. You'd better send him in."

The valet stepped back and held the door open to allow me to pass. I offered him a brief smile of gratitude as I passed over the threshold into what I took to be the drawing room. In fact, it was much like the room in Baker Street from which I'd recently departed, only decorated with a more esoteric flair. Where Holmes might have had a stack of letters on the mantelpiece, speared by a knife, Newbury had the bleached skull of a cat. Listing stacks of leather-bound books formed irregular sentries around the edges of the room, and two high-backed Chesterfields had been placed before a raging fire. Both were occupied, the one on the left by the man I took to be Sir Maurice Newbury, and the other by a beautiful young woman who smiled warmly at me as I met her gaze.

Newbury was up and out of his seat before I'd crossed the threshold, welcoming me with a firm handshake and beckoning me to take a seat on the low-backed sofa that filled much of the centre of the room. He was a wiry-looking fellow of about forty, and was dressed in an ill-fitting black suit that appeared to have been tailored for a slightly larger man. Either that, or he had recently lost weight. He was ruggedly handsome, with fierce, olive-green eyes and raven-black hair swept back from his forehead. He had dark rings around his eyes and a sallow complexion, and I saw in him immediately the hallmarks of an opium eater: perhaps not the most auspicious of beginnings for our acquaintance. Nevertheless, I'd made it that far and I was determined to see it out.

"You are very welcome, Dr Watson," said Newbury, genially. "I, as you might have gathered, am Sir Maurice

Newbury, and this is my associate Miss Veronica Hobbes."

I took the young woman's hand and kissed it briefly, before accepting Newbury's offer of a seat. Miss Hobbes was stunningly beautiful, with dark brown hair tied up in a neat chignon. She was wearing dark grey culottes and a matching jacket – the picture of modern womanhood.

"Would you care for a drink, Doctor?" said Newbury, indicating the well-stocked sideboard with a wave of his hand. "A brandy, perhaps?"

I shook my head. "No, thank you. Most kind, but I'll abstain."

Newbury returned to his seat by the fire, angling his body towards me. "So, how may I be of assistance, Dr Watson? I presume it's not related to one of your journalistic endeavours?"

"Indeed not," I replied, gravely. "I'm here on behalf of an associate of mine, a man named Brownlow. It's connected with that business about the supposed beast that's been seen crawling out of the river. Last night Brownlow had an encounter with the thing, and it rather left him terrified out of his wits. It was… suggested to me that you might be able to help shed some light."

The corner of Newbury's mouth twitched with the stirrings of a wry smile. "And this was not a matter that Mr Holmes was able to assist you with?"

"Holmes is busy," I said, a little defensively. "And besides, it was Holmes who recommended I call. He said you were considered rather an expert in matters such as these."

"I'm sure he did," said Newbury, knowingly.

"Tell us, Dr Watson…" Miss Hobbes interjected, offering Newbury a mildly disapproving look "…did Mr Brownlow give you any indication as to when and where this sighting occurred?" In truth, I couldn't blame the man for enjoying the moment. It was fair to imagine that Holmes himself would have done precisely the same. In fact, knowing him as I did, I'm convinced he would have taken the time to truly relish the irony of the situation.

I smiled at Miss Hobbes in gratitude for the timeliness of her interruption. "Cheyne Walk," I replied. "Close to eleven o'clock yesterday evening. Following the incident he came directly to my club, where he is also a member, and sought me out for my assistance."

Newbury looked thoughtful. "And did he offer a description of the beast?"

I hesitated for a moment as I considered the sheer ludicrousness of what I was about to relate. I felt ridiculous now for coming here and adding weight and validity to this story. How could it be real? Had I simply overreacted to Holmes's rebuttal?

Well, whatever the case, it was too late to back out. "Brownlow described it as having a large, bulbous body about the size of a hansom cab, and eight thick limbs like tentacles upon which it slithered in the manner of an octopus. Now, I'm a little unsure as to the veracity of my friend's description, but given the accounts in the newspapers this morning... well, you understand, I had to come. The poor man thinks he's going insane. He might yet be right."

Newbury glanced at Miss Hobbes. "Oh, I assure you, Dr Watson, that your friend is quite sane. His report is the same in every respect as the others. This 'beast', whatever it is, is quite real."

"Sir Maurice's clerk, Mrs Coulthard, was another of the witnesses," continued Miss Hobbes, smiling reassuringly. "You find us in the midst of a discussion over how best to approach the situation."

"Have you any thought yet as to what it might be? Some sort of primordial beast, woken after years of hibernation? The result of an experiment? A previously undiscovered species brought back from the colonies?" I sighed. "The mind boggles…"

I realise now that these suggestions may appear somewhat ignorant to a reader aware of the facts, but at the time I could think of no other reasonable explanation for what this beast might have been. As Holmes was fond of saying, "Once you've eliminated the impossible, whatever remains, however improbable, must be the truth." If that axiom was indeed correct – and Newbury, also, was right in his assertion that the beast was real – then I could see no other credible explanation.

"I think it would be wrong for us to jump to any conclusions at this stage, Doctor. At least before we've had chance to lay eyes upon the beast ourselves." Newbury glanced at his companion before continuing. "Miss Hobbes and I had only just resolved to take a stroll along Cheyne Walk this very evening. I'm of a mind to catch a glimpse of this creature myself. You'd be more than welcome to accompany us, if you so wished."

"Well, it certainly makes sense to pool our resources," I said. "And I also tend to favour the evidence of my own eyes. I'd be delighted to join you, Sir Maurice." I admit to feeling a certain sense of relief at this rather unexpected development. I couldn't help but wonder what Holmes would make of it all.

"In that case, Doctor, I shall encourage you to make haste to your home and prepare for a cold evening by the river. Warm clothes, stout boots and a firearm would be advisable. We can meet here for an early dinner at, say, six o'clock, and then be on our way." Newbury smiled, and stood to accompany me to the door.

"Thank you, Sir Maurice," I said, taking him by the hand. "And good afternoon, Miss Hobbes."

"Until this evening, Dr Watson," she replied brightly.

It wasn't until I'd already left the house on Cleveland

Avenue that it occurred to me that baiting monsters by the river might have been a rather unsuitable pursuit for a lady. Nevertheless, as I was soon to discover, Miss Veronica Hobbes was most definitely a woman who knew how to look after herself.

So it was that, a few hours later, my belly full of the most excellent beef Wellington, I found myself on the banks of the Thames, shivering beneath my heavy woollen overcoat as Newbury, Miss Hobbes and I took up our positions along Cheyne Walk.

I'd found myself warming to Newbury as we'd talked over dinner, discussing the nature of his work – or rather, as much of it as he was able to discuss, given the secrecy of his role. It transpired he worked in some obscure capacity for the Crown, on one hand aiding Scotland Yard in their ever-constant battle against the criminal elements of the capital, and on the other taking direction from Buckingham Palace itself, performing the role of a state spy and expert in the occult.

That was about as much as I could glean about the man himself, but he talked openly about his catalogue of bizarre experiences, including his encounters with plague-ridden Revenants in the slums; his investigation into the wreckage of *The Lady Armitage* – a terrible airship crash from the previous summer that I remembered well; his run-in with the Chinese crimelord Meng Li; and other, increasingly surprising stories. He was a master at weaving a good yarn, and he held my attention throughout the three delicious courses of our meal. Miss Hobbes, herself a player in many of these exceptional tales, watched Newbury as he related these accounts of their adventures with no small measure of affection.

I came away from that dinner sure that, should Holmes ever decide to hang up his hat, I should readily have another subject upon which to focus my literary endeavours. Moreover, I decided that, despite Holmes's obvious disdain for the man's reputation, if the two of them were to actually meet they would surely find each other's company most invigorating.

I reflected on this as I stood in the shadow of Thomas Carlyle – or rather his memorial statue – at one end of the street, looking out over the Chelsea Embankment. We'd spread out along this stretch of the river, about a hundred yards apart. Miss Hobbes – wrapped in a dark, grey overcoat and wearing a wide-brimmed hat – was between Newbury and I, who, from this distance, I could just make out in the misty evening as a dark silhouette.

This, I understood from Newbury, was the location cited in the majority of the reports, including those of Brownlow and Newbury's clerk, Mrs Coulthard. Most claimed to have seen the creature scale the wall of the embankment and drag itself over the stone lip, pulling itself onto land and slithering off into the alleyways between the serried rows of terraced houses. One report, however, was of the creature also returning to the river by the same means, in or about the same spot. It seemed logical, then, that we should make our observation from this point, and we'd come prepared for a long wait.

Even so, my limbs were beginning to grow weary with the cold. It was a damp, miserable night, and the thick autumnal mist dulled even the glow of the street lamps. It seemed to wreath everything in its embrace, clinging to the trees and the buildings, curling its tendrils across the choppy surface of the Thames. There were but a few people abroad that night, passing along the embankment with their heads stooped low against the inclement weather. They appeared to me like ghostly shapes emerging from the mist, passing from one realm into another as they drifted along beside the river.

We must have waited there for hours without a word passing between us. I checked my timepiece at around eleven o'clock, stamping my feet in an attempt to warm my weary, frozen limbs I was just about to hail Newbury in order to call it a night when I received my first indication that something was afoot.

I became aware of a low, mechanical sound coming from the river, not unlike the clanking of heavy iron chains being dragged through a winching mechanism. At first I imagined it to be a ship drawing anchor, but I could see no masts on the water. I glanced at Newbury and Miss Hobbes, who had evidentially both heard the same noise and had abandoned their posts to approach the embankment. I started after them, wondering if at last we were about to reap some reward from our long vigil.

My hopes were confirmed a moment later when I saw Miss Hobbes start and fall back to the cover of the trees. I ran to her side in time to see two thick proboscises, each about the girth of a man's torso and covered in scores of tiny suckers like those of an octopus, come probing over the stone lip of the embankment. They squirmed and shifted as if feeling for the best possible hold, and then appeared to latch on to the uneven surface, providing purchase for the beast to haul itself out of the water.

It was difficult to ascertain much in the way of detail, due to the gloom and the pervasive mist, but I had already seen enough to set a cold lump of dread in the pit of my stomach. The sheer size of the thing to which such tentacles belonged... I could only stand there beside Miss Hobbes, looking on in abject fear as the beast slowly dragged itself onto land before us.

Newbury had continued to approach the water's edge but was now keeping himself at a safe distance, obviously keen not to find himself caught by one of the thrashing tendrils as the creature heaved itself further and further out of the Thames. The screeching noise continued, and I now realised that what I'd at first considered to be a mechanical noise must in fact have been the sound of the creature itself. I shuddered at the thought of such an infernal beast.

Another tentacle whipped over the side of the embankment, followed closely by a fourth. I had a sense, then, of the immensity of the thing, and as its body finally hove into view I had to fight the urge to run. Brownlow had been correct in his description of the creature and at that point I understood what had so disturbed him about his encounter with the creature the previous night. It was a thing to inspire madness. Simply to look upon it was to question one's own sanity.

As I watched, the monster slipped its bulk over the top of the embankment wall and raised itself to its full height – at least twenty feet tall – twisting and turning as if trying to decide which direction it should now take. I could see very little of it, other than the silhouette of its mass and the gleam of its wet carapace, catching and reflecting what thin shafts of moonlight fell on it from above.

It appeared to settle on a course a moment later, shuffling off in the direction of the nearest side street. It had a curious ambulatory technique, partway between a crawl and a slither, and I couldn't help thinking, despite everything, that the beast was far more suited to water than to land. Nevertheless, it moved with a not inconsiderable momentum, dragging itself along with all the noise of Hades, screeching and grinding as its multiple limbs struck again and again upon the flagstones.

"After it!" bellowed Newbury, his words rousing me from my temporary stupor. I did as he said, charging after it as fast as my numb, tired legs would carry me.

The beast had dragged itself into a narrow opening between two rows of houses, leading to a dark, cobbled alleyway beyond. Now its limbs were splayed around it, grasping at the sides of the buildings, pulling chunks out of the brickwork as it swiftly propelled itself along.

"Stand aside!" called Newbury, coming up behind me at a run. I dived quickly to one side as Miss Hobbes ducked to the other, and Newbury lurched to a stop hurling something high into the air in the direction of the creature.

There was a sudden explosion of bright white light as the flare – for that was what Newbury had thrown – hissed to life, rendering the entire scene in a series of brilliant, stuttering flashes as it spun wildly through the air.

I fell back, awestruck, as I caught my first proper glimpse of the creature, and realised with shock that it wasn't in fact a creature at all. What had at first appeared as some kind of gargantuan, primitive animal was, in the harsh brilliance of the flare shown to be nothing more than a huge mechanical construction. Its metallic limbs, now clearly a series of cleverly segmented iron coils, glinted with reflected light as they writhed and twisted, scrabbling at the walls. Its carapace was dull and black, still dripping with river water and, to my surprise, I saw the startled face of a man inside, peering out through the thick glass of a riveted porthole. I realised it was some sort of amphibious vehicle, and that the man was most likely the pilot. Judging by the appearance of it, I guessed it was a submersible – but a remarkable submersible of the like I had never seen, with the ability to clamber out of the water and scale sheer walls. I wondered at who might have even conceived of such a thing.

The flare struck the back of the machine's carapace and rebounded, tumbling over and over until it struck the cobbles a few feet away and continued to fizz and sputter in the gutter.

I was still standing in awe of the machine when one of the tentacles whipped out and struck Newbury full in the chest, lifting him clean off his feet and sending him sprawling to the ground with a dull thud. It occurred to me later that the pilot had probably assumed he was under attack, and that the flare had been some sort of weapon or explosive device. At the time, however, I was quite unprepared for what happened next.

Miss Hobbes emitted a shrill cry of alarm, but rather than rush to Newbury's aid, she grabbed a large piece of broken masonry and pitched it straight at the strange vehicle. It boomed as it struck the metal hull, causing the pilot's pod to rock back and forth upon the writhing cradle of its legs. In response, the machine reared up, twisting around and releasing its hold on the two buildings. One of its tentacles flicked out and caught Miss Hobbes around the waist, snaking around her and hoisting her high into the air. She looked like a fragile doll in its grip as it swung her around and thrust her, hard, against the nearest wall. She howled pain and frustration, clutching furiously at the iron tentacle in an attempt to prise herself free.

Incensed, I reached for my service revolver, which I'd secreted in the pocket of my overcoat before setting out from home. It felt cold but reassuring in my fist as I raised my arms, searching for a clear shot in the mist-ridden gloom.

Miss Hobbes gave a sharp cry of pain as she was slammed once more against the wall, lolling in the machine's terrible iron grip. Behind me, Newbury was silent and still where he lay on the pavement, unconscious or dead.

I cocked the hammer and took my aim, hoping beyond hope that my bullet would not ricochet and further injure Miss Hobbes. I could think of no other course of action, however; to get entangled in the machine's writhing limbs would mean certain death for us all. I was doubtful my bullets would puncture the vehicle's thick armour plating, but if I could create a distraction I thought I might be able to lure it away from Miss Hobbes.

By this time I was convinced that the people in the

neighbouring houses must have raised the alarm, and I expected the police to appear on the scene at any moment. I hoped for it, concerned that what little I might be able to do would still not be enough.

I squeezed the trigger and braced myself as the weapon discharged. The report was like a thunderclap that echoed off the nearby buildings. I heard the bullet ping as it struck the belly of the mechanical beast, and I ducked involuntarily in case it rebounded in my direction.

Just as I'd hoped, the shot seemed to startle the pilot enough to draw his attention. I squeezed off another bullet, then a third in quick succession. I was pleased to hear the satisfying splinter of glass, suggesting I'd managed to unwittingly strike one of the portholes.

The machine twisted around, releasing its stranglehold on Miss Hobbes and allowing her to slump heavily to the ground. With a terrible scraping of metal against stone, the vehicle lurched out of the mouth of the alleyway towards me. I stumbled back, trying desperately to keep myself out of reach of the probing limbs that thrashed across the cobbles before i_ I stumbled then, catching my heel on a loose paving stone and tumbling backwards, jarring my elbow and sending my revolver skittering across the street.

Panicked I tried to roll out of the way of the oncoming machine, but in my heart I knew it was over. The mechanical beast would crush me utterly beneath its massive bulk.

I closed my eyes, took a deep breath and felt a moment of strange, lucid calm as I waited for it to strike. At least I'd managed to save Miss Hobbes.

But the blow never came. To my amazement the vehicle veered away at the last moment, lurching back the way it had come, towards the river. I leapt to my feet, reclaiming my revolver and staggering after it, but within moments it had slithered over the edge of the embankment, dropping into the water with an almighty splash. I ran to the edge but could see nothing but a frothy ring of bubbles upon the surface.

I rushed back to where Miss Hobbes was struggling to pull herself upright in the mouth of the alley. "Are you hurt?" I asked, skipping the pleasantries.

She shook her head, gasping for breath. "No, not seriously. Please… Maurice." She pointed to the prone form of Newbury. He hadn't moved since he'd been thrown across the street by the beast. I went to his side.

He was still breathing. I checked him hurriedly for broken limbs. Miraculously, he appeared to be mostly unhurt. He'd have a few aches and bruises when he came round, perhaps even a mild concussion, but he'd sustained no serious injuries.

I realised Miss Hobbes was standing beside me and stood back to allow her room. She knelt on the ground beside him and cupped his face in her hands. "Maurice?" And then more firmly, "Maurice?"

Newbury stirred, groaning. His eyes flickered open, and he looked up at us, confused. "Has it gone?"

"Yes, it's gone," I said, with a heavy sigh. "Although we're lucky to be alive. I fear it was a rather abortive encounter."

Newbury grinned as he pulled himself up into a sitting position, dusting himself down. "On the contrary, Dr Watson. Now we know what it is. Tomorrow we'll be able to catch it."

I frowned. "Forgive me, Sir Maurice, but how exactly do you propose to capture a mechanical beast of that size?"

Newbury laughed and took Miss Hobbes's proffered hand in order to pull himself to his feet. "With an equally big net," he replied, clapping me boldly on the shoulder. He glanced at Miss Hobbes. "You look shaken, Miss Hobbes. Are you alright?"

"Yes," she replied, dabbing with a handkerchief at a minor cut on her temple. Her hair had shaken loose and she was flushed. I recall thinking at the time, however, that it was not so much the encounter with the submersible that had shaken her, but her fear for Newbury. "Yes, I'm quite well."

Newbury nodded, but it was clear he was not entirely satisfied with her answer. "Now, I'm sure we could all do with a stiff brandy. Let's repair to Cleveland Avenue where we can rest, tend our wounds, and discuss our strategy for tomorrow."

I found myself nodding and falling into step. I was keen to put some distance between our little band and the scene of the disturbance, and to find somewhere warm to rest my weary bones. I also must admit that, despite the danger, I had found myself quite swept up in the adventure and mystery of it all. There were questions to be answered. Who had that man been inside the strange submersible, staring out at me with such a pale, haunted expression? What was the purpose of the vehicle, and why had the pilot spared my life at the last moment?

I knew I'd be unable to rest until I had the answers to those questions. And besides, I was anxious to know more of these remarkable people with whom I had found myself working. Both Newbury and Miss Hobbes had shown remarkable courage in the face of terrible danger. Not only that, but they had remained entirely unperturbed by the appearance of the bizarre machine, as if they'd seen its like a hundred times before. I was intrigued to know how they planned to tackle the machine the following day, and I knew that whatever scheme was outlined to me that night, I would be unable to resist playing a role.

The following day I woke to a spasming muscle in my left calf. I felt tired and drained, and my body ached as it hadn't done for years. Nevertheless, I also felt somewhat invigorated by the recollection of my adventure the prior evening. It seemed to me as if I'd stumbled upon something momentous, and I was anxious to get to the bottom of the matter.

I washed and dressed and worked the muscle in my leg until the cramping eased. I was badly bruised from where I'd fallen, and my elbow was painful to move. I knew it wouldn't stop me, however. I might have been an old soldier, but I was a soldier still, and I knew how to pick myself up and carry on.

I took a stout breakfast of porridge and fruit, and then set out to call on Brownlow. A short trip on the underground took me across town, and the brisk walk at the other end did much to clear my head. It was a cold, damp day, and the sky above was an oppressive canopy of grey, brooding and pregnant.

Upon my arrival, Brownlow's wife – a willowy woman in her late thirties, who wore a permanently startled expression – informed me that her husband was out, and so I trudged the quarter of a mile to his surgery, where I found him enjoying a momentary respite from his patients. He ushered me into his office and asked the clerk to organise a pot of tea.

It was clear almost immediately that I'd been correct in my assumption that Brownlow would have thrown himself into his work in an effort to dispel his anxiety over the events of two nights previous. He acted as if the encounter had never even occurred, and when I raised the subject he waved me down with a severe frown, indicating that he no longer wished to discuss it. Still, I persisted, and when I began to relate the story of my own encounter with the mechanical beast, he listened quietly, absorbing every detail.

"So I am not, after all, bound for Bedlam," he said, when I'd finished. He did so with a jovial smile, but the relief was plain to see on his face. "Thank you, John."

"You were never bound for Bedlam, Peter. But I do believe you are guilty of overworking yourself. You should consider allowing yourself a holiday with that pretty wife of yours."

He smiled at this and poured the tea. "I think, my dear friend, that I should find such a holiday even more stress-inducing then a late night encounter with a mechanical beast. I cannot abandon my patients."

I sighed and reached for my teacup.

It was approaching midday when I left Brownlow to his patients, feeling as if, for once, I'd been able to lift a weight from his shoulders. Newbury had said he'd need time to prepare for the evening's activities – that he needed to speak with a man named Aldous Renwick – and so, left to my own devices, I decided to head to Baker Street in order to take luncheon with Holmes. I was still rankled with him for his dismissive attitude the previous day, but felt it would not do to let things fester between us. He had, after all, no other friends upon which to prevail if he found himself in need. He was not a man that responded well to prolonged solitude; despite his protestations to the opposite, Holmes needed an audience.

I found him hunched over a leather-bound tome, poring over page after page of arcane diagrams, each of which appeared to depict complex chemical formulas. He was still wearing his ratty old dressing gown and his unlit pipe was clenched between his teeth. Dark rings had developed beneath his hooded eyes, and he appeared gaunt. I guessed he had not been to bed since I had last seen him, let alone the thought that he might have taken a bath or gone for a stroll.

He didn't look up when Mrs Hudson showed me into the room, but waved for me to take a seat. I shifted a heap of newspapers to the floor in order to do so.

"Well, Holmes!" I said, clutching the arms of the chair and leaning forward, hoping to draw his attention from the manual upon his lap. "Last night's activities by the river were quite invigorating."

"Hmm," issued Holmes dismissively, still steadfastly

refusing to look up from his book.

"I saw it for myself," I continued, determined that he'd hear me out. "The beast, that is. Turns out it's a ruddy great machine of some sort, a submersible with legs, containing a pilot. Things looked a bit hairy for a while, on account of the aforementioned pilot attacking Sir Maurice, his associate Miss Hobbes, and me. Had to chase him off with my revolver in the end. You should have seen it, Holmes. Quite remarkable."

At this, Holmes suddenly slammed his book shut and looked up, turning his familiar hawklike gaze upon me. "What was that, Watson? I fear I didn't quite catch what you said."

I issued a long, familiar sigh. "Nothing, Holmes," I said, deflated. "It wasn't important."

Holmes raised a single eyebrow, and then tossed the book he'd been reading on to the floor. It landed with a dull thud on the carpet by my feet. He turned, stretching out upon the divan like a luxuriating cat, resting his slippered feet upon the arm.

I shook my head in resigned dismay. "How is your investigation going?" I asked. "It looks as if you've barely left the drawing room these past two days. Your search for Mr Xavier Gray is not, I presume, proving easy."

Holmes glanced at me, a thin smile forming upon his lips. "Oh, I'd say the investigation is proceeding quite as planned, Watson. The matter has my full attention."

I shrugged my shoulders in disbelief. Despite living with Holmes for many long years and chronicling all of his most notable investigations, his methods could still seem opaque to me.

"What time is lunch?" I asked, leaning back in my chair. "I'm famished and in need of one of Mrs Hudson's hearty broths." I knew it was a liberty, but I felt I'd earned it after the events of the previous evening, and besides, it looked as if Holmes could do with a square meal. Perhaps if I stayed to accompany him, he might actually eat.

"You shall not be disappointed, Watson, if you have it in you to bide your time in that chair for another twenty-six minutes. Beef stew, I believe, with dumplings."

"Ah, my favourite! Let me guess," I said, grinning. "You heard Mrs Hudson place the pot upon the stove, and, over recent months – if not years – you've worked to memorise her routine from the very sounds she makes as she toils. Now, you're able to fathom her every movement from the noises issuing from the basement, and predict the dish and the exact moment upon which she will serve luncheon?"

Holmes gave a cheerful guffaw. "Close, Watson. Very close. She came to inform me just a few moments before you arrived – four minutes, in fact – that she would be serving beef stew, with dumplings, in half an hour's time."

I could not suppress a chuckle. "Well, I'd better pop down and ask if she wouldn't mind setting another place," I said, moving to rise from my chair.

"No need," said Holmes, waving his pipe, "I attended to that yesterday."

"Yesterday?" I asked, incredulous. "Whatever do you mean?"

"I mean that I asked Mrs Hudson to make a special effort to prepare a hearty lunch – your favourite stew, in fact – given that you'd be stopping by after what undoubtedly would have proved to have been a harrowing night on Cheyne Walk, grappling with monsters and such like." He struck a match with a flourish and lit his pipe.

"You astound me, Holmes," was about as much as I could muster.

He was still laughing when Mrs Hudson called us to the dining room for lunch.

* * *

Following my visit to Baker Street, still a little baffled by Holmes's unflappable mood and his apparent lack of progress in his case, I dropped in at my club to pass a few hours of quiet reflection. Duly restored, I called home to collect my revolver – carefully cleaned that morning – before setting out to meet Newbury and the others at Cheyne Walk. It was dark by then and the streets already had an abandoned, desolate air; a thick, syrupy fog had descended along with the darkness to smother everything in its damp embrace, sending the pedestrian population scuttling to the warmth of their homes.

We'd agreed to meet at the very same spot at which we'd encountered the strange machine the previous evening. Logic dictated that this was the most likely place for us to lay our trap. We had, whilst sat around the fire drinking brandy in Newbury's drawing room, discussed the possibility that the pilot might select a different stretch of the embankment to make his ascent that night, following his surprise confrontation with our little band. Miss Hobbes had argued, however, that there must have been some reason why he should so far have chosen to scale the walls at that particular point. All of the witness reports confirmed such was his habit. We'd decided between us that it would therefore make sense for us to stage our trap in the vicinity.

I was, as yet, unaware of the nature of this trap, and it wasn't until I rounded the corner of Cheyne Walk and saw the spectacle of it laid out before me that I began to get some sense of what Newbury had planned.

A large, box-shaped construct, about the height of a man and twice as wide again, sat squat at the far end of the street. Black smoke curled from the top of it, forming a dark, oily smudge, and even from ten feet away I could feel the heat cf its furnace and smell the acrid stench of burning coal. The noise, too, was horrendous: a whirring, clacking cacophony, the sound of spinning turbines, powered by steam. Thick bunches of copper cable coiled from the belly of the portable generator, and a man with tufts of wild white hair was stretching them out upon the pavement, hands sheathed in thick rubber gloves. The cables sparked and popped with the violent electricity that coursed through them. Newbury stood over his shoulder, overseeing proceedings, and Miss Hobbes stood off to one side, watching the river for any signs of movement.

I coughed politely to announce my presence.

"Dr Watson!" Newbury called cheerfully, looking up for a moment from what the other man was doing. I was startled to see his expression alter suddenly from apparent pleasure to immediate concern. "Now, don't move an inch!"

I glanced down to see that, in my haste to join the others, I had strayed dangerously close to one of the live cables. My left boot was only a fraction of an inch from brushing against it, and the slightest adjustment in my posture would have seen thousands of volts hungrily discharge into my body.

Cautiously, I edged away from the live wire until I was comfortable enough to breathe a sigh of relief. I moved over to join Newbury and the man I took to be Aldous Renwick. "So you're planning to electrocute it?" I asked, impressed by the machinery they'd been able to erect in just a few hours.

"Quite so, Dr Watson. When that mechanical beast finds itself entangled in these electrified cables, the resulting surge of power should render it temporarily immovable," replied Newbury.

"Yes, and temporarily deadly to the touch, too," said the other man, gruffly. He straightened his back, laying the last of the cables into position and turning to face me. "When that happens, the last thing you should do is consider touching the machine itself. If you do, you'll be blown clear into the river by the resulting shock. They'll be fishing you out with a net."

Newbury laughed. "Dr Watson, meet my good friend, Aldous Renwick."

"A pleasure," I said, taking his hand.

In truth, I find it difficult to select words with which to adequately describe the appearance of such a unique and eccentric individual. Aldous Renwick defied easy interpretation. As I have already described, his hair was a wild, wispy mess upon his head, and he was unshaven, his lower face covered in wiry grey bristles. His teeth were yellowed from tobacco smoke and his complexion was that of a fifty-year-old, although I placed him closer to forty. He was dressed in an ill-fitting shirt, open at the collar, over which he wore a thick leather smock, such as one a butcher might don while carving meat. Most disturbing of all, however, was the appearance of his left eye, or rather the object embedded in the socket where his left eye should have been.

At first I had assumed that Renwick was wearing a jeweller's magnifying glass, using it to examine the electrical cables with which he had been busying himself, but upon closer inspection I saw that the lens was, in fact, an integral part of the man's face. The device had been inserted into the vacant socket where his eyeball had once been; an artificial replacement, much like a glass eye, but significantly more practical. I soon realised that, although it might have appeared a little ungainly to some, the false eye actually enabled Renwick to see.

I studied the device for a moment as it whirred and clicked, turning as if by its own volition. Deep inside, behind the curved glass lens, a tiny pinprick of fierce red light burned inside his skull. I wondered who had constructed and installed such a thing. It was at once remarkable and utterly disconcerting.

Renwick grinned, his face creasing with a thousand lines. "It's impressive, isn't it, Doctor?"

"It most certainly is, Mr Renwick. Quite remarkable. Tell

me, does it offer the same clarity of vision as the original eye?"

Renwick shrugged. "It suits my needs," he said, glancing over at Newbury. "We're as ready as we'll ever be."

Newbury grinned. "Now to wait for the beast."

We fell back from the edge of the embankment, Miss Hobbes and I posted at opposite ends of the street to ensure that no innocent civilians inadvertently strayed into our trap, just as I had almost done a few moments earlier. The temperature had dropped dramatically, but I'd come prepared for a long wait, and had even thought to bring along a hip flask filled with brandy. I was careful to take only the shortest of warming nips, however, as I did not wish to face the infernal machine again whilst inebriated.

Hours passed. I began to grow weary. I could see the others growing impatient, also, stamping their feet and pacing up and down, anxious for something to occur. At one point Newbury abandoned his post to join me for a moment. I offered him my hip flask, which he received gratefully, taking a long draw. "Perhaps we scared him off," he said, studying the oily river, which stretched away into the night like a black ribbon. "Perhaps he isn't coming back tonight."

"Perhaps," I replied, noncommittally.

"Another hour," he said, quietly. "We'll give it another hour." He trudged off to join Aldous Renwick beneath the cover of the trees.

In the event, it was closer to two before we heard the approach of the bestial machine. Just as the previous night, the first warning was a sound like chains being ratcheted through metal eyelets. I watched, wide-eyed, as the first of the tentacular limbs snaked over the top of the embankment wall. This was swiftly followed by another, and then another, and then finally the hulking body of the submersible, water streaming down its sides as it hauled itself from the river.

"Stay back!' called Newbury, and I admit that I had no

desire to disobey his order. I could feel the trepidation like a dead weight in my belly. What if the trap didn't work? What if the machine proved impervious to the electrical storm, or the pilot chose to take an alternative route entirely? It would all have been for nothing. Worse, we might all have found ourselves once more in terrible danger.

Newbury, of course, was not leaving anything to chance. I watched, surprised, as he suddenly produced a hurricane lantern from somewhere beside him, raising the shutters so that bright, yellow light spilled out, encapsulating him in a glowing orb.

He marched forward, towards the electrical cables, waving the lantern above his head as if he were a matador taunting a bull.

"Maurice, be careful," I heard Miss Hobbes call out in the gloom, and I noted the edge of warning in her tone.

The machine started forward, and then stopped, as if the pilot was uneasy about this unexpected development.

"Over here!" shouted Newbury, waving the lantern back and forth. "Over here!"

The pilot seemed to make up his mind then and the submersible swept forward, its tentacles grinding across the pavement as it charged at Newbury.

With a triumphant cry, Newbury skipped backwards, leading the mechanical beast on.

The sound when the first of the tentacles struck the copper cables was like a thunderclap; a deafening blow that left me reeling with shock. The accompanying flash of sudden, sparking light was almost too much to bear, and I squeezed my eyes shut as it seared my retinas. For a moment everything seemed to take on a dreamlike quality as, struck suddenly deaf and blind, I tried to regain my senses.

When I opened my eyes again a few moments later, the sight was utterly breathtaking.

Unable to halt its momentum, the submersible had slid

fully onto the copper cables and was now caught in the full brunt of the electrical discharge. Blue lightning flickered over every surface, crawling like snakes across the carapace. The tentacles leapt and danced, thrashing about uncontrollably at the mercy of the current. The entirety of Cheyne Walk was lit up by the deadly – but irrefutably beautiful – storm.

"Halt the current!" I heard Newbury bellow, and Renwick rushed to the generator, forcing the lever into the *off* position. A few moments later, the submersible stuttered, gave a last, violent shudder, and then collapsed in a heap upon the ground.

I withdrew my revolver from my pocket and rushed over to where the others were gathering around the downed machine. Miss Hobbes was first to the site, and seemed about to clamber up onto the body of the machine itself in search of the hatch.

"Stand back, Miss Hobbes," called Renwick, running over in order to keep her from getting too close to the machine. "There may be some residual charge. Here, allow me." Renwick approached it gingerly, testing the surface with his gloved hands. He circled the vehicle once before turning to Newbury, a gleam in his single remaining eye. "It's quite something, isn't it? Just as you said."

"Indeed it is," said Newbury, although it was clear there was something else on his mind. "Aldous, the pilot…?"

Renwick frowned, as if he didn't understand the question.

"Will he be dead?" I asked, quietly.

Renwick shrugged. "It depends what protection he had inside." He glanced at each of us in turn. "Only one way to find out," he said. He reached up and took hold of a small metal wheel that jutted from the lower side of the hull and began twisting it, releasing the seal of the pilot's hatch. It loosened off a few seconds later with a pneumatic hiss, and the hatch hinged open with a metallic clang. We all waited with baited breath.

There was a low groan from inside the machine, followed by the sound of a man spluttering and coughing. I glanced at Newbury, who raised an eyebrow in surprise. "I suppose we'd better get him out of there, then?"

Together we worked to turn the hull of the vehicle until Newbury was able to reach inside and drag the pilot out onto the street. He was a sorry mess, shaking and spluttering as he propped himself up on one arm, staring up at us with a blank, pale expression. He was wearing a set of dark blue overalls that were covered in a week's worth of oil and grime, and blood was running freely from one nostril. He wiped at it ineffectually with his sleeve.

I stood over him with my revolver, although in truth it was an unnecessary gesture; there was no fight left in the man, and if he'd tried anything we should easily have been able to restrain him.

"Who are you?" asked Miss Hobbes, her voice more commanding than I'd come to expect from her. She was, if nothing else, a woman of many surprises.

The man gazed up at her, a haunted look in his eyes. "My name is Xavier Gray," he said.

I almost choked in surprise as I tried to assimilate this unexpected information. "Xavier Gray!" I exclaimed loudly.

"You know this man?" said Newbury.

I shook my head. "Indeed not. But I know a man who wants very much to find him. Mr Gray here is the quarry of none other than Sherlock Holmes."

Newbury emitted a rumbling guffaw. "Is that so, Dr Watson? How very surprising."

Gray looked as surprised as any of us. "Sherlock Holmes?" he asked, but it was clearly a rhetorical question.

"Tell us, Mr Gray," prompted Miss Hobbes, "what is the purpose of this machine, and for what reason have you been making these late-night excursions?"

"For them," replied Gray, trembling as he fought back tears. "It was all for them."

"This man is clearly disturbed," said Renwick, redundantly. It was plain for us all to see that Gray was suffering from severe shock.

"Speaking as a medical practitioner, it's clear this man needs rest and a chance to recover from the shock of this evening's events." I said, lowering my weapon. "I imagine we'll be better served by saving our questions until the morning."

"Very well," said Newbury. "May I suggest, Doctor, that you take this man into your temporary custody? I don't believe he represents any real danger, now that his machine has been rendered immobile. I have every faith that you'll be able to tend to his immediate medical needs, and I'm sure Mr Holmes would be only too delighted to hear that we've saved him a job." He delivered this with a wry smile on his lips, and I couldn't help sharing for a moment in his glee. After the manner in which Holmes had dismissed the whole episode it would give me no small measure of satisfaction to deliver Xavier Gray to his doorstep. I could imagine the look on his face.

"Very well," I said. "I shall escort Mr Gray to Baker Street immediately." I glanced at the wreckage of the submersible. "But what of this?"

"Oh, don't worry yourself with that, Dr Watson. I'll send for Sir Charles Bainbridge of Scotland Yard. His men will know what to do with the remains of this most remarkable contraption."

"Bainbridge?" I said, with a smile. "Then we have a mutual acquaintance." I'd worked with Bainbridge almost fifteen years earlier, during the Hans Gerber affair, and again on a number of other occasions during the intervening years. He was a good man, and an even better police inspector.

Newbury laughed again. "I'll be sure to give him your

regards," he said. "Now, Doctor. Let us find you a cab. It's late, and we still have much to do. Our answers can wait until tomorrow."

"Very well," I said, helping Xavier Gray to his feet. "If you'll come quietly?"

The man nodded, hanging his head. "I will," he said, morosely. I decided to take him at his word, although I kept my revolver close at hand, just to be sure.

It was late when we arrived at Baker Street, gone midnight, but I was resolved to rouse Holmes from his bed. We'd passed the journey across town in silence, with just the creak of the carriage wheels and the clatter of horse's hooves to punctuate our journey.

Xavier Gray had remained slumped in the opposite corner of the hansom throughout, as if the life had simply gone out of him. I couldn't help feeling pity for the man, despite the events of the previous evening. I did not then know the nature of the horror that plagued him, but all the same I had some sense that he was carrying an enormous burden upon his shoulders. I decided not to press the matter, and respected his need for silence. Tomorrow, I would push for answers. Tonight I was close to exhaustion, and couldn't bring myself to coerce such a clearly disturbed man.

It was a bleary-eyed Mrs Hudson who came to the door of 221b, wrapped in a black shawl and wearing an exasperated expression. "Oh, Dr Watson. It's you."

"Indeed it is, Mrs Hudson. Please, forgive me for disturbing you at this unsociable hour."

Mrs Hudson gave me a resigned look. "And you think I'm not used to such shenanigans, Doctor? You did, after all, live with Mr Holmes for a number of years."

I grinned. "Is he home?"

"God knows," she said, with a shrug of her shoulders. "But I suppose you'd better come in. Your guest looks as if he's about to catch his death."

I decided not to disabuse Mrs Hudson of the notion that Gray was my guest. It wouldn't do to concern her with the truth that I was leading a wanted man – and a criminal, at that – into her home.

It soon became clear that Holmes was not, after all, at home. Nevertheless, there was little I could do but wait. I ushered Gray into the drawing room and convinced Mrs Hudson to return to her bed. I poured myself a whiskey, deciding it would steady my nerves, and built up the fire in order to banish the chill.

All the while I kept my revolver close at hand, but Gray remained largely silent and subdued.

We'd been there for less than half an hour when I heard a key scrape in the lock downstairs. Footsteps followed on the creaking treads, accompanied by a gaily sung melody, "Tra, la, la, la, la." The footsteps halted outside the door. "Hello, Watson!" said Holmes, breezily, before the door had even been opened.

Of course, this was not a difficult deduction. Holmes knew Mrs Hudson's habits well, and that she would already be in bed. She would not have allowed anyone other than I to wait here for Holmes, and since it was evident that someone inhabited the drawing room – probably from the spill of light beneath the door – it had to be me.

The door swung open and Holmes's beaming face appeared in the opening. He was wrapped in a dark brown cape and was wearing a top hat. "Ah, I see you have a visitor," he said, removing his hat and strolling boldly into the room.

I stood. "Indeed I do." I indicated the sorry specimen crumpled in the chair opposite. "This, Holmes, is Mr Xavier Gray.'

Holmes looked from one of us to the other with a wide-eyed expression. "I... well... is it really, Watson?"

Xavier Gray glanced up at Holmes. "Dr Watson is correct, Mr Holmes. I am indeed Mr Xavier Gray," he said, his voice low and moribund.

"How extraordinary," said Holmes. "How very extraordinary." He seemed genuinely surprised by this development. He stroked his chin thoughtfully. "This business with the unusual beast?" he asked, after a short moment of reflection.

"Quite so," I said, proudly. "You were wrong to dismiss it, Holmes. It's proved to be the most remarkable of cases. The beast was in fact a bizarre, amphibious submersible being piloted by Mr Gray."

"Indeed?" said Holmes, without even a flicker of irony. "Well, perhaps I was wrong to be so dismissive, Watson. If it wasn't for your tenacity..."

"Don't mention it, Holmes," I said, with a smile. "So what now? I'm afraid we haven't questioned him yet regarding his motives. I fear he's rather in the grip of a severe case of shock."

Holmes nodded. "Very good, Watson. If I could prevail on you for a short while longer, I'll send for Mycroft immediately. Of course, you're welcome to the spare room this evening, if you should wish it?"

The thought of my old bed reminded me of just how tired I was. By this time it was almost two o'clock in the morning. "Thank you, Holmes," I said, nodding in gratitude. "The spare room will be most appreciated."

I waited with Gray while Holmes bustled off to make the necessary arrangements. He returned a few minutes later, looking rather pleased with himself. "Mycroft will be here shortly. Now, Watson, if you'd be kind enough to pour Mr Gray a brandy?"

"What was that?" I said, somewhat startled. I'd been

dangerously close to drifting off before the fire.

"A drink for Mr Gray, Watson. Make it a substantial one."

With a sigh, I pushed myself out of my chair and crossed to the sideboard. When I turned back a moment later, glass in hand, I was annoyed to see Holmes had helped himself to my seat, opposite our visitor.

"Mr Gray, I should like to talk with you," said Holmes, his voice low and even.

Gray seemed not to hear his words, or otherwise chose not to engage with them.

Holmes leaned forward in his – or rather, in my – chair. "I know what became of your family Mr Gray."

At this the other man's demeanour seemed to alter entirely. He stiffened, lifting his head to stare directly at Holmes, who smiled calmly and waved at me to deliver the brandy. I placed it on the side table close to where Gray was sitting and retreated, moving round to stand behind Holmes.

"I didn't kill them," Gray said, gritting his teeth, and I was startled to see tears forming in the corners of his eyes as he spoke. His fists were bunched so hard by his sides that his nails were digging into the flesh of his palms, drawing little beads of blood. "Despite what they might say, I only wanted to protect them."

"I believe you," said Holmes, levelly. "It was immediately clear to me upon examining their remains that you were not to blame. Rather, it was the work of a criminal organisation, a network of thieves and robbers known as the 'Order of the Red Hand'. All of their typical hallmarks were in evidence." He paused, as if weighing up his own words. "I'm very sorry for your loss," he added, almost as an afterthought.

Xavier Gray reached shakily for the tumbler of brandy I had provided for him and drained it thirstily, shuddering as the alcohol did its work. He returned the empty glass to the table, wiping his mouth with the back of his hand. "I tried to save them," he said, and his eyes implored us to believe him. "I tried to help. But I wasn't strong enough. I couldn't stop them. They held me back while they did it. They made me watch." He began to weep openly then, tears trickling down his pale cheeks. "And all for what? For a few measly pounds. I only wish they'd killed me, too. Then I wouldn't have to live with the memory."

Unsure of what else I could do, I collected his glass and poured him another generous measure. The story unfolding before me was not at all what I had expected.

"And so you decided to take matters into your own hands?" prompted Holmes, leaning back in his chair and making a steeple with his fingers.

"I didn't know what else to do," said Gray between sobs. "It was all I could think of. All of those machines, those weapons, just hidden there in storage, covered in dusty tarpaulin. No one would know. Those ruffians needed to pay for what they'd done."

Confused, I glanced at Holmes, who shook his head minutely to indicate that I should refrain from interjecting with any questions.

"So you took the submersible and set about searching for the perpetrators of the crime?"

Gray nodded. "Yes. I knew they wouldn't lie low for long. People like that never do. And so I made my nightly excursions in the stolen submersible, hoping to find them."

"In the very same location where your own family perished at their hands?"

Gray nodded. "Cheyne Walk. That's where they set upon us. I pleaded with them to stop. I tried to reason with them. I promised to give them everything if only they would spare the lives of my wife and children. But it was as if they were punishing me for only having a few pounds in my wallet. They wanted to make me pay, one way or another. And so I wanted to make them pay in return."

"It would never have been enough," said Holmes. "You would never have been able to live with yourself."

"You think I can live with myself now?" said Gray, burying his face in his hands. "I have nothing left to live for."

I hardly knew what to say or do. I'd seen men like this before, broken because of a grave loss. It was clear that Gray had been driven to do what he had because of grief, and that temporary, blinding madness it inspires.

I was still somewhat unsure of the full picture, but in listening to the conversation I had managed to piece together something of the story. It seemed to me that Xavier Gray had been the victim of a terrible, random crime, and that a gang of thieves had set upon him and his family in the street. His family had been brutally murdered before his very eyes, and as a consequence his mind had snapped. He had stolen the experimental submersible from – I assumed – the government facility where he worked, and had set out to seek revenge. It was a shocking tale, and I felt no small measure of pity for the wretch. I cannot say I wouldn't have done the same in his circumstance.

I jumped at the sound of a cane rapping against the front door, down in the street below.

"Mycroft," said Holmes, leaping out of his seat and disappearing to welcome his brother.

We remained silent for a moment. I heard Mycroft bustling into the hallway downstairs. "I'm sorry," I said to Gray, watching as he downed the remains of his second brandy.

"So am I," he replied, and I knew the words were not really intended for me.

Mycroft entered the room then, ahead of Holmes, and I once again found myself taken aback by the sheer presence of the man. He was heavyset, with an ample waist and a broad, barrel-like chest, and taller even than his brother. He looked decidedly put out at finding himself there at Baker Street at nearly three o'clock in the morning, and his forehead was furrowed in a deep frown.

"Watson," he said, levelly, by way of greeting. "I understand my thanks are in order." His tone was businesslike and clipped.

I smiled and gave the briefest of shrugs. "You're welcome," I said. "I did only what I felt was necessary."

"You did me a great service," said Mycroft, quickly, before turning to Gray, who was still sitting in the armchair opposite, clutching an empty glass. "Come along, Gray. It's over now."

Xavier Gray looked up to meet Mycroft's intense gaze. "Is it?" he asked, softly, before placing his glass on the side table and getting to his feet. "I don't think it shall ever be over."

Mycroft didn't respond, other than to place a firm hand on Gray's shoulder and to steer him swiftly towards the door. "Goodnight, Dr Watson," he said, without glancing back. "Until next time."

Holmes saw his brother and their charge into the waiting carriage, before returning to the drawing room, a sullen expression on his face. "A dark business, Watson," he said, quietly. "A dark business indeed."

"I'm just pleased that it's over," I said, stifling a yawn.

"Oh, I think for Mr Xavier Gray, Watson, the pain is only just beginning."

On that note, I repaired to my old room with a heavy heart, intent on a long and restful sleep.

The next morning I arose late to find Holmes had been up and about for hours. Indeed, I had my suspicions that, as I knew he was wont to do, he had not visited his bed at all.

"Ah, Watson!" he said jovially, as I poked my head around the drawing room door. He was sitting with the morning newspapers, snipping away with a pair of silver scissors, taking cuttings for his scrapbooks.

"Morning, Holmes," I said, somewhat taken aback by his jollity.

"Come and sit down, Watson! We'll have Mrs Hudson rustle you up a late breakfast." The thought was most appealing.

"Tell me, Holmes, have you had word from Mycroft?"

Holmes nodded. "Indeed I have, Watson." He returned to his clippings.

"And?" I prompted, exasperated.

He glanced up from *The Times* with a mildly confused expression.

"Xavier Gray?" I said. "There are those of us still anxious to understand his story," I said, taking a seat opposite him. "As well as your role in the matter," I added, for in truth that was my real motivation.

Holmes set down his scissors. "Ah, yes. Of course. Xavier Gray, Watson, was a government scientist and spy. He was working on a number of highly sensitive projects in the area of mechanised warfare, when, a week ago, he suddenly disappeared."

"Disappeared?" I echoed.

"Quite so," replied Holmes. "His superiors were, of course, concerned for the man, and even more for the sensitive information he was party to. Had he defected? Had he been captured and taken prisoner? The usual means of investigation turned up nothing. His home had simply been abandoned, and his family were gone, too."

"And now we know why," I said, gravely.

"Indeed. But at the time, the men responsible for tracing him had been unable to turn up any evidence of where he might have gone. Mycroft feared he might have fled somewhere untraceable in order to sell his secrets to a foreign agency, taking his family with him. In desperation, he called on me to investigate."

"And?"

"I soon discovered what the others had, of course, missed. Gray's family – his wife and two young boys – had been horrifically murdered just days prior to his disappearance. It appeared to be the work of the criminal gang I spoke of, the Order of the Red Hand, a network of robbers and thieves who had set upon them in the street and cleared out their pockets before disappearing. The bodies were still lying unidentified in the morgue."

"But why did Gray believe he was under suspicion? Last night he was most anxious to clear his name when you raised the matter."

"Once I had discovered the truth about his family, the imbeciles at the Yard were quick to proclaim his guilt, despite my evidence to the contrary. They simply could not fathom why a man might flee in the aftermath of such harrowing events, unless he was himself the killer or somehow connected with the perpetrators."

"That's preposterous!" I said.

Holmes laughed. "An all too familiar story, I fear, Watson."

"One can hardly blame him for taking matters into his own hands when faced with that as an alternative. I should imagine any man in his position might have chosen to do the same."

"Grief drives people to do terrible things, Watson, as you well know."

"Indeed," I said, quietly. "What will happen to Gray now?"

"Most likely an institution, I'd wager. At least until he's had time to recover from the shock and torment that drove him to such extreme ends."

"Extreme ends indeed. I can only imagine that, when he attacked Sir Maurice, Miss Hobbes and I, he'd mistaken us for the very same criminals who had attacked and killed his family. Particularly when Newbury tossed a flare in his direction."

"I believe you'd be safe in that assumption," said Holmes. "I imagine he saw only what his shattered mind had conjured."

"And what of the Order of the Red Hand?"

"Ah," said Holmes, brightly. "Their story is far from over. We shall face the Order of the Red Hand again. I am sure of it."

"I have no doubt you're right," I said, knowingly. "Well, that's an end to a remarkable secuence of events, Holmes," I continued, with a sigh. "And a most satisfactory resolution. For both of us."

"Indeed," said Holmes, rising from his seat and crossing to the fireplace to search for his pipe and Persian slippers. "I believe the old adage, Watson, is 'to kill two birds with one stone'."

"Quite so," I agreed. "It is almost as if..." I paused, hesitating to give voice to a nagging doubt that had been plaguing me since I'd woken that morning. "It is almost as if someone masterminded the entire thing."

"Really, Watson?" said Holmes, laughing. "You do have a tendency towards the fanciful."

"Hmm," I replied. "So where were you last night while all of the excitement was going on?"

Holmes smiled, returning to his seat and beginning to meticulously stuff the bowl of his pipe with shag. "A violin concerto. German. It was quite exquisite, Watson. The company was only in London for one night. It was truly not to be missed. Not under any circumstances."

"A violin concerto!" I exclaimed, astounded. "Really, Holmes!"

Holmes laughed. "Now, Watson. Breakfast!" he said, lighting his pipe and ringing the bell for Mrs Hudson. "There's a little matter I wish to discuss with you, regarding a missing jewel..."

* * *

The story of the Higham Ruby is a tale for another time, of course, and following the peculiar events of which I have just given account would seem entirely prosaic.

I sent word to Newbury that the matter had been successfully concluded and took pains to outline the story recited by Holmes, regarding Xavier Gray's unfortunate circumstances and the true nature of the mechanical beast we had fought. I received a brief note of thanks from Miss Hobbes, who explained that Newbury had been detained with other matters but wished to extend his thanks for the part I had played in proceedings, and to reassure me that the submersible stolen by Gray had been given over to the appropriate authorities.

It would be nearly two years until I once again encountered Sir Maurice Newbury and Miss Veronica Hobbes, in connection with the incidents I have previously set out in "The Case of the Five Bowler Hats". Events at that point would take a decidedly more sinister turn, and perhaps if I'd had the foresight I might not have wished so readily to find myself engaged in another mystery with that ineffable duo.

As it was, I'd found myself most invigorated by my association with Newbury and Miss Hobbes, and knew that, should the circumstances again present themselves, I would most definitely enjoy the prospect of joining forces with them once again to investigate a mystery of the improbable.

Moreover, as I tucked into Mrs Hudson's excellent breakfast, I was content to know that for once in the long history of our friendship, I had been able to successfully surprise Mr Sherlock Holmes.

THE SACRIFICIAL PAWN

LONDON, OCTOBER 1902

"Unhand me, you darned scoundrel!"

The familiar voice reverberated throughout the old manor house like the bark of a cornered dog. Sir Maurice Newbury looked up from where he slumped against the wall of his makeshift cell, and smiled.

Despite the circumstances, he was relieved to hear the voice of his old friend, Charles Bainbridge, to know that the chief inspector was still alive. He'd been worried that the people responsible for their capture might have proved less inclined to keep Bainbridge alive when they'd discovered he didn't have what they were looking for. Thankfully, that seemed not to be the case. So far, at least.

Newbury heard boots thundering in the hallway on the other side of the door. There were at least three of them, he estimated, along with their uncooperative prisoner. Consequently, he decided it wasn't the time to try to make a break for it, especially given his own rather beleaguered condition. He'd have to bide his time for a while longer.

The bolt grated in the lock, and then the door to the room was flung open and Bainbridge was shoved rudely inside.

"God *damn* you!" he exclaimed loudly, as he stumbled

and caught himself on the edge of the fire surround, barely managing to keep himself upright. The door slammed shut behind him, allowing Newbury only the slightest glimpse of their black-robed captors.

Bainbridge glanced around warily, taking in his surroundings. His eyes fixed on Newbury, who remained slumped in the corner on the other side of the room. Bainbridge's relief was immediately evident from the look on his face. "Newbury! Thank goodness you're still alive!"

Newbury grinned, and then winced as the gesture set off a series of sharp pains in his head. He'd taken quite a beating as he'd tried to evade capture, and even after three days, he could barely move without being reminded of it. Then, of course, there were the further beatings he'd received twice daily ever since he'd been holed up in the room. "I see the rescue attempt is going exactly as planned, Charles?" he said, with a chuckle.

Bainbridge sighed and crossed the room to stand over him, limping ever so slightly as he walked. Newbury realised Bainbridge wasn't carrying his cane. That meant yet another hope of escape was dashed. He must have lost it in the fight or had it confiscated by their captors.

Newbury glanced up at his old friend. Bainbridge looked as if he'd put up a good fight, which was entirely in keeping with what Newbury would have expected; Bainbridge wouldn't have taken lightly to being set upon and bundled into a hansom in the dead of night. The front of his shirt was torn and he was sporting a bruised and swollen eyelid. Newbury felt a brief pang of remorse.

"I'm sorry, old chap. Miss Hobbes and I have been searching for you for days," said Bainbridge. He sounded a little sheepish, and he unconsciously stroked his bushy moustache as he spoke; a nervous gesture Newbury had seen a hundred times before. "Thought you'd gone off on another of your... episodes. We imagined you'd eventually turn up in one of those blasted Chinese dens you seem so intent on inhabiting. Miss Hobbes and I have spent hours searching in back rooms all across the city, expecting to find you half dead, in a stupor, or worse." He paused, looking Newbury up and down appraisingly. "Mind you, half dead appears to be a fairly fitting description. What the devil happened, Newbury?"

Newbury expelled a long, plaintive sigh. "Devil is quite the word, Charles," he said, running a hand through his hair. "Sit down and I'll tell you everything." He glanced at the door. "I don't imagine we'll be hearing anything more of our captors for a while yet."

Bainbridge shrugged and – evidently realising there was no furniture in the room upon which to take a seat – lowered himself to the floorboards beside Newbury, groaning quietly at what Newbury took to be the result of another recent injury. He couldn't help feeling responsible for Bainbridge's suffering, and would have preferred to avoid involving his friend in the whole wretched affair, but in the end he'd felt he'd had no choice.

The room they were in had once been a bedchamber – and a grand one at that – but had long since been stripped bare and turned into a makeshift holding cell. The windows were boarded and barred, the oilcloths had been torn up and staunch bolts had been fitted to the other side of the door. There was nothing left in the room that could be used as a weapon. Newbury had checked. Even the fire grate had been emptied of coal. Every inch of the room was now familiar to Newbury, from the dark oak panelling to the untreated floorboards. Three days spent locked within its four walls had left him with little else to do but study his surroundings and try to conceive a means of escape. At least, now, things finally seemed to be coming to a head.

"Well? Are you going to enlighten me?"

Newbury turned his head to regard the chief inspector. "Tell me, Charles, what did you learn of our captors during your abduction?"

Bainbridge furrowed his brow in thought. "Very little. They came out of nowhere. Three of them, dressed in black robes, with hoods obscuring their faces. They set upon me on Wardour Street with a blackjack. I put up the best fight I could, but one of them caught me with a blow to the head and before I knew it I was being restrained and bundled into the back of a hansom. They forced a cowl over my head and went through my pockets as we barrelled off into the night. I've no idea how long I lay like that in the footwell. An hour, maybe more. None of them said so much as a word, and every time I made a sound I received a sharp boot in the ribs for my effort." He shook his head. "Anyway, next thing I know, we're in this big house and I'm being goaded along the passageway to this room." He sighed. "I must admit, I'm relieved to see you here, Newbury. At least now I know it's more than just an opportunistic robbery. I'd feared I might end up dumped in the Thames with a knife in my belly by the end of the night, all for the sake of the contents of my wallet. At least this way we have a fighting chance of effecting an escape. But who are these people? What do they want with us?"

Newbury steeled himself for his friend's response before he spoke. "Cultists, Charles. They're demon-worshipping cultists from an organisation known as 'The Cabal of the Horned Beast'."

"Cultists!" Bainbridge spat the word. "Good God! As if I hadn't seen enough of this devil-worshipping claptrap in my time…"

Newbury raised his hand to still Bainbridge's outburst and the chief inspector – red-faced – fell quiet. "They're dangerous, Charles. They have very unusual beliefs, centred around the worship of obscure entities from ancient pagan mythology. This isn't your typical, run-of-the-mill cult. They're very serious and they have money and influence. Their members number in the hundreds and their influence is felt far and wide. Do not underestimate them."

"Pah! Surely you're not telling me these people are actually in possession of other-worldly powers? That's too much, Newbury, even for you."

Newbury raised an eyebrow. "Too much? Surely, Charles, your mind is no longer as closed to such matters as it used to be?" It was a rhetorical question, but he let it hang for a moment before continuing. "But no, that's not what I'm saying at all. Whether they have genuinely harnessed occult power, or whether they simply *believe* they have, matters little. They're just as dangerous regardless. Perhaps more so, because of their arrogance, because they're driven by their beliefs. And besides, their wealthy patrons ensure the Cabal's coffers are always brimming with funds enough to feed their arsenal. They have some bizarre and dangerous weapons. Some of them very unconventional indeed."

"But why now, Newbury? What's inspired them to take action against you now?"

Newbury sighed and rubbed at the three-day-old bristles that were beginning to irritate his throat. "Because I stole something from them, Charles, and they want it back very much indeed."

"You *what*?" Bainbridge sounded utterly indignant. "Do I take it you were acting on behalf of Her Majesty?"

Newbury shook his head, slowly. "I was acting on behalf of a dear friend."

Bainbridge exhaled slowly, and Newbury could tell he was struggling to contain his fury. 'Well, I won't even begin to attempt to decipher your motives, Newbury. I can only put my faith in your judgement and trust you would never endanger yourself and your friends without good reason."

"I can assure you, Charles, it was for the very best of reasons."

Bainbridge eyed him for a moment, as if weighing him up. "Very well." He winced as he stretched his legs out before him. "So tell me, what *is* this mysterious object that's caused these fools to become so agitated?"

"A book," said Newbury. "A very old and very rare book."

"All this for the sake of a book!" Bainbridge guffawed loudly. "I hope it's a ruddy good read!"

"Hardly," said Newbury, with a wry smile. "It's in ancient Aramaic. A book of rituals and incantations, entitled *The Cosmology of the Spirit*, the only original copy known to exist. There are others, of course, but all of them are missing vital passages. This, the earliest surviving example of the text, was uncovered centuries ago by a crusader, who brought it back to Scotland from the ruins of Constantinople. It languished for half a century in the vaults of a highland church before passing into the hands of a hermeticist named John Charterton. Charterton was a pragmatic man, and realising what he had in his possession, he sold the book for a king's ransom and retired on the proceeds. It's said that when the true nature of the book came to light, the Vatican attempted to acquire it through means both legal and illicit. The stories claim they raised a small army of agents to act on their behalf, but by then it was too late, and the book had disappeared, along with the mysterious man who had purchased it." He coughed and attempted to moisten his dry lips.

"The next thing anyone heard of the manuscript it had passed into the hands of an aristocrat named Henry Carvill almost a hundred years later. Carvill was a renowned occultist and went on to found the organisation that today is known as 'The Cabal of the Horned Beast', within whose headquarters we now sit. The manuscript has been held in their vault here in London ever since."

"Fascinating, Newbury," said Bainbridge, in a tone that made it clear he thought the lecture to be anything but. "You do have a taste for these musty old books." He shook his head, indicating that, in truth, he already knew the answer to his next question. "So, do I assume that you've had the good sense to copy these all-important missing passages, and that now you'll be able to return the original book to its owners to secure our release?"

"No, no, Charles. I fear it's not that simple. The book itself is the key, the true artefact. The words it contains are irrevocably entwined with the pages upon which they are written. The two are inseparable. Without the original manuscript, the words themselves mean nothing."

Bainbridge expelled a heavy sigh. "I feared you'd say something like that," he said. He offered Newbury a weary smile. "So, where is it now?"

"I told them that you had it."

"You *what?*" Bainbridge exclaimed, looking utterly flabbergasted. He stammered for a moment. "You... you *what?*" he repeated.

"I'm sorry, Charles," said Newbury, his voice low and even. "I didn't want to get you mixed up in all of this. But I needed to get a message out, to let you know where I was. I knew that you and Miss Hobbes would assume the worst, believing that I'd once again succumbed to the lure of the opium dens. As a consequence, I feared I might be dead before you discovered the truth. So, during one of the many beatings I've been forced to endure, I set them on your trail as a means of alerting you to what had occurred."

"Well, a damn lot of good it's done you, Newbury! Look at us both! I can hardly help you escape from in here. All you've actually managed to achieve is that we're both now trapped in the lion's den."

Newbury smiled sadly. "I'm truly sorry, Charles. I couldn't see what else to do."

Bainbridge's shoulders slumped. The fight had gone out of him. "You know I'll always help you, Newbury, any way I can. But this is a dangerous game you're playing…"

Newbury inclined his head in acknowledgement. "I know that, Charles." He could tell that Bainbridge was furious with him, but also that, in a way, he understood. Newbury had taken the only option he'd had left. Well, *almost* the only option… he might have remained silent, therefore sealing his own fate but ensuring the safety of his friends. He wondered if Bainbridge would have made the same choices.

The chief inspector pulled himself up on shaky legs. "Well, there's little use in sitting here like a pair of old men. Have you tried to prise the bars off that window?" He crossed the room, grasped hold of the iron grille and gave it a sharp tug. It didn't budge.

"It's no use, Charles. I've been over this room a hundred times. They have us trapped. There are no means of escape. But I need you to trust me. All will be well."

"All will be well!" Newbury could hear the incredulity in Bainbridge's voice. "People like this, Newbury, like these cultists – they're not rational. I mean… what have they even got planned for us? Something diabolical, I imagine."

"Well, eventually, I suppose, they'll want to sacrifice us to their pagan gods. They hold a belief that the lifespan of every human being is predetermined, that the moment of a person's natural death is a fixed point in time. They also maintain, however, that if the correct rites are observed, then the early death – the sacrifice – of a person can release the unspent potential of that life, the years that belong to that body but have not yet been lived. When they're done with us, they'll kill us for our remaining years, given the opportunity."

"Well, they won't get much from me!" said Bainbridge,

finally forgoing his anger in favour of a hearty laugh. "They'd be better off with a younger model." He was clearly astounded by the absurdity of it all. He crossed to the fireplace, gazing down at Newbury. "You see what I mean? Irrational poppycock!"

Newbury grinned, weighing his next words carefully. "They won't kill us, so long as they believe we still have the book. The book is more important to them."

Bainbridge shook his head. "So, truthfully, where is the book?"

Newbury frowned. "It's better that you don't know, Charles. For a whole variety of reasons."

"I'm beginning to feel like there's a lot I don't know." There was a warning note in his voice. The tone of their conversation had shifted once again.

"I could argue just the same, Charles," said Newbury. "All that time you've been spending with the Home Secretary and his new bureau…"

"State business! There's a difference, Newbury. You're gambling with our lives over a triviality."

Newbury clenched his fists in frustration. He wished he could tell his friend the truth: that he'd done it for Veronica, that he'd stolen the book to help her sister, Amelia, and that somehow, incredibly, the rituals it contained were helping to heal her, to calm her tempestuous, clairvoyant mind. But Bainbridge believed Amelia to have perished in the siege of the Grayling Institute earlier that year, and Newbury had given his word to Veronica that he would not reveal the truth to anyone – not even Bainbridge. "I can assure you, Charles, that it's anything *but* a triviality…"

"That's all well and good, Newbury, but what I was–" Bainbridge's reply was cut short by a thunderous bang from further up the hallway, followed by angry shouting and cries of alarm. He glanced at Newbury with a quizzical expression.

"Ah, here comes the cavalry!" said Newbury, his face splitting into a wide grin.

"What? I'm not following you, man! What's going on?" There was the sound of pounding feet from outside the cell door, accompanied by grunting and the soft thuds of blows being struck.

"Stand back, Charles!"

Bainbridge did as he was told, stepping to one side just in time to avoid being caught in the wake of the splintering door as it caved inward and a body came tumbling through, sprawling to the floor at Newbury's feet.

The body belonged to a thing that had once been a man, but had been so debased, so *altered*, as to no longer resemble a human being in any conventional sense. Both of its hands had been replaced by lethal-looking steel pincers, and its lower jaw had been removed, exchanged for a brace of fierce enamel tusks that had been wired directly into its skull. They opened and closed spasmodically as the man-thing struggled to right itself.

Transparent tubing erupted from six evenly spaced points on its chest, coiling round beneath its arms and disappearing into two metal panels on its back. Strange, pinkish fluid coursed and bubbled through the pipework, and what flesh remained was covered in scrawled runes and wards.

The creature twisted its head to glare at Newbury, and he was struck by the sheer terror in its eyes. He couldn't help feeling a deep sense of pity for this thing that used to be a man. He wondered if there was enough intelligence left for it to be aware of its situation, if the former human being knew to what atrocious depths it had sunk. Clearly the creature had been somehow manufactured by the Cabal to guard their lair.

Newbury watched in appalled fascination as the man-thing rolled on to its back and used its pincers to lever itself up on to its feet once again.

Simultaneously, a black-robed figure leapt through the ruins of the shattered doorway. It looked identical to those who had set upon Newbury in Chelsea and the others he had encountered at the house since his incarceration. In its right hand the cultist was brandishing what looked – to all intents and purposes – like Bainbridge's missing cane. Its face was shrouded in the shadows of the hood.

For a moment the two figures circled one another, the man-thing's vicious jaws snapping open and closed, its deadly pincers raised. Then, seeing an opening, it rushed forward, charging the cultist. The robed figure demonstrated lightning-fast reactions, ducking and weaving out of the way of the snapping pincers, which threatened to decapitate it at any moment, slashing at the air where the cultist's head had been only seconds before.

In response the cultist lashed out with a sharp kick, striking the man-thing on the left knee and causing it to buckle over and howl in pain. An elbow followed swiftly to the side of its head and it staggered woozily, almost losing its balance.

The robed figure wasted no time, taking its opponent's momentary disorientation as an opportunity to bring its weapon to bear.

The cultist twisted the head of the walking cane in its hand, causing the wooden shaft to begin to unpack itself with unerring mechanical precision. Four thin panels levered open, beginning to revolve at speed, spinning around a central glass chamber that began to pulse with blue electrical light. Newbury smiled. So it *was* Bainbridge's cane.

Seeming to recover itself, the man-thing lurched forward, again raising its right pincer and opening its jaws as if it intended to pin and gore the cultist. The robed figure was too quick, however, and danced out of the way, raising the shimmering lightning cane, thrusting it forward and down so that the sharp metal tip penetrated the soft flesh of the man-thing's gut. There was a terrifying *clap* as the weapon discharged its ferocious electrical storm directly into the creature's belly. Its body shuddered violently as the power coursed through it, causing its pincers to spasm open and closed, dancing electric light sparking between them.

After a moment, the charge dissipated and the man-thing's corpse slumped back to a heap on the floor, the shaft of Bainbridge's cane still protruding from its midriff. The stench of charred meat filled the room.

Newbury grinned. Bainbridge was staring at the scene, mouth agape. The hooded figure turned towards them and with one swift movement, raised their hands and folded back their cowl, revealing the pretty face beneath.

"Miss Hobbes!"

Veronica offered Bainbridge a lopsided grin, shaking out her long brown hair. "Hello, Sir Charles." She reached down, grabbed the handle of the lightning cane and wrenched it free from the still-smouldering corpse of the abomination on the floor. She twisted the head sharply to the left and the cane repacked itself, becoming once again nothing but an ornate walking stick. She held it out to Bainbridge. "I think you must have dropped this."

Bainbridge took the cane from her, staring at it in bewilderment as if he didn't recognise it or know what to say. "I'm… I'm astounded, Miss Hobbes. Thank you."

Veronica chuckled, turning her attention to Newbury, who had remained slumped on the floor throughout the proceedings, looking up at her, filled with admiration.

"I got your message," she said, reaching down, clasping his arm and hauling him to his feet. He wavered there unsteadily, clinging on to her for fear he might black out at any moment.

"Your message!" Newbury turned to look at Bainbridge, who was eyeing him from across the room. "The message you said you'd despatched? The reason you sent these devil-worshipping oafs after me in the first place! It wasn't a message for me at all, was it? It was a message for Miss Hobbes!" He regarded them both, a look of consternation upon his face. "*I* was the message. I was never anything but a sacrificial pawn!"

Newbury grinned. "Oh, I wouldn't go that far, Charles. You were excellent company, too."

"Of all the…" Bainbridge had turned a particularly bright shade of cerise. He opened his mouth to speak, but no words were forthcoming.

"I told you, Charles – I had little choice. I knew Veronica would discover what had happened and would follow you here. It had been three days, and I was sure my own trail would have grown cold. I counted on Miss Hobbes realising it was too much of a coincidence that you should be abducted too, and that she would strike out immediately to find you."

"And by extension you, too, Newbury," replied Bainbridge.

"Quite so."

"Well, you've got some nerve. I'll give you that."

"I'll take that as a compliment, Charles."

"It ruddy well wasn't meant as one." replied Bainbridge, but he was laughing as he said it.

Newbury could hear a commotion breaking out throughout the house now, raised voices and the distant clamour of fighting. He glanced at Veronica, who indicated the figure standing in the doorway, two uniformed men by his side. "I went immediately to Inspector Foulkes, who mustered a small army of constables. They're rooting out the cultists as we speak."

"Thank you once again, Miss Hobbes," said Bainbridge, turning to Inspector Foulkes, who was watching the exchange with interest. "Well, Foulkes? Don't just stand there! Round up the lot of these scoundrels! Newbury tells me we're likely to find evidence of all manner of bizarre practices to charge them with, not least human sacrifice and treason. And then there's

the assault of a police officer, and kidnapping, of course…"
His voice trailed off as he bustled through the doorway and
cut on to the landing beyond, where Newbury could hear
him snapping out orders to the gaggle of uniformed men
awaiting him.

Foulkes met Newbury's eye and shrugged, a broad grin
on his face. "I'm glad you're well, Sir Maurice." He glanced
after Bainbridge. "Best get after him," he said, and then
disappeared the way he had come, hurrying to catch up with
the chief inspector.

Newbury turned to Veronica, and then stumbled, barely
able to support himself after three days with very little food and
water, and round after round of torturous beatings. Veronica
stepped forward and caught him by the shoulders, holding
him upright. "Are you alright, Maurice?" The concern was
evident on her face. "I mean, I know you're hurt…"

"I knew you'd come," he said, smiling warmly. "I knew
you'd work it out."

"It was a hell of a risk," she said, although it sounded more
like a compliment than an admonishment. "And the look on
Sir Charles's face…"

Newbury laughed, loudly, and then collapsed into her
arms as the world closed in around him and unconsciousness
finally took hold.

CHRISTMAS SPIRITS

LONDON, DECEMBER 1902

They were still in the room.

He could sense them there, watching him with their blank, impassive eyes. They'd been there for hours, ever since he'd returned from the White Friars. Earlier, he'd convinced himself they were mere phantoms, nothing but products of his unconscious mind, but now he was beginning to doubt his own veracity. Were they in fact real, physical entities? Malign spectres that had come from the realm of the netherworld to torment him? He was no longer sure.

He'd tried calling out to them to provoke a response, but his words had fallen on deaf ears, echoing around the otherwise empty house. He'd received only silence in reply; only the same eerily unwavering, blank-faced stares. So he had smoked another of his cigarettes – the carefully crafted, opium-tainted cigarettes he'd taken to carrying in a silver case in his breast pocket – and allowed himself to drift away into the temporary seclusion of an opium dream.

Now, however, this short-lived reprieve had reached its inevitable end and the three figures still stood in judgement by the window, resolutely refusing to be dismissed from their vigil.

With a weary sense of inevitability, Newbury knew all of this before he'd even opened his eyes. He could feel the cold hostility of their stares, boring into him.

Newbury's eyes flickered open and he drew a hand over his stubble-encrusted chin, issuing a long, heartfelt sigh. His lips were dry, his tongue thick in his mouth. It was late and he'd been unconscious for some hours. Outside, everything was still, quiet. He imagined a thick blanket of silence had smothered the street, as if the swirling, frozen fog had descended on the city and muffled everything, shutting out the world. Everything out there was covered in a layer of crunchy, hoary frost, crisp and white, as if, in the cold, it was somehow renewed, made fresh again.

Everyone else, he supposed, was at home in bed, preparing themselves for the morning's festivities. He knew he should be doing the same. His home was usually his haven, his place away from the concerns of his chaotic life, from the Queen, from all the usual murder, vice and danger that typically occupied his time. Today, however, it was no haven. Today spirits had invaded his home. Whether or not they were figments of his mind mattered little: still they were there, still they were judging him.

Newbury stirred, massaging his aching neck. He chose not to look to the three figures by the window, but turned his attention instead towards the dancing flames in the grate. They spat and popped as they hungrily consumed the firewood that Scarbright had stacked there earlier.

Scarbright. Newbury couldn't help but suppress a smile at the thought of the man. Bainbridge had made it more than clear that he had only intended to loan the butler – his own, personal manservant – to Newbury for a couple of weeks, but months had now passed and Scarbright was still there, at Cleveland Avenue, still cooking and cleaning and managing Newbury's affairs. He'd proved a constant, reliable aide, and

Newbury had to admit that he'd grown rather fond of the man.

Newbury knew that Bainbridge had already taken steps towards finding a replacement butler for his own household. He might have been an expert in dealing with the capital's criminal elements, but the chief inspector struggled to even make a decent pot of tea for himself. It wasn't likely he'd settle for temporary arrangements for more than a few months.

That Scarbright was no doubt reporting back to Bainbridge on Newbury's activities was almost irrelevant; Newbury had long ago ceased to be concerned by his friend's well-intentioned duplicity. There was little that he'd ever consider keeping from Bainbridge, and very little that Scarbright could tell Bainbridge that Newbury wouldn't admit to himself. Bainbridge already knew of Newbury's continuing experimentation with occult ritual and his ongoing abuse of the opium poppy, and in turn, Newbury had been made fully aware of what Bainbridge thought of such things. As a result, they had come to an uneasy, unspoken understanding on the matter: Bainbridge would continue to berate him, while Newbury would continue to ignore the said reprimands in return.

Newbury would see his friend in the morning, when the weary widower would venture across town to join him for Christmas dinner. It had become something of a tradition for the two bachelors to celebrate the season together, although this year they were to be joined by a third companion, a recent addition to their small circle. His name was Professor Archibald Angelchrist, and he worked in some opaque capacity for the government – a scientific advisor, or something of the sort. Bainbridge had been spending an increasing amount of time with the Home Secretary in recent months, helping to establish a new investigative bureau (the remit of which Newbury was still a little unclear of) and, during the course of this work, he had first encountered, and then come to know, Angelchrist.

Consequently, Newbury had got to know the man in the months that followed and, while perhaps still a little wary of one another, they had quickly become friends, if not yet confidants. He seemed like a decent sort of fellow – with a sharp mind and an even sharper tongue, and Newbury found himself enjoying the man's company immensely. When, therefore, Newbury had become aware of Angelchrist's situation – the fact that he would be spending Christmas alone – it had seemed only appropriate to invite him to Cleveland Avenue to join the festivities there.

Scarbright, who had already retired for the evening, would spend the morning preparing a goose, before being granted the afternoon off to visit his relatives in Shoreditch. The three remaining men would then no doubt concern themselves with food, drink and hearty banter. Newbury wished that Veronica could have joined them, too, but she had other more pressing familial concerns to attend to.

Newbury had always enjoyed Christmas. As a boy, he'd learned to love everything about the season, from the rich, spiced puddings prepared by the household cook, to the spirit of cheer that seemed to sweep up all the people of the great metropolis. Perhaps what he'd loved most about the day itself was not the neatly wrapped parcels filled with wonderful gifts, but the effect it had on his father.

Christmas day was the only day of the year on which he had his father's full attention. The only day during which the man stopped working, hung up his boots and spent the day before the fire, watching, listening, and smiling. Newbury marvelled at how the man's whole demeanour would soften, how his expression would become less troubled, how the worry lines around his mouth and eyes would seemingly melt away. He could still see that smiling face in his mind's eye now, if he concentrated, underlit by the flickering light from the grate.

Together the two of them had roasted chestnuts over

the fire and spent hours talking about books and reading Dickens's Christmas stories. His father had filled his head with wondrous tales of adventure and foreign lands, stories that Newbury had never forgotten. Stories that still inspired him and filled him with a deep longing for those distant countries, where adventure and excitement waited for him around every corner. He had cherished those hours. Even in the years that followed, during his father's declining days, Newbury had taken care to be at his side each Christmas day, no matter what else might be vying for his attention, where else he was supposed to be. He had learned that much from the man – that Christmas was a sacred time. Not, to him, in the religious sense, but as a time to rest and take stock of one's life. To be with loved ones. To be still, if only for a day.

His father had died years ago, of course, but Newbury had continued to observe the many trappings of Christmas. Carollers, Dickens, mulled wine, gaudily decorated fir trees – to Newbury these were the essence of the season, and he kept it well each year. And these days he surrounded himself with family of a different kind; Bainbridge was as much a brother to him now as anyone else alive or dead. And Veronica... well. Veronica was something else again.

Recent weeks, however, had left Newbury with a heavy heart, and while he'd made every effort to engage his enthusiasm for the celebrations, he had found himself unable to truly embrace the spirit of the season. His mind was on other things. Troubling things.

His ritualistic experimentation had continued to yield results, and his drug-fuelled visions had become increasingly prescient. Alarming things lurked just around the corner. Newbury had seen into the future. Consequently, he was haunted by more than simple apparitions.

He looked up. The three figures were still there, watching him from across the room. They had every appearance of being genuine, physical entities, and Newbury felt the hairs on the back of his neck prickle in fear, despite himself. It was certainly not outside the realms of his beliefs that spirits such as these should manifest themselves before him. But there was still doubt... still that niggling thought that his mind might yet be playing tricks upon him. Was it the effects of the weed? Or perhaps it was something worse, a consequence of the rituals he'd been performing, some sort of diabolical side effect?

Newbury eyed each of the spectres in turn, searching their faces for any sign of why they might be there, any clue as to the reason for their sudden appearance earlier that evening. One moment he'd been alone, smoking his pipe and reading his tattered old copy of Dickens's *The Signalman*, the next the three interlopers had been standing in the shadows, menacing him from across the room. They were all the more terrifying for their startling familiarity, for adopting the guise of his friends, both old and new.

Templeton Black was there, lounging against the wall in his rumpled black suit, pencil thin and with a pale, almost unearthly, complexion. He had a shock of startling grey hair, and he was young – as young as Newbury remembered him. As young as he was the day he'd died.

The affair at Fairview House had been one of the worst of Newbury's career, and he knew from the few words that they'd exchanged on the subject that Bainbridge felt entirely the same. That day, Newbury had lost not only an assistant, but also a dear friend. Templeton Black had barely been more than a boy, having celebrated his twenty-first birthday in Newbury's company only weeks before his death. Looking at his pale face now, glaring back at him blankly from across the room, Newbury felt a sharp pang of guilt. He should have protected the boy. He should have *done* something. He should have been able to prevent it from happening.

Even now, years later, he found it hard to reconcile himself to what had occurred. The whole case had been a mess. The house, supposedly haunted by a malicious, murderous spirit, had in fact been rigged with traps and devices to spring mechanical death upon the unwary. Rather than a malign spirit, Fairview House had been inhabited by a madman, a lunatic hell-bent on living out his supernatural fantasies, and Newbury, Bainbridge and Templeton Black had been nought but unknowing playing pieces in his disastrous game.

The insane inventor and his bizarre creations had savagely murdered Black, who had sacrificed himself so that Newbury and Bainbridge should live. It had been a disaster of the highest order. As far as Newbury was concerned, it should never have happened. It should have been him. Templeton Black should have lived. Newbury should have not.

Whether he acknowledged it or not, the whole experience had scarred Newbury. And what was worse – what compounded the matter – was that he'd allowed it to happen again.

Earlier that year, the young reporter George Purefoy had died at the hands of the renegade doctor, Aubrey Knox. He had been murdered in the most excruciating manner, disembowelled alive, his intestines strung out to form a vast, grotesque pentagram, a sacrifice to some abominable agency to which Knox subscribed. Knox had hoped to divine the future in the boy's blood. Now, through less diabolical means – but no less dangerous – Newbury was attempting to do the same. That he was doing it for the best of reasons – the protection of the realm and the people he cared for – made it no less of a moral crime. He had engaged in occult practices in a manner in which he had always promised himself he would not.

Was that why Templeton Black, or at least the spirit wearing his persona, was here now? Was his old, dead friend somehow judging him? Was Black sending him a warning?

"I'm sorry," Newbury said, quietly. He could barely look

the apparition in the eye. "I'm so sorry."

Templeton Black – or the thing that purported to wear his guise – smiled. He took a step forward, holding his hands out before him in a placatory gesture.

"What is it you want from me?" Newbury said, and he could hear the tremor of fear in his own voice. "I don't know what you want."

The spectre frowned, but the look did not carry with it any malice. There was concern evident in those pale, ghostly eyes. Newbury realised with a start that what the apparition wanted was forgiveness.

"But it was me! It was my responsibility! You were only a boy... You were..." He trailed off, unable to continue.

Black smiled once again and shook his head. His lips remained tightly shut. He raised his right arm and pointed at Newbury.

"Me? You want me to forgive *myself*?" Newbury shook his head emphatically. "It doesn't work like that, Templeton. It's never worked like that! I can't forget what happened, what *I* allowed to happen to you."

But the apparition was changing before Newbury's eyes. The fine, black suit was beginning to crumble and peel, curling away from the skeletal figure beneath. Black opened his mouth and dark, autumnal leaves began to spill out into the room, swirling away as if excited by a gust of wind that Newbury could neither feel nor hear.

"Templeton...?" Newbury called, but the wind seemed only to increase in ferocity in response, and the figure at the centre of the maelstrom, the spirit of his dead friend, seemed transformed now into nothing but a scattering of dry leaves. Moments later, Templeton Black had been swept away entirely, becoming dust once again, becoming nothing but a memory.

The heavy curtain drapes, which seconds earlier had been

whipping about violently in the storm, fell still across the window. The room was utterly silent.

Newbury realised he'd been holding his breath. He rocked back in his chair, forcing himself to breathe, calming his nerves. He reached for his brandy glass but realised, with dismay, that it was empty. He glanced over at the sideboard where the bottle stood invitingly, but he didn't want to get out of his chair, to leave the comfort and safety of the fireside, at least while the two remaining spectres were still in the room.

"What do you want?" he shouted over at them, despairingly. And then more softly, a plea: "Leave me in peace."

In response, the second of the spirits stepped forward, drawing Newbury's attention. The appearance of this figure – a larger, more rotund character than Templeton Black – was perhaps even harder for Newbury to palate. For this apparition took the form of Sir Charles Bainbridge, his dearest friend.

The doppelgänger was uncannily accurate, to the extent that, had Newbury not suspected otherwise, he might have mistaken the spirit for the real thing. Just like the real Bainbridge, this spectre leaned heavily on its cane, its bushy moustache twitching as it regarded him reprovingly.

Newbury had known Bainbridge for only a relatively short span of years. They'd met soon after Newbury had been inducted into Her Majesty's service, and although Bainbridge had never spoken of it, Newbury suspected the police chief had been tasked with keeping a watchful eye on the new recruit.

Whatever the reasons, the two men had spent a great deal of time together in the early days of Newbury's career and had soon forged a lasting friendship. In the years that followed they had been through much together. Bainbridge had been with him at Fairview House, of course, but there were innumerable other instances, too, including the time they had hunted a depraved serial killer through the slums, or their investigations into a phantom cab on the King's Road, or *The Lady Armitage* disaster of the prior year.

Latterly, their relationship had been pushed to its limits, with Bainbridge unable, or at least unwilling, to understand Newbury's continued use of the opium poppy, nor his reasons for dabbling in the occult sciences. Bainbridge wasn't aware, though, of what had passed between Newbury and Veronica, and the effort Newbury was making to protect them all. Newbury had seen something during one of his opium dreams. Something terrible and indistinct, lurking just around the corner, a disaster waiting to strike. And Veronica's sister, Amelia, had seen it too.

While Bainbridge wasn't so closed-minded as to rule out the potential of the occult sciences – as so many others in his profession did – Newbury knew he would be inclined to dismiss Newbury's visions as hallucinations inspired by the drugs. Veronica, however, had grown to understand the nature of such things through her sister, and had latterly pressed Newbury to continue with his experiments, to attempt to get to the bottom of whatever danger it was that they faced.

Of course, Bainbridge had experience of the occult, and what it could do to a man. He'd known Aubrey Knox in the days before the doctor had gone rogue, back when he was a brilliant scientist working on behalf of the Crown. It was Bainbridge's belief that Knox's interest in the occult had fed his hunger for power, and had eventually led him into a spiralling descent of ritual and depravity. It had also been made clear to Newbury that the Queen herself harboured similar opinions on the matter and that, while she had engaged Newbury specifically as a counter against enemies of the Crown who may engage in such dubious pursuits, she was also wary of his interest in such matters.

Both Bainbridge and the Queen had been burned by their experience of Knox and as a consequence they were simultaneously nervous and protective of Newbury. As far as Newbury was concerned, such anxieties were entirely misplaced. Understandable, he supposed, but nevertheless misplaced.

Newbury met the apparition's gaze. If the spirit proved true to the nature of the man whose form it had adopted, it would be far less forgiving than Templeton Black.

In the event, however, it was not the apparition's demeanour that disturbed Newbury, but the sudden alteration in its appearance. As he studied his friend's face, he saw Bainbridge's eyes begin to bruise and sink. His flesh became pale and lifeless. It was as if he were watching the man succumb to a terrible wasting disease.

Bainbridge staggered back, leaning all the more heavily on his cane. He was growing thinner and more haggard with each passing moment. His eyes seemed watery and distant, as if he had suddenly lost focus, or was seeing something else in the distance, something that wasn't really there. He clawed at his own face, became nervous, irritable. He no longer looked like Newbury's friend, but the denizen of some hellish infirmary ward or else Bedlam itself.

And all of a sudden it struck Newbury what was happening to the spectre. He'd seen these symptoms before, manifesting themselves in the patrons of the opium dens he often frequented. This was the curse of the poppy, taken to its extreme. This was a man wasting away because of his addiction, driven only by his hunger for a drug that offered him no sustenance. This was what Bainbridge feared would become of Newbury if he didn't find a means to end his own relationship with the drug.

"You're wrong," Newbury said, but his voice lacked conviction. "You're wrong."

The spirit turned its head and gave the weakest of smiles, before Newbury noticed that its legs had begun to boil away into a cloud of thick, blue smoke. The vapour seemed to seep from the floor, billowing upwards and slowly consuming the figure, swallowing Bainbridge until all that was left of him was the vague impression of a man, a smoky silhouette that soon dispersed to nothing.

Newbury hung his head, exhausted. The alcohol, the poppy and the long hours were beginning to take their toll. He longed for his bed, to be free of the visitations that now plagued him.

There was only one of them left now. Newbury could hardly bear to look at it. This was the spirit he feared most of all, the one that had taken the form of Veronica Hobbes, his fellow adventurer, his assistant, the woman he loved.

If Templeton Black had come in search of forgiveness, and Bainbridge had come to dissuade him from the poppy, what had Veronica come for? Had she appeared merely to torment him? To show him what he could not have?

Newbury lifted his head and offered the apparition an accusatory glower. "And what of you, spectre? Why do you wait until last of all?" He didn't expect a reply. "Am I now Ebenezer? I've already been granted echoes of the past and the present. Do you now come to show me my future?"

The expression on the spirit's face was pained. Newbury felt his chest tighten. Whether in fear, or with something else entirely, he wasn't sure. The spirit had captured all the beauty of Veronica Hobbes, all of her delicate strength and femininity, in its efforts to recreate her. It – she – was dressed in a flowing white gown of intricately worked silk that trailed across the floor as she moved. Her dark hair hung loose around her shoulders.

As he watched, the thin figure placed her hands upon her left breast, crossing her palms over her heart.

Time seemed to stop.

It was as if the two of them, Newbury and this ghostly vision of Veronica, had become momentarily trapped within a bubble, a universe all of their own. Everything around them was still and silent; the rest of the world had been shut out. At that moment, nothing else even existed

Newbury watched in awe.

The lights dimmed until only Veronica was visible, standing alone in the otherwise impenetrable darkness, clasping her hands to her breast. She was limned with a soft, ethereal glow, a white haze, shimmering as if burning with an inner light of her own.

She opened her mouth to speak, but the only sound to pass her lips was the *tick-tock, tick-tock, tick-tock* of a clock, which grew in intensity until it filled the entire room, until Newbury had to raise his hands to cover his ears, until it seemed to drown out even his very thoughts.

Tick-tock, tick-tock, tick-tock.

It was a dreadful sound, the sound of a life counting out its final moments; the sound of impending doom; the sound of the reality rushing by without them as they were trapped in this abstract domain. There was nothing but Newbury, Veronica, and the ominous ticking of the clock. And all the while, Veronica stood facing him, her mouth open, her hands clasped to her breast, tears streaming down her pale cheeks.

Newbury screamed, a wordless, terrified scream. He screamed until his lungs burned, screamed so that he might hear something other than the insistent *tick-tock, tick-tock, tick-tock* of the clock. But even that was no use. Nothing could drown out that terrifying, insistent sound.

"I don't know what to do," he whispered, putting his head in his hands. "I don't know what to do."

Tick-tock, tick-tock, tick-tock.

Then, as suddenly as it had begun, everything was still.

Newbury sobbed in relief. Around him, everything was quiet, save the crackle and spit of the fire in the grate. He glanced up. The apparition had gone. The beautiful, terrifying vision of Veronica had disappeared. The gas lamps burned warmly in their glass bowls. The room had returned to normal. He was alone.

Newbury reached for his empty glass, and realised he was shaking. Pushing himself out of his chair, he crossed the room to the sideboard, still glancing nervously over at the window where, just a few moments earlier, the spectres had stood over him in an unwelcome vigil.

He poured himself a large measure of brandy and gulped it down quickly, welcoming the long fingers of warmth that it spread throughout his chest. His heart was still hammering. He felt light-headed. Had he really seen anything at all? What had it all meant? There had been three spirits, each representing either his past, present or, he realised with a horrible sinking feeling, his future.

But surely that was ridiculous, the result of too much Dickens, of a late night on a full stomach and indulgence in his opium-laced cigarettes. He looked again to the window. There was no sign that there had ever been anything there at all. It must have all been in his mind, a concoction of his fevered imagination. It had to be!

Yet in his heart he didn't really believe that. The thought sent a cold shiver running down his spine. For if it hadn't been in his mind… well, that didn't even bear thinking about. What had the third apparition been trying to tell him? Was Veronica in danger? Was the sound he'd heard, that *tick-tock*ing, the minutes of her life slowly ticking away? He had no way to be sure. But somehow he knew it had something to do with that terrible thing he had seen, that darkness which he knew was coming.

Of all the things he had seen that night, it was this that terrified him the most: the notion that Veronica might be in jeopardy. There was only one answer. He had to continue with his experiments. He had to continue to explore the boundaries between the real world and the spirit realm. Only then could he find a way to prevent whatever it was from occurring. Whatever that might mean for him – whatever the spectre of Charles had warned him of that very evening – he would do it to protect Veronica.

Newbury glanced over at the carriage clock on the mantelpiece. It was close to three o'clock in the morning. Bainbridge and Angelchrist would be there in a matter of hours, full of festive cheer, and Newbury had every intention of joining them in their celebrations. He had placed neatly wrapped gifts for each of them beneath the tree. There was one there for Veronica, too, but that would have to wait awhile. He would speak nothing of the night's events. That would only inspire enquiry from Angelchrist and concern from Bainbridge. No, he would keep his little commune with the spirits to himself for now. He could see no good in laying it out for the others.

Sighing, Newbury set about banking the fire in anticipation of retiring to his bed. He was weary and in need of good company. He only hoped that the spirits were done with tormenting him for the night. It was, he thought to himself with a smile, Christmas day, after all. And despite what Dickens might have him believe, Newbury knew that Christmas was a time to spend with his friends in the present, not the ghosts of the past or the spectres of the future.

As he turned down the lights and crossed to the door, he couldn't help looking over towards the window once more, just to be sure. He was relieved to see nobody there, lurking in the shadows.

It was going to be a good Christmas. He was sure of it. But the New Year was an undiscovered country, and he feared whatever it might bring.

STRANGERS FROM THE SEA

"Ah, there it is."

Sir Maurice Newbury ran his fingers along the raised spines of his bookcase until they came to rest upon a particular battered tome. He levered the book out of its home between two similar volumes and carried it across to his chair by the fire, into which he flopped languidly, the book upon his knee. The leather was flaking and the gold print of the title was faded, but still discernible: *Hermeticism in the Modern Age.*

A half-smoked cigarette, tainted with sweet-smelling opium, dangled from Newbury's bottom lip, and his suit was rumpled and unkempt. His pupils were narrow pinpricks staring out of dark, bruised pits, and his flesh had taken on a pale, milky complexion. Detritus surrounded him: heaps of scrawled notes, piles of old books, dirty crockery and empty claret bottles – the signposts of days that had passed in a blur of drug-fuelled research.

Newbury hefted the book, blowing dust off the top of its pages. Then, taking another long pull on his cigarette, he rested the spine in his left palm and allowed the book to fall open. The pages fanned, and as they finally came to settle upon a chapter involving ritual embalming and the transmogrification of the spirit, something dislodged and fluttered to the floor by his feet. Frowning, he bent to retrieve it.

It was a cream-coloured envelope, covered in faded, spidery scrawl. Newbury's eyes widened at the familiar handwriting. It belonged to Templeton Black.

Black had been a dear friend and former assistant, who had died four years earlier during a botched investigation, and Newbury had never quite forgiven himself for what had occurred. He blamed himself utterly for the young man's death and not a week went by when he didn't feel a twinge of regret, wishing he could somehow turn back the clock, live those days over again with the benefit of hindsight.

Newbury turned the envelope over in his hands. His heart skipped a beat. The letter was unopened. How long had it sat there, hidden inside that dusty old book, waiting to be discovered? The postmark was smudged and unreadable.

Trembling, Newbury closed the book and placed it on the floor beside his chair. He took the cigarette from between his lips and flicked what remained of it into the fire. Then, settling back, he ran his finger along the inside of the envelope and carefully extracted the letter within.

There were two pages, each of them covered in the same scratchy, looping handwriting. He swallowed, his mouth dry. How could he have ignored a letter from Templeton? He supposed that, at the time, it had been nothing unusual, a note written in haste between meetings. Something, perhaps, that Templeton would have dashed off quickly to impart some information or other, soon forgotten as the pair of them moved on to the next investigation, the next adventure. Now, though, it was like receiving a letter from beyond the grave, a communication lost in time.

Newbury exhaled, realising that he'd been holding his breath. With a sigh, he smoothed the first page and began to read:

August, 1897
My dearest Sir Maurice,

Knowing you as I do, I don't expect you shall bother to read this
letter when it lands upon your doormat. Indeed, it is my full
and firm belief that it will end up heaped amongst the similarly
discarded notes on the drawing room carpet at Cleveland
Avenue, never to be seen again. (I am often amazed by your
ability to disregard your missives in such blatant fashion. I'm
sure it must drive your unlucky correspondents to distraction.)
   Nevertheless, I felt it necessary to impart a few words,
despite this anticipated outcome. Think of this largely, then,
as a cathartic exercise on my own part. There are things that
need to be said – things that I need to say – and in my present
condition, I wonder if perhaps I will have no other opportunity
to say them.
   And who knows! Rather than discard the unopened envelope,
you might fortuitously tuck it inside one of your dusty old tomes
to serve as a bookmark, and then happen upon it one day
unexpectedly, years from now. I hope then that its contents will
prove entirely irrelevant, and if I'm still about in the land of the
living, we can share a drink and laugh over it, marvelling at
my youthful temerity.

Newbury sighed and gave a hearty chuckle; Templeton had
known him so well. He smiled at the fond memory, although
he also felt a twinge of deep regret as he considered that last
sentiment. How he would dearly love to be able to share such
a moment with his old friend. To sit and laugh over a drink at
his club. If only things had been different. If only...
   He read on:

   The view from my convalescent bed here in Richmond is not
so bad: the rolling hills of Yorkshire in the distance, a picturesque

little town, a castle. I've known worse, and the people seem cheerful enough. Perhaps we should both venture a little further afield from time to time; London can be an oppressive sort of place, and I wouldn't want our little episode by the sea to put you off.

(Ah, a slight accident. Please excuse the rather unsightly smear of cigarette ash towards the bottom of the page. The nurses here are, for some God-awful reason, opposed to the old Guinea Golds, and thus I'm sneaking a quick smoke as I scrawl this note on the veranda, unbeknownst to the matron.)

Newbury grinned. This was very much like the Templeton Black he remembered.

I am, I'm told, lucky to be alive. Although the doctor (a handsome devil if ever I saw one) has explained there is little he can do to relieve my symptoms. And so my convalescence has become a waiting game as the infection runs its course. One way or another, the doctor believes it will be over within the week. I cling on to that thought. It represents blessed relief, whatever might become of me.

The fever itself comes and goes. Some days it is almost too much to bear, and I feel as if I am close to combusting from within, as if there's a fiery inferno inside my chest and the pressure is mounting all the time, seeking a way out. In those moments I long for unconsciousness, but it rarely comes.

When the fever is not raging the days drag by with little to hold my interest, and although there are periods of severe discomfort, it is the nights I dread.

I fear I'm suffering from the most awful night terrors. Ridiculous for a man of my age, I know, but I'm assured they are simply a result of the infection, fever-dreams caused by the invading parasites.

In them, we're back at Maltby-by-the-Sea, and I can taste

the fresh, salty air on my lips. The place is near-deserted, just as I remember it, but nevertheless I have the overwhelming sense of being observed. Whatever I do, wherever we go, there's a pervading feeling of being watched. Something malign is hounding us, and yet despite this sinister understanding, we go blithely wandering about the place, as if searching for trouble.

(I have come to understand that this, of course, is exactly what we do. It is our modus operandi, our reason for being. We attract trouble like magnets attract iron filings, and we revel in it.)

The townsfolk act as if there is nothing untoward to concern them, offering hollow smiles as they turn us away, ignoring our questions. Yet all the while, terrible plans are afoot. Evil things are brewing. Night falls, and we take refuge at The Angel Hotel.

That's when the strangers come lurching from the salty spray, trailing seaweed and foul-smelling water as they seek us out, coming to drag us to our doom beneath the waves. We struggle as we're pulled from our beds, but there are too many of them and they smother us, carrying us back to the beach, where the townsfolk are arrayed to watch, grinning and staring.

I thrash as I'm dragged into the water, try to call out, but the shock of the icy embrace is too much and the water floods my lungs. I panic as I try to breathe, try to push myself towards the surface, but they hold me down, and soon the light begins to dim.

This, I know, is their revenge. They have come for us because of what happened, because we know their secret, and because they cannot allow us to live.

It is then that I wake, gasping for breath.

Newbury sat back in his chair, memories stirring. This letter, then, had been written during the aftermath of that very investigation, following their return from Maltby-by-the-Sea. They'd been called north to investigate a spate of missing people in the little seaside town on the east coast. The townsfolk had proved largely obstructive and unhelpful, even when another of their number – a young woman called Florence Partington who had recently moved to the town from Darlington – had disappeared from under their noses.

Black had maintained all along that something untoward was going on, and that the townsfolk were either too afraid to discuss it, or complicit. Despite this, the two of them had been unable to uncover a shred of evidence, other than a series of unusual footprints in the wet sand and a torn shred of a woman's nightgown in the churchyard.

This had gone on for some days, with people's attitudes towards Newbury and Black growing increasingly hostile. It was made abundantly clear to them both that they were not welcome in the town. Nevertheless, neither of them could shake the feeling that there was something obvious they were missing, that the strange behaviour of the town's inhabitants and the pervading undercurrent of tension were connected with the unexplained disappearances.

Newbury had finally brought the matter to a head, when – to his horror – he had discovered the truth about the locals: that they were not, in fact, locals at all. They were *things* that had come out of the sea, shambling creatures from beneath the waves that had cast a glamour upon the town, taking on the appearance of normal people, acting out normal lives. To what end had never been made clear, but one thing was certain – any outsiders who came to settle in Maltby, any real people, were swiftly despatched, dragged out to sea in the night to be silenced.

Newbury had broken the spell and revealed the strangers for what they really were: monstrous humanoids with bloated white flesh, jagged teeth and glossy black eyes, trailing seaweed and salt water in their wake. They were impersonators, living a lie, and they had to be stopped.

These things, these *strangers*, had turned on Newbury and Black, and Black had almost become another of their victims, manhandled to the bay and forced beneath the dark and shifting waters. Newbury had come to his aid, however, fighting the beasts off with a cattle prod and effecting their escape.

Cold, wet and bedraggled, they had fled the town and taken shelter in a derelict barn for the night.

When they returned to Maltby the following day, accompanied by a small force of policemen, the town had been deserted. The entire populace had seemingly returned to the water during the night, leaving Maltby as a ghost town, eerily abandoned.

It was then that Black had collapsed and been rushed to a doctor in the neighbouring town, sporting a terrible fever and a hideous rash that began to emerge in blotchy patches all over his body. The doctor had managed to stabilise him, reducing the fever, but the rash, it seemed, was the result of an infection caused by Black's exposure to an unusual algae during his brief foray into the sea. There was no obvious treatment other than to manage the fever, and so Black had been sent to Richmond to recuperate, and for a while the doctors had been uncertain as to whether or not he'd survive.

Newbury recalled the anxiety of those weeks, the horrible uncertainty over whether his dear friend would live or die. At the time, Black had seemed his usual, flippant self, taking it all in his stride, joking and laughing on the few occasions Newbury managed to head north to pay him a visit. Newbury had always wondered how Black had been able to remain in such high spirits during such a trying time. Clearly, though, there were things that had preyed on his mind, things he'd needed to put in writing because he'd felt unable to say them out loud.

Newbury turned the sheet of notepaper over and continued to read.

Anyway, enough of that. You do not need to hear talk of such things. The business in Maltby is over and done with now, and my dreams are naught but silly fictions. You need not trouble yourself with them. Although I must add that I find it ironic that the strangers who did their best to finish me off might inadvertently have succeeded, despite your best efforts to haul me from their fishy embrace; the infection continues to spread. Rest assured, though, that I will continue to fight it, and with any luck I'll be fit and by your side again in a few weeks, ready for another adventure.

And so we come to the crux of my letter. I worry now that my words will seem steeped in melodrama, that you'll consider my concerns boyish and unfounded. Yet I will state them here regardless, because I must: I fear for you, Maurice.

I fear you are treading a path that will lead towards not only your unhappiness, but your detriment in every respect. Your obsession with the hermetic arts grows almost daily, it seems, and your recent engagement in its practices has left me deeply concerned for your well-being.

Understand that I have no doubt regarding your intentions. The results of your endeavours, too, cannot be disputed – the ritual you performed in Maltby, for example, served to unveil the strangers for who they truly were, to save lives. Yet I saw the toll it took on you, saw how much of yourself you had to sacrifice in order to dispel their glamour. (Not to mention the unspeakable mess you made of your hotel room when you eviscerated that peacock.)

I cannot help but think back to Old Mab, the witch we encountered in the woods, the woman who had given herself up to the trees. She had lost herself in the darkness. You said then that you understood the temptations she had faced, that she had allowed herself to be gradually eroded by her desire to help others, to wield forces she did not fully understand.

My fear is that you walk that very same path, and that you, too, will lose your way. I say this now because I see that you are balanced upon a precipice, and that there is still time for you to step away.

I ask only that you consider my words, as my dear friend and confidant. If I am to die here in Richmond, I would do so knowing that I have warned you of what I consider to be the greatest danger you face. All the strangers from the sea, wood witches, ice spirits, clockwork golems and other villainous creatures we have faced are as nothing when compared to this.

I am tired now, and the nurses will be along soon to berate me for spending too long on the veranda in the cold. Forgive me if I seem maudlin, but I urge you to heed my words. There will be choices to be made, and for your own sake, I hope you make them well.

I hope that we shall meet again, Sir Maurice.

Your friend,
Templeton Black

Newbury allowed the pages to slip from his fingers. They fluttered to the floor. There was a hollow sensation in the pit of his stomach, a gnawing sense of emptiness and regret. Tears came then, in floods, and Newbury cupped his face in his hands, his body wracking as he shook with emotion.

Would things have been different if he'd bothered to read the letter all those years ago? Would he have made different choices? Perhaps he might have prevented the dreadful events that followed? How could he ever know?

Black had pulled through, of course. He had shaken off the infection and returned to London, and nothing more had been heard of the strangers who had once come from the sea. Together, he and Black had shared many more adventures, before that fateful day at Fairview House, before his friend was cruelly snatched away from him by the machinations of a madman. Yet Black had never mentioned the letter, had never aired his concerns again, not even when Newbury had involved him in matters pertaining to the occult, to his fascination with the hermetic arts and rituals. And now it was too late. Far too late.

Wiping his eyes, Newbury stooped and retrieved the letter. He folded the pages and slid them carefully back into the envelope. Next, he picked up and opened the book, and placed the envelope carefully inside. He stood and crossed to his bookshelves.

"I'm sorry, Templeton," he said, his voice cracking. "I'm sorry, but I made my choice a long time ago, and now I have to live with it. People are depending on me. Veronica's depending on me. I can't let her down, no matter the consequences. I let *you* down...' He paused, taking a deep breath. "And I won't allow it to happen again."

He placed the book carefully back where it belonged on the shelf and returned to his seat.

He reached for his silver tin and sought out another cigarette, which he lit with an ember from the fire. He took a long, steady draw, and allowed the smoke to plume from his nostrils. The sweet taste of the opium was reassuring on the back of his tongue.

The past, he told himself, was a closed book. Now he needed to look to the future. What other choice did he have?

Sighing, he reached out his hand for the book at the top of the nearest pile – *The Cosmology of the Spirit* – but then stopped short, his fingers resting lightly upon the cover.

Something had caught his eye: another dusty old book, resting open and upside down on the hearth, sprinkled with soot from the fire. It had lain there for some months, abandoned in lieu of more pressing matters. Newbury grinned.

"Perhaps just for today, Templeton," he said. He snatched up the other book enthusiastically – a copy of H.G. Wells's

The Time Machine – and stubbed out his cigarette on the arm of his chair. "Perhaps just for today."

Chuckling, Newbury eased himself back into his Chesterfield, and settled down to read.

THE ONLY GIFT WORTH GIVING

♛

LONDON, DECEMBER 1903

Winter had stolen across London. It had rushed in without warning to sweep away the mild, autumnal afternoons and leave deep drifts of crisp, white snow in their place. It had frozen pipes, sent animals scurrying to their seasonal hibernations and covered everything in a layer of thick, hoary frost.

At least, that was how it seemed to Sir Charles Bainbridge as he trudged steadily through the bitterly cold afternoon towards the home of his friend and companion, Sir Maurice Newbury. One moment the days had seemed long and mellow, orange leaves turning to mulch beneath his boots, the next they were short, dark and cold, and snowflakes were swirling on the icy gusts outside his window.

Perhaps, he reflected, he was just getting old. The days seemed to pass so much faster than they once had. Or perhaps it was simply because he was so damn busy. He preferred the latter option, but he feared the former was probably true. These days the cold made his bones ache and his blood freeze in his veins, and he longed for nothing more than a glass of brandy and a warm fire.

Today, however, was not a day for retreating from the

world. Today he had more important things to see to than his own comfort.

Bainbridge had spent the last three days investigating – rather unsuccessfully, if he was honest with himself – one of the most brutal murders he had yet encountered in his long and onerous career. A man had been discovered stripped and bound to a lamp post, left as bait, Bainbridge had come to realise, for the roving Revenants that still plagued many of the deprived districts such as Whitechapel and Shoreditch. It was clear from the body – or at least, what remained of it – that the victim had been slashed at least once across the belly with a sharp knife, probably in an effort to draw enough blood to attract the dreadful creatures. It was evident, too, that the Revenants had come en masse, devouring much of the poor sod while he was still alive, rending the flesh from his bones with their savage, yellow teeth.

There hadn't been much of him left when Bainbridge had arrived at the site the following morning, but the snow and the chill had largely preserved the scene, much to the chief inspector's dismay.

There was no doubt it was anything but an execution – a particularly grisly one, at that – but Bainbridge had so far been unable to as much as identify the victim, let alone establish a motive or a perpetrator. The swarming Revenants had disturbed any tracks that might have been left in the snow as they'd set about their gruesome feast, and the uniformed constables he'd assigned to the task had not yet turned up the dead man's clothes. Consequently, all he had to go on was a flayed, half-eaten corpse, so ravaged it was barely distinguishable as a human being at all. It could have been any of the hundreds of young men reported missing in the city every day.

Bainbridge gave a heavy sigh and brushed flakes of snow from where they'd settled on his bushy grey moustache. His breath was coming quick and sharp from the exertion of the walk, steaming in the frigid air before his face. He felt hot and bothered beneath his heavy black overcoat, despite the chill and the numbness in his extremities.

The case was giving him sleepless nights. He had no idea who was responsible for the man's death, and he was struggling to imagine who might have been able to even conceive of such a dreadful method of execution. He'd always found it difficult not to take these things personally – his failure to spot the means by which to approach the case, his inability to perceive a way around the lack of evidence. But he had to admit, as it stood, he was no closer to solving the case after three days than he'd been in the first few minutes after arriving on the scene.

Now, though, it was Christmas Eve, and he was on his way to visit Newbury, his feet crunching on the thick blanket of snow that had settled over large swathes of the city.

He wondered how his old friend was faring. Newbury had been avoiding him of late. Bainbridge was astute enough to see *that* at least. He supposed he couldn't blame Newbury. As close as they were, there was only so much berating a man could take, and Bainbridge had been free and forthcoming with his admonishment. He knew he shouldn't do it – that it did neither of them any good – but he just couldn't help himself. He simply couldn't sit idly by and watch his dearest friend throw his life away through ritualistic drug abuse.

Not that his words ever seemed to get through. Newbury could be as stubborn as Bainbridge himself, and even less immovable when he wanted to be. Yet Bainbridge couldn't help wondering whether there was more to it than simple addiction or rebellion. Was something – or some*one* – else exerting an influence on him? More recently, too, Newbury had retreated into one of his camnable black moods, locking himself away in his study and refusing to emerge for days at a time. Bainbridge simply didn't know what to make of it. Perhaps that was simply the price of genius? Perhaps the *ennui* came hand in hand with the remarkable flashes of insight. He supposed he'd never know for certain.

Unconsciously, Bainbridge's hand strayed to his overcoat pocket, patting it gently as if reassuring himself that the little package inside was still safe and secure. He couldn't prevent a smile from tugging at the corners of his mouth as he imagined the look on Newbury's face as his friend unwrapped it. It was the perfect Christmas gift. Perhaps it would be enough to cheer Newbury and stir him from whatever dark depression had taken hold of him.

The snow was swirling in dancing eddies all around Bainbridge, and he bowed his head against the icy gusts. The streets of Chelsea were near deserted, save for the occasional lonely figure drifting through the snow, featureless silhouettes against the sulphurous glow of the street lamps. A steam-driven carriage hissed by, its wheels creaking and thundering as they skittered and slid over the icy cobbles, its exhaust funnels belching black fumes that melted the snow in a wide trail behind it. Bainbridge found himself envying the occupants as their faces flickered past, wide-eyed as they took in the snowy scene all around them. He wished now that he'd taken one of the police carriages, but foolishly he'd sent the drivers home to their families to enjoy the festivities. Sometimes, he considered, altruism didn't pay.

Still, he was nearly there now. He trudged on, his ankles damp from where his feet sank in the powdery snow.

Bainbridge felt his spirits lift as Newbury's house hove into view a few moments later. Warm orange light spilled out into the street from the bay window at the front of the property, conjuring up thoughts of a crackling fire, a brandy and a rest. He forged on, plodding as fast as he could against the driving wind.

As he approached the house, Bainbridge could see that the curtains were half drawn against the inclement weather and the encroaching darkness. He hoped Newbury was at home and hadn't suddenly been tempted away to his White Friars club He wasn't, after all, expecting Bainbridge until the morning, and Newbury did generally make an effort to celebrate the season.

Bainbridge mounted the red stone steps at the front of the house and rapped loudly on the door with the end of his cane He noticed, with a faint smile, that the paintwork was marred with innumerable little indentations, each one a perfect crescent, the result of his prior visits. He brushed himself down as he waited for a response, shaking off the light dusting of snow that had settled over him as he'd walked.

A moment later, just as he was raising his cane impatiently to knock for a second time, he heard the creak of footsteps in the hallway. "Hurry along, Scarbright! It's rather chilly out tonight."

The door creaked open on hinges in need of a good oiling, and Bainbridge felt a welcome flood of warmth from within.

"Sir Charles?" Newbury's valet – Scarbright – sounded utterly incredulous, as if taken aback that the chief inspector might actually be out there in the swirling snowstorm on Christmas Eve. He stood for a moment in the doorway, staring at Bainbridge as if he couldn't quite take it in.

"Well, don't just stand there, man! Step aside so I might come in "

Scarbright blinked at him, and then realisation seemed to dawn on his face and he stepped back, beckoning Bainbridge inside. "Of course, my apologies. It's only that I believe Sir Maurice wasn't expecting you until the morning, sir."

Bainbridge grinned as he handed over his hat and cane and began unbuttoning his coat. "Oh, don't fret so, Scarbright. I'm not staying. I simply have something for Sir Maurice that couldn't wait."

"Even on Christmas Eve, sir?"

"Quite so, Scarbright," replied Bainbridge, failing to entirely hide his displeasure at the fact the valet considered it appropriate to question his motives. He shook out his coat, spattering water and ice droplets over the polished floorboards. Then, having extracted the small package from inside one of the pockets and dropping it into his jacket pocket instead, he handed the still-dripping garment to the valet. "Now, be a good chap, Scarbright, and organise some tea."

Scarbright smiled wryly as he folded the coat over his arm. "Of course, Sir Charles. Sir Maurice is... *relaxing* in the drawing room."

"Ah, like that, is it?" replied Bainbridge. "Well, I'll get in there and stir him up a bit. It doesn't do to let him fester, Scarbright."

The valet raised a single eyebrow in response. "I'll see to that tea, Sir Charles," he said, before turning and sloping off down the passageway towards the kitchen.

Bainbridge smiled to himself. Scarbright had always shown an unerring sense of loyalty, and it was obvious he liked Newbury. It was for this reason that Bainbridge had acquiesced to him remaining indefinitely at Cleveland Avenue, instead of returning to Bainbridge's own employ.

Of course, Newbury thought it was all his doing, and often ribbed Bainbridge about the way in which he had stolen the chief inspector's servant from under his nose, turning Bainbridge's "spy" – given to Newbury on loan after his housekeeper had walked out on him – into a loyal, dedicated valet. Bainbridge had allowed this little myth to grow, aware that Newbury needed this victory if he were to ever truly accept Scarbright as anything other than Bainbridge's informant. The irony was, of course, that Scarbright had long since ceased to inform Bainbridge of anything useful at all. Not that Bainbridge had wanted to spy on his friend in the first place It was simply that he wished to keep a watchful eye on Newbury, in order that he might intervene if the situation needed him to, or if Newbury went and got himself into trouble with his employers. Which, Bainbridge considered, had happened on more than one memorable occasion in recent months.

"Stop loitering in the hallway and come and warm yourself by the fire, Charles. And tell Scarbright not to bother with that tea. I need brandy!" Newbury's bellowing voice carried down the passageway from the drawing room, eliciting a loud guffaw from Bainbridge. So much for the surprise. He might have known Newbury would have anticipated the identity of his unexpected caller. There'd be some obvious giveaway, no doubt; the *click-clack* of his cane, the way he rapped on the door, the simple odds that Bainbridge would be the only one of Newbury's friends to call at such an hour, on Christmas Eve, in the snow.

Bainbridge wasted no time in accepting Newbury's invitation, and, still feeling damp and cold from his excursion, swiftly made his way along the passageway to the drawing room. He didn't bother to knock before pushing open the door and stepping over the threshold.

Inside, it was warm and welcoming, although filled with the thick, syrupy aroma of opium. Smoke hung in the air like a viscous shroud, clinging to the ceiling and causing Bainbridge to splutter and cough, wrinkling his nose in distaste.

A fire burned heartily in the grate, and the curtains were drawn against the weather. The room was in some disarray, with scattered newspapers and leaning piles of leather-bound books covering every conceivable surface. Specimen jars filled with things that Bainbridge had no desire to identify nestled amongst these towering stacks, and Christmas presents wrapped in gaudily coloured paper were heaped in a pile in one corner, ready for the festivities the following day. Very much unlike Newbury himself, Bainbridge mused, who looked as if he had no intention of engaging with the seasonal cheer.

He was currently lounging on his sofa, his head resting upon one of the arms, his feet balancing upon the other. His collar was askew, his hair a tangled mess, and he was blowing smoke rings into the air above his head, watching them drift away languorously and melt into the corners of the room.

He turned his head fractionally to glance at Bainbridge, and although his expression was far from unwelcoming, he did not appear overjoyed to see his friend standing over him. He returned to blowing smoke rings for a moment before speaking.

"I suppose you're going to berate me and tell me to put this out immediately?" said Newbury, waving his opium-tainted cigarette lackadaisically in Bainbridge's general direction. Blue smoke curled from the end of it, describing twisting ribbons in the air.

"Do what you will," Bainbridge replied, in what he considered to be a very reasonable tone.

Newbury twisted around sharply to look up at him, a question in his eyes.

Bainbridge chuckled and shrugged. "Well, it's your ruddy house, and God knows I've stated my case enough times before. Besides, it's Christmas. It wouldn't do to get into a row."

"Are you feeling quite well, Charles?" asked Newbury, this time with a wry smile.

Bainbridge sighed, and then issued a barking cough as he inhaled a lungful of the thick, sweet-smelling smoke. "Well, you *could* do the decent thing and at least open a window."

Newbury laughed loudly and swung his feet down from the sofa. He leaned over to the coffee table and crumpled the remains of his cigarette into the ashtray, before hauling himself to his feet and crossing to the window. A moment later the room was filled with a cool, swirling gust, which stirred up the fire and banished the worst of the clinging smoke.

"If I'd realised it was that easy to have you extinguish your foul cigarettes, I'd have been more reasonable about it before," said Bainbridge, with a chuckle. "It seems all that shouting was unnecessary."

"Well, as you said, it *is* Christmas," replied Newbury, with a shrug. Bainbridge watched as Newbury shifted a pile of books to make room for them both to sit by the fire. He'd lost weight, and he was looking a little gaunt.

"You're not yourself, Newbury," said Bainbridge, his tone a touch more serious than before. "You usually relish this time of year."

"I'm bored, Charles," said Newbury, waving his arm dramatically. "I have no interest in commonplace murder and petty villainy. After everything that's happened… well, I simply cannot muster any enthusiasm for the mundane. I crave stimulation. I crave adventure." He dropped into a Chesterfield and ran a hand through his unkempt hair, issuing a heartfelt sigh. "Nothing seems to hold my attention." He shook his head, as if recognising how impetuous he sounded. "Oh, pour us a drink would you, Charles?"

Bainbridge sighed as he made his way over to the sideboard and began searching around for two clean tumblers. "Listen to yourself Newbury! So damn melodramatic. You make it sound as if the world has suddenly stopped turning. As if you've somehow managed to solve every conceivable mystery of interest, and now you've found yourself redundant!"

"Haven't I?" asked Newbury.

"Newbury, it's been *two months*! Hardly a lifetime. And if we're honest with one another, we both know you needed the rest. You're simply growing stir-crazy because you refuse to leave your ruddy rooms." Bainbridge glugged brandy into the glasses as he talked. "And besides, it's not as if *I'm* not busy.

You could always give me a hand if you're at a loose end."
He collected the glasses and crossed the room, passing one
to Newbury before lowering himself into the chair opposite.
"Well, with the very best of the season and all that," he said,
raising his glass in Newbury's direction.

Newbury smiled. "I take it you're still coming to dinner
tomorrow?"

Bainbridge took a long swig of brandy, rocking back in
his seat with an appreciative sigh. "You just try to stop me!
I wouldn't risk missing one of Scarbright's Christmas feasts."

Newbury laughed. "And Angelchrist?"

"I believe so," he said. "Although in truth our paths haven't
crossed for a number of weeks. We were supposed to meet at
the club for dinner this week, but I had to postpone because
of an incident in Shoreditch."

"Ah, yes. The Revenant murder."

Bainbridge was a little startled by this revelation that
Newbury was already aware of the case he was investigating.
"Yes... indeed so. But how did you know?"

Newbury shrugged. "As I explained, Charles, I'm bored.
And I make it my business to remain informed, even if, as
you so eloquently put it, I 'refuse to leave my ruddy rooms'."

Bainbridge flushed. "Then no doubt you're already aware
that the investigation has ground to a halt? Not that it ever
really got started."

"Indeed," said Newbury.

"And you had no thoughts of offering your assistance?"
Bainbridge felt at risk of losing the good mood that had
so far possessed him that afternoon, but he fought away
his aggravation. That was Newbury all over: dismissive
of Bainbridge's work, unless there was something in it that
caught his attention, some peculiar or occult element that
somehow made it stand out from the norm.

Newbury looked away, staring into the leaping flames of

the fire as if he was instead staring through a window into another world. "I can't see how I could be of assistance to you, Charles. Truthfully. People do terrible things to one another, and sometimes we're able to punish them for it. Sometimes, if we're lucky, we're even able to prevent it. But this time, I think you're simply going to have to accept that you're unable to attribute this horrible, random act of violence to any particular villain, as galling as that may be."

"Perhaps," said Bainbridge, softly. He took another swig of his brandy and allowed himself a little inward smile. So Newbury wasn't aware of the entire picture, then. He could draw some satisfaction from that, at least.

"Is that why you're here tonight? To solicit my help with your case? If so, Charles, I'm afraid you're wasting your time. There's nothing in it for me. Nothing I can get my teeth into."

Bainbridge placed his tumbler on the coffee table between them – or rather, on the pile of old newspapers that covered its surface. "Not at all, Newbury. I simply came to give you a gift."

He watched as Newbury's face fell in disappointment. "A gift? I... well, thank you, Charles." Newbury turned to glance at the heap of parcels in the corner. "Although I fear I'll have enough brandy and cigars to last a lifetime after tomorrow."

Bainbridge couldn't prevent himself from grinning. "Ah. I fear it's not that sort of gift, Newbury." He reached into his pocket and retrieved the small package he had placed there earlier. He handed it to Newbury. "Happy Christmas, dear chap."

Newbury offered him a confused expression. "But you're coming to dinner tomorrow, Charles. Is it not traditional for us to exchange gifts over a glass of port after dinner?"

Bainbridge laughed. "Just open the damn thing, Newbury!"

Shrugging, Newbury reached inside the small manila envelope and withdrew the object inside. His eyes widened in surprise as it dawned on him exactly what it was. "It's made of bone!"

"Human finger bones, to be precise. Five of them."

Newbury almost leapt out of his chair, dropping the envelope and turning the object over in his hands. He held it up to the light, studying it closely with a sudden gleam in his eye.

Bainbridge had received the thing that morning, left for him in the same unmarked envelope at the Yard. His reaction, upon opening it, had been quite the opposite of Newbury's; he'd recoiled in fascinated horror, dropping the artefact immediately upon the open ledger on his desk. It was a talisman or occult token of some kind, a pentagram formed from a grisly assemblage of human finger bones, bound together with thin leather strips. The bones had been artificially bleached, and black script had been meticulously etched on to the smooth surfaces, written in an arcane language that Bainbridge – or anyone else at the Yard, for that matter – could not identify. And so he had brought it to Newbury, partly to ask for his help in identifying its purpose and meaning, but mostly because he knew it would arose his friend's interest, particularly when he had occasion to read the accompanying note.

"It's fascinating," said Newbury, still scrutinising the object beneath the nearest wall-mounted gas lamp. "Where did you get it?"

"Someone left it at the Yard for me this morning," said Bainbridge, leaning back in his chair and watching Newbury with an amused grin. "But you haven't seen the best part yet, Newbury. Take another look inside the envelope."

Newbury carefully placed the talisman on the cluttered mantelpiece beside the cat skull and specimen jars, and hurried back to where he had been sitting, scooping up the discarded envelope and fishing around inside until he found the little notecard. He pulled it free, tossing the envelope away again and then turning the card over so that he might read its message.

Bainbridge watched as Newbury's face lit up in abject shock and surprise. The chief inspector had, of course, already committed the contents of the note to memory. It was written in a beautiful, flowing script, just four simple words on a cream-coloured notecard. Nevertheless, they were four words that would quicken Newbury's heart and resurrect his enthusiasm for life, four words that would alter his opinion of Bainbridge's case and send him running to collect his coat, despite the inclement weather, despite the date:

Regarding your corpse…
Clarissa

"She's back!" Newbury exclaimed, and Bainbridge could hear the excitement in his voice.

"It does rather seem that way," replied Bainbridge.

"Lady Arkwell, here in London once again. I believed her lost, dead…" he trailed off, evidently unable to find the appropriate words.

"We all did, Newbury."

Lady Arkwell, or Clarissa Karswell, had proven to be a thorn in Newbury's side during the course of the prior eighteen months. He had battled with her on numerous occasions and even, during one particular affair, formed a temporary alliance with the woman in the face of a common enemy. She purported to be a foreign agent, but as yet, Newbury had been unable to ascertain to which nation or organisation she was affiliated. The truth was, she had continued to outwit Newbury at every stage, even, it seemed faking her own demise in order to throw him temporarily off her trail. Yet here she was, back in London and making the first move, using Bainbridge to re-engage Newbury as if anxious to continue with their little game. Bainbridge had often wondered if there wasn't, in fact, something more to it than that, but that was nothing but idle speculation; he'd only met the woman on one occasion himself, and even then, he hadn't known it was her until well after she had already gone.

Newbury, for his part, seemed genuinely invigorated by the challenge and always rose to the occasion, whenever she showed her hand. He'd confided in Bainbridge more than once that he found the woman to be a complex, unfathomable creature whose motives were dubious and opaque, but with whom he was incurably fascinated. She was neither nemesis nor friend, and Bainbridge found it hard to put his finger on exactly *what* she was. As far as he could tell, Newbury had yet to fathom that one himself, either.

Whatever the case, it was clear Newbury had a deep admiration for her, as well as a great deal of respect. He'd mourned her passing as if she'd been a close personal friend, which, in many ways, Bainbridge supposed, she probably was. It was clear Newbury had felt the loss of such an admirable opponent keenly. Such was the unusual nature of the relationship between them. Now, as Bainbridge had anticipated, the news that she was alive and returned to London had been more than enough to rouse him from his ennui.

"Regarding your corpse…" Newbury glanced up from the note to glower at Charles. "She means the corpse you found tied to that lamp post in Shoreditch?"

Bainbridge nodded but didn't say a word.

"And you allowed me to spout all of that nonsense about giving up and accepting you would never find the killer? All the while with this in your pocket!"

"You seemed on such a roll, it was a shame to stop you," Bainbridge replied cheerily.

The two men stared at each other for a moment across the

drawing room, and then, almost simultaneously, they both broke out into heaving guffaws of laughter.

A moment later, when the laughter had subsided, Bainbridge stood and crossed to where Newbury was once again standing by the mantelpiece, examining the gruesome talisman. He put a hand on his friend's shoulder. "You want to see it? The corpse, I mean."

"I thought you'd never ask."

Bambridge chuckled. "Fetch your coat then. It's cold out."

Newbury raised his eyebrows in surprise. "What? Now?"

"Why wait?"

"Because it's snowing, and it's Christmas Eve!"

Bainbridge rubbed his hands together before the fire. "There'll be plenty of time for all that nonsense tomorrow. You're not seriously telling me you'd rather remain here to play parlour games, are you? Not when there's a case to be getting on with, and Lady Arkwell, somewhere out there in London, waiting for you to make the next move."

Newbury eyed his friend for a moment, a wide smile spreading across his face. "Quite right, Charles. Quite right. To the morgue it is!"

Bainbridge watched as Newbury bustled around for a few moments, collecting up all the necessary articles he needed for an excursion into the snowy evening. He couldn't help smiling to himself for a job well done, both on his part, and on the part of the mysterious Lady Arkwell. Her timing could not have been more perfect. He had no idea how she was connected to the dead man – whether her little parcel was intended as an admission of guilt or a helpful pointer in the right direction – but at this point he wasn't all that concerned, either. The important thing was the effect it had had on Newbury. They could worry about Lady Arkwell's motives later, together.

"Right. I think we're ready to face the storm," said

Newbury, standing by the drawing room door, trussed up in his woollen overcoat and holding Bainbridge's own overcoat in his gloved hands.

"More than you might have imagined," Bainbridge replied, quietly. If the other man heard, he made no mention of it.

Bainbridge crossed the room to join his friend in the doorway, taking his still-damp coat and slipping it over his shoulders.

"Oh, and one more thing," said Newbury, putting a hand on Bainbridge's arm. "Merry Christmas, Charles."

Bainbridge felt all of the tension suddenly drain out of him. Here, before him, was his old friend, ready to face the world by his side. For now, at least. "Merry Christmas, Newbury," he said, and together, the two of them made their way down the hall towards the blizzard, relishing the opportunity to spend their Christmas Eve together at the morgue.

Neither of them, Bainbridge reflected, could have been happier.

A RUM AFFAIR

♛

I

The crisp, white snow crunched beneath her boots as she tentatively approached the scene, Newbury beside her.

The man lay abandoned on Curzon Street, isolated and alone. He had suffered the most horrific of deaths: his stomach burst open by a legion of tiny mechanical spiders, hatched in his gut. The glittering creatures still scuttled about in the ruins of his innards. Beneath him, the blood was a crimson shadow upon the blank canvas of the snow.

"How did they get inside of him?" asked Veronica, disgusted.

"I have no idea," said Newbury, quietly. "But I intend to find out."

II

It was five days before Christmas, and Veronica was once again in the morgue.

"The fourth victim in as many days," said Bainbridge, frowning, as if he expected Newbury to simply pluck the solution from thin air.

"Each killed from within by these tiny brass beasts," said

Newbury, turning over one of the gleaming spiders in his palm.

"And all worked for the same firm of solicitors," said Veronica, trying not to look at the corpse. Its face was livid purple and fixed in an anguished scream.

"Yes," said Newbury, thoughtfully. "And all had theatre ticket stubs in their pockets."

III

"Could someone be targeting your employees?"

Tarquin Grundy shrugged. "Perhaps. We handle all manner of cases, Sir Maurice: criminal, domestic, corporate. We're regularly on the wrong end of threatening remarks."

"Anything specific?"

"A rival firm, Jones & Jones. They have a habit of getting a little too close to the criminals they represent. I'd wager they're not above a spot of espionage."

"We'll look into it," said Newbury. "What else?"

"There *was* a recent matter," continued the solicitor, "involving a newspaper publisher, Julian Petrie. We acted for the prosecution. He threatened our man as he was sent down, with death."

IV

On Bedford Square, close to the solicitor's office, a street vendor in a top hat was selling bowls of hot, spiced punch to passers-by. His solicitations echoed off the nearby buildings. People swarmed.

Veronica waited in the queue, smiling. She exchanged coppers for steaming bowls.

Together, the three investigators sipped at their drinks beneath the boughs of a snow-covered oak, staving off the brisk chill.

"I'll look into this Petrie fellow," said Bainbridge.

"While we pay a visit to Jones & Jones," said Newbury.

"And don't forget," said Veronica, grinning. "Someone has to arrange a visit to the theatre..."

V

The offices of Jones & Jones were unsavoury, dilapidated, but with a veneer of elegance that suggested the firm had recently lavished money upon them. The solicitors themselves, however, were unable to maintain this implied respectability; shabby and coarse, the two men ogled her and cursed Grundy for his accusations. Newbury drew the interview to a close within minutes, taking her arm and leading her out into the street.

"Thank you," she said.

"For what?" asked Newbury.

"Getting me out of there."

He looked perplexed. "Well, it's clear they didn't do it."

"Why?"

"They lack the subtlety," he said, grinning.

VI

Petrie, it transpired, had not fared well in prison, and had been found swinging from his belt in a cell two days earlier.

"A dead end," said Bainbridge, sighing. "Literally."

"Not necessarily," said Newbury. "He might have had friends."

"Not many," replied Bainbridge. "He was sent down for blackmail. He'd alienated most of his acquaintances."

"What of his newspaper?" asked Veronica.

"The *Mayfair Chronicle*," said Bainbridge. "That's next. Perhaps there might be some residual loyalty amongst his former colleagues."

"Enough to start a murderous spree in revenge?" said Newbury, doubtful.

"I've known people commit murder for less," replied Bainbridge, darkly.

VII

Newbury escorted her to the theatre, where they witnessed a seasonal spectacular replete with moaning spectres, murderous shenanigans and clockwork splendour; entire set pieces that came alive before her eyes – a revolving stage, a mechanical hound, a sword-fighting brass idol with six limbs.

Backstage, they found the engineer responsible for such marvels, hunched in his dimly lit workshop. He claimed to know nothing of the solicitors who had visited the theatre and then died, nor of the spiders which had killed them.

"Is it him?" she asked afterwards, unsure.

"It could be," said Newbury. "But what is his motive? And how?"

VIII

"My investigations at the *Mayfair Chronicle* turned up little," said Bainbridge. "Petrie was universally reviled, tolerated only because he paid the salary bill. I could find no motive for revenge. Indeed, many of the men working there argued Grundy had done them a great favour."

"Likewise, I fear Jones & Jones is a dead end," replied Newbury. "They lack the means and initiative, and I do not believe they represent a viable professional threat to Grundy's business."

"The engineer at the theatre?" said Veronica.

"We cannot prove a connection," said Newbury, "or a motive. I fear I'm at a complete loss."

IX

Ever since she'd been a little girl, Veronica had adored Christmas; the scent of roasting chestnuts, the crisp winter air, plentiful gifts wrapped in gaudy paper. As a child she'd strived to bring the season to life for her sister, Amelia, who was often bedridden with her illness.

This year she had the opportunity to do so again, to recapture the magic of their youth and spend the day in secretive solitude in Malbury Cross. She only hoped the unsolved deaths would not intervene; she feared it might be Amelia's last Christmas, and she wished to be at her side.

X

They held a conference at Chelsea, taking tea before the fire.

"Well, I'm damned if I have any notion of what's going on," said Bainbridge, morosely.

"And we've another two people dead," said Veronica. "We're no closer to discovering how those machines got inside of them." She took a sip from her teacup.

"That's it!" said Newbury, laughing, jumping to his feet. He had that wild look in his eye that Veronica knew so well. He'd been struck by inspiration.

"What is?" she said.

"I'm in the mood for a bowl of hot punch," he said, heading for the door.

XI

The sweet vendor knew it was over as soon as he saw Newbury stalking through the snow. He abandoned his stall and fled; Newbury gave chase, wrestled him to the ground, bloodying his nose in the process.

He struggled desperately, but when he saw Bainbridge

standing by with his cane, and Veronica wielding her hatpin, he relented. "I'll talk," he said, sobbing. "I'll tell you everything."

Newbury hauled him to his feet. "Most satisfactory," he said. "We can converse on the way to the Yard."

"I want a solicitor."

"I think it's a bit late for that," said Bainbridge, wryly.

XII

"So you're saying he was spiking their drinks with those tiny machines?" said Bainbridge.

"Indeed," replied Newbury. "They were barely noticeable amongst the fruit and spices in his punch. He reserved the poisoned bowls for the colleagues of his patron, Grundy. They'd discovered Grundy had been falsifying evidence to aid convictions."

"And once inside, the little machines would activate and burrow their way out?" asked Veronica.

"Precisely. Hours later, they'd kill the victim. Grundy procured the machines from the engineer at the theatre."

"Remarkable," sighed Bainbridge.

The clock chimed.

"It's nearly Christmas!" said Veronica.

Newbury grinned. "Right! Who's for punch?"

A NIGHT, REMEMBERED

LONDON, 1929

"A ticket for the *Argus*? I'm getting a bit old for this sort of thing, you know, Mr Rutherford. Besides, I don't have a particularly good track record when it comes to boats. There was that dreadful business on board the *Olympiad*, and I was, of course, aboard the *Titanic* when she went down. Are you sure you want to curse the *Argus* to a similar fate?"

The man – a dapper-looking fellow in his late sixties, with silver hair swept back from his forehead and a youthful physique that belied his age – delivered this with a playful twinkle in his eye.

"I wasn't aware you were on the *Titanic*, Sir Maurice," said Rutherford, failing to hide his surprise. "Was Miss Hobbes travelling with you at the time?"

Newbury shook his head. "No. Mercifully, I was alone."

"A mission?" prompted Rutherford. He wasn't really supposed to delve into Newbury's past case history – many of his exploits were now considered state secrets – but he was intrigued, and he couldn't really see what harm it could do. They were, after all, sitting alone in the Whitehall offices of the British Secret Service. It was unlikely they were going to be overheard.

"In a manner of speaking. There was a woman…" said Newbury, with a distant smile.

"A woman?" asked Rutherford, surprised.

"Yes. But not how you think. It was never like that." He paused for a moment, as if conjuring up her ghost. "Well. Not really. Her name was Clarissa Karswell, and she was one of the most remarkable women I ever met," continued Newbury, wistfully.

"Praise indeed, given the nature of your usual company," said Rutherford.

"Quite. Miss Karswell was certainly a unique example of her sex. She was an agent, of sorts, although it was never entirely clear for which agency she operated. Perhaps, in hindsight, she worked only for herself. She was known to others by the code name 'Lady Arkwell'."

"And you had been charged with bringing her in?" asked Rutherford, withdrawing his silver cigarette case from his jacket pocket and offering it to Newbury.

Newbury declined with a polite wave of his hand, so Rutherford took one of the thin American cigarettes for himself and pulled the ignition tab, watching it flare briefly to life.

"A long time ago. Just after the turn of the century. Her Majesty the Queen tasked me with locating Ms. Karswell and bringing her to heel." Newbury chuckled quietly to himself. "I never managed it, of course. We danced an intricate waltz over the years, sometimes finding ourselves diametrically opposed, on other occasions joining forces to battle a common foe." He sighed. "Even now, I miss her terribly. I could always count on her to liven things up a bit. She, Mr Rutherford, was the one that got away."

Rutherford frowned. "So this 'Lady Arkwell' – she was the reason you were aboard the *Titanic*?"

Newbury grinned. "She was travelling under an assumed

name. Her intention – I believe – was to smuggle some stolen relics into New York. They were the spoils of a British expedition to the Congo – the famed expedition that uncovered the ruins of an ancient civilisation in the jungle, still overrun with giant, carnivorous birds. I encountered those wretched things on more than one occasion, and I can tell you, Mr Rutherford, they were beautiful, but deadly creatures. That, however, is another story entirely..." he said, smiling playfully.

"Anyway, it appeared that Miss Karswell had purloined the priceless artefacts from the British Museum, and she hoped to pass them off to a coterie of rich American collectors upon arrival in New York." Newbury shrugged. "They never made it to America, of course. Now they're languishing somewhere at the bottom of the ocean."

"They were lost with the ship when she hit the iceberg?" Newbury grinned. "Ah, so you don't know."

"Don't know... what, exactly?" Rutherford realised he was leaning forward in his chair, drawn further and further into Newbury's burgeoning tale. He took another draw on his cigarette, allowing the smoke to plume from his nostrils.

"What really happened. The reason the *Titanic* went down," said Newbury, with an amused grin.

"You mean to say she didn't strike an iceberg?" Rutherford frowned. "It's well established. The reports all say—"

"Reports are written, Mr Rutherford, by those who survive, and published by those who wish to control the opinions of others," said Newbury, cutting him off. "I, on the other hand, was there, and saw it with my own eyes. I felt the chill embrace of the water as it clutched at me and tried to drag me to a watery grave. I watched the *Titanic* sink beneath the waves."

Rutherford stared at Newbury, utterly fascinated. "So what did happen, Sir Maurice? If she didn't strike the iceberg... Something must have done for her," he said.

'Oh, it most certainly did. And to this day, I'm still not

entirely sure what it was," replied Newbury. "It was the most dreadful thing, a thing of nightmares…" He broke off, and for a moment looked unsure as to whether he would continue. "I'm rather getting ahead of myself," he said, finally, reaching for the glass of water Rutherford had placed between them on the low table. He took a swig of it, and then peered disapprovingly at the glass. "Haven't you anything stronger?"

Rutherford laughed. "There's a bottle of brandy in Major Absalom's drawer," he said, rising from his seat. "I'll fetch it."

"Good man," said Newbury, draining the water and sliding the glass across the table. "Water will never do."

Rutherford rummaged around in the top drawer of his superior's desk until he found the bottle he knew to be hidden there. He'd have to replace it before Absalom discovered it was missing, but it would be worth it. It wasn't every day he was able to coerce such a legendary figure into giving up one of his tales. He crossed to the table and glugged out a generous measure, before dropping back into his seat.

Newbury reached for the glass. "My thanks to you, Mr Rutherford."

"So, you were saying?" said Rutherford, trying his best not to sound impatient.

"The iceberg, yes." Newbury drained half of the brandy from his glass, and then placed it back on the table with a satisfied sigh. "Well, I was in the first-class saloon when it happened, taking a whisky and keeping a watchful eye out for Ms. Karswell. I'd checked the passenger manifests before boarding, but I'd been unable to discern under which assumed name she'd been travelling. I myself was operating under an alias – one of the reasons my own name did not appear on those same manifests when the roll call of the dead was published later – and so there I was, scanning the faces of the other passengers, hoping to catch sight of her familiar profile and her startling red hair."

Newbury was staring into the middle distance now, and Rutherford tried to imagine what the man was seeing: the sumptuous interior of that great vessel, filled with the bustle and murmur of people, each of them ignorant of the horrors about to occur.

"I felt the ship judder as it struck something, and then a few moments later the engines cut out and we shuddered to a halt. There were a few concerned glances between passengers in the saloon, but mostly people seemed content to carry on as they were, lost in their own world of polite conversation and unnecessary etiquette. I, on the other hand, being incessantly inquisitive, decided to head up on deck to see if I could ascertain what had happened.

"It was frigid out there on the deck, and in the moonlight the ice floes glittered like a carpet of sparkling diamonds. Beside us, the peak of an immense iceberg loomed out of the water, casting a dark shadow across the ship. It was so close that, at first, I assumed that we'd struck it, but as I approached the railings and peered over the edge, I saw that was not in fact the case."

"Then what was it?" asked Rutherford, his voice barely above a whisper.

"A submersible," replied Newbury. "a massive, cylindrical, underwater vessel, listing just beneath the surface of the waves. It was clearly drifting, derelict, and there was evidence of huge scars in its flank."

"Scars?" asked Rutherford.

"Yes, deep parallel scratches in the metal. I had no idea what weapon could have left such a mark. It was clear to me, however, that it was the wreckage of this submersible that the *Titanic* had struck as she attempted to navigate the ice."

"I don't understand," said Rutherford. "Why cover it up? Why did all the reports claim it was the iceberg that did for the ship?"

"Because the thing that had destroyed the submersible was still there, in the water, waiting for us," Newbury replied, shuddering at the recollection. "We didn't know that at the time, of course. The captain ordered the engines to be restarted, and the ship moved off again."

Newbury reached for his glass and took another long swig of his drink. He looked pale, as if by forcing himself to relive those fateful moments he was once again stirring up powerful emotions he had long ago suppressed.

"Unbeknownst to the passengers, of course, the *Titanic* was at this point taking on more water than she was capable of withstanding. The engine rooms were already filling with water. We were doomed from that moment, even before the creature struck."

"Creature?" Rutherford echoed, surprised.

"Indeed, Mr Rutherford. A beast of the sort you have never imagined, and you should hope that you will never meet." Newbury met Rutherford's gaze and held it for a moment, and the look in his eyes was so intense that Rutherford knew that he was deadly serious. After a moment he turned away.

"For a while I stayed there, huddled on the deck against the spray, watching the dark waters churn far below with the passing of the great liner. Everything seemed to return to normal, and I could have almost believed that I'd imagined it all, the vision of the drifting submersible and the tortured scream of rending metal I had heard as the ship had struck it. But then the *Titanic* began to list dramatically to the right, and it was at that point I realised she was going down. The engines cut again, and this time there was an outbreak of panic amongst the passengers below."

Newbury smiled sadly. "The reports were quite accurate about this, I fear, Mr Rutherford. The whole affair was terribly mismanaged. First-class passengers, now startled from their dreary existence beneath, began to spill out on to the deck, pouring forth in a torrent of shrill chatter and evening wear. Some of them were wearing lifejackets and carrying their belongings – others were still dressed only in their finery.

"The crew were panicking now, too, of course, and were calling for women and children to take to the lifeboats. It came to me then that I had to find Miss Karswell. I had to ensure she took her place upon one of those rafts. She was a brave and stubborn woman – not unlike Miss Hobbes – and she would not volunteer herself for a place unless goaded, believing that she stood a better chance than most in the water and giving her own place up for another. I knew this because I knew her. The *Titanic* was sinking, however, and I would not allow such a remarkable woman to go down with the ship. I had to find her."

"And did you?" asked Rutherford, crushing the stub of his cigarette in the cut-glass ashtray on Major Absalom's desk.

Newbury nodded. "Yes. But I was too late. The press of people on deck was already proving untenable. I pushed my way through the chaotic morass of limbs, searching the crowd for a glimpse of her face. The lifeboats were being lowered and cast adrift, many of them only half full, but I knew she would not yet be aboard one of them.

"As I fought my way towards the other end of the deck I heard the very fabric of the vessel groan beneath me, and the ship lurched. I was nearly knocked from my feet by a sudden jolt, only keeping myself upright by virtue of the metal railing, which I grabbed at frantically to hold myself steady. When I looked up again, I saw her."

Newbury took a deep breath. Rutherford could see that he was trembling, and so took up the bottle of brandy, refilling Newbury's glass.

"Thank you, Mr Rutherford. I think I might indulge in one of your American cigarettes after all, if I may?"

"Of course." Rutherford placed the open tin on the table

beside Newbury's glass. Newbury reached forward and took one. He studied it for a moment, and then pulled the ignition tab and took a long, deep draw.

"She was standing no more than thirty feet from me, a stricken look upon her pretty face. She looked entirely lost and alone, and I think perhaps more vulnerable than I had ever seen a woman look before, or since. It was the look of a woman who knew she was going to die, and was furious at her own impotence to do anything about it.

"It took a moment for her to see me there, still clinging resolutely to the railing, and when she did her eyes widened in shock and she opened her mouth as if to call to me. I pushed myself away from the railing, intent on fighting my way towards her, when the first of the tentacles came lashing out of the water, whipping across the deck just in front of me and sending me sprawling backwards across the deck."

"Tentacles? The creature?" said Rutherford, appalled.

"Indeed so. The limb of some dreadful Leviathan from beneath the waves. It must have been as big as the ship itself, and as its limb thrashed and splintered the deck before me, I realised it was wrapping itself around the ship. I glanced round to see more of the thick, slimy proboscises flicking over the railings, curling around the funnels. Whatever the thing was, it had the ship in its clammy embrace and, as the deck lurched beneath me once again, I understood that it intended to drag the *Titanic* down into the watery depths."

"Good Lord," said Rutherford. "I had no idea. How did you get away? And what of Ms. Karswell?"

"I scrambled unsteadily to my feet. By now I'd realised that the ship was lost. Even before the beast had struck she'd been taking on too much water. Everybody was screaming, throwing themselves overboard in an effort to escape the thrashing limbs of the creature or make it to the life rafts, which were now spreading out in a concentric circle around the *Titanic*, cast adrift on the midnight ocean.

"There was no sign of Clarissa. Either she'd gone overboard, or she'd been caught in the devastation caused by the thrashing beast. I tried to find a path through to where I'd last seen her, but the deck was splintered and broken and proved impassable. The ship was being dragged down quickly now, tilting wildly, and I was left with little choice. I had to try my luck in the water. I could only hope that Clarissa had done the same."

"Were you wearing a lifejacket?"

"No I was still in my evening suit. I shed my jacket and threw myself overboard, hoping beyond hope that I could get myself clear before the ship was entirely submerged and I was pulled under by the current."

"But what about the beast?" asked Rutherford. "Weren't you afraid that it might try to drag you under too?"

Newbury shook his head. "No. The beast was too busy with the ship. That was the far greater prize. I was but a mote compared to the immensity of the creature and the ship. It would barely have noticed me as I splashed into the ice-cold water, gasping for breath."

"Did you make it to one of the lifeboats?"

"I did. The women dragged me aboard, shivering and barely able to speak, and when I looked round the last thing I saw before unconsciousness took hold was an immense, cyclopean eye beneath the surface, glaring up at us as we rowed frantically away from the drowning ship."

"So this creature – it was responsible for the damaged submersible? And so, indirectly, for the loss of the *Titanic*?" said Rutherford, barely able to comprehend the gravity of the tale that had just been laid out before him.

"One can only assume," said Newbury, "but it seems the only likely explanation. One might even imagine that the submersible was left there purposefully, as if the beast had sensed our approach and had laid out its trap."

Rutherford slumped back in his chair, shaking his head. That a creature so terrible might still exist out there in the ocean depths… no wonder the truth had been covered up. If it were ever to get out that monstrous things such as that were prowling the depths of the Atlantic ocean, no one would ever set foot aboard a steamship again. He wondered how many other vessels lost at sea had suffered a similar fate.

And then it struck him. Newbury had not told him what had become of the woman. "Ms. Karswell," he said, urgently, "did she also make it to one of the lifeboats?"

Newbury glanced away, unable to look Rutherford in the eye. "No," he replied, solemnly. "She did not. I searched for her on the rescue ship, and again when we returned to shore, but she was nowhere to be found. I hoped for many years that, somehow, she had found her way to safety, that she might find a way to reach me, but it's been so long… and I've heard nothing. Not even an idle word in a report, or the slightest fleeting reference. And believe me, I've looked. No, Mr Rutherford. I fear Miss Karswell was lost to the icy depths when the *Titanic* went down, and the world is a much emptier place without her."

"I'm sorry," said Rutherford, unable to find any other words. He could see from the expression on Newbury's face that the man was still deeply pained by the loss. But then… He felt in his pocket for the note. Could it be?

Newbury sighed. He took the ticket that Rutherford had given to him earlier, glanced at it again, and then cast it onto the table beside his drink. "I hope you can understand, Mr Rutherford, my less than enthusiastic response to your suggestion that I take a cabin aboard the *Argus*. What is it for, anyway? What's the nature of the mission, that an old man like me might be dragged out of retirement?"

"Well, that's just it, Sir Maurice. We don't really know,"

said Rutherford, failing to suppress a grin.

"I'm sorry?" said Newbury, perplexed.

"The ticket was delivered here this morning, addressed to you. It was in a plain manila envelope, and the only other thing it contained was this note." He handed the folded slip of paper to Newbury. "We had no idea what it might mean," Rutherford continued. "At least, not until..." he trailed off, watching the other man as he studied the note.

Newbury was silent for a long moment. "Well, I'll have to go, won't I?" he said, grinning broadly. Then he was laughing, and Rutherford could see the misty tears forming in the creases of his eyes. "Can't see as I have any choice." He handed the slip of paper back to Rutherford.

Rutherford beamed. "No, Sir Maurice," he said, laughing. "I can't see that you do." He glanced down at the piece of paper in his hand, the single, neat line of copperplate written there in black ink, an invitation to an old friend:

ARE WE TOO OLD TO DANCE?

THE MAHARAJAH'S STAR

LONDON, FEBRUARY 1933

Rutherford hadn't expected the house to be quite so impressive.

It was Georgian, and had probably once been a farmhouse, but sometime in the course of the last century it had been swallowed by the expanding girth of the metropolis. Now it was surrounded by regimented ranks of Victorian terraces, just another old house on the outskirts of London, a relic of a bygone age. That, he supposed, was progress.

He took a long draw on the stub of his cigarette and then flicked the still-smouldering butt out of the window. He was sitting behind the wheel of his car, the engine gently sighing as it settled after the long drive. He was tired and cold. He hoped the professor would offer him a hot drink, but in truth he was expecting a frosty reception. The whole situation was rather delicate. The professor had been a much-respected government agent. To have someone go poking around in his past, asking questions about events that happened thirty years earlier... Well, Rutherford knew how *he* would feel about it if it were him.

Rutherford stretched his aching neck and climbed out onto the pavement, locking the car door behind him. His breath made ghostly shapes in the frigid air as he tramped up the gravel path towards the front door. It swung open before he'd even had chance to mount the steps and an elderly butler peered out, his balding pate gleaming in the sunlight. "Good morning, sir. May I be of assistance?"

Rutherford cleared his throat. "Yes. I'm here to see Professor Angelchrist. Is he home?"

The butler narrowed his eyes. "Your name, sir?"

"Peter Rutherford. I'm here on behalf of the British government. I believe the professor may be able to help with my enquiries."

"Very good, sir. Please come in. I'll see if the professor is available for visitors."

Rutherford smiled and stepped into the hall, dipping his head to avoid bashing it on the low beam over the door.

Inside, the cavernous hallway was dimly lit and ticked ominously with the workings of innumerable clockwork machines. Rutherford sensed movement in the dark recesses behind the staircase, but couldn't discern anything because of the poor light. He waited by the door for the butler to return, feeling a little uneasy.

"Professor Angelchrist will see you in the drawing room, Mr Rutherford," the man said when he reappeared a moment later, giving a slight wave of his hand to indicate the way.

Rutherford thanked him. He passed along the hallway, stopping before the drawing room door. He rapped loudly, twice.

"Come." The voice from within the room was stately and firm, but cracked with age.

Rutherford pushed the door open and stepped inside.

The professor was sitting by the hearth in a leather armchair that seemed to dwarf him, giving Rutherford the impression he was smaller than he probably was. His hair was a shock of startling white, and he wore a short beard and wiry spectacles. Dressed in a morning suit, his liver-spotted hands were folded neatly on his lap. He looked up and smiled at Rutherford, beckoning him to the chair opposite his own.

"Good day to you, Mr Rutherford. I hope you'll forgive me if I don't get up." He held out his hand and Rutherford reached over and shook it firmly. "These old legs aren't what they once were."

Rutherford smiled. "Of course," he said, taking his seat.

"You're here on behalf of the government, eh? Secret Service, by the look of you." The old man's eyes flashed with amusement, but then he looked suddenly serious. "You've come for it, haven't you?"

Rutherford frowned. Direct and to the point. He hadn't been expecting that. "*It*?" he said, feigning ignorance.

"Come now, Mr Rutherford. Let us not patronise one another. I know you're here for the Maharajah's Star. I always knew someone would come, one day. I'm only surprised it's taken so long." The old man leaned forward in his chair, fixing Rutherford with a firm stare. "That is why you're here, isn't it?"

Rutherford shrugged, and nodded. "So you admit you have it here?"

Angelchrist gave a crooked smile. "What do you know of the Star, Mr Rutherford?" he replied, avoiding the question.

So, they were going to play a game. Rutherford found himself warming to the old man. "That it once belonged to the Maharajah of Jodhpur, a man renowned for his love of beautiful things. During the course of his reign the Maharajah amassed a great wealth of treasures from all around the world. Precious jewels, ancient relics, famous works of art. That sort of thing. But the Star was always his most prized possession, so valuable, so precious that none of his servants were even allowed to look upon it. No one but the Maharajah himself even knew what it was. He kept it locked inside a specially constructed cabinet in his treasure room, and he kept the key on his person at all times, even when he slept. Legend has it many thieves foolishly attempted to steal the Star, but the Maharajah wise to these interlopers, had installed a hundred clockwork warriors in the treasure room. Anyone who broke in was cut to ribbons by their flashing blades."

"Very good," Angelchrist said, reaching for his pipe and knocking out the dottles in his palm before discarding them in the fire. "Go on."

"When the British went in after the '57 rebellion they discovered the palace had been ransacked. The treasure had all gone, the clockwork warriors had been destroyed and the Maharajah lay murdered in his bed. But the thieves had failed to locate the key that still hung around the neck of the Maharajah's corpse. It was retrieved by the British soldiers and eventually found its way back to London on the airship *Empress's Grace*. The treasure could not be traced, however, and although the occasional, solitary item turned up on the black market, it remained a mystery as to what had become of it."

Rutherford paused as the butler appeared in the doorway bearing a silver tea tray. Angelchrist beckoned him in, and the butler came forward and set the tray down on a low table. He beat a hasty retreat. "It's about this point in proceedings when your name, along with those of Sir Maurice Newbury and Miss Veronica Hobbes, is first mentioned."

Angelchrist grinned. "Sir Maurice Newbury! What a remarkable fellow."

"Did you know him well?"

Angelchrist nodded. "Oh, yes. Newbury, Miss Hobbes and I, along with Sir Charles Bainbridge, were involved in far more than just the matter of the Maharajah's Star. Newbury opened my eyes, Mr Rutherford, to the secret world that exists in the shadows, just beneath the veneer of civilisation."

"So what of the Star?" Rutherford prompted.

"You must understand that in those days, thirty years ago, the government and the monarch were at odds with one another. Publicly, of course, all was well, but beneath the surface a power struggle was taking place. In 1902 I was working for the fledgling Secret Service. Newbury and the others were agents of the Crown. But we knew one another well and had helped each other on many occasions." Angelchrist paused for a moment while he lit his pipe. "When word came that the Maharajah's treasure had turned up in London in the hands of a criminal gang, both myself and Newbury were charged with retrieving it. As we had on so many prior occasions, we agreed to pool our resources. It didn't take us long – with the help of Bainbridge and Scotland Yard – to discover where the treasure was being held. It had arrived on a steamship, disguised as cargo, and was in the possession of a gang of smugglers and pirates who maintained a warehouse out by London Docks."

Rutherford nodded. So far, everything Angelchrist had said confirmed what was written in the reports of the time.

"Well, the four of us – Newbury, Miss Hobbes, Bainbridge and I – stormed the place with a handful of bobbies for back-up. The smugglers put up quite a fight. It transpired they'd been operating out of the warehouse for some time. The place was heavily fortified, protected by a huge, flightless, carnivorous bird they'd brought back from the Congo, along with an army of mechanically reanimated pygmies. Well," Angelchrist said, around the mouthpiece of his pipe, "Bainbridge and I dealt with the bird, leading it a merry dance around the docks before felling it with a shot to the head. Newbury, Miss Hobbes and the bobbies were left to handle the pygmies in the meantime. They must have ripped through the place like tornadoes, as a veritable army of the mechanised corpses lay sprawled upon the ground when Bainbridge and I returned a short while later. There was, of course, no sign of the criminals response He – fled amongst the chaos, we presumed – but we found the Maharajah's lost treasure locked in a subterranean vault beneath the warehouse."

Rutherford nodded. He didn't know whether Angelchrist was embellishing the story or whether the original report had been light on detail, but this was the first he'd heard of the terror bird and the reanimated pygmies. He reached for the teapot and began pouring the tea. "And the Star? The reports state that you retrieved the cabinet but found it empty."

Angelchrist grinned. "Well, I suppose we were a little… ecoromical with the truth. The Star was there, in the cabinet, just as the stories suggested it would be. We turned the treasure over to the Crown as we'd been instructed, but the Star – well, we all agreed to bring it here for safekeeping. It's been in my possession ever since."

Rutherford frowned. How could a man so celebrated, with such an impeccable service record, do something such as this? To steal and hide a national treasure? Not only that, but Sir Maurice Newbury, too, conspiring along with him. Rutherford could hardly credit it. "Where is it?" he asked.

Angelchrist laughed. "You're holding it now," he said.

"What?" Rutherford looked down at the teapot in his hands. "Surely not…" he said, trailing off. Yet even as he spoke he saw that the old, clay teapot was etched with a rough five-pointed star, around which two lines of Sanskrit had been crudely engraved. "My God!" he said, setting it down upon the tray. "You're telling me this is it? This is the Maharajah's Star? It's just an old, worthless pot."

Angelchrist was still laughing. "But that's exactly the point, my dear Rutherford. The inscription, roughly translated, means 'That which the heart treasures most cannot be measured in gold'. It was the Maharajah's secret. The Star was worthless, but it served as a reminder to him that all of the treasure he had amassed, all of that wealth, meant nothing.

Not really. They were nothing but pretty trinkets."

Rutherford leaned back in his chair, staring at Angelchrist in disbelief.

"It was also one of the finest security measures ever devised," Angelchrist continued. "The true power of the Star was the very fact the world believed it to be a treasure of unimaginable value. While it remained locked in the Maharajah's cabinet, guarded by those hundred clockwork warriors, it was the only thing on the mind of thieves and vagabonds throughout all of India. It represented the ultimate prize. The Maharajah knew that while the true nature of the Star remained a secret, all of his other treasures were safe. His enemies had eyes only for the Star."

Angelchrist reached for his teacup and brought it to his lips before continuing. "Newbury knew this. And he knew that the Queen was only really interested in baubles and trinkets. She, like all those other thieves who had tried to take it over the years, was enamoured with the notion of the Star as a treasure. She wouldn't recognise its intrinsic value, even if she did know the truth. So Newbury suggested I take the Star into safekeeping, that we put it about that the Star was still lost. That way the criminal elements throughout the world would have something to keep them occupied while we focused on keeping the Empire safe. He was that sort of man, Mr Rutherford. Always concerned with what was best, what was *right*. It worked, too – there have been many criminals over the years that have sought the Star, dedicating their lives to finding it. The last thing I heard, an albino count from Romania was in London, devoting all of his not-inconsiderable influence into tracing what became of the pirates who stole it."

Rutherford shook his head in disbelief. He couldn't take his eyes off the teapot. It was a simple, utilitarian object that had been at the centre of a mystery for well over a century. So many people had given their lives in pursuit of the Star. Yet

Rutherford couldn't help thinking that perhaps Newbury had been right. Perhaps it was best to preserve the enigma of the Star. To leave those people searching.

"I suppose you'll be taking it with you?" Angelchrist said, his voice level.

Rutherford met his gaze. "I... no. I think, perhaps, it would be in everyone's best interests, Professor, if the Star were to remain here with you. Let's forget we ever had this conversation. We'll enjoy this cup of tea, and then I'll take my leave. I think that would be for the best."

Angelchrist chuckled. He clamped the mouthpiece of his pipe between his teeth. "Good choice, Mr Rutherford," he said. "Good choice indeed."

Rutherford reached for the teapot. He was thirsty, and it was going to be a long drive home.

THE ALBINO'S SHADOW

LONDON, AUGUST 1933

I

"I even heard he'd been resurrected from the dead by a blood infusion from some heathen witch doctor. They say he's not even a man anymore, but some sort of pale spirit, half ghost, half juju."

Major Absalom rocked back in his seat and fixed Rutherford with a look of absolute sincerity, peering out from beneath his heavy, furrowed brow and bushy eyebrows. He chewed thoughtfully on the end of his pipe, smoke dribbling from his nostrils like the exhalation of a dormant dragon.

Rutherford smiled. He'd always thought the Major was a little too credulous for his own good. "You sound as if you actually believe all these myths about this 'Monsieur Zenith' character," he said, before taking a long draw on his cigarette. He blew the smoke casually from the corner of his mouth, watching his superior officer with interest.

Absalom's frown deepened. His whiskers – which curled impressively from his ears to meet his moustache – twitched as he considered Rutherford's words. "To be truthful with you, Rutherford, I'm not even sure I believe the man himself isn't a myth. I mean, really..." he sighed, leaning forward again and placing both of his palms on the leather surface of his desk.

Rutherford watched him, amused. "I hear the Yard have attributed scores of cases to him over the years. He's one of the most wanted men in the Empire."

Absalom snorted.

"You're not a believer, then, sir?"

"Be that as it may, there are others," Absalom coughed, as if not wishing to give voice to the names themselves, "who do believe he's out there, and moreso, that he's harbouring sinister intentions towards them."

Rutherford stubbed out the remains of his cigarette in the cut-glass ashtray on Absalom's desk and folded his hands on his lap. "Does the Prime Minister have any evidence to support his claim?"

Absalom raised an eyebrow in surprise. Clearly, he hadn't expected Rutherford to be so well informed. "Of course he doesn't," he said, resignedly. "Simply that he asserts to have received a telephone call from the villain in question."

"And?" Rutherford prompted.

Absalom shrugged. "Only that Monsieur Zenith told him to expect a change in his fortunes."

"It's not a lot to go on," said Rutherford.

"Indeed it's not," agreed Absalom, "and to be honest, if it were anyone else, I should be counselling equanimity. However, we're talking about the Prime Minister. We need to show we're taking it seriously."

Rutherford nodded. "And, of course, rule out the potential of a real threat," he said, smiling.

"Yes, yes, yes," replied Absalom, with bluster. "Goes without saying." He stroked his whiskers absently.

"So you want me to pay a visit to Downing Street, speak with the Prime Minister?" asked Rutherford.

"God, no," said Absalom, grimacing. "Wouldn't want to

lumber you with that. I'll take care of the PM." He rocked back in his chair. "No, I want you to look into this Monseiur Zenith character, see if you can't get to the bottom of what's going on. I want to know who he is and what his game is. If," he added, with a roll of his eyes, "he even exists at all, that is."

Rutherford grinned. "I know just where to start," he said.

II

Rutherford paused for a moment at the end of the garden path, chewing on the stub of his cigarette.

The house was just as he remembered it from his visit six months earlier, when he'd called on the professor to interview him regarding the matter of the Maharajah's Star; old, immaculate and somewhat incongruous, nestled as it was amongst its modern counterparts. *Not unlike its owner*, Rutherford mused with a grin.

The interview had proved successful, but not at all in the manner Rutherford had expected. After hearing Professor Angelchrist's tale, Rutherford had ended up throwing in his lot with the retired agent, helping him to perpetuate a decades-old lie about the whereabouts of an ancient treasure.

It was during the course of the ensuing conversation that Angelchrist had first mentioned the "albino prince". It had been only a fleeting reference, a cursory remark to demonstrate another point, but for some reason it had lodged in the back of Rutherford's mind. Now, with hindsight, he realised that Angelchrist could not have been referring to anyone else. It had to be Zenith.

He had no idea whether the professor would know anything more about Rutherford's alabaster-skinned quarry, but regardless, it was the only lead he had. If Angelchrist proved to be a dead end, Rutherford would be forced to go back to Absalom empty-handed.

Rutherford filled his lungs with sharp, sweet tobacco smoke, dropped the stub of the cigarette on the path and crushed it underfoot. He exhaled slowly through the corner of his mouth as he walked towards the door, which – as he'd expected it might – swung open before he'd even had chance to put his boot on the bottom step.

Angelchrist's elderly, bald-headed butler peered out through the narrow crack, a suspicious frown on his face.

"Good afternoon. I'm here to see Professor Angelchrist," said Rutherford, genially.

The man's expression altered almost immediately as he seemed to recognise Rutherford's voice. "I fear I did not recognise you for a moment, Mr Rutherford. I do beg your pardon." The door opened fully and the butler gave a slight smile as he beckoned Rutherford into the house.

Rutherford smiled. "I imagine the professor receives a great many visitors," he said. "You couldn't possibly be expected to remember them all."

"No sir," said the butler in a droll voice. "It was the… well, it was the *act*."

Rutherford couldn't help but laugh at the butler's derisory tone. He reached up and removed the offending item – a wide-brimmed fedora he had purchased in New York a few years earlier – and handed it to the other man as he stepped over the threshold, ducking his head beneath the low beam.

The butler took the hat without further comment, closing the door behind them and following Rutherford into the house. He placed it carefully on a nearby hat stand and held out his arm for Rutherford's overcoat.

The hallway was shrouded in darkness, and Rutherford could hear the groaning and ticking of myriad clockwork machines in the shadowy recesses. A large, potted aspidistra stood at the foot of the staircase, and a wooden, life-sized figure of a caveman loomed down eerily from the landing above.

Rutherford had a sense that the house was crowded with the accumulated detritus of decades, paraphernalia of a thousand long-forgotten adventures. He longed to explore, to go rummaging and digging amongst all of this wondrous stuff, to unpick the tales attached to each item.

"If you'd like to come this way, sir," said the butler, interrupting his reverie, "I'm sure the professor will be delighted to speak with you."

Rutherford nodded, and followed behind the other man as he led them through the winding bowels of the house, past the propped-up case of an Egyptian mummy, a strange-looking contraption labelled the *aetheric calibrator* and a display case filled with primitive effigies and dolls. Atop this display case sat a large brass owl, which turned its head to follow them as they passed, clacking its metallic wings and chirruping noisily.

"Ignore the owl, sir," said the butler. "It has eyes only for the lacquered furniture, damnable thing."

Rutherford tried not to laugh.

A moment later, the butler stopped abruptly outside a panelled door, and rapped loudly three times. He turned the handle and pushed the door open for Rutherford. "In here, Mr Rutherford," he said, shooing Rutherford in. "You make yourself comfortable, and I'll organise some tea."

"Thank you," said Rutherford, realising for the first time that he didn't actually know the butler's name. He stepped over the threshold into the dimly lit room beyond.

Professor Angelchrist was sitting in a chair by the fire. He might not have moved in the intervening six months since Rutherford's previous call – he sat in precisely the same position, a book balanced neatly upon his lap. He looked up when Rutherford came into the room, and smiled warmly. "Welcome back, Mr Rutherford. It's good to see you again."

"Likewise," said Rutherford, crossing the room to shake Angelchrist by the hand.

"Please, take a seat, and tell me how I might be of assistance to you," said Angelchrist, waving Rutherford to the chair opposite. "Is it with regards to the Maharajah's Star?"

"In a manner of speaking," replied Rutherford, settling into his seat. "I remember that, during my previous visit, you told me of an albino prince from Eastern Europe who'd been searching for the Star."

"Ah, yes. Monsieur Zenith," said Angelchrist, with a tight smile. "What an interesting fellow."

"So he's real, then?" asked Rutherford, sensing a story.

Angelchrist laughed. "Oh, yes, Mr Rutherford, as real as you or I." He folded his book shut and placed it neatly on the side table. "I met him once," he continued. "He came here but a week after you, searching for the Star."

Rutherford couldn't hide the surprise on his face. "He came here?"

Angelchrist laughed again. "Indeed. He was quite charming, in his own way. Resourceful, too. He'd followed the trail of the Star and, like you, Mr Rutherford, he'd established that I was the last person to see it before it disappeared. He came here to ask me for it."

Rutherford blanched. "Did he threaten you, Professor?"

Angelchrist chuckled. "Oh, no. Not at all. He was a perfect gentleman. When he discovered the truth about the Star, he was most amused. He seemed to have an appreciation for the irony of the situation. He stayed for a while, telling me something of his exploits, of his long search for the Star, and then left without further ado."

Rutherford frowned. This didn't sound like the behaviour of a hardened criminal. "Did he leave you a calling card or a forwarding address? I've been tasked with finding him. A threat has been made, you see, and it seems likely that Monsieur Zenith may be behind it."

Angelchrist shook his head. "This was some months ago

now, Mr Rutherford. A man like Monsieur Zenith does not stay still for long," he replied.

"Nevertheless… do you have any notion of where I might find him?"

Angelchrist shook his head. "I fear not."

Rutherford gave a resigned sigh. "Then I thank you for your help, Professor. You've been most helpful." He stood, brushing himself down. "I suspected I was hoping for too much that you might be able to put me on the albino's trail."

Angelchrist chuckled. "Ah, now I didn't say that, Mr Rutherford. If you want to find Monsieur Zenith, then there's someone I think you should talk with."

Rutherford dropped back into his seat, intrigued. "Who?"

"Miss Veronica Hobbes," said Angelchrist.

"Miss Veronica Hobbes?" echoed Rutherford, surprised.

"Indeed. Miss Hobbes has, over the years, had cause to pit her wits against Monsieur Zenith on a number of occasions," said Angelchrist.

"Alongside Sir Maurice Newbury?" asked Rutherford.

"And alone," replied Angelchrist, nodding. "If there's anyone I know who could assist you in this matter, it's Miss Hobbes."

Rutherford grinned. "Do you know how to reach her?"

"Indeed I do, Mr Rutherford," said Angelchrist, heaving himself up out of his chair with a groan. "You wait here for Casper to bring the tea, and I shall make a telephone call."

III

They met at a restaurant in Kensington, sitting by the window in the shadow of a broad awning. It was a brisk morning and Rutherford would have preferred to sit inside, but the lady seemed intent on sitting out. She sipped at her Earl Grey and watched him over the brim of the teacup, seemingly impervious to the cold.

He watched her in turn, as if they were circling opponents, sizing each other up. After a moment, she spoke. "Well, Mr Rutherford?"

He was about to answer when the waiter bustled over and began describing the specials with great bonhomie. Rutherford found none of the proposed delicacies fired his imagination, so ordered a simple salad, and only then so as not to seem impolite. In truth, he would have been happy to subsist on nothing but strong coffee and cigarettes.

The waiter hurried off again and the woman – Miss Veronica Hobbes – waited patiently as Rutherford slowly extracted a cigarette from his silver tin, lit it with a match and took a long, welcome draw.

She was not at all what he'd been expecting. He wasn't sure what he *had* been expecting, but it hadn't been this. He supposed he'd imagined she'd seem older, more like Angelchrist, a relic of a bygone age.

In fact, she was far younger than Angelchrist, and although she was in her early fifties, she had the look of an attractive woman ten years her junior. Her hair did not yet show signs of turning to grey, remaining a dark, voluminous brown, and aside from a tiny, sickle-shaped scar on her left cheek, her skin was unlined and unblemished. Her eyes were striking and full of life and energy.

Strangely, Rutherford thought he could hear a faint ticking sound as he leaned closer to her across the table, as if she were harbouring a small carriage clock in her handbag. He decided it would be impolite to enquire.

"Thank you for coming," he said, sincerely. "I imagine you know who I represent?"

She smiled knowingly and took another sip of her tea. "I know that you work for the Secret Service, if that's what you mean?" she said, quietly, so that they might not be overheard. "I know that you're on the trail of the albino prince, and that you don't have any idea of where to begin, or whether he even actually exists at all."

Rutherford laughed. "Yes," he confirmed. "That's about the size of it, Miss Hobbes." She was clearly more informed than he'd anticipated, too. He made a mental note not to underestimate this striking woman. "Although Professor Angelchrist assures me as to the corporeal nature of the villain," he added.

Miss Hobbes smiled and placed her teacup gently on its saucer. "Oh, he exists, Mr Rutherford. I can very much attest to that."

Rutherford blew smoke from the corner of his mouth, watching as it was quickly dispersed on the frigid breeze. "The professor mentioned you'd had occasion to go up against Monsieur Zenith during your time in active service?"

Miss Hobbes laughed, and her face lit up in amusement. "He does have a way with understatement," she said.

"Indeed?" prompted Rutherford.

She sighed, indulgently. "One does not simply trifle with Zenith, Mr Rutherford. To him it's all a game, you see? All of it. He revels in the tête-à-tête. Once you engage, it becomes a battle of wits, a game of chess, played out across many years and many continents."

"And you, Miss Hobbes – you entered into this game with the albino?"

"I had little choice. Our paths crossed during an investigation, and he became… *intrigued* by me. In the years following the war, barely a month would go by without our meeting once again. His criminal activities were diverse and reckless, but never, ever, boring. Stolen works of art, voodoo cults, ancient curses, flesh golems and clockwork shop dummies – just a few of the nefarious schemes to which I found myself in opposition." Miss Hobbes paused as the waiter delivered her sandwich to the table. "Another pot of tea, please, waiter," she said, with a smile. "Earl Grey." She glanced at Rutherford. "I've developed something of a taste for it. It's all Maurice will ever drink."

Rutherford laughed. "And how did Sir Maurice feel about all of this attention you received from Monsieur Zenith?"

Miss Hobbes raised a single eyebrow. "Oh, Zenith was only ever interested in the game, Mr Rutherford. I just happened to be another of the players." She picked at her sandwich. "Over time, his interest waned. Perhaps I became predictable, too easy to anticipate? Now, I believe, he has engaged another playmate. Nevertheless, I often wonder if, perhaps one day, I shall hear from him again."

"I thought you had retired, Miss Hobbes," said Rutherford.

"People like us never retire, Mr Rutherford. We simply grow older, and slow down." She smiled. "Here comes your salad."

Rutherford stubbed out the remains of his cigarette as the waiter placed the plate on the table.

"I need to find him, Miss Hobbes," he said, once they were alone again.

"Yes, I daresay the Prime Minister has suffered a few sleepless nights of late," said Miss Hobbes, wryly.

Rutherford grinned, despite himself. "Yes, I daresay he has."

"I fear Monsieur Zenith is a wily devil, Mr Rutherford. He shall not be easy to find."

"I don't doubt it, Miss Hobbes. But do you know where I can even begin my search? You mentioned that Zenith has engaged another in his games."

Miss Hobbes grinned. "Indeed. There's a man, a detective, who lives on Baker Street." She reached for her handbag. "Let me give you his address."

IV

The detective reclined in his chair and regarded Rutherford appraisingly. He was handsome, with a square-set jaw, fine dark hair swept back from his forehead and the solid-looking physique of a boxer. He was dressed in an unassuming black suit, the collar left open while he relaxed by the fire. Rutherford felt a little uncomfortable beneath his penetrating gaze, but was nevertheless drawn to the man, who – he'd decided – was harbouring a fierce intelligence behind his piercing blue eyes.

A large bloodhound was curled up by his feet, and his housekeeper – a bumbling, rotund woman whose propensity for malapropisms, even in the scant few moments in which Rutherford had met her, seemed utterly at odds with the calm sophistication of her employer – was making tea.

He'd come here directly following his meeting with Miss Hobbes, on the off-chance that he'd find the detective at home, and much to his surprise he'd been admitted and ushered into the detective's consulting room. He sat there now, before the dying embers of a warming fire, studying the detective's face for any signs of a reaction. He had, moments earlier, imparted the news of Monsieur Zenith's threat to the Prime Minister.

"Zenith is a dangerous foe indeed, Mr Rutherford. You should watch your step," said the detective, folding his hands upon his lap. He was wearing a thoughtful expression.

Rutherford smiled. "I'm sure I've faced worse," he replied, without humour.

The detective shook his head. "I sincerely doubt that, Mr Rutherford. Zenith is dangerous because he cares little for his own existence. He lives only for the thrill of the chase. To him, all of this – life, criminality, danger – is a game. A game he insists he will win, at any cost, even his own life."

"You make him sound utterly insane," said Rutherford, weighing up the detective's words. They seemed to chime with the opinions expressed by Miss Hobbes earlier that morning. The portrait he was assembling of this albino prince was one of a deranged genius, intent on finding an exciting way in which to die.

"Not insane," replied the detective. "Simply bored. Weary of this world, and looking to fill his hours with excitement. He craves those things most others fear. He commits his crimes not for political or penury gain, but because he is searching for distraction, for thrills. When he is not being tested in such a way, he succumbs to a fatalistic state of ennui, and gives himself over to his favoured intoxication, opium."

"He's an opium eater?" asked Rutherford, surprised.

"Indeed. A most voracious one at that," replied the detective. "But do not let that fool you, Mr Rutherford. He is at his most dangerous when his mind is not distracted. That's when he cooks up his most diabolical schemes, his most dangerous endeavours. He will look to push himself ever closer to the precipice, raising the stakes, and in turn, the reward. The greater the danger, the bigger the thrill."

"You've faced him many times before?" asked Rutherford.

The detective laughed. "Oh yes, Mr Rutherford. On countless occasions. He might have killed me more than once, save for his unusual moral code and his desire not to forgo a worthy opponent. Zenith obeys only his own rules, and they are close to unfathomable."

"I see that I have my work cut out," said Rutherford, with a sigh. "But tell me, do you think he's serious?"

"In his threat to the Prime Minister?" The detective paused, and then his shoulders heaved in a resigned shrug. "Impossible to say. I find it hard to imagine what he could possibly hope to gain from such an undertaking, other than sheer amusement. I doubt he'll be considering murder – although he certainly has before. No, I imagine his scheme will be to somehow discredit the Prime Minister and force a resignation. Assuming, of course, that he even has anything on the man. It wouldn't be unlike Zenith to fake a controversy just to stir things up a little." The detective smiled wistfully.

"You sound as if you almost admire him," said Rutherford.

"Oh, I do, Mr Rutherford. In many ways. Yet in others I find him utterly despicable. I will, when the opportunity arises, take every measure to see him locked behind bars. My moral code is not as complex as the albino's, and while I recognise and perhaps even appreciate his genius, I still see, nevertheless, a criminal mind at work. One day he will overreach, and I will be there to catch him when he falls."

"You'll help me, then?" asked Rutherford. "You'll assist me in locating Monsieur Zenith and bringing this threat against the Prime Minister to an end?"

The detective sighed. "Alas, Mr Rutherford, I find myself entangled with a prior engagement, and one of equal importance to the security of the realm. The Master Mummer is once more afoot in London, and I'm working with the Yard to put a stop to his schemes. We believe he intends to cause a train to derail as it pulls into King's Cross Station, and to use the ensuing panic as cover for a transaction of some sort. As yet, we're not entirely sure as to the nature of that transaction, but I have a fear he's looking to smuggle one of his associates into the capital as part of some even bolder strategy." The detective met Rutherford's gaze. "Even now, the Yard is working to ascertain which train has been sabotaged and targeted. I may be called upon at any moment."

Rutherford nodded. "I quite understand," he said. "Your dedication to the protection of the nation does you credit. I see that your reputation is well earned."

The detective chuckled. "Perhaps." He reached for his briar pipe, which was resting on the arm of his chair. He watched Rutherford in silence for a moment. "I fear you are not yet fully aware of the danger you are facing, Mr Rutherford. Once you engage Zenith, you will be unable to disentangle yourself from his web. You will find yourself in the midst of a battle of wits, from which the only way out is to win. Unless, of course, he grows tired of you and sees to it that you are dead."

For the first time, Rutherford realised that the detective was actually afraid of the albino. He felt suddenly cold. "Nevertheless, I cannot put my own safety above that of the Prime Minister," said Rutherford, steadfastly. "I have a job to do."

The detective nodded, sucking on his pipe. "Very well, Mr Rutherford. I shall tell you what you need to know. As I explained, Zenith is a consummate opium eater. He keeps a Japanese manservant known as Oyani, and it is this man whom he charges with the maintenance of his addiction. Oyani will need a regular supply of the drug for his master. Therefore, if you wish to find Zenith, you need only look for the Japanese."

Rutherford smiled. He was sure the detective was making it sound simpler than it was, but this – finally – was the lead he'd been searching for. "My thanks to you," he said.

"Don't thank me yet," said the detective, quietly. "In time you may feel quite differently about the matter."

Rutherford sighed. He'd have to cross that bridge, he decided, when he came to it.

V

It had taken him three days to find the Japanese, three days during which there had been no more threats made to the Prime Minister via his private telephone line, but throughout which the politician had continued to press Major Absalom for any sign of progress.

Ever the diplomat, Absalom had assured the Prime Minister that Rutherford was on the trail of the villain, and that the matter would soon be brought to a close. The Major had then telephoned Rutherford in the dead of night to unleash his own barrage of threats, berating him for his failure to locate the man whom Absalom himself considered to be nothing more than a myth. As Rutherford had discovered, however, his superior did not take kindly to being reminded of this fact, which, of course, he now deemed to be utterly inconsequential.

Thankfully, the newspapers were yet to get hold of the story, and so it only remained – so Absalom had put it – for Rutherford to bring the matter to a swift conclusion. Locating Zenith had now become Rutherford's sole aim. He had barely been home in the last week, and he could feel the pressure of the situation bearing down on him like a pressing weight upon his shoulders. He could almost sense Absalom's whiskered presence looming over his shoulder, watching him as he worked.

Thankfully, the detective's steer had proved to be a good one, although the consequent tour of London's less than salubrious establishments of intoxication – the Chinese-operated opium dens – had been a taxing and largely unrewarding business. Rutherford's questions had led him to become embroiled in two brawls, and at least one attempt had been made on his life as he'd lounged on a divan in a place called "Johnny Chang's", pretending to be lost in an opium dream while in fact keeping a watchful eye on the comings and goings of the clientele. The would-be assassin had been nothing but a child – a Chinese boy in the employ of the owners of the house, charged with despatching any unwanted visitors and making off with their wallets. Rutherford had shown the boy the back of his hand, before making a swift exit from the establishment in question.

Finally, however, the net was closing on Monsieur Zenith. From where he now sat, lounging upon a daybed in the semi-darkness and beneath a fog of thick, sweet-smelling smoke,

Rutherford could see the little Japanese manservant deep in conversation with one of the Chinese attendants. If Oyani knew he was being watched he gave no outward sign of it, continuing with his master's business – the procurement of a new supply of opium – quite readily.

Rutherford had been forced to make a pact with the devil in order to secure this trap. The owner of the house – Meng Li – was one of the most notorious Chinese crime lords in the Empire, and his men had identified Rutherford as an agent within minutes of him entering the iniquitous den. This, in itself, had not surprised Rutherford, but the fact that Meng Li himself had chosen to pay him a visit was more cause for astonishment. Not only that, but the man had seemed to know all about Rutherford's search for the Japanese manservant of Monsieur Zenith.

"You search for Oyani, whose master is the white ghost, he of pale flesh and crimson eyes," Meng Li had said, standing over Rutherford as he reclined on the daybed, feigning delirium. To Rutherford the crime lord himself had appeared somewhat wraith-like, with sunken eyes, jaundiced skin and a long, dripping moustache and beard. His flowing silken robes skimmed the floor as he moved, giving the impression he was floating on a carpet of billowing opium smoke. It was impossible to discern his age from his appearance, but his voice spoke of untold decades, perhaps longer.

"I do," Rutherford had responded, knowing that lying to this man was in no way an option. He would have been dead before he had finished his sentence.

"Then I can help you, Mr Rutherford, in your quest," Meng Li had continued, with a smile, "for a price."

"Name it," Rutherford had said, perhaps even then knowing that he was involving himself in something decidedly inadvisable.

"Only that I may call upon you, Mr Rutherford, if I should

find myself with need to," Meng Li had said, in a tone so reasonable that Rutherford had almost missed his meaning. *Quid pro quo.* If he chose to accept this man's help, he would be in his debt. That, in itself, might prove to be deadly. But what choice did he have?

"I accept your offer," Rutherford had replied, with a bow of his head.

"Very wise, Mr Rutherford. The hand of Meng Li, once extended, is not to be shunned," the crime lord had said, with a broad grin. "Now, let us speak of Oyani."

So it was that Rutherford had been granted leave to lay in wait for the manservant for what transpired to be his daily visit to the opium den. Now, only a few hours later, he watched as Oyani concluded his business, slipping the small package of opium into the folds of his coat and handing over a sheaf of notes.

Rutherford made ready to follow him, gathering his coat and checking his revolver in his pocket. With luck, the Japanese would finally lead him to Zenith.

As yet, Rutherford had no idea what he would do when he found him.

VI

Oyani had travelled on foot, and as such had proved relatively easy to trail. He'd made little attempt at concealment, and Rutherford had kept to the shadows, keeping pace with the manservant, but at enough of a distance that Oyani would not – he hoped – become aware of his presence.

They had crossed town for at least two miles before arriving at St. John's Wood, ducking down unfamiliar side streets and alleyways, at one point taking a short cut across a small, leafy park.

Eventually, Oyani had come to a stop before a large

Georgian building that bore the legend *BROUGHAM MANSIONS* on a small, brass plaque. It was an impressive edifice that had clearly once been the home of a well-to-do sophisticate, but had now been broken up into a series of luxury apartments. Zenith, Rutherford considered, must have taken up temporary residence in one such apartment.

Rutherford watched from behind a tree on the other side of the road as Oyani dug around in his pocket for a key, slipped it into the lock and opened the door to the foyer. He disappeared inside.

Moments passed. Rutherford hesitated, trying to decide on the best course of action, and then, just as he was about to step out from behind the boughs of the great oak, Oyani appeared once again in the doorway. The manservant glanced from side to side, shrugged, and then announced, loudly to the street at large: "Won't you come in, Mr Rutherford? You are, after all, expected."

Rutherford bristled with shock. *Expected?* But... how did Oyani know Rutherford's name? Or that he'd been followed here? Had the Chinese attendant tipped the manservant off, back in the opium den? Rutherford tried to think on his feet. What should he do?

"Monsieur Zenith awaits you in the drawing room," said Oyani, and Rutherford knew, then, that he had been outplayed. The game had already begun, and Rutherford was already one move behind.

He took a deep breath, forcing himself to remain calm and level-headed. He stepped out from behind the tree. "Thank you, Oyani," he said, with a smile. "Tell your master I should be only too pleased to join him."

Oyani bowed, and then disappeared inside once more, leaving the door hanging open for Rutherford.

So, this was it. Behind that door was the man he had heard so much about, the man who had threatened the Prime Minister, and who many – including the head of the Secret Service – believed to be nothing more than a phantom, a ridiculous myth. Rutherford knew now, beyond a shadow of a doubt, that he was dealing with a man of absolute genius, a master manipulator; a man so adept at managing his reputation that he'd been able to construct an entire mythology around his very existence.

Rutherford took a deep breath, and then set out to meet him.

As he crossed the road and approached the door, he became aware of the strains of a violin emanating from one of the first-floor apartments, a soulful lament, played by an exceptional hand. He followed the sound, through the grandiose entrance hall, up the immense central staircase and towards an open door that led into one of the apartments. Steeling himself, he stepped inside.

Oyani was waiting to greet him, and wordlessly ushered him on into the drawing room. He slipped his hand into his pocket, feeling the comforting butt of his revolver against his palm.

The room was dressed after the appearance of its owner: in swathes of ebony and startling white. The floor was laid in a chequerboard of alternating black and white marble, whilst the walls were washed in brilliant white paint. Black drapes hung across the window, and a low divan sat in the centre of the room, covered in a crimson throw. A tall, gilt-framed mirror hung above the fireplace, in which leaping flames licked gently at a wooden log.

Monsieur Zenith himself stood with his back to Rutherford, dressed from collar to toe in immaculate black, his right arm moving slowly back and forth with the ebb and tide of the strains of his violin.

Rutherford sensed the door closing behind him as Oyani retreated, leaving him alone in the room with the albino.

"Don't you think it's sublime how a simple phrase on the violin can describe such exquisite pain?" said Zenith, his voice a low, epicurean drawl.

Rutherford remained silent, studying Monsieur Zenith's back. His grip tightened on the revolver in his pocket. After a moment, the violin playing ceased.

"Oh, do put the gun down, Mr Rutherford. You shan't be needing it," said the albino, pompously. "I should consider it very bad manners indeed if you were to shoot me on our first date." He turned then, glancing back over his shoulder, and Rutherford was granted his first proper glance at the albino's face.

He was stunningly handsome, with a profile that might have been hewn from the purest Carrara marble. His thin, sensuous lips were drawn in a tight smile, and his eyes were orbs of the deepest crimson. His white hair was short and swept back from his forehead, and he was dressed in pristine evening wear – a black suit and velvet cape, with a red silk cravat – even at this time in the mid-afternoon.

"I'm here–"

"I know why you're here," said Zenith, cutting him off abruptly. He lowered his violin and bow, placing them on a lacquered sideboard before turning and crossing the room. He flicked his cape out behind him and dropped onto the divan, stretching out like a supine cat. At no point did his gaze leave Rutherford's face. "But let's not talk of such prosaic matters, Mr Rutherford. Let us get to know each other a little, first of all."

Rutherford sighed, withdrawing his hand from his pocket. He glanced behind him, located a high-backed chair and dropped into it. "You cast a long shadow, Monsieur Zenith," said Rutherford, calmly.

"For one so pale?" replied Zenith, wryly. "Yes, I understand you've heard the testimony of a number of my acquaintances.

And yet still you came. I find this… most satisfactory."

Rutherford must have frowned, because Zenith allowed himself an amused smile.

"Am I not everything you expected, Mr Rutherford? Do I disappoint?"

Rutherford hardly knew how to respond. "I have yet to form a full and proper opinion, Monsieur," he replied, levelly.

Zenith laughed, and his long eyelashes flickered. "Quite so. I do enjoy it when people are honest with one another. Don't you? Saves all that ridiculous posturing."

"Then allow me to ask you an honest question, Monsieur."

"Be my guest."

"Why? Why threaten the Prime Minister?"

"Oh, this again," said Zenith, waving his hand and affecting an air of disinterest. "Why not?" he said, in response.

"But what could you possibly hope to gain? Was it blackmail you had in mind?"

"Nothing so prosaic, Mr Rutherford." Zenith looked him in the eye. "If we're still being honest with one another, perhaps it's time I confessed. I never had any intention of seeing it through. The threat to the Prime Minister was a bluff, a flippant sham, a fake." He laughed. "Does that surprise you?"

"No," said Rutherford. "No, it doesn't surprise me. But it nevertheless intrigues me. I still wish to know why."

Zenith smiled again. "Excellent. I see, Mr Rutherford, that you shall do quite well."

Rutherford felt his heart skip a beat. "I beg your pardon?"

"I'm bored, Mr Rutherford. Peter. I can call you Peter?" Rutherford nodded his assent. "My detective friend is otherwise engaged, and I find myself in need of… company."

"You have Oyani," said Rutherford.

"Ah, but I require a very particular sort of company, Peter. You see – this world, I find, is a dreary place, when all is said and done. I need a companion who can offer a diversion, a distraction from the tiresome, day-to-day business of living."

"A plaything, you mean?" asked Rutherford, harshly.

"Not at all," said Zenith, with a conciliatory tone. "That's quite the point. Rather someone who might offer up a challenge, who might present at least a modicum of intelligence."

"So… your scheme, the reason for your threatening telephone call to the Prime Minister – it was all to draw someone out, bait for a new opponent for your infernal games?"

Zenith sighed contentedly. "And you answered the call with perfect aplomb."

Rutherford swallowed. His mouth was dry. So all of this – all of those conversations with Angelchrist, Miss Hobbes and the detective, his parley with Meng Li – all of it had been a kind of extended job interview, a test by which Zenith might identify his latest opponent in the grand game of his life. By finding him, by following Oyani here, Rutherford had effectively volunteered himself for the position. "What if I do not agree to this risible business?" he asked.

"Then, of course, your precious Prime Minister will find his darkest secrets spread across the evening headlines."

"So I'm to become a sacrificial lamb?"

"Oh, don't look at it like that, Peter. We'll have fun, you and I. Two kings commanding our legions of knights and pawns, each trying to stay one step ahead of the other." Zenith swung his legs down from the divan, pulling himself up into a sitting position. "So, Peter. Do we have an understanding?"

"I don't see that I have any choice," said Rutherford, resignedly. "Unless, of course, I reach for my revolver and shoot you now."

Zenith scowled. "I should hope you would not prove so uncouth," he said, standing. "You'd make a terrible mess of the décor."

Rutherford laughed. In spite of everything, he was strangely attracted to this most unusual of criminals. "We have an understanding, then," he said. "The Prime Minister will rest easily tonight."

"Oh, I shouldn't have thought so," said Zenith. "Not knowing the sorts of things he gets up to after nightfall."

The door opened, and Rutherford turned to see Oyani waiting in the hallway to show him out.

"Until we meet again, then, Peter," said Zenith, extending his hand. Rutherford took it and held it for a moment. It was surprisingly warm.

"Good day, Monsieur Zenith," he said, and then turned and followed Oyani to the door.

VII

The red telephone box stood like a bright sentinel on the street corner, the herald of a new age. Rutherford smiled to himself as he opened the door and stepped inside, regarding the primitive machinery before him, all dials and coiled cabling. He'd spent time in New York a few years earlier – during the height of the tensions with the former colony – and the holotube technology the Americans had developed quite outstripped the more traditional telephony system still in place across England. Nevertheless, it would suffice for his needs.

He lifted the receiver to his ear. "Operator? Yes, Whitehall 1212, please. Thank you."

The telephone buzzed at the other end. After a moment, it clicked, and a woman's voice spoke on the other end. "Yes?"

"Hello, Ginny. It's Peter. I need to speak with Absalom," he said. The woman was Absalom's secretary, Ginny Roberts.

A pause. And then: "I'm afraid he's busy, Peter. In with the PM. He's not accepting calls."

"He'll want to accept this one, Ginny. Trust me."

"Sorry Peter. No can do." She sighed. "You know how he is." she said, apologetically.

"Very well. Can you give him a message for me, then?"

"Of course."

"Can you tell him the threat to the PM has been eliminated?"

"Yes. I'll tell him right away." She paused again. "Is everything quite well, Peter?"

"Yes, everything's fine, Ginny. Don't worry. Just pass on the message for me, if you will."

"Yes, I will. 'The threat to the PM has been eliminated'," she parroted. "Good job, Peter."

"Thank you, Ginny. See you later?"

"Not tonight, Peter. I'm off early for the weekend. Going dancing with Eve."

Rutherford laughed at the sheer normality of it all. "Well, you have a good time, Ginny. Watch out for yourself."

"Goodbye, Peter."

"Goodbye." He replaced the receiver and leaned back against the inside of the telephone box. His heart was hammering frantically in his chest. It was over. The job was done. The Prime Minister could sleep safely in his bed.

For Rutherford, however, it was only just beginning. The game was afoot, and he had no idea when, or how, Zenith would make the next move. The strange thing was... he actually found himself relishing the idea. The notion of meeting with such a remarkable character again filled him with a thrill of anticipation. He remembered the words of Miss Veronica Hobbes, spoken in the restaurant just a few days earlier: "His criminal activities were diverse and reckless, but never, ever, boring."

To Rutherford, there was promise in those words.

Rutherford pushed open the door of the telephone box and stepped out into the brisk afternoon. He turned his collar up against the chill, and started off down the road. He would catch a cab back to Whitehall, where he'd offer Absalom just enough of the facts to put the Major's mind at rest.

Then, he decided, he might see about a game of chess at his club. After all, he was going to have to get some practice.

OLD FRIENDS

LONDON, DECEMBER 1933

"Good morning, Professor."

Rutherford leaned back against his car door, watching as the two men – the aged Professor Angelchrist and his immaculately dressed butler – traversed the path to the end of the garden. Their steps were tentative and steady, and Angelchrist was leaning heavily on his ebony cane, his exhalations forming ghostly shapes in the chill winter air. Late morning sunlight was slanting through the overhanging branches of a nearby oak tree, dappling the frosty path. The ice crystals twinkled like diamonds scattered haphazardly across the ground.

'And a good morning to you, Mr Rutherford," replied Angelchrist, glancing up for a moment from where he'd been carefully following his own steps. "This is a... unexpected pleasure."

Rutherford grinned. He reached into his pocket, his fingers closing on his silver cigarette case. He half extracted it before changing his mind and allowing it to fall back into place. "I thought you might enjoy a short drive," he said, non-committally.

'Did you indeed?" said Angelchrist, with a knowing smile. Clearly, he suspected an ulterior motive. The old man was still sharp, and Rutherford had to suppress another grin. "Well, I don't suppose it could do any harm, now that I'm up and about." He'd reached the front gate of his property and rested there for a moment, his hand on the stone gatepost. He was wrapped in a warm winter overcoat and was wearing a bowler hat and black leather gloves. He was labouring slightly for breath, and Rutherford wondered how long it had been since he'd last left the house. He hoped the trip wouldn't be too much for the old man.

Rutherford pushed himself away from the car and smoothed down the front of his coat. He walked around the vehicle and popped open the passenger door. "If you need some more time…?" he said.

"Nonsense," said Angelchrist, with a dismissive wave of his hand. "I'm quite ready, Mr Rutherford." He pushed himself away from the gatepost, shrugging off the concerned hands of his butler, who was fussing around him, trying to take his elbow in order to prevent a fall. "I must admit, I'm rather intrigued about the true purpose of your visit."

Rutherford laughed. Angelchrist was as direct and to the point as ever. He chose not to respond to the comment as he watched Angelchrist cross the pavement towards the waiting car.

"A most unusual conveyance, Mr Rutherford," said Angelchrist a moment later, as he lowered himself heavily into the passenger seat.

Rutherford closed the door and circled the back of the car, sliding easily into the driver's seat. "It's a recent model," he said, twisting the key in the ignition and causing the throttle to choke and splutter, until the engine finally bit, roaring noisily to life. "It's powered by oil rather than coal."

"Remarkable," replied Angelchrist, with a raised eyebrow. He propped his walking stick against the dashboard and fastened his seatbelt. "I do miss my dear old motor car," he said, wistfully. "We had some adventures together, let me tell you. She proved a reliable friend for many years. Although she was never quite the same after that incident with the Squall." He paused for a moment, reflecting. "Mind you, neither was I."

"The Squall?" asked Rutherford, absently, glancing in the wing mirror.

"Horrible, bat-like things, they were, and they really did give us a run for our money. That was – what, more than twenty years ago now. Seems like a lifetime."

Rutherford had never heard this tale before, and was tempted to press Angelchrist for the full story. But it would have to wait for another occasion. They were already running behind.

He glanced out of the window at the butler, who was standing like a bemused sentry at the gate. Rutherford offered him a quick wave, before releasing the handbrake and easing his foot down on the accelerator.

The car purred away from the kerb. Snowflakes had begun to flutter on the breeze, and they dashed themselves against the windscreen with desperate abandon. Rutherford watched them disintegrate where they fell, before sweeping them away with a flick of the wiper blades.

"How are you, Professor?" he asked, once he'd finished swinging the vehicle around in a U-turn in order to head back towards Central London.

"Tired, Mr Rutherford. And old. But I admit, you've piqued my interest." He glanced sidelong at Rutherford, who kept his eyes fixed firmly on the road ahead. "What is the purpose of this little outing?"

"I was hoping you could tell me more about Sir Charles Bainbridge," said Rutherford, levelly.

"Aha! I knew you had an ulterior motive for dragging me out of the house!" said Angelchrist, laughing. "What is it you're getting at? What do you wish to know?"

"I'm interested in hearing more about your friendship," said Rutherford, "how you met Sir Charles, and likewise, Sir Maurice and Miss Hobbes."

"May I enquire as to why?" said Angelchrist, although it was clear from his tone that he was not in any way put out by Rutherford's questioning. He was an old hand at interrogation and the ways of the Service, and he appeared more amused than perturbed. Besides, Rutherford imagined it provided him a rare opportunity to talk.

"Let's call it... idle curiosity," replied Rutherford. "I'm sure everything will become clear. I'd ask that you indulge me for just a little longer."

"Very well," said Angelchrist, amused. "I'll play along with your little game, Mr Rutherford. But let me be clear – my relationship with the people you mentioned did not begin with friendship."

"It didn't?" said Rutherford, frowning. "I understood you were firm friends for many years. When we spoke about the matter of the Maharajah's Star–"

Angelchrist held up a hand to silence him. "I said it didn't begin with friendship, Mr Rutherford. That came a little later. At first things were fairly antagonistic between us, particularly between myself and Miss Hobbes. I represented an unknown quantity, you see. Perhaps even a threat."

"A threat?" queried Rutherford.

Angelchrist nodded. "In 1902 the Secret Service was a fledgling operation. Sir Charles had been brought in to consult for the Home Secretary, but I was the man charged with actually putting the team together. There was a great deal of ill feeling amongst the Crown agents, who were suspicious of our motives. They thought we were looking to usurp them. Even the Queen herself worked to fuel their discontent. She turned us into enemies."

"For what purpose?"

"To undermine us. To stunt the growth of our organisation. You must remember that the climate was one of utter paranoia. The Queen held sway over an absolute autocracy, and she feared the Secret Service was an attempt by the government to make a grab for power. So she turned her agents against us, instructed them to block us at every turn. She tried to make enemies out of us in order to protect her own interests."

"So… you and Sir Charles were on opposing sides?" said Rutherford, intrigued.

"So the Queen would have had it. In truth, Charles never accepted her position on the matter. He was the first to come round, when he saw the good work we were doing. It was around this time that he'd begun to question the motivations of the monarch and to see the value in an independent network of agents. Of course, we were not entirely without prejudice ourselves, but we certainly had the best interests of the nation at heart. Charles and I became staunch allies, despite the Queen's insistence to the contrary, and soon after we developed into firm friends."

"What of Sir Maurice, then?" asked Rutherford.

"Newbury trusted Charles. It's as simple as that. And, I suppose, he too saw evidence of our good work. He welcomed me into their circle, and before long I was visiting Newbury's Chelsea home to while away long evenings with him and Charles," said Angelchrist, with a distant smile.

"But Miss Hobbes was much less forthcoming?" said Rutherford, echoing Angelchrist's earlier statement. He was surprised by this news; in his – admittedly limited – experience, Miss Hobbes had always proved perfectly charming and approachable.

"Indeed," said Angelchrist, "although I cannot blame her. It was my fault, you see. I didn't give the woman enough credit. I didn't deem it appropriate to include her. And so her suspicions found fertile ground in my evasiveness, and she feared I was involving her friends in nefarious schemes – schemes, in fact, that might endanger their lives and risk the retribution of the monarch." He sighed. "It is one of my biggest regrets, Mr Rutherford, that those suspicions led Miss Hobbes into harm's way. Had she died, I might never have been able to live with myself."

"You're talking about the Executioner?" asked Rutherford, softly. He'd read the reports of the time, of how a murderess had run rampant through the capital, executing Crown agents and excising their hearts as grisly trophies. Miss Hobbes had been her final victim.

Angelchrist nodded. He was silent for a moment, and Rutherford was unsure whether he was avoiding further discourse on the topic, or simply ordering his thoughts. "So, you know of the Executioner," he said, a moment later. "Then you understand that Miss Hobbes had good reason to distrust me. In her eyes I was largely responsible for what became of her."

Rutherford eased on the brake as they approached a junction, and then took a right turn, exiting onto a broad, empty road. The surface was dusted with fresh, white snow. He gunned the accelerator and moved away, steadying the wheel with both hands as the tyres slipped on the wet road. "But reparations were eventually made?" he said.

"Yes. It was during that business with the Undying that Miss Hobbes and I finally came to an understanding," said Angelchrist, seemingly happy with the more positive direction the conversation was taking.

"Go on," prompted Rutherford.

Angelchrist glanced across at him. "Are you aware of the Undying, Mr Rutherford?"

Rutherford shook his head.

"Then what I'm about to tell you may be quite disturbing. I know already that I am able to rely on your discretion," said Angelchrist, pointedly.

"Of course," said Rutherford, intrigued.

"Very well. You may already be aware that my family has a... dark and chequered past?"

Rutherford shook his head again, keeping his eyes on the road. 'No. I wasn't aware of that."

Angelchrist chuckled quietly to himself. "I come from a long line of peers, many of whom were known to have indulged in somewhat dubious practices. Back in 1902, my last surviving relative – an uncle – passed away of natural causes, leaving me to inherit the family seat, an old pile up in Oxfordshire."

"You own an estate in Oxfordshire?" said Rutherford, surprised.

"I once did. I long ago donated it to a far more worthy cause. At the time, however, I was quite taken with the notion of living out my dotage in a place like that." Angelchrist laughed. "I moved in with the idea of weekending at the house, remodelling it to suit my needs. I'd thought to spend my week in London, in a rented flat, and to use the old house as a place to escape to when time and duty permitted. The house itself was relatively sound – for a fifteenth-century mansion – but the grounds had been left to go to wrack and ruin. I began my renovations by having the woods cut back and the lake dredged and reshaped."

"And I'd wager you found something unexpected?" prompted Rutherford.

Angelchrist gave him a sly look. "Quite so, Mr Rutherford. A hansom carriage at the bottom of the mere."

"A hansom carriage?" repeated Rutherford.

"Indeed. With some surprising – and somewhat grisly – cargo on board."

"A corpse?"

"In a manner of speaking. The remains of an unidentifiable creature," said Angelchrist.

"Due to its condition?" asked Rutherford.

"No. Although I grant you, it had clearly been there for some time. More because it appeared to have some... human qualities, but was taller and broader than a man, with long bony protrusions along its spine and sharp, black talons at the tips of its fingers. It appeared that the hansom had been pushed into the mere with the corpse already in the back."

"With a view to concealing it," Rutherford surmised.

"Quite so," said Angelchrist. "Well, I sent directly for Newbury. As you know, he's something of an expert when it comes to such things."

"Was he able to establish the true nature of the corpse?" said Rutherford, glancing over at his passenger. Angelchrist was staring thoughtfully out of the window, seeing ghosts in the snow.

"He came immediately, on the very next train, bringing Sir Charles and Miss Hobbes along with him. He donned a diving suit and went down to the wreck, but found nothing further of note. He could not identify the creature, but knew of a man in London who might help; a zoologist at the Natural History Museum who specialised in the study of unusual or previously unrecorded beasts. We had the remains moved forthwith, and the very next day we followed them back to the capital." Angelchrist was toying with his cane, rolling it back and forth between his palms as he recalled the details of his tale.

"Well, the findings were quite remarkable," he continued. "Newbury's specialist – a Mr John Farrowdene – proved that the creature was, in fact, human. The evidence was irrefutable. The young man – victim, volunteer, I do not know – had been so altered through surgery and selective breeding that he was barely recognisable as a man at all. What was more, this wasn't the first example of its kind the zoologist had seen; there were at least two others like it, and he showed us what was left of them, stored in a taxidermist's room deep in the bowels of the museum."

"Who could have done such a thing?" said Rutherford, disgusted by the very idea.

"I'm surprised you need to ask, Mr Rutherford. It transpired the creatures were the result of an abominable eugenics programme sponsored by the Queen. The surgeons in question had been experimenting with life extension, and with the weaponising of human beings. The programme had been deemed a failure, however, and had been shut down a couple of years earlier. What the Queen and her cronies didn't know, of course, is that a number of the test subjects had escaped into the sewer systems beneath London, where they'd formed a bizarre and primitive community. They'd begun to breed amongst themselves."

"Good Lord," said Rutherford, shaking his head. He'd known that Queen Victoria had, in her later years, begun to pursue all manner of increasingly desperate avenues to combat her degenerative condition, but experimenting on her own people in such a way... it seemed so barbaric. "And the hansom cab? Why had it been dumped at the bottom of your family's mere?"

"Ah," said Angelchrist. "It seems my late uncle had been somehow involved in establishing the aforementioned programme for the Queen. The corpse in the hansom was – he believed – the last evidence of their gruesome experimentation. A most inefficient means of covering his tracks, but then he always was an arrogant blighter."

Rutherford flicked the lever behind the steering wheel to increase the frequency of the windscreen wipers; the flurry of snow was now making it difficult to see. He leaned forward, peering out of the windscreen. "So, what was it about this particular matter that helped to bring you and Miss Hobbes to an understanding?" he said.

Angelchrist laughed again. "Danger, Mr Rutherford. It's

surprising what being trapped together in the sewers by a horde of mutants can do for your relationship with a lady."

"You went down there?" said Rutherford.

"We did," replied Angelchrist, "and discovered an entire colony of the creatures. At first they proved damn hostile, too – particularly after Charles attacked one of them with his cane."

"A colony? Right there beneath the capital?" Rutherford tried unsuccessfully to keep the incredulity out of his voice.

"Quite so. At least thirty or forty of the creatures, living in squalor amongst the dank, foetid tunnels down there. They'd built a kind of shanty town from scavenged materials, huts and hammocks and the like. They separated us and dragged us to holding pens, such as the kind one might imagine would be employed by those uncivilised natives of the Amazon basin. Miss Hobbes and I were held in one pen, while Charles and Newbury were held in two others." Angelchrist chuckled. "To be honest with you, Mr Rutherford, we all thought the game was up. The creatures were so strong and determined. There was little hope of effecting an escape. So, with nothing else to do, I used the opportunity to make my peace with Miss Hobbes."

Rutherford nodded. He'd been in similar situations himself, and he recognised the impulse – or rather the need – to set things right before it was too late. "What happened?" he asked.

"Newbury," said Angelchrist. "Newbury happened. He was so calm and collected, even in the direst of situations. He established that, despite all indications to the contrary, the creatures still understood English. And he reasoned with them. He made a deal. He explained who we were and that we represented no real harm."

"They accepted his word?" said Rutherford, incredulous.

"They might have been creatures, Mr Rutherford, but they

were not monsters, despite their appearance. Newbury made it clear to them that we would protect their secret; we would not report our findings, and their underground home would not be disturbed. They allowed us to walk free." Angelchrist sighed, leaning back in his seat. "And as far as I'm aware, none of us ever did repeal our word. We never spoke of it again, not even amongst ourselves."

"So they're still there, down beneath us now?" said Rutherford.

"Quite possibly," replied Angelchrist, levelly. "I've heard reports over the years, sightings of 'bogeymen' in the sewers or alleyways of the city, and I admit to you, I've taken heart from such things. It gives me hope that their colony is still alive and flourishing. After everything that was done to those people, it is the least we can hope for."

"And Sir Charles, Sir Maurice and Miss Hobbes? What happened next?"

"They all became very dear friends. We had many adventures together over the years. I've never known a finer group of people. A family, really. Although... it's been a while..."

"When was the last time you saw any of them?" asked Rutherford.

"Too long. Years," replied Angelchrist, his voice cracking. "You know how it is, Mr Rutherford. Time has a habit of running away with you. Before you know it, years have passed. You've been so absorbed in your own small corner of the universe that you've drifted apart from your friends, and you barely noticed that they'd stopped calling. We were all so busy trying to save the world..." He trailed off, unwilling or unable to continue.

The two men remained silent for a time, drifting on through the deserted streets of the capital. The snowstorm had gathered momentum now, and the view through the car windscreen was a chaotic haze of fluttering white. They turned a corner, and then – swerving to avoid another, oncoming car – Rutherford slowed and gradually drew the vehicle to a stop outside a large Victorian terraced house.

"We're here," said Rutherford, quietly.

Angelchrist frowned and leaned over, peering out through the driver's side window. He narrowed his eyes, as if straining to see through the blizzard. "But... I recognise this house. This is... it's Charles Bainbridge's house!" He glanced quizzically at Rutherford. "Why have you brought me here? After all this time?" He sounded confused, as if he'd been caught off guard. "I don't understand."

Rutherford smiled. "You said yourself it had been too long, Professor. Now's your chance to put that right. Your friends are waiting for you inside."

"Friends? You mean...?"

"Sir Charles, Sir Maurice and Miss Hobbes, yes," said Rutherford. "All of them. You're expected."

Angelchrist issued a long, contented sigh. He searched Rutherford's face, unable to suppress his joy. Slowly, the corners of his mouth twitched until a wide grin was playing across his face. "But why?"

"Merry Christmas, Professor," said Rutherford. He reached for the handle and popped open the door, shivering as flecks of snow swirled in on an eddy, spotting his face and arm. He climbed out, his feet crunching on the newly settled snow. Angelchrist was clambering out of the vehicle on the passenger side. Rutherford glanced up at the house; saw the shadowy forms of three people standing in the bay window, watching. He raised a hand in salute.

"Are you joining us, Mr Rutherford?" asked Angelchrist, coming to stand beside him, looking up fondly at the figures hovering in the window. "I'm sure you'd be more than welcome."

"Oh, no," replied Rutherford, taking a step back towards

his car. "I wouldn't be able to keep up."

Angelchrist laughed. He put a hand on Rutherford's shoulder. "Thank you," he said. "Thank you so very much."

Rutherford nodded, and then turned and slid back into the driver's seat, pulling the door shut behind him. He watched for a moment as Angelchrist trudged carefully towards the house, leaning on his cane. The door was open now, warm light spilling out across the street.

Grinning, Rutherford turned the key in the ignition, gunned the engine, and quietly steered the car away into the snowy afternoon.

A TIMELINE OF THE
NEWBURY & HOBBES UNIVERSE

1930s   A Night, Remembered
The Maharajah's Star
The Albino's Shadow
Old Friends

STORY NOTES

(The following story notes assume readers have already read the stories included in this volume, and include spoilers.)

THE DARK PATH

I've wanted to explore the story of Newbury's previous assistant, Templeton Black, for some time. Templeton's death at Fairview House is one of Newbury's biggest regrets, one of the things that defines him, and every mention of Templeton so far has been focused on the way he died.

When it came to deciding on the contents for this collection, I knew I wanted to open with something new, and that seemed like the perfect opportunity to bring Templeton properly to life, to give him an opportunity to shine. "The Dark Path" is his story, really. Newbury serves as a catalyst, but Templeton's the one who saves the day. His relationship with Newbury is very different to Veronica's, almost a role reversal, with Templeton being the louche, boozy, seat-of-the-pants sort of guy, and Newbury being the more staid, professional one.

The story itself is a mirror of Newbury's own fascination

with the occult, and foreshadows the path he eventually takes himself. There'll be more to come from Templeton in the future.

THE HAMBLETON AFFAIR

This is the first Newbury & Hobbes short story I ever wrote, and it's an early indicator of the different directions I've always planned to take with the stories.

I started writing this within half an hour of finishing *The Affinity Bridge*. I think I was so fired up from finishing my first full-length novel that I didn't want to stop. The case is referenced in the closing pages of the novel, and I essentially just picked up the conversation between Newbury and Bainbridge from that point and ran with it. I suppose it's a bit of a twisted love story, really, recited by Newbury long after the event. At the time it felt like quite a different type of tale for Newbury, *sans* Bainbridge and Veronica, and I guess I was testing the format a bit. It appeared in the UK limited edition hardback of *The Affinity Bridge* as a bonus story.

THE SHATTERED TEACUP

This was the first of a number of Christmas stories I've written for Newbury and the gang.

What I consider to be a "traditional Christmas" is essentially Victorian – plum puddings, mistletoe, presents under the tree – the fault, I think, of Charles Dickens, who popularised many of these notions with his Christmas stories. It's become a bit of tradition for me, too, to write a Newbury & Hobbes story at Christmas time.

This one was originally written to go inside a Christmas card, which was sent to my friends and family. There's a gag hidden in the story, too – an ongoing friendly rivalry with my brother, Scott, over who can outdo the other by referencing a story from our youth – about a shattered mug. Go and watch his movie, *The Tournament*, if you want to see how he got me back.

WHAT LIES BENEATH

I don't think I'll ever stop experimenting with ways to tell different Newbury & Hobbes stories, and this was one of the first. It's told in an epistolary format, but the twist (and I'm assuming you're reading these notes *after* you've read the stories) is that the letters are all being written to the corpse of their author's murdered wife. I've always been intrigued by epistolary stories, and there's another, of sorts, later in the books.

I think this was the first Newbury & Hobbes story not to feature any steampunk or fantastical elements – it's a simple horror story about a man's jealousy and dangerous obsession with his wife.

THE LADY KILLER

In some ways this is the newest story in the collection, but in others it's one of the oldest, too. The mysterious spy, "Lady Arkwell" – or Clarissa Karswell, as Newbury comes to know her – was born out of a desire to have a recurring sparring partner for Newbury, someone who could turn up in a number of stories and mix things up a little bit between Newbury and Veronica.

This, really, is Clarissa's origin story, and I wrote the first half of it a couple of years ago, before shelving it to get on with what I was really supposed to be doing – writing the new novel. It sat there for some time, although references to Lady Arkwell started to show up in other stories, almost as if I was unconsciously seeding her into the saga.

Again, when it came time to decide which stories to include

in this book, this one seemed like a natural choice, so I went right back to the start of Clarissa's tale and started over. This story is the result. It won't be the last we see of Clarissa Karswell.

THE CASE OF THE NIGHT CRAWLER

If you hadn't realised by now, I'm a huge fan of Sherlock Holmes. I can't recall the genesis of this story, other than the fact I'd always wanted to dabble with a Holmes story, and couldn't resist making it a crossover – something I'd later go on to explore in more depth in my Sherlock Holmes novel, *The Will of the Dead*, which features Bainbridge as a main character.

The story was originally written for a convention chapbook for Teslacon, and revised for inclusion in my *Encounters of Sherlock Holmes* anthology.

It was a great deal of fun to have Watson team up with Newbury and Veronica instead of Holmes, but to make sure Holmes was there in the background, pulling the strings, circling Newbury as a bit of a rival. Watson ends the story thinking he's finally got one over on Holmes, but Holmes, of course, knew what was going on all along, and just wanted to make sure he was free to attend a violin concerto.

THE SACRIFICIAL PAWN

This story serves as a prologue, of sorts, to the fourth novel in the series, *The Executioner's Heart*. In that book, Newbury has managed to obtain a rare and dangerous book of ritual magic, *The Cosmology of the Spirit*, which he's using to "heal" Veronica's clairvoyant sister, Amelia.

It's also a reference to one of my earliest pieces of published fiction, a novella I wrote for Telos Books for their Time Hunter series, *The Severed Man*. That book features a secretive devil-worshipping cult known as "The Cabal of the Horned Beast", and they reappear here for the first time since 2004. What I found interesting about writing this one was the fact the cult, although clearly the "bad guys", are the ones who are hard done by. It's Newbury who steals from them, provoking them into seeking revenge. We see that revenge played out in full in *The Revenant Express*.

CHRISTMAS SPIRITS

Another Christmas tale. This one has its roots even more firmly in Dickens – it's essentially a riff on *A Christmas Carol*, with Newbury, befuddled by opium on Christmas Eve, hallucinating the spectres of Templeton Black, Bainbridge and Veronica: past, present and future. There's some foreshadowing of what's to come in *The Revenant Express*, and it was the first time I'd properly written about Templeton Black, albeit as a ghostly spirit.

STRANGERS FROM THE SEA

Another recent tale, this, written for the charity anthology *Storyteller*, a tribute to the fantastic writer Matt Kimpton.

I wrote this straight after "The Dark Path" and wanted to do something else with Templeton Black, something that picked up on the themes of that other story and showed Newbury later, already lost to his obsession with the occult.

The genesis of the story was lovely, too – a friend called Nick Campbell found a page in an old children's book listing loads of wonderful old titles, most of them forgotten and long out of print. A group of us began riffing on the titles, imagining what stories might have belonged to them. It was Stuart Douglas of Obverse Books who jumped in and suggested he pull together an anthology as a tribute to Matt, with each author taking a title from that list and writing a new story. This one is mine.

THE ONLY GIFT WORTH GIVING

Yet another Christmas tale! This one's set later in the series, though, after the events of the sixth novel. Things have changed for Newbury, Veronica and Bainbridge, and Newbury's fallen into another of his black moods. Bainbridge pays him a visit on Christmas Eve, however, with the only Christmas present he knows will rouse Newbury from his depression – a new case.

This one was written for the *Newbury & Hobbes Annual 2013*, which was a ridiculous amount of fun to put together. It was written long before I ever got round to finishing "Lady Arkwell's Deceit", but echoes the already-planned ending of that story, with the enigmatic Clarissa Karswell sending Newbury a note to reignite their little game.

A RUM AFFAIR

This one was also written for the *Annual*. I was playing around with form again here. I'd been writing a long sequence of "drabbles" – one-hundred-word stories – that built into a longer narrative, and decided to write a story in twelve mini-chapters, one each for the twelve days of Christmas. I love the discipline of writing precisely like this, carefully choosing every word and sticking to the rules. It's quite a challenge, but it's something I do a lot. I have notebooks full of these things, mostly featuring Newbury and Lady Arkwell. One day I'll collect them all into a book.

A NIGHT, REMEMBERED

I wrote this story around the time of the centenary of *The Titanic*, but this is the first time it's seen print. It was written entirely at a writer's retreat, fuelled by coffee, doughnuts and the good company of other writers.

It features what's probably the last appearance of Lady Arkwell, chronologically speaking, but it's the first time Peter Rutherford appears in the Newbury & Hobbes story. He's a character I created for my novel *Ghosts of War*, a British spy who represents the next generation of secret agents. Here, he's charged with interviewing an older Newbury about what *really* happened the night the *Titanic* went down, and passing on another of Lady Arkwell's notes.

THE MAHARAJAH'S STAR

This might be my favourite of the short stories I've written to date. It represents a kind of nexus point in my fictional universe, the point where everything came together and I realised that all of my stories were really all part of one big saga. It features Peter Rutherford interviewing Professor Archibald Angelchrist – an aged, retired Secret Service man – about an adventure he once had with Newbury, Veronica and Bainbridge.

Angelchrist was a key character in my *Doctor Who* novel, *Paradox Lost*, and then later in *The Executioner's Heart*, but this was his first appearance.

I like how it takes the form of smaller, nested stories that all come together at the last moment – and the fact it's got terror birds and reanimated pygmies in it. It's the story I typically bring out for readings and events.

THE ALBINO'S SHADOW

There are few greater pleasures in life than sitting down to read an issue of the Sexton Blake Library. For years I've been addicted to these pulps, which had their golden age in the inter-war years. They're rip-roaring adventures, full of larger-than-life heroes and villains.

The best of these villains, and, in my humble opinion, one of the best fictional characters ever created, is Zenith the Albino. He's a gentleman prince from Eastern Europe, who smokes opium-tainted cigarettes and always wears immaculate evening wear, treats women with the utmost respect and has a rather relaxed attitude towards life and death. He appeared in over forty novels and novellas during the 1920s and 1930s.

This story was written for a new anthology of Zenith stories, and I decided to pitch him against Peter Rutherford, my British spy of the same era. Of course, it was too good an opportunity not to have Rutherford seek the advice of Veronica, amongst others, when going up against such a dangerous foe.

What I was also doing here, and in these other Rutherford stories, is showing the changing of the guard, the handing over of the baton from Newbury and Veronica to the next generation. Rutherford is clever enough, and respectful enough, to know that he can learn a great deal from those who have fought such battles before.

OLD FRIENDS

I suppose this is quite a sentimental story, really, but I'm a romantic at heart.

I was doing two things here. Firstly, exploring Angelchrist's history with Newbury, Veronica and Bainbridge to really get to the bottom of his place in the saga, his relationship with the key characters. Secondly, showing another side to Rutherford, and how he thanks Angelchrist for all of his help by reuniting him with his old friends at Christmas. It felt like a good note to end the collection on, the point where Rutherford goes it alone, leaving the old guard to retire in peace, finally able to simply enjoy one another's company at Christmas, safe in the knowledge that someone else is out there now, looking out for the interests of the British Empire.

ACKNOWLEDGEMENTS

"The Dark Path", "Lady Arkwell's Deceit" and "A Night, Remembered" are original to this volume.

"The Hambleton Affair" first appeared in the limited-edition hardback of *The Affinity Bridge*, published by Snowbooks in 2008.

"The Shattered Teacup" first appeared in a limited edition chapbook for Christmas 2008, given away by the author as a Christmas card.

"What Lies Beneath" first appeared in the limited edition hardback of *The Osiris Ritual*, published by Snowbooks in 2009.

"The Case of the Night Crawler" first appeared as a limited edition chapbook for Teslacon II, published by Percepto Press.

"The Sacrificial Pawn" first appeared in *Team Up*, published by Obverse Books in 2011.

"Christmas Spirits" first appeared in the hardback edition of *The Immorality Engine*, published by Snowbooks in 2011.

"Strangers from the Sea" first appeared in the charity anthology *Storyteller*, published by Obverse Books in 2013.

"The Only Gift Worth Giving", "A Rum Affair" and "Old Friends" first appeared in *The Newbury & Hobbes Annual 2013*, published by Obverse Books in 2012.

"The Maharajah's Star" first appeared in the charity ebook anthology, *Voices From the Past*, edited by Scott Harrison and Lee Harris, published by H&H Books, 2011.

"The Albino's Shadow" first appeared in the anthology *Zenith Lives!* edited by Stuart Douglas, published by Obverse Books in 2012.

ABOUT THE AUTHOR

George Mann was born in Darlington and is the author of over ten books, as well as numerous short stories, novellas and original audio scripts.

The Affinity Bridge, the first novel in his Newbury & Hobbes Victorian fantasy series, was published in 2008. Other titles in the series include *The Osiris Ritual*, *The Immorality Engine* and the forthcoming, *The Revenant Express*.

His other novels include *Ghosts of Manhattan* and *Ghosts of War*, mystery novels about a vigilante set against the backdrop of a post-steampunk 1920s New York, as well as an original *Doctor Who* novel, *Paradox Lost*, featuring the Eleventh Doctor alongside his companions, Amy and Rory.

He has edited a number of anthologies, including *The Solaris Book of New Science Fiction* and *The Solaris Book of New Fantasy*, and has written new adventures for Sherlock Holmes and the worlds of Black Library.